"Here's what we're going to do, Praxle," said Teron. "I'm going to hold your right hand, and any time you lie to me, I'm going to break one joint of one finger. If you try to cast a spell or do anything else untoward, I'll break your finger joints one after another until you stop. Shall we begin?"

"Do I have a choice?" asked Praxle.

"Of course you have a choice. You may choose how many fingers I break before you cooperate."

Praxle paused, set his jaw, and let out an exasperated sigh. "I hope you understand how hard this is for me," he said. "I deal in information, which means that I acquire it instead of dispense it. On those rare occasions that I give knowledge to others, I charge my clients dearly for the privilege." He glowered at his interrogator through narrowed eyes.

Teron tilted his head slightly. "I deal in death. No charge." He reflected for a moment, then added, "Pain is just a hobby."

THE
WAR~TORN

THE ORB OF XORIAT

THE WAR-TORN • BOOK 2

EDWARD BOLME

THE ORB OF XORIAT

THE WAR-TORN TRILOGY • BOOK TWO

©2005 Wizards of the Coast, Inc.

Distributed in the United States by Holtzbrinck Publishing. Distributed in Canada by Fenn Ltd.

Distributed to the hobby, toy, and comic trade in the United States and Canada by regional distributors.

Distributed worldwide by Wizards of the Coast, Inc. and regional distributors.

Cover art by Wayne Reynolds
Map by Dennis Kauth
First Printing: October 2005
Library of Congress Catalog Card Number: 2004116908

9 8 7 6 5 4 3 2 1

ISBN-10: 0-7869-3819-6
ISBN-13: 978-0-7869-3819-3
620- 95013740-001-EN

U.S., CANADA,
ASIA, PACIFIC, & LATIN AMERICA
Wizards of the Coast, Inc.
P.O. Box 707
Renton, WA 98057-0707
+1-800-324-6496

EUROPEAN HEADQUARTERS
Hasbro UK Ltd
Caswell Way
Newport, Gwent NP9 0YH
GREAT BRITAIN
Please keep this address for your records.

Visit our web site at www.wizards.com

Dedication

*For my wife, who had, at best, the vaguest
idea what she was getting into.
You are the greatest.*

Acknowledgments

*Thanks go to a number of people for this
book: my wife, for holding the family together
when everything else was falling apart;
Mark Sehestedt, for working with me above
and beyond the call of duty to make this
happen; and everyone involved in making
Eberron a reality, for giving me—
and you—a new sandbox to play in.*

Novels by Edward Bolme

*Title Deleted for Security Reasons
The Steel Throne
The Alabaster Staff*

ELDEEN BAY

N W E S

WHISPER WOODS

THE STARPEAKS

AUNDAIRIAN BORDER CHECK

AUNDAIR

WROGAR KEEP

DASKARAN FERRY

DASKARAN

THALIOST

REKKEN-MARK

FAIRHAVEN

SILVERCLIFF CASTLE

THRONEHOLD

THRANE

FLAMEKEEP

LATHLEER

ATHANDRA

THE BURNT WOOD

BLUEVINE

THE CRYING FIELDS

PASSAGE

GHALT

GALLAISE GAP

THE MONASTERY of PASTORAL SOLITUDE

SIGILSTAR

ARULDUSK

MASTER KEY

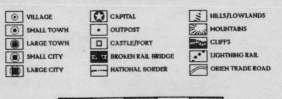

⊙ VILLAGE	✪ CAPITAL	HILLS/LOWLANDS
◉ SMALL TOWN	• OUTPOST	MOUNTAINS
◉ LARGE TOWN	☐ CASTLE/FORT	CLIFFS
▣ SMALL CITY	BROKEN RAIL BRIDGE	LIGHTNING RAIL
▦ LARGE CITY	- - - NATIONAL BORDER	ORIEN TRADE ROAD

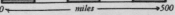

0 ← miles → 500

TABLE OF CONTENTS

PROLOGUE

How sad, thought Keiftal, rubbing his stubbly chin, that such a beautiful sunrise should herald the end of this monastery.

He looked out at the open fields of the Galtaise Gap. The dawning sun shone upon a sea of steel. After almost two weeks of waiting, the Thrane army was ready for an attack upon the monastery, intent on wiping out Keiftal and his fellow monks. The red eastern sky glinted off the helmets of thousands of Thrane troops, making it seem as if the lush green fields ran with blood. Huge siege engines stood as stark silhouettes against the east.

In a sense, it was beautiful. The Thrane army was arranged in a rigid structure, a pattern of death and destruction, an orderly arrangement intended to cause chaos.

Keiftal rang the bell, raising the alarm, calling the monks forth to battle, even though he knew it was pointless. Against these odds, the monks would hardly acquit themselves well. If they awaited the foe, flying boulders and firebombs would destroy them as they stood, yet if they charged unarmored through a rain of arrows to face a hedge of spears, their strength would be wasted. The only victory they could win would be to remain true to their sacred vows.

1

"Dol Arrah," he prayed, "Radiant Mistress of Honor, you know I had hoped someday to merit the title of Master in your service. I do not ask for special dispensation for myself, but if it be your will, please spare your monastery this day and allow us to continue to serve you as we have done for nigh two thousand years."

The Thrane army was almost fully ordered. Keiftal estimated that the battle would begin in less than an hour. He drew a deep breath and let it out slowly.

The Grand Master stepped up beside him. "Any sign of reinforcements?" he asked.

"None at all, master," said Keiftal. "I don't understand. The Prelate knew they were marching. We sent word when the Thranes moved, and he vowed to send reinforcements. Without them, the monastery will be destroyed."

"We serve Dol Arrah," said the Grand Master. "Trust in her to deliver us."

"I trusted in her servant the Prelate to deliver reinforcements," Keiftal said.

Time passed as each side performed their rituals. The monks of the monastery gathered outside, stretched and meditated, each moving in his individual rite, all preparing to acquit themselves well on their last day. The Thranes stood in unison, a rigid organic whole as their officers exhorted them to their duty.

The Grand Master ordered the monks forward with a wave that struck Keiftal as a gesture of resignation. They closed on the Thranes, loosely ordered to present a poor target for archers and trebuchets. It was a long walk to the Thrane lines, but by the time they arrived, they would be warmed up, while the Thranes would be stiff from standing still.

Then Keiftal heard a voice. *Run*, it whispered.

He stuttered his step, slowing. *Run*, the voice repeated. Airy, feminine, commanding. Keiftal felt fear rising in his heart. He stopped, his pulse racing, his breath fast and shallow. He looked around.

The voice spoke once more. *Run,* it insisted. *It's here.*

Keiftal staggered back, seized by trepidation. He looked about for a threat and found none.

Blinking rapidly, he found himself back at the monastery with one trembling hand seeking stability against a solid wooden pillar. He had only a vague panicked memory of retreating that far. He saw his fellow monks marching toward the Thrane lines. He looked once more at the invading forces, and then, on the horizon near the enemy camp, he saw something.

His eye was drawn inexorably toward it, even though he didn't know what it was. He saw a flash of black, a burst of darkness fierce and stark against the rising sun.

And he felt a great depraved eye opening to gaze upon the land, a vast snarling mouth yawning to swallow the world. Already hovering on the brink of panic, Keiftal averted his eyes and dived behind the pillar.

He hunkered like a child, knees drawn tight, eyes crushed closed as an otherworldly maelstrom wracked the battlefield. He covered his ears and shrieked, but he could not block out the horrid sounds that resounded in the dawn.

As he passed out, the last thing he heard was the screams of the lost.

SHADOWS OF THE LAST WAR

CHAPTER 1

Evening, the 28th of Olarune, 998 YK

Teron walked across the blood-hued grass as the last sliver of the sun began to sink below the horizon. Although he was light of frame and stood on the shorter end of average, his tightly packed muscles gave him weight. His short-cropped black hair and beard framed a face taut with tension and a pair of blue eyes as cold and dead as a hanging convict. His skin, the color of oiled walnut, blended with the well-washed gray of his simple canvas outfit.

Although he walked with a cat's gentle step, in this area he felt as stealthy as a drunken orc. The grass creaked beneath his bare feet. It was not the brittle crunch of dead vegetation, but still a far cry from the whispery rustle of healthy growth. Too much had happened here for the ground to ever be whole again.

The rolling grassy plains held little resemblance to the rest of Aundair. Even those Aundairian towns that had been utterly razed by the Thrane army were fairer in comparison. The grass of the Crying Fields bore an unhealthy red hue. Under the light of the setting sun, it seemed the color of fresh blood. The tone stood as a reminder of the cost of the Last War, of the countless dead in the dozens of battles that had been fought here for the control of the southern portion of the kingdom.

As Teron walked the ruined meadows, he paced a familiar cerebral landscape, a drear and brooding path of mental flagellation. He hearkened back to the Last War, and the guilt and pain and shame whipped his soul, serving to purge and purify his mind.

So much blood shed, he thought, with every nation locked in a brutal struggle for dominance. So much carnage spread over so many decades, yet for all the brutalities, only the Crying Fields bear this terrible scar . . . a cold reminder of how far we have fallen from grace. The Sovereign Host has cursed us for what we are. For what we have done, they have cursed this place above all the lands.

Rather, he reminded himself, taking a rare side excursion in his dark thoughts, this place was cursed above all lands save Cyre. Then again, Cyre has the advantage of being truly and completely dead. Ah, to be dead instead of merely scarred, twisted into a dark revenant of the Last War. Ruined by one's choices. Ruined, like the monastery, and forever doomed to lurk in this blighted land, fighting the old battles, again and again.

Mists twined around his ankles as he walked. At first, the mists merely swirled in the wake of his stride, but as the night deepened they began to writhe of their own accord, manifesting from nothing and rising like sinister serpents to tarnish the darkness.

Somewhere, an indeterminate distance away, Teron heard a wail. He couldn't tell if it was several voices crying out in unison or one voice shredded into strips. After a few steps, the sound was followed by a faint howl of triumph.

Teron glanced up at the moons. Several were below the horizon, the rest spread across the luminous Ring of Siberys like tokens on a shaman's necklace. Sedate Olarune lingered on the horizon, waxed full, pregnant with power. Her pale orange color seemed to mock the sun. Slow-moving Vult hung almost directly overhead, while splinters of Sypheros and Barrakas lurked in the moody hues of the sunset.

He pressed on, moving quickly across the rolling hills. The noises around him grew in strength and clarity. Groans, shrieks, shouts. The darkness was almost complete, the colors draining from the sky, and the tiny secluded vale that Teron sought was just ahead. As he crested the last hill, he paused to look back toward the remnants of the ruined monastery. It stood on the hilltop, its jagged lines looking like a shivered fang. Faint glimmers of light shone from a few windows, twinkling like stars brought from the sky to live in Aundair.

Teron smiled cynically. There were a few left, he supposed, a few glimmers of hope. Keiftal was one. He knew the old man was watching, staring into the darkness. He always did. Then there was that young boy who scrubbed the pots; he counted. Definitely Flotsam, such good-heartedness in such an ugly wrapping.

He descended into the shadowy draw, out of sight of the monastery. Down where no one could see, ask questions, come looking... find out. More sounds crawled through the night—the bitter clash of swords, the whetstone flare of spells, the shouts of the desperate, and the pitiful wails of the dying.

It was fully dark, and the tendrils of mist rose and congealed into a fog, thick and somehow greasy. Teron took a deep breath, let it out, then stripped off his shirt. Soon his test would come, but tonight he would practice.

He slowly spun one hand at his side, stirring the supernatural mist. Burgundy curls of smoky energy coalesced as he did so, trailing from his hand like the tresses of a lover. The familiar nausea returned to the pit of his stomach, and he steeled himself to endure the torment.

A translucent figure loomed out of the mist, glowing faintly. It looked human enough, arrayed in old-fashioned Thrane armor, but the utter madness in its glowing eyes spoke otherwise. It opened its black pit of a mouth, and Teron heard a wail of anguish crawl forth as if from an infinite distance.

Teron clenched his fist as the apparition readied a hazy, shifting sword.

● ● ● ◉ ◉ ● ●

A light rain drizzled on the nighttime streets of Wroat. The mellow golden glow of the everbright lanterns washed across the wet cobbles, adding some cheer to an otherwise cold and damp evening. Caeheras wiped his sleeve across his brow and turned from the main road into a side street and then again into a wide alley. As he left the last of the everbright lanterns behind, he pulled a torch from his pack and ignited it with a tindertwig. It flared to life, illuminating the dark alley. Caeheras didn't need the torch. His elf eyes easily pierced the darkness. But he figured he was being followed, and the least he could do was make it easy for those shadowing him.

He moved through the alleyways with practiced ease. He knew the area well—far enough from the Street of Worship to avoid any unwanted interlopers, near enough to the Foreign District and its plethora of diplomatic bodyguards that the presence of the city constabulary was still greatly diminished.

Caeheras didn't want interruptions. At least, none that he hadn't planned.

He found the appointed court, a narrow square surrounded by multistory warehouses and manufactories. A wagon, empty of anything save a crumpled tarp, stood against the wall to one side, its empty harnesses dangling in a puddle. A few open crates and barrels littered an area near the center of the quadrangle. In the far corner from Caeheras stood an array of smaller wooden boxes filled with new goods. Caeheras noted the subtle emerald sheen of a warding spell protecting them against theft. The wizard who owned that particular building was well known for his inventive and vengeful methods of dealing with thievery, and the boxes stood unmolested.

Caeheras placed the torch on the ground in the center of the square, then walked across to the warded boxes and stood with his back to them. Their warding spells were as good as a

Deneith bodyguard for protecting one's back. He pulled his cloak a little tighter and waited, shifting his weight from one foot to the other to keep warm. As expected, he soon heard approaching footsteps.

Caeheras smiled as his richly dressed client stepped into the square. Though taller and a tad more robust than many gnomes, the newcomer was still a good two heads shorter than Caeheras.

"Praxle," said Caeheras.

Praxle's smile shone in the darkness. "A torch," he said. "How rustic. I never would have thought you were a romantic, Caeheras."

"The Undying Court reminds us that the old methods often work best."

"Indeed," answered Praxle. He stepped to the center of the plaza so that the torch illumined him from below. "I didn't think I'd be hearing back from you for another year or two, maybe longer."

"I, uh, I work fast."

Praxle blinked, his mouth open in amused surprise. He doffed his cap and swept it low in a formal bow. "Caeheras, I am truly impressed. You've found the answer already?"

"You brought the payment?"

Praxle slid a hand into the folds of his rain cloak and pulled out a small pouch. He reached in and removed a gem. Across the plaza, Caeheras couldn't tell what kind it was, but he saw the tell-tale sparkles as Praxle turned it between his fingers to catch the torchlight. "My answer is yes, if your answer is yes. Good wages, especially considering how short a time you worked on it."

Caeheras wiped his sleeve across his brow again, then ran his hand through his sodden hair. "I found its location for you," he said, "but I had a bit of a problem."

"I don't pay you to find problems, Caeheras," said Praxle. "I pay you to find information."

"That is true, Praxle," said Caeheras, "but I ran into some extra expenses. This was very difficult, you see. Very difficult. And my fee has gone up. A lot."

Praxle clucked his tongue. "A contract is a contract, Cae-heras," he said, "and I'm very disappointed that you'd think otherwise. But if you give me what you have, we'll see about paying you a bonus for your efforts."

"No," said Caeheras. "I need the entire fee up front. If you don't have enough with you, we'll consider what you have a down payment." Caeheras drew his thin rapier, and as he did, three armed humans entered the quad, cutting off Praxle's escape routes. "Make your choice, Praxle."

Praxle smacked his lips. "Caeheras," he said as he looked over the other thugs, "this is definitely a breach of contract. We agreed that neither of us would bring anyone else in on our meetings."

"The contract price changed," said Caeheras, "so I felt some other changes might also be wise."

Praxle shook his head. "I'm very disappointed, Caeheras."

"That I worked things to my advantage?"

"No," said Praxle with a weary sigh, "that you forgot with whom you're dealing."

Caeheras started to retort but only uttered one unintel-ligible syllable before concern clouded his brow.

Praxle looked at the thugs surrounding him. "Since Cae-heras didn't teach you one very important lesson, I will. So remember this, each of you, and it will serve you well: When-ever you deal with one gnome, you deal with all of them." He made a small hand gesture, and the noise of a tiny bell chimed in the night. The warded boxes behind Caeheras faded away, the illusions unraveling into a thousand tiny motes that glit-tered like diamond dust being swept away by a whirlwind. In the boxes' stead stood a half-dozen gnomes armed with cocked crossbows. At such short range, each was powerful enough to send a bolt of iron-tipped wood clean through someone's breastbone. At the same time, the tarp on the wagon rustled, and three more gnomes stood up from beneath it, each armed with a brace of hand crossbows. And above, someone spoke an arcane hex, and light suddenly shone forth to bathe the entire square.

Praxle smiled and drew a blade from beneath his cloak. It shone wetly in the light. "Did I ever mention that my uncle is an herbalist?" he asked as he turned the blade back and forth. "Brews all kinds of interesting substances. Helps counter-balance all the overwrought strength of too-big folks like your hired hands."

Caeheras glanced at his compatriots. One was clearly ner-vous, looking skyward and wondering what other hazards might await them beyond the magical light. The second, the most veteran of the group, was calm, accepting. The third, however, looked like a cornered beast and tensed herself to strike.

"Wait, you three," said Caeheras. "No hasty actions. The clever d'Sivis has the better of me this day." He smiled ruefully at the gnome and tilted his head. "I thought it was a breach of contract to bring someone else along."

Praxle shrugged. "If we'd just done our business politely, you never would have known they were here. Just remember who first broke the agreement."

"We could both make more gold . . ." started Caeheras.

"I have . . . enough wealth," said Praxle in a long-suffering tone. "With what I pay you, you should know that. So give me what you have, and I'll give you your payment."

Caeheras winced in defeat, reached into his cloak and pulled forth a small sheaf of parchment, carefully wrapped in waxed paper and tied with twine. "That's terribly generous of you, Praxle, considering the situation," he said.

"The situation hasn't really changed, Caeheras," said the gnome. "It's just become clearer to all involved." He held out both hands and spoke, loudly enough that the gnome on the rooftop could also hear. "Attend, people. Caeheras and I must conclude our business, so no—"

A loud twang interrupted Praxle, and a long arrow from above suddenly pierced Caeheras's neck and imbedded itself inside his shoulder. He stumbled forward, guttering, one hand rising to his neck as the other, clutching the papers, pointed accusingly.

For the merest instant, Praxle wondered which of his people had loosed the deadly shaft. Then he saw the fletching on the arrow and heard the flat twang of other bows loosing. Interlopers! He knew that at least one arrow was aimed at him, standing as he was perfectly exposed in the center of the square.

Praxle moved, but not fast enough. He felt a burning flash of pain strike his thigh just above the knee. His leg gave, causing him to stumble and fall on top of the torch. Rolling quickly off the oily fire, Praxle snatched up the torch and flung it into the air as hard as he could, incanting words of power. The firebrand twirled ten feet upward, then exploded in a blinding starburst of brilliant sparks as Praxle's frantic spell caught up with it.

Praxle already had a hand up to shield his eyes from the flash, and he used the distraction to scramble, his leg twitching painfully with every move, toward Caeheras. As the light from the flare died, Praxle saw a shadow sweep down from above and snatch the bundled papers from Caeheras's trembling hand. The mortally wounded spy fell to his knees, the shock and betrayal fading from his eyes as blood welled through his fingers.

Praxle jerked his head about to follow the shadowy figure. At that moment, another arrow grazed the gnome's scalp and shattered on the cobbles. He rolled to one side and scrambled for the cover of the empty crates, wedging himself into the gap between two of them as another arrow imbedded itself in the wood.

Breathing heavily—both from fear and from the pain in his leg—Praxle glanced at the quivering arrow. Making a quick judgment of the archer's location, Praxle wove another incantation, then leaned out from his cover. His sharp gnomish eyes saw someone rise up on the rooftop, bow in hand, and Praxle let fly with his spell.

A wad of acid, conjured into existence and held into a missile by the thinnest sheath of mystic energy, flew from Praxle's outstretched hand. Praxle paused, poised to duck back behind his cover, saw the archer draw the bow . . . and heard the distinctive splash and sizzle of the acid hitting the mark. Confident that the archer would be out of the fight for at least a moment, Praxle stuck his head out to find the thief who'd stolen the papers from Caeheras.

There he was, climbing a knotted rope dangling down the wall of the warehouse on the far side of the quadrangle. He was thin, almost wiry, and dressed head to toe in dark gray, a shade that faded almost to nonexistence in the dim rain-washed light.

Praxle glanced about. Caeheras lay dying in the open, and Praxle could see two or three other gnomes likewise slain, as well as one of Caeheras's thugs. A bristled clot of arrows showed where two other gnomes huddled for cover against the unknown archers. Praxle glanced back at the thief then scrambled over to where the other gnomes were cowering.

"Get your bows ready," he hissed, clamping one hand on his injured leg. "Tinka's on top of that wall!"

"Then why doesn't she blast that damned bandit while he's climbing?"

Praxle looked up again, wary of new arrows. "Probably waiting for the best time," he answered. "Wait until he's close to the top of the rope and—"

A high-pitched scream interrupted him, and a small flailing shape dropped past the thief and landed with a thud on the cold cobbles.

"Tinka!" yelled Praxle as the gray clad thief disappeared onto the roof. He turned to the gnomes with him. "You, see if she's alive," he said. "You, see who else is left."

"But—"

"Shut up and do it!" said Praxle. He rose and limped over to Caeheras's body. "They're smart, whoever they are, so they're already making a getaway."

Caeheras was still breathing, a testament to his vitality and willpower. The elf lay in a pool of rainwater, one that grew redder with every passing heartbeat. His eyes tried to focus on Praxle as the gnome kneeled beside him.

"Caeheras, you know that wasn't me, right?" Praxle asked.

Caeheras nodded slightly.

"You're not going to make it, friend," he said. "You've lost too much blood. So tell me what you know, and I'll pay double the fee to your kin."

The elf closed his eyes in defeat. "Aundair," he whispered, his breath burbling in his chest. "Prelate . . . has it."

"Which prelate?" persisted Praxle in a whisper. "Answer me!"

"Hey, Praxle," called one of the other gnomes. "Jeffers caught one of the elf's sidekicks!"

Praxle turned his head. "Shut up!" he snapped. He turned back to Caeheras, imploring. "Who is it?"

"Monastery," said Caeheras. "Crying Fields. He—"

The rest of the answer got swept away as the elf's last breath rattled its way to freedom.

THE PATHS WE WALK
CHAPTER 2

Keiftal whistled tunelessly to himself, the feel of the breath between his lips somehow giving him comfort. He had aged many years since the destruction of the monastery, since the nascence of the Crying Fields. The wrinkles in his face were only marginally blurred by his stubbly beard, and the whole tired affair was framed by short-cut, unkempt gray hair.

He turned his head back and forth, scanning the crimson-tinged grasslands. Occasionally he broke his slow, shuffling stride to tug on the reins of the mule that followed dolefully along behind him.

He could feel the grass creaking beneath his sandaled feet. It felt maddeningly wrong. A hint of the smell of mortification insinuated itself into the air, both sweet and nauseating like the lingering perfume of a shameful tryst. The scent never failed to bring back memories of the aftermath of the destruction of the monastery, those horrible summer days as the bodies of the dead had bloated in the sun, attracting vultures and maggots until the corpses' bellies had opened up at last to vent their foul gases.

The few remaining monks—there'd been six—had done what they could to bury the dead respectfully, until, with the passing weeks, the task had proved too great to bear.

He remembered how the youngest of them had committed suicide, unable to face another day of the grotesque undertaking. That afternoon, the rains had come. Keiftal wept with relief at the sight, hoping that the blood would be washed away. And for a while it was.

For a while.

He looked up and saw vultures circling him in the sky and wondered if he had, at last, gone mad with the weight on his soul. "Why won't the memories leave me in peace?" he cried into the empty air. "Sovereign Host, why can I not sleep one night without hearing the screams of the dead?"

He stood there, weeping bitterly, wheezing between clenched teeth. Tears squeezed out from his tightly shut eyes. One fist beat his breast while the other, seemingly forgotten, firmly held the mule's tether. He cursed the events of that day and prayed for deliverance.

Then a sensation wormed its way past his grief, a persistent but distant interruption like someone far away calling for his attention. He mastered his emotions and realized that the mule was tugging insistently on its tether. He opened his eyes and looked around, but saw no threats.

He looked at the mule. It was acting a little skittish, but of course most animals avoided the Crying Fields. Keiftal looked up.

"Well, will you look at that?" he mumbled. "The vultures are still there. They're not visions after all. Come, now," he said to the mule in a voice suddenly more brassy and cheerful, "let's go see what they've found, shall we? Maybe it will be some good news."

The mule snorted and shied away.

"Oh, now, don't give me that. Even this place can hold good news. Sometimes."

He led the mule over the gentle slopes toward the center of the vultures' lazy circles. As he crested the last rise, he saw what he hoped to see: a body lying curled almost into a fetal position on the corrupted turf, half-naked, unmoving. Two vultures closed in, walking slowly. Their bright red heads leaned forward, peering hopefully at a potential meal.

Keiftal shuffled toward the body in a geriatric jog, pulling the recalcitrant mule forward. The vultures skipped away, spreading their funereal wings like cloaks and croaking at the intruder.

Keiftal staked the mule's tether to the ground, then kneeled by the body. "Oh, Teron," he said, rolling the young monk onto his back, "why do you do this to yourself?"

Teron was pale, his skin covered with the salty residue of dried sweat. A trail of dried blood ran from his nose and down one cheek. Pale bruises covered his arms and torso. As shallow as Teron's breathing was, Keiftal clearly smelled that he'd thrown up at some point. Teron's tight muscles held their position as Keiftal rolled him over, and the elderly monk gently stretched Teron's limbs out into a more relaxed posture. First he unbunched the arms, then he stretched the legs. Once Teron looked comfortably supine, Keiftal tried to unclench the young man's fists. After a few moments, he gave up. He massaged the young man's chest and sunken belly until Teron's breathing became more regular. He tried unsuccessfully to pry Teron's jaw open, so instead he settled for pouring a trickle of water from his wineskin onto the young man's bared teeth. He watched the small trickle run down the teeth and behind his cheek, then he saw Teron's neck move as he reflexively swallowed. He poured a little more water into Teron's mouth in this fashion, then sat back and surveyed the little vale in which Teron lay.

The grass was beaten down for yards and yards in every direction. In some places, the turf had been worn down right to the dirt. Further up the slope, patches of grass were pockmarked and ashen. Near the top of the rise, one section of turf had been ripped from the ground like the scalp from a skull.

"I'd understand, Teron," muttered the old monk, "if you had a prayer of changing anything out here. But this isn't self-purification. This is self-destruction."

Keiftal gathered his strength. Once steeled to the task, he pulled Teron into a sitting position and then tried to maneuver his own body into a position where he could lift the young man. Eventually he settled for sitting beside Teron and rolling over, pulling Teron over on top of him. He pushed himself up onto his hands and knees. With more grunting and fussing, he eventually got Teron situated properly across his shoulders. He crawled slowly over to where the mule was staked. Gripping the mule's leg with one hand to help pull himself up, Keiftal rose first to his knees, then to his feet. He leaned across the back of the mule with his burden, then awkwardly pushed Teron up over his head, getting his monastic robes caught between the unconscious monk and the mule's saddle blanket. With much tugging and grumbling, he extricated both his robe and the blanket from between Teron and the mule. With a look of exasperation he flipped the blanket carelessly over Teron's body.

He kicked the stake out of the ground and staggered back toward the monastery, the mule in tow. "I'm getting too old for this," he said.

He paused, turned, and cuffed Teron across the back of the head. "You should be, too. Do you hear me?"

Teron lay unmoving.

"Bah," groused Keiftal. "You never listen."

⊙ ⊙ ⊙ ⊙ ⊙ ⊙ ⊙

Praxle watched as the lightning rail pulled into the station at Wroat. It was a huge construction, aesthetically unpleasing and brutal of form, yet beautiful in inspiration and power. The harness coach came first, a large armored carriage with bulges and pipes that made it look like the nose of a boil-infested horse. At the very front of the harness coach was the catch-and-kill, a reinforced bladed spike. Its strength and magically augmented sharpness ensured that no matter what beast might be standing astride the conductor stones when the lightning rail came, the harness coach would be able to plow right through its pieces.

Electric discharges encircled the harness coach, shooting from vents and connecting with each other as well as the conductor stones beneath. The pattern often looked like a harness and only added to the appalling equine image.

Passenger coaches followed behind the harness coach, hooked together into a caravan by linkages and a rather dubious-looking catwalk. They were also constructed of metal, armored against natural disasters or the possibility of raiders. Each coach had conductor stones beneath it, and lightning arced between them and the mated conductor stones laid out in the ground beneath. Despite the haphazard actions of the lightning, the coaches hovered in place, and the ride was as smooth as that offered by a horse-drawn carriage.

Praxle half-turned to the half-orc that towered over him. "Come, Jeffers," he said. "Let's find my cabin and get away from these crowds."

Jeffers picked up Praxle's copious luggage and followed his master onto the lightning rail. The two moved through the caravan of coaches until they found the luxurious private suite that Praxle had rented. Once inside, Jeffers poured Praxle a snifter of brandy and then proceeded to unpack those things that Praxle might require on the two-day journey to Aundair.

Praxle sat by the window and put his feet up, occasionally taking small sips of his drink. Soon the coach got under way, accelerating slowly but smoothly. They left Wroat and soon were speeding along the vast Brelish countryside.

Jeffers finished arranging the room, then left and fetched some food.

Praxle stared out the window as the lightning rail sped along. He didn't hear the constant actinic crackling of the magical fields propelling the caravan along the plinths. His eyes did not see the Howling Peaks slowly sailing past his window like great stone galleons of a bygone age. Nor did he smell the savor of the Brelish stew that Jeffers had procured.

"You look pensive, master," said Jeffers as he refreshed Praxle's drink. "May I ask what troubles you?"

"The Orb of Xoriat, of course," he said. "After so many years, I'm on its track at last. Unfortunately, I am not the only one. Caeheras let his lips slip, and somehow the Shadow Fox found out."

"Who is this Shadow Fox, master?" asked Jeffers.

"We don't know," said Praxle. "We—the University gnomes!— we don't know. He's some sort of Cyran bandit, and that's the extent that we've been able to find out. Everyone knows *about* him but no one seems to know anything *of* him, other than he operates out of Thrane, primarily in Flamekeep."

"Are you of the opinion that the Cyrans may be able to reach the Orb first?" asked Jeffers.

"I don't know, because I don't know who sent them. Who would be desperate enough to hire the Cyrans, anyway? Working with Cyrans is like asking a viper to suck the venom from a scorpion's sting." Then Praxle found the thread and started to pull, and the veil obscuring the truth started to unravel. "Of course no one hired the Cyrans. That means they're acting on their own. So the Cyrans know about the Orb. Wait, Jeffers, do you remember that hireling you pinched after the ambush?"

"Yes, I do, fairly well, master. A bit of a rake, two short swords, as I recall."

"His accent was that of a Cyran, was it not? And he acted so calm during the whole fiasco, he escaped the Shadow Fox's ambush unscathed."

"Indeed master, and if I understand your implication, I would indeed hazard that he was acting at the behest of the Shadow Fox, and that he himself brought extra information to Caeheras, hoping to purloin the Orb directly from him."

Praxle nodded. "So he brought extra information to Caeheras, and the Shadow Fox hoped to snatch the Orb from him. But when Caeheras went to me instead—albeit with the intent of gouging a higher price—he brought the plan to the Shadow Fox." Praxle grinned slyly. It all made sense. "Well, then, the Cyrans think they've pulled a perfect escapade, don't they? But they don't know that Caeheras whispered his dying secret to me." Praxle paused and looked over at the half-orc. "Do you remember what the Cyran looked like?"

"I was not as close to him as you were, master, so I claim no particular credit to the accuracy of my memory."

"Sit here in front of me," Praxle said.

The half-orc obeyed.

Praxle closed one eye and spun his hands in tiny, intricate circles, creating wisps of magical energy. With the ease of endless practice, he split his attention between his eyes. The open eye guided his hands as they layered the magical energies onto Jeffers' face; the closed eye looked into the past, probing Praxle's memories for the required image. As he worked, the wisps took shape and then began filling in with details as Praxle's fingers flew through their elaborate gestures. Hair. Eyes. A nose. The sardonic smile the Cyran had given in parting. The stubble on his chin, outlining a small scar. Praxle plumbed the depths of his mind and brought it all back, weaving it into an illusion of startling clarity.

At last Praxle finished. He looked proudly on his handiwork. "Take a good look at this man, Jeffers," he said as he handed his retainer a small mirror.

"Remarkable, master, as always. This is indeed his face."

Praxle shrugged. "I make a habit to study faces," he said. "Well, then, this Cyran may be on this very run—probably in one of the lower-class carriages. I want you to find out if he's here."

"And if he is, master?" asked the half-orc.

"He will have a tragic accident."

"It will be a pleasure, master."

"Thank you. Here, let me make this easier for you . . . ." Praxle made a few more mystic passes, and the illusion faded from Jeffers's face. "Keep the mirror with you. Look into it if you need a refresher. You'll see the Cyran's face looking back at you."

"Thank you, master," said Jeffers as he rose. "I believe we have several hours before the next stop. I'll report back shortly."

The latch clicked as he closed the door.

My, thought Praxle, seeing the landscape outside the window for the first time, the countryside looks peaceful. I shall have to invest myself in some Aundairian wine. It would be an excellent accompaniment to success.

⊙ ⊙ ⊙ ⊙ ⊙ ⊙

Teron walked into the meditation garden, paused, and spied a familiar figure sitting on a bench and watching the flowers sway in the scant breeze. He smiled at the thought of the aged master using such a simple meditation. It had been one of the first practices Teron had learned, and it remained an excellent way to calm the mind and find simple peace—watch the flowers until you sway with them.

"Keiftal," he called, but the elder monk did not reply.

He walked down the stone path that circled Keiftal's bench, his footsteps barely disturbing the pebbles. As he walked, he fluffed his thick tunic. His gray canvas uniform was drenched with the sweat of his workout, and it clung to his skin. Unfortunately, all that the fluffing did was make the wet tunic colder as it pressed to his back once more.

He walked around and squatted in front of his mentor, arms resting easily on his knees.

"Teron!" exclaimed the aged monk with a warm smile.

Teron rocked back just a little. "It's me. No need to shout."

Keiftal laughed heartily, but with a bit of a hollow sinus sound. "Especially not here, I suppose," he said. Then he went silent, staring at the face of his student, love and regret mixing in his wrinkled gaze.

"You wished to see me, honored one?" asked Teron. He noted that Keiftal dropped Teron's gaze as soon as he spoke, and he regretted breaking the moment.

"I did, my boy," he said. "But," he added, his slurred S sounds coming from behind his teeth, "don't call me honored one. That's a title for nobles, not a simple old man like me."

Teron bobbed his head, then let it droop as he fiddled with a stone on the path. "You always say that. But you're my teacher, and—"

"Back flip!" barked Keiftal.

Teron sprang. His hands whipped up. He pinwheeled his arms for angular momentum as he arched his back. In a flash he landed, feet shoulder-width apart, left arm raised defensively, right fist cocked at his floating rib for a powerful counterpunch.

"Good," said Keiftal. He reached over and took his staff, planting one end on the rocky path a mere hand's span away from Teron's front foot. "How many times do I have to tell you to look at your elders when you speak?"

Teron smiled abashedly. "Too often, honored one."

"Four basilisks!"

Teron flew into the ritual form. Eyes closed, he relied on his kinesthetic sense to maintain balance and position. He erupted in a whirlwind explosion of kicks and punches, the canvas of his tunic and pants popping with each extreme acceleration. Twelve punches, twenty blocks and eight kicks later, he entered the second half of the form, structured as the exact reverse of the first half. He came to rest at last, facing Keiftal with his feet shoulder width apart and his right fist cocked again. His eyes were still closed, though the crease in his brow clearly illustrated the fiery gaze that burned behind the lids. Keiftal looked down at his staff. Teron's foot stood but a span away.

Keiftal looked around and found they were indeed alone in the garden. "Your mastery of the art has been improving, Teron," he said, his voice somewhere between a murmur and a stage whisper. "There is still some room for improvement, I'm sure, but it is getting harder and harder for me to find it."

Teron relaxed his stance. "Thank you, honored one."

"You are perhaps the best student I have seen come through here."

"I *was* one of the best, master."

"You *are*. This monastery was founded well before Galifar united the Five Nations, my boy, and your petulance will not break the foundation laid by generations of masters. By the standards we've held for almost two millennia, you exhibit what is perhaps the finest mastery of technique I've ever seen."

"Thank you, honored one," said Teron, hardening his heart so the compliment rolled off, unfelt.

"I should clarify. You exhibit excellent martial technique. Here we teach that mastery of the outer motion must be balanced with mastery of inner stillness. You are very weak in that regard."

"I have passed my meditation requirements, Master Keiftal," said Teron.

"You have. And you have not thereafter made any effort to improve yourself in that arena. You've thrown all of your energy into bettering your combat abilities. Now while your, um,"—he glanced around again—"your situation excuses that to a degree, the fact remains that you have all but abandoned meditation and the pursuit of inner peace."

"As you wish," said Teron, hoping that his noncommittal answer might end this unwanted scrutiny of his inner workings.

"You do not let go of the world and embrace peace, Teron. Instead, you fight the world, hoping to crush your way to peace. But it cannot be done."

Keiftal looked into Teron's eyes and saw the steely disagreement therein. He sighed. "Do you know why we have not rebuilt the Monastery of Pastoral Solitude, my boy?"

"I've always assumed it was because Prelate Quardov hates us."

Keiftal cocked an eyebrow. "It's that obvious, is it?"

"Yes, it is."

"I suppose in a way, we merit his distaste," said Keiftal with a half-smile. "We've never rebuilt it as a reminder to ourselves both of the results of violence, for violence made a ruin of this beautiful monastery; and the costs of failure, for our failure to protect this place brought it to what it is now. But of course, this monastery is part of Prelate Quardov's purview. Its welfare is his responsibility. Has been since before it was destroyed. So I imagine that leaving this place as it is has become rather a sore reminder to him of how he failed to protect his charges."

"That's not the whole of it," said Teron.

"Now the training for your class was rather different from what we normally teach," said Keiftal. "I know we told you that the monastery ruins were to serve as a reminder to your—to you and your comrades, that is—a reminder of what you were fighting for. But if you look at it, my boy, you'll see that even that approach ties back to the cost of violence and the price of failure."

"That's not what I mean," said Teron.

"Then what do you mean, my boy?"

"I mean that if his reverence wanted to repair the monastery, he would. But he doesn't want to. He has a reason of some sort."

Keiftal sucked on his teeth. "Well, my boy—"

"You're not going to tell me, are you?" asked Teron, resignation in his voice. He watched emotions rage across Keiftal's face—shame and anger, bitter sadness and righteous indignation.

At last the elder monk mastered his face and looked about. "Do you know why we *have* rebuilt this garden?" he asked.

"No, honored one. Why?"

"To show that even here, even in our derelict home set smack in the middens of this ruined land, even here there is hope for renewal and rebirth. Even here there we can coax forth peace and beauty." He looked into Teron's eyes again and saw his words dash themselves against his quiet defiance like a toasting glass against a brick wall. He shook his head sadly. "Why do you do it, Teron?" he asked.

"Do what?"

"Go into the Crying Fields? The Last War is over, my boy. Can you not accept that?"

"I can, honored one. But peace cannot accept me."

Keiftal started to reply but paused, trying to get a mental grip on Teron's words.

"It keeps me sharp," said Teron, hoping to steer the conversation away from his unexpected admission. "I don't want to rust like a neglected blade."

"Your skills are . . . well, there must be better ways."

"I don't know of any. Who's left who's had the training I've had? No one. How can I hone my skills sparring against people I know are no threat? It's the closest I can get to the war."

Keiftal started to answer, thought better of it, then took a deep breath and forced it out. "You are right, my boy. Now I know your training has been harder since . . . well, since. But the shadows of the Crying Fields, they may look threatening and all, my boy, but they're just . . . they're just shadows!"

Teron looked into his mentor's eyes. "Not always," he said.

THE MONASTERY OF PASTORAL SOLITUDE
CHAPTER 3

It was an hour before dawn, and ghostly wails and cries drifted across the Crying Fields like foul pollen. Teron lay on a thin grass-filled mattress in his ascetic monk's cell. A sheen of sweat glistened on his skin in the light of the moons, and the night air cooled it so that his skin had the feel of a corpse. His quickened breath hissed between his teeth, and his hands clenched and unclenched as his legs twitched and pumped.

A cat appeared in the open window to his cell, leaping silently to the sill from somewhere outside. Its gray fur had black stripes and blended in very nicely with the moonlight and shadow. Its tail twitched as it aligned its ears to Teron. It sat and surveyed him for a while, and its ears slowly swiveled back, revealing its discomfort. The tail lashed even more. At last it crouched low and leaped through the darkness to the supine form. It landed heavily on his sternum, using the momentum of the jump to gather itself and leap immediately again for the low table in the corner.

The impact startled Teron from his sleep. He yelled, his voice tight and controlled but full of fear. He blocked an unseen strike as he sat up, then his frenzied eyes cast wildly about in the darkness. His gaze came to rest at last on the nearly invisible shape of the cat.

"Meow," said the cat, in a voice that sounded far more like a kitten than a tom.

Teron blew out his lungful of air, half laughing and half relieved, and flopped back down to the mattress. He drew in a deep breath and stretched, running his hands through his hair. He heard the tomcat leap to the floor and walk over, then felt the heavy, padded step of the cat as it climbed onto his chest and settled down, kneading into Teron's skin with its long, sharp claws.

Teron scratched the cat's wide head, ruffling its dirty hair. "How do you always know when I need you to wake me up?" Teron asked. He found his answer in the half-lidded eyes of the cat. It started to purr, an uneven, raspy sound like a steel-booted gnoll slogging up a steep pile of gravel.

"Phew," said Teron. "What on Eberron is that, Flotsam? Your breath smells like you ate a goblin chirurgeon's gloves!"

Teron spent a long time stroking the cat, focusing on rubbing the tom's muzzle and the base of its ears. The cat drooled, its saliva slowly collecting on its chin, dripping onto Teron's chest and pooling at the base of his neck. Teron didn't mind, though. The chance for his touch to bring pleasure instead of injury and death was well worth the nominal annoyance of some cat spittle.

Eventually he worked his hands down the cat's back, massaging its muscles and scratching its pelt. The sky began to lighten in the east.

With the massage completed and the monastery starting to awaken, the cat knew its time was up. It stood, arched it back, licked Teron's stubbled chin in thanks, and returned to the windowsill to groom itself and watch the day begin.

Teron rose slowly and easily. He limbered up, bending and stretching to get his blood flowing, then popped his neck, his back, his ankles, and finally cracked his knuckles all at once. When he was finished, he stepped over to the small window of his cell, placing his hands on the sill on each side of the cat. He looked at the growing dawn with a disinterested eye. The sky was a sickly hue, a wan excuse for a sunrise as was so often the case in this cursed portion of fair Aundair.

The tomcat meowed.

"I know, Flotsam," said Teron. "I wake up feeling pretty much the same way." He blew out a lungful of air.

"Let's go see what's in the larder, shall we?" he asked, and as he turned to leave his room, the cat hopped down the outside of the window.

● ● ● ◉ ● ● ●

Outside the wreckage of the front gate of the Monastery of Pastoral Solitude, Prelate Quardov's carriage rattled to a stop. A roil of dust billowed about as the coachmen hopped off the rear of the carriage and trotted over to its ornate doors, windows sealed from within. In unison they opened the double doors, and a step automatically dropped into place for the single passenger.

Inside, the prelate blinked at the sudden onset of the bleary late morning sunshine. He extinguished the sole lamp in the carriage with a sigh of regret. He disliked the monastery—more so, he hated it. Visiting the place was a flagellation of torment. It reminded him of many things he'd rather forget, things that should have been abandoned in the past to wither and die, unremarked, unremembered. The Last War, the Quiet Touch, and . . .

He glanced out the open doorway; within the overgrown courtyard of the monastery, Quardov saw Master Keiftal leading several other monks to greet their visitor.

He scowled, wanton loathing in his heart, but finally mastered his face and exited the carriage, descending the folding wooden step with the sedate pace of a swan.

He stood fully and surveyed the surroundings—the broken stone walls, the charred remnants of the gate, the sickly yellowed sky, and the blood-red grass all around. Dissatisfied as usual with the area, he worked the wax-and-cotton plugs from his ears.

As he did so, a limpid wind stirred the air, bringing the echo of a warbling wail to Quardov's ears. "They make no difference," he grumbled to himself, fingering the waxen plugs in his hands.

"Why is it that no matter how hard I try to seal my ears, I can always hear those noises?"

"I cannot explain it, my reverence," said Keiftal, drawing closer.

"Excuse me?" asked Quardov.

"I said I cannot explain it, good prelate."

"Explain what? Why the gnome is coming?"

"You asked why you hear the noises, my reverence," said Keiftal, slight confusion furrowing his brow. "I cannot explain it, other than to say that this place in unnatural in many ways, and natural ways of opposing its influence may not be particularly effective."

"You heard that?" asked Quardov. "Yet you tell me you're half-deaf at best."

"Mm. Perhaps my reverence spoke rather more loudly than intended," said Keiftal, blushing.

"Be that as it may," said Quardov, forcing much more joviality into his words than he felt, "I shall have to take care to watch my words while you are around, old man."

"Shall we—" began Keiftal.

"Yes," replied Quardov tersely. He strode forward to the monastery, trying hard to look at nothing. At last his annoyance got the better of him, and he glanced at Keiftal. "Why do you linger here?" he asked.

"Excuse me, my reverence?" said Keiftal, trotting beside Quardov like a well-trained dog. His slurred voice boomed in the empty courtyard.

Quardov stopped and turned to face the monk directly. "I said," he repeated, enunciating carefully, "why do you linger here? You condemn yourself to remain trapped in the pain of the past. We must forgive our neighbors, but forgiveness does not come when we immerse ourselves time and again in the pain of the past. Forgiveness begins with forgetting."

Keiftal nodded, but his brows, with their long wiry hairs, wrinkled pensively. "But my reverence," he said, "how can we forgive something that we do not remember?"

Quardov's face pinched in annoyance, then he regained his composure and clasped his hands, one fist inside another, behind his back. To him, the Crying Fields were a blight upon Aundair, and so, therefore, was this monastery, this twisting knife, this ruined relic that remained here in the face of all reason and kept the painful memory fresh. He wished he could remove the whole area from the world, cut it away and burn it like a gangrenous limb. Even walling it off would have been preferable. "Let us finish our business that I might leave this foul place," he said.

"As my reverence wishes."

The party crossed the courtyard, wending its way through the larger stones scattered years ago by the collapse of sections of some of the buildings, to what had become the main hall. This portion of the monastery had suffered less than other sections—especially the former Great Gallery—although it still had a few holes in its walls and roof from Thrane trebuchets.

Quardov entered the main hall and exhaled in relief when the monks closed the doors behind him. "Very well, then," he said, turning to Keiftal and raising one gentle hand to his forehead, "has that blasted University gnome yet arrived?"

Keiftal's brow creased with concern. "He has, my reverence, and—"

"Then fetch him," he said. "Where have you stashed the academic little beast?"

"Actually, I'm right here," said a bright voice.

Quardov's heart skipped a beat, and he turned to look down the long hall. Light slanted in from several open doors, and Quardov watched as a small silhouette drew closer and then stepped into view, illuminated by the slanting light.

"Praxle Arrant d'Sivis, University of Korranberg, at your service, your reverence," said the gnome, sweeping his hat off his head and wafting the scent of clove in its wake.

"Ah, here he is," said Keiftal. "Praxle d'Sivis, this is Prelate Quardov Donrain, Patriarch of the Faithful in Fairhaven, High Archdeacon of the Cathedral of the Heavens, Blessed Apostle of the Church of the Sovereign Host, and Keeper of the Divine Wrath. My reverence, this is Praxle, famed son of the dragon-marked House Sivis and respected lecturer of the University of Korranberg."

Praxle bounced forward and kissed the prelate's ring. Quardov's eye twitched once with the realization that, Praxle being as short as he was, he didn't have to bow to do so.

"My apologies to all if I stampeded your formal introductions by introducing myself," Praxle said. "It was not my intent at all."

"Professor d'Sivis," said Quardov, a gracious if ungenuine smile smearing itself across his lower face, "it is a pleasure to make your acquaintance. Our thanks to you that you have troubled yourself to visit our humble monastery."

"Humble is the word, all right," said Praxle. "This place has seen better days. What in the name of the Mockery happened here? Um, begging your pardon, your reverence, I . . . I didn't mean to let my mouth run off like that."

Quardov smiled. "It is of no worry, my good gnome. As a priest, I assure you that I deal with the Dark Six on a regular basis. Mention of their names bothers me not, and in fact it may be said that those gods are certainly more at home in this . . . territory than are those that we serve." He gestured back down the hallway in the direction from which Praxle had come. "If you would be so kind as to accompany master Keiftal and me, we have a comfortable room in which we may talk."

With a swish of his silken robes, Quardov strode down the hall. Praxle followed, while Keiftal trotted to keep up with Quardov, casting frequent glances over his shoulder at the gnome.

"Don't look so flustered," said Quardov. "We'll meet in the choral chamber. Go open the door and shoo away anyone else who's there. Now."

Keiftal scurried ahead, leaving Quardov alone to gather his composure again. His gaffe, Keiftal's bumbling introductions, and Praxle's casual demeanor had put the staid cleric off kilter, and he was determined to regain control of the conversation.

He needed to control the situation; the very presence of a University gnome was enough to send chills up his spine.

Quardov swept past Keiftal into the choral chamber, Praxle following a bit behind. The chamber was done all in wood, perfectly cut, lustrously polished and immaculately dusted; even the exterior stone walls were paneled over in oak. The arches in the room bespoke acoustic architecture. The room had been built for the pure pleasure of creating and enjoying vocal music. A thick carpet with a geometric design covered the floor and dampened the footsteps. Heavy, dark curtains covered the narrow windows that reached from floor to ceiling. Only a corona of light around each drapery proved that the sun still shone. Two simple iron chandeliers, each with a trio of ever-bright lanterns, provided a soft glow that failed to fully illumine the room.

Praxle whistled appreciatively, and the room resonated with the sound. "This room, the . . . choral chamber, you say? Now this is beautiful. Simply beautiful. You've done a masterful job of repairing it."

"We have not repaired anything, if you please," said Keiftal, glancing nervously at the prelate.

"Careful, easy now. You don't have to talk so loudly, especially not in this room," said Praxle. "Well, then, what did you do to protect it? How did you manage to keep this place from getting wre—well, damaged like the rest of the buildings around here?"

"The choral chamber never suffered any of the harm that fell upon our monastery," explained Keiftal, his voice still too loud in the well-designed room. "It was divine providence, I am certain."

"And likely the last miracle the Sovereign Host will ever grant this place," added Quardov.

Praxle walked over to one of the windows and pulled the curtain back. Light flooded into the room, seeming to bleach the wood of its color. "Gack. Nothing but blood-red grass," he said, and let the curtain fall closed again. "I can see why you leave the curtains closed. You have a choice between dim and somber or well lit and disturbing." He turned back to the men. "My apologies, but I did not have time to research this area thoroughly before coming. What happened here?" he asked, gesturing about.

Prelate Quardov took a long, deep breath and let it back out. "Everything happened here, my good gnome," he said, running his hand through his salt-and-pepper hair. "During the Last War, Thrane and Aundair fought over this ground two score times or more. It was all warfare, naught but death and destruction, and of very little interest to a spiritual person."

Praxle sat on the carpet and folded his legs. "In truth, I'm not a particularly spiritual person, your reverence," he said, leaning his elbows on his knees. "Take no offense, but I have a deep and abiding interest in history and in things that have definitively happened, far more than in philosophical debates over subjects that can neither be proved nor disproved. I'd love to hear the history of this place, particularly during the Last War."

Quardov hung his head and considered what to say, but just as he started to speak, Keiftal's rough and untrained voice rolled over his words.

"It happens, good gnome, that I've lived here through a majority of the Last War. I'll be happy to tell you all of what happened here."

"Keiftal . . ." warned Quardov quietly.

"Please do," said Praxle with a smile. He glanced at Quardov, his pleasure obvious. "My ears are piqued."

"Well, I can't give you all of it. I only began my learning here in, hmm, 939, I think, after my mother was killed on the Brelish frontier. I know there had been some fighting over this ground prior to that, but I don't know the details. I passed my final student test in . . . let's see, that would have been 943. The Thranes attacked that summer, and my master, he . . . he sped up our training to ensure we would be on the battlefield. You see, the problem was that we—the Aundairians as a whole, not this monastic order, of course—we had Tower Vigilant to the north and Tower Valiant to the south. No, wait, reverse that, Valiant north and Vigilant south, I think. Oh, but that doesn't matter. The point is that we had nothing between them, nothing guarding the Galtaise Gap except this monastery."

Praxle raised a hand politely, stopping Keiftal in his dissertation. "Forgive me, my good man, but I am not overly familiar with the geography up here. What's the Galtaise Gap?"

"Ah," said Keiftal, and he began gesturing dramatically on a large imaginary map in the air. "There are two ranges of hills sitting on our side of the Thrane border. The Thranes say otherwise, of course, but that is immaterial. These hills run north-south, and create a bit of a natural boundary. Towers Vigilant and Valiant stand in the lowlands just on our side of these hills. Now for Thrane to attack either of these towers would involve either marching straight across the hills, or else marching through the gap and then around the hills. Do you see?"

Praxle nodded.

"Of course, the towers are fortified, and the Thranes would need to bring siege engines to attack them effectively. Large, heavy things, difficult to get through rolling hills and annoying to drag the long way around. Instead, the Thranes decided it was easier to strike straight through the Galtaise Gap and make for Ghalt."

"Why didn't Aundair build another tower in the Gap?" asked Praxle.

"The crown attempted to do so a few times, but each time the Thranes would attack and destroy whatever progress had been made in construction. But even if a tower had been completed, I doubt it would have changed the Thrane strategy much, other than to make them bring siege equipment and sappers along. I do believe their long-term goal was to seize Ghalt, threaten the lightning rail line, cut the Orien trade road that connects southern Aundair to the rest of the nation, and then perhaps launch an attack up the rail line from the south to take Marketplace and the southern portion of the kingdom." He paused and nodded, glad to share his interest in history with someone.

Praxle leaned forward, cupping his chin in one hand. "Keiftal, my good friend, with all due respect, you're thinking too small. Thranes think bigger than that."

"What do you mean?"

"If I remember right, the lightning rail passes Ghalt, then goes to Passage, then continues northeast to Fairhaven, right?"

Keiftal nodded.

Praxle smiled. "I'll bet you anything they intended to raze Ghalt to the ground and push through to Lake Galifar. They get there, they cut the lightning rail north and south and isolate Passage against the coast. A quick siege, take Passage, and the southern half of Aundair falls. Issue terms of surrender to Fairhaven, then turn the army south into Breland. *That* is how a Thrane thinks."

Keiftal stared at Praxle for a moment, his mouth flapping as he grasped the concept. "I . . . I thought you didn't know much about our geography," he said, for lack of any better commentary.

"Not the details, no," said Praxle. "But I've spent a lot of time studying the history of the Last War, especially the campaigns of Thrane."

"Really?" said Keiftal. "Why Thrane in particular?"

"Thrane Military Studies was the only empty chair in the University faculty," said Praxle.

Keiftal laughed, while Quardov, having been completely ushered out of control of the conversation, forced his face into a reasonable imitation of a mirthful grin.

"Seriously, though, I believe strongly in studying one's enemies. After our people allied themselves with Breland thirty or forty years ago, Thrane truly became our enemy. And," Praxle added, rising to his feet, "thanks to the good relations between Breland and Aundair, the Aundairians—you—became our friends." He beamed as he looked at the two clerics, but Quardov took the opportunity to commandeer the conversation.

"This has all been very interesting, brother Keiftal, but I am sure that such a learned gentlegnome did not travel across

Khorvaire so that you could prevail upon him to listen to you practice your history lecture. Let us—"

"Oh, not at all," interrupted Praxle. "This is fascinating."

"You're just saying that to be polite to brother Keiftal," said Quardov. "But he is a good monk, humble and obedient if headstrong, and his ego needs no fawning praise. Pay him no further mind."

Praxle set his mouth in disappointment. "As you wish," he said. He sauntered over to the curtains again, and pulled one aside. He placed one foot on the windowsill and let the curtain fall behind him, partially concealing him from the two priests. "That is one of the strangest views I've ever seen," he said. "Don't you think, your reverence?" He maneuvered his hands through the gestures of a spell, hoping that Quardov's answer would help conceal the small arcane noises of his action.

"I have long since grown more than weary of the spectacle," said Quardov. "I would be happier if the grass were either to regain its normal hue or to die."

Unseen behind the curtain, Praxle mouthed a few words.

"Quardov! Prelate Quardov!" came a voice, seemingly a long way down the hall.

Quardov stepped to the door and cracked it open. "What?" he bellowed.

"Prelate Quardov, the marn shurrn parvirmenir serembluten!" mouthed Praxle, a gleeful smile on his face. "Parumbleren megomnownan right away!"

Quardov sighed wearily. "I can't discern a word they're saying. Would that they'd simply come down here and tell me directly."

"Maybe they know you wish privacy," said Praxle.

"Respect my wishes? They should do so more often. If you will excuse me, Professor d'Sivis, I shall return anon."

"Not a problem." As soon as the prelate glided out of the room, Praxle reappeared from behind the curtain. "Well then, enough staring out at the red fields," he said. "Tell me, Keiftal, we were discussing the Galtaise Gap?"

"Yes, indeed," said Keiftal, eager to help cover for Quardov's absence. "The Thranes had it in their head that this was the way to invade Aundair, and they did it repeatedly. I've lost count of how many battles I've been involved in, all fought for control of this area. Some were small, like when the master took all of us students out to ambush a Thrane scout patrol. That was our final test, you see. Then about thirty years ago, those were the huge battles. Biggest armies I've ever seen, thousands of pennants fluttering, tens of thousands of spear points shining in the sun, shield walls that seemed to run from here to the horizon. And when the cavalry charged, the whole ground trembled with the impact. Then the smoke and dust filled the air, and you couldn't see more than a few hundred yards in any direction at best, and everything was shouting and yelling and utter chaos." Keiftal paused, his eyes lost in the past. "Those were the biggest, and after that the battles started getting smaller again. I think both sides were losing soldiers faster than the populace could breed them."

"And in all that time, the Thrane generals never succeeded in their campaigns?" asked Praxle.

"They succeeded to greater and lesser extents," said Keiftal. "Many of their victories were too costly for them to continue. Others weren't. For example, in the winter of 941 they defeated the main force just north of here. Then they bypassed the monastery and marched straight for Ghalt. They actually burned part of the town, too, from what I heard. Massacred the people who wouldn't join the Church of the Silver Flame. But the remnants of our army reformed here, and we caused them such supply problems that the Thranes had to withdraw before Ghalt fell.

"They seized the monastery itself in 977," added Keiftal. "Held it for a few weeks until the Quiet Touch killed all their officers."

"The Quiet Touch?" asked Praxle. "What's that?"

"The Quiet Touch is, well—"

"The Quiet Touch is not something we discuss openly," said Quardov as he reentered the room and shut the door behind him. "My abject apologies for the interruption. We shall have no more such distractions."

"So you took care of whatever problem they had?" asked Praxle.

Quardov smiled bitterly and nodded. "It appears that my presence was not needed after all."

"How thoroughly annoying," said Praxle. "Well then, this . . . this Quiet Touch . . . is it some kind of summoned spirit?"

"No, not at all," began Keiftal. "It's a . . . well . . ." He cast a glance at Quardov.

"It is a magic spell developed by the Arcane Congress," said Quardov, "a ritual that required a number of mages to perform. It . . . smothers its victims, rendering them unable to breathe or speak. Hence the name."

"I see," said Praxle, carefully eyeing Quardov.

"Never mind that," said Keiftal, stampeding his overloud words across the conversation. "Those are the two major times that the monastery failed to hold the Galtaise Gap. Many of the Thrane invasions were stopped right here, or near here. Our martial training is very good."

"It sounds like there's been a lot of bloodshed here," said Praxle.

"Indeed, a modern tragedy," said Quardov. "Likewise is it a tragedy that Keiftal has dragged you back into a discussion of war. I am sure you are here for more . . . academic purposes than to dredge yourself through such an ugly bit of history."

"Tell me, Keiftal," said Praxle, utterly ignoring Quardov, "some of the people I spoke to in Ghalt say that this area is cursed. They say the tainted grass is some sort of divine condemnation for the amount of blood spilled here during the Last War."

"Oh no, not at all," answered Keiftal.

"Why do you say that?" asked Praxle.

"Because if it happened slowly, over time, then that would be a reasonable conclusion."

"Keiftal?" said Quardov.

"But it didn't," continued the monk.

"Keiftal," said Quardov again.

"Rather the change came upon us rather suddenly, over a few weeks at most."

"Keiftal!"

With this last outburst, Praxle gestured, and Keiftal looked over at his prelate. "I'm sorry, my reverence?"

"Attend me, my son."

"As you wish. I apologize if I was warming overmuch to my subject." Keiftal hurried himself over to Quardov's side.

"Not at all, my son," said Quardov as Keiftal approached. "I was just beginning to fear you might be boring our guest with an excess of events in which he and his people had no part. After all, he is here on business, and we must accommodate him."

"Pray continue," countered Praxle. "This is becoming truly fascinating. Do you think something happened that caused the grass to turn red?"

"Absolutely. It all started in the wake of the Thrane invasion of 974. A terrible time. It set the stage for the fall of the monastery a few years later. The Thrane army was marching, and we were awaiting word on reinforcements."

"And what happened?" asked Praxle, involuntarily stepping forward.

Quardov rubbed his upper lip with his thumb and forefinger, then rested his hand across his lower face to cover his mouth. "Say nothing more on the subject," he said under his breath.

"The Thrane army had some sort of magical device," said Keiftal, his voice quaking. Lost in memory, he did not notice Quardov's sudden glare. "It was very powerful, whatever it was. It killed people by the thousands."

"What happened to it?" asked Praxle, his eyes gleaming.

Prelate Quardov clamped Keiftal's elbow in an iron grip. "We do not know, my good gnome," he said. "Presumably the device was either consumed by its use, or removed by the Thranes after the battle. I understand it was not to be found in the aftermath."

Praxle pursed his lips. "I see. Well, we can always hope it consumed itself; such a powerful artifact could be quite . . .

destabilizing." He stepped over to the window and pulled the curtain open again. "I would hate to see somewhere else become as blighted as this place."

Quardov sniffed. "You came here with a purpose, professor d'Sivis," said the prelate. "Shall we table these military reflections and address your University's needs?"

Praxle raised his free hand dismissively. "I find myself fatigued, good prelate. While this conversation has been most diverting, it is a very long trip from Zilargo. I would prefer to have a bath first, and perhaps a good midday meal while we address the University's research. Would you please arrange these things for me? I am happy to pay for whatever inconvenience this shall incur."

Quardov pressed his lips together in annoyance. "As you wish. I shall have one of the monks see to your needs, although I fear our board may be somewhat less sumptuous than what you are used to in Korranberg."

Praxle let the curtain drop. He faced Quardov and gave a gentlemanly bow. "I thank you, your reverence. We shall speak later."

❀ ❀ ❀ ❀ ❀ ❀ ❀

High above the ground, the Shadow Fox hung on the side of the monastery, her feet braced on opposite sides of one of the tall, thin windows.

She pulled her ear away from the small tin cone she had pressed to the windowpane and glanced down. She saw the curtain swaying near the ground, and thanked whatever gods might be listening that she'd decided to climb high rather than hunker low.

THE NOOSE TIGHTENS

CHAPTER 4

Dressed only in a pair of simple pants and drenched with sweat, Teron pressed his body closer to perfection. His toes rested on the windowsill of his lonely cell as he did pushups on his clenched fists. Sweat ran down the sides of his face, dropping from his nose and forehead to the floor. He tried to focus on the little rippling rings each droplet made in the growing puddle to turn his mind away from the trembling weakness that grew in his exhausted muscles.

He could feel his concentration starting to slip as it usually did when he neared one thousand repetitions. Awareness of his continued effort forced its way into his mind. He paused from the rhythmic up and down motion, bent his hips to rest his back, and took several deep breaths.

Only then did he become aware of the cat.

Flotsam sat on the sill, and its lashing tail repeatedly struck Teron across the ankles. A low growl emanated from its throat.

Teron glanced over his shoulder, but the angle was all wrong. He pushed off with his feet, dropped his shoulders into an easy somersault, rolled to a standing position, and stepped over to the tom.

"What is it?" he asked. "I'm late for the midday meal."

He reached out and stroked the cat's fur. It took no notice of the gesture, and Teron could feel the tension in its muscles. He looked out onto the Crying Fields, following the cat's gaze. His eye scanned the area, but he saw no sign of birds or rodents.

"You see something," he said quietly. "I guess eating can wait."

❋ ❋ ❋ ❋ ❋ ❋ ❋

"Keiftal?" Prelate Quardov reached out and tapped the elder monk on the shoulder.

The monk started, surprised by his superior's appearance in his cell.

"We need to talk, my friend," said Quardov.

Keiftal put down his pens, set aside the parchment that he was illuminating, then stood from his small desk to face the prelate. He dropped his eyes for a moment and licked his lips as he shifted from foot to foot. "I'm sorry, my reverence," he said, fear and sorrow filling his eyes.

Quardov winced at Keiftal's excess volume and patiently held up one hand, gesturing him to lower his tone.

"I didn't intend to tell the gnome so much about the Thrane Sphere," Keiftal said. "You may remember that the whole incident was . . . well, a very difficult time for me. I often get too wrapped up in my memories. If you said something to restrain my tongue, I didn't hear it, and for that I apologize."

Quardov smiled, his gentle gaze itself a benediction. "It is all right, my friend. I understand."

"You do?" asked Keiftal, hope in his eyes.

"Of course I do," he said. "It was a very traumatic time for everyone. But Keiftal, my good servant, there is a more important issue we face, and I require your assistance in the matter."

Keiftal wrung his hands and leaned forward. "Of course. How may I be of service?"

Quardov paused to consider his words. "The gnome wishes to meet with me in private, ostensibly to speak with me about his University's business here. However, he will no doubt press me with further questions about the . . . Thrane Sphere and the incident that you began to describe. Much has happened over the last twenty-odd years, and I have . . . so many duties and responsibilities. Well, to be frank, much of the details have slipped from my mind. Before I speak with him, I must ensure that I have the facts accurately summarized in my own mind, if you would be so kind as to check my memory."

"As you wish, my reverence," said Keiftal in a stage whisper so loud it sounded more like he was gravelly hoarse.

"Well, then," said Quardov. "Let us start with the Thrane Sphere. What exactly happened to it after the battle?"

"I recovered it, my reverence. I sent you that private missive, inquiring after its disposition."

"I know that," said Quardov. "I can't remember precisely what we finally chose to do with it. The general plan, yes, but . . ."

Keiftal looked at his superior with no small concern. "We hid it in the catacombs," he said, "under the flagstone in the corner of the false tomb."

"Ah, the false tomb," said Quardov.

"Yes, my reverence."

"Probably smart to keep it away from the dead bodies. Wouldn't want them rising up, would we?" Quardov winked.

"Uh, yes, my reverence," said Keiftal. "I mean, no."

"Thank you for your time, my child," said Quardov. "I must go to meet with our good professor d'Sivis."

He strode from Keiftal's small chamber but paused and turned just outside the door.

"Master Keiftal," he asked, "do you think that the gnome believed what I said about the Quiet Touch?"

"I rather doubt it, my reverence," said the old monk. "But that was a clever answer in any event. I doubt he'll be rude enough to question your veracity."

Quardov nodded, then departed. As he walked the shadowed corridors of the main hall to the room where Praxle had asked to meet, magical motes peeled away from his skin, leaving a slight trail of shifting colors in his wake. It looked almost like he was dissolving in the darkness. By the time he reached the door to the meeting room, the last vestiges of the spell had completely unraveled.

He opened the door.

Inside, prelate Quardov ceased his pacing. "There you are, professor d'Sivis. I was becoming concerned that you had lost your way."

"Pray forgive my tardiness, prelate," said Praxle, smiling as he closed the door behind him.

⊙ ⊙ ⊙ ◉ ⊙ ⊙ ⊙

Teron stalked across the blighted grass, bare feet making a rustling noise as they crushed the stiff blades. His face was a blank mask as he scanned the ground. After leaving his cell, he'd found a large area of depressed grass just on the other side of a rise, indicating that several creatures of some sort had lain there, observing the monastery. Multiple tracks left the area. He'd chosen to pursue the one that headed for the monastery.

Are they beasts? he wondered. Surely spies wouldn't risk having so many people skulking about in broad daylight? Unless they were shapechangers.

He followed a trail of disturbed vegetation, turned stones, and other faint marks, pausing every five to ten paces to kneel and inspect the ground more closely. The tomcat Flotsam moved nearby, scenting the air. Were he not so exhausted from his workout, he'd follow the trail at a crouching trot, head low to the ground, but his legs would not withstand such additional abuse, and he doubted he could spare the time to rest up. If only he could find a decent footprint in the hardened ground, he'd better know what his quarry might be . . . and whether the whole monastery might be in danger.

The trail turned to one of the windows in the choral chamber, then emerged again. Teron paused and inspected the window and casement. The pane was only as wide as his forearm was long, and the stone frames extended outward a good span or more from the glass. The surfaces were wide and close enough for even an inexperienced climber to scale with little difficulty.

He ran his fingers carefully up and down the stonework outside the windows. He found a piece of moss clinging to the casement and noted that the top edge of the patch had been partially turned down. Teron stood, letting his fingers trace the casement, and found a few lighter slashes on the stone, where some grit had scratched the dirty surface of the building. Matching marks marred the other side of the window, as well as a small piece of dark fuzz snagged on a ragged piece of mortar.

He exhaled with deep concern. He'd hoped the trail had been made by a rat or a lingering squad of Karrnathi zombies still fighting the Last War. Such intrusions were not unheard-of in this section of Aundair. Those that prowled the Crying Fields were dangerous but manageable. But this proved that he was facing a real threat—a sentient creature with stealth and forethought. And it answered, at least in part, why people would risk a daylight intrusion. More activity meant more to spy on.

He looked up the height of the window. Two and a half floors over his head, the casement came to a point. It looked like it would be a difficult climb from there to the roof. Perhaps, he surmised, the infiltrator had chosen to find another way, or perhaps the infiltrator had successfully scouted a route and left to gather comrades. Either way . . .

Concentration once more wiped all expression from his face, and he continued tracking the intruder's footsteps. As he passed near the ruins of the Great Gallery, he stopped, got down on his hands and knees, and inspected the ground. Flotsam stepped up next to him, sniffing the dirt.

Two paths crossed the one he was following. One of those paths indicated that more than one person had used it, or that someone had used it multiple times. He studied the area, looking for hints on which path was the newer. He was able to dismiss one of the crossing paths—the one probably left by a single person—as older. The other he was not so clear about.

He sat back on his heels, lacing his fingers and pressing them to his lips. Should he follow the one or the many? The larger group was clearly more powerful, but their size meant they might not be as great a threat. They could be neither as small nor as stealthy as a lone operative. The Quiet Touch had proved that lone people could be very dangerous indeed. But he had no way of knowing whether the single person was a scout, an assassin, a diversion, or a rearguard.

He chose to follow the single track, for no other reason than that he had already been following it and was getting used to the person's style of movement. He tightened the drawstring of his tunic, hoping to stem off the annoying feeling of hunger.

The trail led into a denser section of rubble toppled from the ruined building. He followed the trail by hopping from stone to stone; his bare feet made almost no noise as he moved, and he was able to keep the suspect trail pristine.

The trail wound expertly among the rubble, always following the path that offered the most concealment and created the least noise. This infiltrator moved like he did, he realized. He gained respect for his opponent—and also relaxed somewhat, for this realization made it easier to forecast the track.

The trail led to a portion of the monastery that was a near-total wreck, the former cathedral of Dol Arrah. The cathedral had stood five stories tall before the war, with towers rising far above that; a stirring sight when one realized how very old the cathedral was. One of the first large projects undertaken by House Cannith after they revolutionized construction with their dragonmarks and magewrights, it had once sported a lofty sanctuary, balconies across the ceiling and down several of the walls, huge stained-glass windows, soaring pillars made from the trunks of mammoth Karrnathi pine trees, and well over a hundred hand-carved benches. The foundation of the cathedral was a complete level of its own, all stonework, and filled with room after room of illuminated manuscripts, catechisms, studies in exegesis and theology, and histories of the lives of the faithful. Below that lay the tombs of past leaders, martyrs, and teachers. It was said that the faithful in the cathedral had been therefore supported by the scriptures and the bones of the holy.

Naturally, the Thranes, being beholden to the Silver Flame and not the Sovereign Host, had bombarded the cathedral in 918, destroying its priceless history, unique architecture, and timeless beauty in a matter of days. Perhaps they had hoped that so doing would break the will of the resident monks. From his talks with Keiftal, Teron knew that the travesty had only incensed the monks to further greatness, although the cathedral had never been used for any purpose since. At least not until the resurrection of the Quiet Touch.

Teron glided up to the ruined side of the cathedral. The foundation with its empty galleries of scribes' cells was imbedded into the ground, with only small windows here and there to let in natural light. The sanctuary floor started roughly at the height of Teron's hip, but the walls rose higher, and the ruined stained-glass window over which he needed to climb was almost as high as he could reach.

Did you go up to the sanctuary floor or down to the scriptorium? he wondered. I could answer that if only I knew what drew you here in the first place.

* * * * * * *

"How did your interviews go, master?"

"Flawlessly, Jeffers," answered Praxle, shutting the simple wooden door behind him as he entered their guest quarters. "Flawlessly. There's nothing like a little illusion to find the truth, as they say."

"What did you find out, if I may be so bold, master?" asked the half-orc. He opened a hard leather case and pulled out a cut-crystal bottle and a gnome-sized brandy snifter. He filled the glass and handed it to his master.

"The Orb of Xoriat is concealed in the catacombs, Jeffers. Where is that, you wonder? So did I. So I had a very nice chat with our friend Prelate Quardov. First I enquired after his position in the church and all the important tasks that he performs. Well, then, once he was well-buttered, I pressed him for the history of the monastery, especially all the famous heroes and saints that might be buried here, and among whose number I was *certain* he would eventually take his rightful place."

Jeffers sniggered.

"And, after all that plying, he told me that he would not be buried with the local saints, but in Fairhaven."

"Why would that be, master?"

"Because the catacombs are in yon cathedral, that utterly ruined scrap heap. No one goes in, so the tombs lie unattended. In truth, it makes a twisted kind of sense to bury something like the Orb in there. No one wants to enter such an unsafe area, and if the Aundairian religious elite do nothing to clean it up, then, it's clear to all that there is nothing of value there."

"Except for the saints," said Jeffers.

"I know," said Praxle, a confused lilt in his voice. "That's a dichotomy of Quardov that I haven't yet unraveled. He's snubbing everyone buried there, in a way, yet he's managed to twist it around to where everyone seems to believe that he's being respectful by letting it all rot. Kind of like this whole monastery."

"My word, master, it appears that Quardov's tongue was far more effusive than I had surmised."

Praxle snorted, a jaded and longsuffering note. "Not as such," he said. "I persuaded him that I had a research grant from the University, and that if he could spare me the trouble of trudging all the way to Fairhaven and digging through their huge library of musty old tomes, I'd be happy to apportion my expense account with him."

"You bribed him."

"Jeffers, a cleric is above such menial temptations," said Praxle. They shared a laugh.

"Well, then, somewhere beneath the cathedral are the catacombs," said Praxle. "Tonight, you and I will see what we can find."

The half-orc pulled out a large traveling case and undid the latches. He opened it and pulled out a small lantern with a colored lens, a set of lock picks, a crowbar, and a wide broadsword with a serrated blade. He fished around in his kit bag and grabbed a whetstone, then sat on a chair and started honing his blade. "Why did you not demand the Orb outright, master?" he asked. "It does rightfully belong to the University, does it not?"

"Yes it does, but as they say, possession finds ways and means to keep itself." Praxle stepped over to the window and gazed out, surveying the ruins of the cathedral. "The prelate is very defensive about the Orb, make no mistake. I know I frustrated him by pressing about military matters earlier, which is why I took such pains to fawn all over him just now. No, he'd never admit they had the Orb, and he certainly would never turn it over. I'll have to resort to other means."

"Won't that cause trouble when they discover the Orb's missing?"

"It won't matter, Jeffers. Because then I'll be the one who has possession."

THE CATACOMBS
CHAPTER 5

Teron's training, his rigorous indoctrination, his faith, and his instinct all told him to proceed forward alone, that to do otherwise was to rely on someone else who would prove weaker than he. Nevertheless, his intellect carried the day. He did not know whom he pursued, the threat they posed, or their intent. He had never been within the confines of the cathedral ruins. No one in the monastery went there. As near as he could tell, he was the only one in the Monastery of Pastoral Solitude who was even aware that intruders were here—and he was exhausted from his afternoon workout. He had to inform someone, even if it risked exposing his presence to whomever lurked within the debris of the cathedral.

Regret and self-reproach cursing him even as he did it, he found several fist-sized chunks of masonry and threw one as hard as he could at the main hall. He followed it with another and then a third. The rocks sailed through the air and cracked against the exterior wall, one by one.

One of the brothers of the monastery poked his head out, looking around for the source of the disturbance. Teron raised his arms over his head, crossing the forearms to form an X. *Invaders.* The brother clenched a fist at his shoulder. *Understood.*

Teron held both palms up, dropped them, then raised one hand turned sideways. *Unknown people. Less than ten.* The brother signaled that he understood. Teron pointed his arm at the ruins of the cathedral, then swept it down. The brother clenched a fist a third time and disappeared back into the building.

Teron turned back to the ruins. He ran his fingers along the wall leading to the broken window over his head, looking for any traces or imperfections that would indicate the intruder had climbed the wall. He found none. He stooped down to the small window that led into the basement. The window had once been an iron lattice filled with small diamond-shaped panes. The lattice was badly broken and had rusted, but Teron noted that the ironwork along the bottom of the opening had been pushed flat, and some of the cracks in the rusted iron showed a sliver of shiny metal, untouched by the weather.

Teron glanced at the broken glass on the sill and the ground outside the window, then at his bare feet. He knew there was likely more broken glass inside. He prayed he could land gently enough that none of it would pierce his soles. With a shrug of resignation, he slipped through the small window and dropped noiselessly to the stone floor.

He landed in a crouch, hearing the creak of stressed glass beneath his toughened feet. He held his position for several heartbeats, listening intently and staring straight at the darkest shadow he could find. Soon his eyes adjusted to the gloom of the sunken scriptorium level of the cathedral foundation and details become clearer. He saw a rectangle of darker black—an open doorway. He glanced at the floor, the illumination given by the slanting shaft of sunlight revealed that footsteps had broken the layer of dust and ash that had lain here, undisturbed save by the occasional rodent, for so many years.

A small shadow moved at the window as Flotsam peered in and meowed.

"I don't like it either," whispered Teron. "I just wish I had your eyes."

He dropped his breathing into a slow and easy cycle, the air flowing noiselessly in and out of his lungs. He moved forward in attack stance, a ready half-crouch. His feet moved gently, stepping one after the other in a rolling gait designed to provide steady pressure and thus minimize the creaking of the floorboards. His aching muscles protested the further abuse in the wake of his workout, but he ignored their warnings.

He left the room and entered the hallway beyond. The gloom deepened. He focused his eyes on nothing, knowing that his peripheral vision grew more reliable as the darkness deepened. The trail, he noted, had broadened. The dust was disturbed by the passage of multiple tracks.

I thank you, Lady, that you led me here, he prayed. *I might not have been able to follow the trail otherwise.*

He continued toward the center of the ruined structure and the darkness deepened. Occasional small holes in the decaying wooden flooring of the cathedral above admitted a secondary glow from the shafts of miasmic sunlight that pierced the ruined sanctuary.

As he continued slowly, he realized another reason why the interlopers chose to strike in broad daylight—at night, the light of their lanterns might be seen from afar as they explored, but in the daytime, the sunshine obliterated any such telltale glow.

The trail moved into an apse in an area so dark he could only sense its openness by the changes in the behavior of the air. He heard voices—faint, distorted. For a moment he wondered if he was hearing the agonies of the Crying Fields, almost never heard in the daylight but somehow persistent here, hidden from the sun . . . but after careful consideration, the timbre of the voices was not one of hate and suffering.

It's them, he thought. I must be at a stairwell of some sort, and they on a lower level where they think their voices will go unheard.

He lowered himself to the ground. His muscles were somewhat tight from skipping the warm-down stretching after his workout, and they acceded unwillingly. He tapped around the floor with his fingers in a broadening circle and found the top stair of the descending flight. Feeling around to locate the balusters, he rose again and descended the stairs as silent as a viper, fingers lightly tracing the handrail. He felt his heart preparing to quicken, felt the sensation of adrenaline infusing into his tired, uncertain muscles. His stomach growled, sounding to him as loud as a great cat's mating call. He tightened his tunic once more.

The catacomb level was carved out of the ground itself and laid with quarried slabs. The stone stairs were built in a gradual spiral wide enough to bear a coffin, pallbearers, and light-bearing acolytes, all at once. The steps were shallow and expertly placed. Teron lost his sense of direction by the time he was halfway down. However, as he reached the bottom of the stairs, he realized that he could see faint shapes in the darkness, and he knew he was getting close to the intruders and their lanterns. In this perfect darkness, even the faintest indirect light was visible.

He heard a few more words whispered among the strangers. Turning his head, he figured out which direction the sound was coming from. The quiet conversation ended, then Teron heard a grating sound as of sand and stone. He glided closer, slowly, one finger trailing along the wall to ensure his path was straight.

He heard quiet shuffling ahead, and the smothering darkness waned ever so slightly as more reflected light spilled into the hallway. His pace quickened.

At that moment, his stomach chose to make the loudest of its protestations.

He froze. So did the others.

He heard someone start to whisper, but the sound was immediately cut off by a sharp, "Tch!"

Teron held his position, although his muscles were very unhappy to freeze in a ready stance. For many long moments he stood there. The light neither rose nor faded, and the only thing Teron heard was the ringing in his ears.

Somewhere in the darkness he heard the sigh of steel gliding out of a well-oiled scabbard—then footsteps, a slow, stealthy gait born of the hunter's confidence. He tried to use his peripheral vision to watch for motion, but his eyes were having trouble seeing anything in the unchanging darkness, and his mind was starting to imagine it saw the apparitions of the Crying Fields.

The shadows shifted, or so he thought. He tried to move his head around to discern whether or not he saw a human silhouette—

Blue eyes flashed briefly, looking like Flotsam's eyes seen at night.

Magic! Teron lunged forward in the darkness, intent on landing the first blow, for he knew that the other, with magically augmented vision, had spotted him in the near-pitch black.

He cleared the handful of yards between him and his quarry, trailing his right hand along the wall to maintain his bearings. He hooked his left fist at the center of his foe, an unskilled blow of power and momentum rather than precision. Relying solely on sound and peripheral vision, Teron's first blow struck wide of where he'd hoped. He felt it land a glancing blow just below the ribs. At the same time, Teron felt himself run into a partially raised blade, and the steel ripped through his tunic and across his left side, skipping along his ribs and opening skin and muscle.

Teron heard tense words, not quite shouted but filled with urgency, but he could not attend to the meaning. His concentration was consumed by his kinesthetic sense, tracking where his body was in comparison to his opponent and the walls. The wounded monk knew that the intruder had the benefit of vision, but he certainly didn't have the same close-combat training. If he did, he wouldn't be using a slow and awkward weapon like a longsword for interior fighting.

Teron sensed the sword rising, so he spun in close and low, his back to his foe's chest. The right arm came down, and as the arm hit Teron's shoulder, he hooked his right arm around the enemy's sword arm, immobilizing it. A strike with the open left hand sent the sword clattering down the hall. He smashed the back of his head into his opponent's nose, then stomped his left heel on the other's foot and was rewarded by the sound of breaking bones.

Teron turned to finish the enemy off, but his speed and strength were hampered by his exhaustion, and the enemy managed to pull away from him with a howl of unbridled agony. Teron shoved him out of the way, satisfied that he was out of the combat. As he turned to face the next threat (or at least his best guess as to where the next threat would come from), he staggered slightly as his muscles protested the exertion.

He heard a voice, and then the universe turned white.

Despite his training in fighting blind, the sudden transition from pitch dark to piercing daylight had a disorienting effect on Teron. He shut his eyes, but all he could see was a glaring red afterimage. He gave ground, spinning his arms in a defensive ring, until he backed into the stone wall of the corridor. He tried to force his aching eyes back open and glimpsed a glowing object fly past him and down the hallway. There was a shadow ahead of him, lit from behind.

Then he felt an impact in his abdomen, and a burning sensation that was all too familiar—he'd been impaled. He grimaced in pain, his eyes squinting against the light. One hand ran to his side and clutched the end of a quarrel embedded in his gut. Blood welled out from the wound and soaked into his tunic and the waistband of his pants.

"We gotta go!" said a dusky voice. "Now!"

"Where's Rander?" someone asked, half whispering. "Rander! Where are you?"

"I'll bet he knows," replied a light female voice.

Teron blinked several times, and through the haze of his tortured eyesight, he saw a shadow drawing closer to him, brandishing a crossbow.

"Where's Rander, monk?" said the shadow. "Which way did you throw him?"

"Careful, Grameste," warned the first voice, "that monk might still be dangerous."

Teron said nothing. He leaned against the wall, panting. He didn't have to feign his fatigue or his pain. He tightened his grip on the quarrel that seemed to devour his side.

Grameste moved closer, then she turned her head and paused as he spied Rander and the effect of Teron's handiwork. "Oh my—" she began, stretching her neck forward to see better.

With one smooth motion, Teron drew the quarrel from his side and speared the end of the bolt into Grameste's head, piercing the weak spot of the skull just behind the ear. She jerked, but Teron kept his grip and followed it up by striking the pointed end of the quarrel with his other hand, driving it fully into the woman's brain, killing her instantly. The only noise she made was a slight squeak—then a long, slow exhale as she slumped to the floor.

For a moment, stunned silence reigned.

"Sovereign bitch!" said one of the intruders, a tremor of fear in her voice.

Teron's eyes adjusted to the light, and he stood. He saw three people left. One was a spellcaster of some sort, probably female, holding a staff aglow with magical light. The second figure he could see only partially, as it held a bulls-eye lantern focused directly at the wounded monk. The third was a male, judging by his silhouetted build.

Teron ignored the trembling in his legs, the burning sensation in his side, and the trickle of blood that worked a red trail down his trousers. He flexed his shoulders to pop a few vertebrae in his upper back, then settled into combat stance and began to advance upon the strangers. His calf tried to cramp, so he paused in his approach to stretch it out. He concealed his momentary weakness by shifting to viper stance.

The male stepped forward. He exhaled slowly, belying his tension. "I'll take care of this wretch," he said. "Oargesha, you and Fox take the back way out of here, just to be safe."

"Just buy us some time, Roon, and then follow," said the wizard. A woman. Her voice betrayed her sex.

"A few moments will be enough for us," said the third, the one with the dusky voice, "but perhaps too much for you. I've heard monks can be fast. Bleed him some more, hobble him, or strike his eyes before you follow."

"Be careful," said the wizard.

"Aye, Oargesha," said the rearguard.

The shadow with the lantern set it on the floor, still facing Teron, then the two intruders turned to leave, with only Roon watching their back. Unfortunately, Teron knew Roon would be enough. His exhaustion, the two wounds, the cramp that threatened to return, and the fact that they knew these catacombs gave his opponents the edge they needed.

Since he could not beat the three of them, Teron let the two go. There was no point in fighting a battle that could not be won. Instead, Teron focused his whole being on ensuring that Roon died. Narrowing his focus in this manner brought Teron a pure, almost joyous clarity. He had a purpose, it was readily attainable, and nothing else mattered.

Roon stepped closer, drawing two short swords. The left blade he held inverted, with the blade extending down his forearm, while the right he dangled behind his back.

The two faced each other for several long breaths, the only sound an occasional flick or pop from the lantern's untrimmed wick.

He's trained, thought Teron, as he studied Roon's stance. Lead blade ready to block any strike and wound me in return, rear blade hidden so I won't see a change in grip. Good stance, but not relaxed. Tense breathing. He's trained but not experienced enough to be a master of his techniques.

Teron took a deep breath and clenched his teeth as a wave of dizziness swept over him. With time, he mused, I could find his weakness, find the slow move, but time is not a luxury I have, not bleeding the way I am.

Roon flashed forth, thrusting straight from the hip with his rear blade. Silhouetted as Roon was, the blade never entered the lamp's light, and it took Teron a split second to see what was happening. Teron twisted his arm in a rolling block to guide the deadly point away from his vitals, but he was a little too slow and the point sheared into his arm below the shoulder. Roon followed the strike with a forehand slash, trying to draw the blade of his inverted sword across Teron's body. Teron ducked the strike, and Roon's fist glanced off the top of his head. Roon pulled back, and Teron felt the inner edge of the blade draw a line across his shoulder—whether by accident or design he did not know.

Teron spun and tried to hook Roon's heels with a leg sweep, but his trembling leg made him a little too ponderous. He only caught a part of Roon's foot, and the burglar stumbled out of range.

Teron rose, slowly and not at all in the manner in which he'd been trained.

Roon smiled, and did a taunting little shuffle step. "Looks like you'll be meditating on nothing soon, friend," he said.

Teron cursed himself for his lack of concentration. Roon must die, he thought. That is my purpose. He focused himself, trying to channel his energy into his aching limbs. He felt the rise of a familiar wave of nausea building in his gut.

Roon charged again, this time leading with his front weapon, a stepping forehand slash followed by a backhand thrust. Teron feinted, then dodged right. His left hand hooked upward to brace Roon's wrist, while his right hand punched Roon squarely on the elbow. There was a flash of red and the sound of ligaments and cartilage breaking under the impact as the joint gave way. Roon yelped, and his planned combination move with his rear sword became a wild, flailing swing that carved a light cut across Teron's chest.

"Dolurrh!" cursed Roon. He staggered back, the sword dropping from his nerveless left hand. He looked confused, fearful.

Teron leaned forward and vomited up a small wad of stomach juices before he regained command of his uneasy esophagus.

Roon's eyes lit up with the possibility of escape.

Seeing this, Teron swallowed hard and pushed out every ounce of energy his spirit had left, forcing the power into his fists. His face contorted with rage, pain, and tormented intensity. He lunged forward, reversed his direction and feinted a kick with his left leg, then reversed again, launching a roundhouse kick with his right. It connected squarely with Roon's thrusting sword, although between the thrust and the force of the kick, the sword's blade opened a long, nasty gash along Teron's shin. The monk used his momentum to spin around and, with a loud cry, he struck Roon as hard as he could with both arms, his hands molded into veritable spear points.

His strike landed true, hitting Roon just below the breast on each side. He heard a loud crack but was unsure if he had broken Roon's ribs, his own fingers, or both.

The last thing he remembered was seeing the sweep of the lantern light as he fell to the floor.

❋ ❋ ❋ ❋ ❋ ❋ ❋

High above the earth, a small falcon stooped to a dive, falling closer and closer to the ground and the two mounted women who awaited it. The raptor swooped out of the dive at grass level, beating its wings and rising again to land on Oargesha's outstretched wrist.

Oargesha turned to the Shadow Fox and shook her head.

The Fox set her mouth in a grim line and exhaled, a sigh that was almost a growl of frustration. "Rander, Gramm, and Roon. This was . . . a very expensive excursion."

Oargesha tried to look at the Shadow Fox, tried to meet the weight that hung in her leader's eyes, but couldn't. "I can't believe you just left him like that."

"I had to. This bag is more important than all of us. Do you understand that? If we'd stayed, maybe we'd be dead, too."

Oargesha hung her head. "We knew following you wouldn't be easy, Fox," she mumbled. She cast a longing look back toward the Crying Fields. "But . . . oh, I don't . . . Fox, what was all this for?"

The Shadow Fox looked at the heavy, black leather bag that they had stolen. Although roughly rectangular in construction, it bulged with something large and round inside. "I'm not sure," she said.

Oargesha looked at the Fox, her chin quivering. "What do you mean, you're not sure? Don't you know?"

The Shadow Fox met Oargesha's eyes. "No, I don't. The message that we took from Roon's elf friend didn't say much about the Black Globe other than it was a powerful artifact with the ability to effect dramatic changes in the world."

"You mean maybe we could use it to try to restore Cyre?"

"Possibly." She grasped the bag's handles, which she had draped over the saddle horn, and pulled. When she tugged on the heavy handles, the bag did not react naturally. It resisted moving as if it were extremely heavy, but when she got it moving, it gathered an inertia that defied instinct. As she hefted it up to her lap, the bag kept moving upward, and she had to wrestle it down until it sat, quiescent, in front of her.

She glanced at Oargesha. Oargesha shrugged.

The Fox tested the heavy latches that held the bag closed. "Locked," she said. "No surprise. We'll have to open it later. That's probably best, anyway. If we opened it here, we'd spend our time looking at it instead of getting away." She patted the bulging leather and then pushed the bag back down to its resting place, draped over her saddle horn. "So. We have five horses, two of us, and one Black Globe. We should be able to make good time. Barring magical intervention, we'll make Ghalt before anyone can pass word to the authorities."

Oargesha nodded.

The Fox paused, looking around even though there was nothing to see but red-tinged grass out here at the fringe of the Crying Fields. "Come to think of it, let's not ride to Ghalt. It's the nearest town, and when the pursuit starts asking questions, folks there might remember seeing two women with five horses. And I don't know about you, but that's where I stole mine."

"Then where do we go?" asked Oargesha. "Hook around and make for Athandra?"

"No, that'll take too long. No decent roads, plus we'd be spending too much time near the Monastery of Pastoral Solitude. They'll be scouring the land east, I'm sure." She considered her options, then made her choice. "We'll cut north by northwest from here, skipping Ghalt altogether. Instead, we'll find the Orien trade road and push hard straight to Lathleer. Once there, we can reappraise our situation. I'd like to switch modes of transportation if possible, and see if maybe we can get a couple of dim-witted sots to join us on the trip to Fairhaven. Once there, we'll hook the lightning rail to Thrane." She drummed her fingers on her saddle, nodding to herself. "I think that's our best bet. It's fast, and it doesn't retrace the route we took here. There's no way to know whether or not any of the people we lost might still have had their lightning rail passes with them."

Oargesha fought back some tears. "Right." She sniffed. "Let's go."

The Shadow Fox paused a minute before spurring her horse. "It's hard for me, too, Oargesha. Just remember that they died for a good cause."

Oargesha said nothing as she flicked the reins.

* * * ◉ * * *

Praxle reclined on his thin mattress, idly practicing his cantrips as the sun crept toward the horizon. Jeffers was on the floor beside him, testing the bulls-eye lantern, trimming the wick and checking the lenses. Praxle paused in his practice when he heard footsteps approaching. "That's odd," he said. "Last time they only sent one to summon me."

Jeffers looked over at Praxle, then stood and set the bulls-eye lantern on the side table. An instant later, the door rattled as someone pounded on the other side. "Praxle d'Sivis!"

"One moment," Praxle called. "Let me finish dressing."

He snapped his fingers and pointed Jeffers to the corner behind the door. He made some shuffling noises, then opened the door until it rested against his firmly planted foot. He made a show of adjusting his trousers.

Outside the door stood Prelate Quardov, Master Keiftal, and roughly a half-dozen monks in black. Quardov did not look happy. Each of the monks wore an absolutely blank expression.

"Well, this is unexpected," said the gnome. "I thought I wouldn't be summoned until the evening meal. Pray tell, what can I do for you?"

"Do not insult us by acting innocent," said Quardov.

A flash of panic flew from Praxle's heart to his loins, but he quickly mastered the emotion. Had his bribe to Quardov somehow backfired? Had they heard Jeffers's whetstone? "I'm sure I don't know what you're insinuating," he said, carefully moderating his voice for that perfect balance of respectful caution and carefree innocence. He slid his hands into his pants pockets.

Quardov smirked. "You thought these people were just a bunch of Aundairian countryside simpletons, ignorant of the duplicity that festers in the big cities. You were wrong."

"I'm afraid I still don't understand," said Praxle. He pulled his left hand from his pocket. His mind raced. Did they know he'd glamered himself to appear like Quardov?

"Your visit here has proven to be more than academic," said Quardov.

Praxle spread his arms wide—helplessly, innocently. With this gesture, his left hand was concealed from view behind the door, and he flicked a small potion to Jeffers, who stood motionless in the corner.

Obviously annoyed at Praxle's continued protestations, the prelate stamped his foot. "You came here to steal the Thrane Sphere!" he yelled. "And by the Five Nations, you will burn for your blasphemy!"

The suddenness and ferocity of the accusation caused Praxle's face to blanch. "What's the—?"

"Don't even try such a tactic with me!" bellowed Quardov, the veins bulging out beneath his pale skin. He pointed a finger atremble with ire. "Arrest him! Arrest them both!"

The black-garbed monks leaped past Quardov and into the room. Two of them seized Praxle and ratcheted his arms into joint locks. He struggled, but one of them planted a thumb at the base of his ear and pressed, bringing such pain that the gnome relented.

The other four fanned out. One of them slammed the door fully open, but the room was otherwise empty.

"Where's your companion?" asked one of the monks.

"I sent my domestic out to collect some local flora and fauna," said Praxle. "The university wants samples of the oddities found here."

Quardov glided into the room. He picked up the bulls-eye lantern that Jeffers had set on the side table and held it out accusingly. One of the monks offered Quardov the newly-honed serrated sword from the luggage case. Quardov ran a finger along the edge, clucking his tongue, then pulled his hand back and rubbed the whetting oil between his fingers.

"And these?" he asked. "Are these the tools you use to collect samples of grass, Professor d'Sivis?" He handed the blade back to the monk, then placed his hand on the lens of the lantern. "And this lantern is still warm. Is it really that much of a challenge to find weeds around here?"

"I can explain," said Praxle.

"There's no need to explain." Quardov gestured, and one of the monks holding Praxle pressed his thumb into the soft spot behind the gnome's ear again.

Praxle hissed in pain.

"You come here and verify for yourself the existence of the Thrane Sphere by its effects upon this landscape," said Quardov, casting a dark look at Keiftal. "You impersonate me by means of illusion to discover where the Sphere is secreted. Oh, yes, little gnome, that came to light once your colleagues committed their crime. Then you use your scholarly ploy to press me for details on our past so that you can learn about the catacombs. Once you have these details, you send your compatriots to recover the Sphere while you linger here playing the innocent historian." Quardov stepped over to Praxle and bent down to look him square in the eyes. "It was a very good plot. Indeed it was. Unfortunately for you, your compatriots were spotted. I am pleased to tell you that some are dead. And now you will tell us where the rest of them went."

Quardov stood and began to leave the room.

"But there's nothing to tell," protested Praxle. "We've been in the monastery all day!"

Quardov halted in the doorway and turned his head. "You've been in the monastery all day? Why, dear gnome, I thought you sent your companion out for samples."

Praxle tried to think of an answer—any answer—but failed.

CHAPTER 6

Quardov led a procession through the heart of the monastery and across the courtyard to a little-used outbuilding. As they entered, a scruffy tomcat rounded the corner. It arched its back and hissed at Quardov, then stopped, sat, and watched the procession pass before scampering off.

The black-clad monks followed Quardov into the building. Two of them held Praxle's arms in debilitating joint locks. The gnome dared not struggle. Two more moved over to iron manacles dangling from a massive beam in the ceiling. They opened the cuffs and clamped them around Praxle's small wrists.

The cuffs were built for a human frame. They hung just low enough so that Praxle's feet could still touch the floor. His arms, however, extended straight into the air, with his shoulders pressing on his ears.

"Find out everything he knows," said Quardov. "Leave no marks."

"My reverence," said one of the monks, flexing his fingers, "we never leave marks."

Quardov ignored the comment and turned to leave, Keiftal following after him.

As they crossed the courtyard, Keiftal struggled to keep even with the prelate. "Would you like to speak to Teron, now, my reverence?" he asked, peering at Quardov's face.

Quardov drew up short, his lip curled in loathing. "Teron? Why is he still here?"

"What would you have us do with him, prelate?" asked Keiftal.

"I don't know," said Quardov. He fluttered one hand in vexation. "Send him home."

"This is his home," said Keiftal. "He was just a lad when he first arrived. We raised him, taught him, trained him in the ways—"

Quardov raised one hand. "I *know*," he said. "Do not presume to remind me."

"Then why do you wish us to send him away? He is the last of—"

"I know he's the last, and damn his soul, he lingers so!"

"He is—"

"He is a freak!"

Keiftal backed away. "Wh—what do you mean?"

Quardov stabbed one accusing finger in the direction of the monastery. "Anyone who went through that . . . that *training* so easily is not someone who is in full possession of his faculties! He—" Quardov paused. "He shouldn't exist. I don't trust him, nor would I trust any of his kind."

Keiftal nodded. "As you wish, my reverence, but I still suggest you speak with him. He might offer some additional insight into the gnome's fellow conspirators."

Quardov clenched his teeth. "You speak too loudly, Keiftal," he said. "You have ever since the first day you brought that damnable Sphere to me."

* * * 🌀 * * *

Teron groaned. The light tormented his eyes and gouged its way into his mind. His restless legs kicked weakly, pulling the sheet from his body, and his stomach felt like a single knot of rope.

He felt a cold cloth placed on his forehead, then a second cloth, sodden with water, placed at his lips. He gathered his wits and sucked on the cloth. An unseen hand took it and replaced it again. Teron drank more, then managed to squeeze out the word, "Enough."

He forced his breathing and heartbeat to become regular. He started clenching and unclenching his fists in a slow cycle, willing his body to cooperate.

A deep breath, and then he stretched, first his arms, then his shoulders, then his torso—

"Hsst!" Two biting pains in his sides brought him fully to consciousness.

"I wouldn't do that, brother," said his attendant.

"You could have . . . told me earlier," managed Teron.

"I didn't know you'd forgotten it."

Teron laughed, a single chuckle more like a cough than a true laugh. "I didn't know either," he said. "What happened?"

"I wasn't there, brother. If you'll be all right alone for a moment, let me fetch the master and the prelate. They've been asking after you."

Teron nodded weakly, and he heard sandaled footsteps depart the room.

He lay there for a while, trying to recollect his thoughts and memories, and inventory his known wounds. Then he realized that he was in no imminent danger and that his best course of action right now was simply to rest, so he tried . . . and failed, because after a few moments of calm, his brain started working on the memories again.

Soon he heard footsteps approaching. He opened his eyes just long enough to see Quardov, Keiftal, and one or two others enter the room. Most of the people stopped at Teron' side. One person—Teron recognized master Keiftal, thanks to his shuffling step—went around his cot to the other side.

The imperious voice of the prelate split the air. "Tell me what happened."

"I was about to ask you the same thing," said Teron.

"I insist you tell us. Now."

"My reverence," said a voice that Teron recognized as the attendant, "he is very weak. He has lost a lot of blood."

"Tell me what you know," said Teron. "I'll see if you're right."

The prelate sniffed, clearly annoyed. "One of the . . . *brothers* . . . claims that he saw you give the signal for invasion and then repair into the scriptorium below the cathedral. He went for assistance. While he was gathering others, he chanced to see a glowing, pulsating object shoot from the scriptorium window and arc over the rise."

Teron raised one hand halfway, then let it drop.

"You wish to add some keen insight?" said Quardov, who, although he'd been annoyed at having to speak, now showed affront at being interrupted.

"I think . . . it was a bird familiar . . . with a light spell."

"That would make sense, my reverence," boomed Keiftal, his nasal voice swamping the room. "The flapping wings of a bird would seem to make the light flicker, would they not?"

"Enough," said Quardov. "As the witness and the others exited the building, they saw a pair of thieves exit the scriptorium and flee up the same rise. They gave chase, but the pair chanced upon a quintet of horses and rode away."

"Brought there . . . by the familiar," said Teron.

"Yes, quite," said Quardov. "I'm sure we were all aware of that." He sighed. "Then the brothers searched the scriptorium and the catacombs. They found you and took you for dead. But . . . you were not. They also found other bodies. The thieves you killed?"

Teron nodded.

"One had a rather unusual injury—black burns upon his breast. Burnt through to the bone, I am told. Tell me, how did you manage that?"

Teron opened his eyes. Quardov loomed over him. On the opposite side of the bed, Keiftal gazed down on him with a look of grave concern. Teron closed his eyes again and let his head sink back on the pillow. "I don't remember. One of the thieves probably had a torch, and I used it for a weapon."

"A torch?" said Quardov. "We found no torch, but instead a bulls-eye lantern. Are you suggesting that the thieves took a torch, but left a lantern? Preposterous!"

"It could have been a wayward spell, my reverence," said Keiftal.

"You will tell me what happened!" said Quardov.

Teron didn't react. Instead, he paused for a heartbeat, and then started softly snoring. He twitched one hand for good measure.

"We should let him sleep, my reverence," said the attendant.

Quardov growled and stomped from the room. As his steps faded, Teron popped his eyes back open and caught Keiftal's sleeve as the old master shuffled his way around the bed.

"Keiftal," he whispered. "How many bodies did you find?"

The old monk glanced down the hallway, then raised two fingers.

Teron scowled.

❀ ❀ ❀ ❀ ❀ ❀ ❀

Quardov waited until Keiftal had left the hospice and shut the door behind him. "That was an utter waste of my time."

"I apologize, my reverence," said Keiftal. "He has been badly injured."

Quardov closed his eyes and clenched his jaw. "And now we have nothing to do but wait."

Praxle's shrill scream echoed through the air.

Quardov snorted and began to walk down the hall. "At least such sounds are no strangers to this place."

"My reverence," said Master Keiftal, trotting around to be in front of the prelate, "We should not wait."

"Don't stand so close to me," said Quardov.

Keiftal retreated a step or two.

"We must wait, Keiftal," Quardov said. "What other choice do we have?"

"We must pursue!"

"With what?" asked Quardov. "The thieves fled on horseback. Magebred horses, no less, and five in number, so even if we did have a nag in the stable, they'd still get away! We could send a runner to alert the military, but what would they find?

Nothing! We can give them no more than, 'Watch for a large spherical object,' and that is hardly helpful in matters such as this! By the Sovereign Host, we don't even know what the thieves look like! What more would you have me do, you impudent wretch? This is all your fault anyway! You were to safeguard that Sphere!"

"Send Teron after them."

Quardov laughed, a hysterical laugh of bitter grief and unbearable stress. "Do you really think that one monk is going to outperform the entire Aundairian military?"

"That's what he does," said Keiftal. "You said yourself that you didn't think the military would find anything. He's much more . . . unobtrusive than a battalion."

"We cannot use him," said Quardov. "The thieves fought him in the catacombs. They know what he looks like."

"And he knows what they look like," said Keiftal. "He's the only one who does."

Quardov opened his mouth to respond, but the words didn't come. He saw the logic and found himself running out of energy. He chose to make a small concession and said, "You make some sense, Keiftal. For a change. But despite your reasoning, it will be too late. He will be too slow in recovering from his wounds."

"You are right, my reverence," said Keiftal. "It will take too long for him to recover naturally."

"What are you saying?"

"I suggest that you lay your hands on Teron and petition Dol Arrah to heal his wounds."

"What?" gasped Quardov. "Heal him? Heal that . . . that . . . that travesty? His kind weren't even supposed to survive the war!"

Keiftal's eyes widened. "What? What do you mean?"

"Don't you understand?" The prelate lowered his voice to a hiss. "They are an embarrassment, an affront, a festering blight on the fair face of Dol Arrah! The Quiet Touch never should have been. We never should have allowed them to be!"

Quardov paced back and forth, turning like a wild dog on a short tether. He took a deep breath and continued. "Don't you see? That's why we sent them on their final missions. When the Treaty of Thronehold was being negotiated and peace was approaching, we sent them out on suicide missions. Remove key Thrane military personnel to advance our position in the coming peacetime and blot out their foul existence from our history! They should all be dead, gone, vanished from the face of Eberron, and he, he has the gall, the temerity, the cold vindictiveness to live!"

Keiftal stood, his mouth agape. Then he shook off his surprise, swallowed hard, and looked at Quardov with a cool, detached gaze. "Then, my reverence," he said, "the Thrane Sphere is as good as lost."

* * * * * * *

Praxle fought to lose consciousness, strove to dive into blissful blackness, but the broken rafters wouldn't let him. The rafters dangled him like a fish on the line. They summoned the fingers. The fingers sent searing fire up and down his body, bouncing him back and forth between the abyss and the light. Praxle tried to remember, but he couldn't. There was only pain and the dread of pain.

Someone asked a question, but it meant nothing to Praxle. He would have answered, but he couldn't. His head hung to the rear, forcing his mouth open, and now it was gone dry. Or maybe it had been the screaming that did it. He raised his head just enough to try to swallow, to get some fluid back in his parched mouth. He failed at that but chanced to see his arms stretched before him. They were trying to dive, but the rafters pulled them away.

He heard words: "You've pushed him too far. He's incoherent." He was uncertain what the words meant, but someone was banished away. Praxle hoped that didn't mean that he'd failed the rafters somehow and that more pain was coming. He felt a hand grab his hair and pull his head erect, then someone dumped a small pail of water over his head. Praxle gasped, and then his tongue licked up all the water that was within reach. Another half pail of water quickly followed, and Praxle was aware enough to capture a mouthful or two. With that, he was able to rouse himself and clear his mind.

His wrists were chafed where the manacles were clamped, and his shoulders and elbows ached from supporting the weight of his body. His knees quivered from weakness, but he forced himself to stand nonetheless—partially to relieve the pain in his wrists but more so to make it easier to breathe. His head weaved back and forth as if it were too heavy for his neck, which, truth be told, it was.

The room was empty, save for one black-clad monk. The interrogator stood in front of Praxle, appraising him with a critical eye and a passionless face. He caught Praxle's gaze, and seeing that the spark of sanity had returned, he bowed his head slightly. "I apologize if this interrogation is being done in an unprofessional manner," he said. "Uses such as this are not our primary reason for learning pressure points. Thus we are not taught how to employ them in these situations. I fear we have taken more of your time than is necessary, yet there is much time still to be spent here. For that I am sorry, but I have more I must learn from you."

"I've told you all I know," said Praxle.

The monk smiled. "It would take a lifetime for you to tell me all you know," he said. "But in this case, I will spare you the punishment for lying to me."

"There's nothing else you can learn from me . . . about . . . whatever happened here."

"So you say. But I have been directed to find out for myself if that is true. Shall we continue?"

"I'd rather not," said Praxle.

"Acquiescence would have been easier for both of us," said the monk. "It would have given you the illusion of influence, and me the illusion of cooperation. Now we have neither." He reached out and took Praxle by the elbows, pressing his thumbs onto the vulnerable nerves.

As Praxle stopped writhing, he felt a light triple tap on the top of his head. He looked up, but saw nothing but the rafters.

The monk grabbed Praxle's hair and pulled his head forward again. "Stay with me," he said, "and we will finish more quickly. We would both like that, wouldn't we?"

Praxle nodded. "Yes, we would," he said, and started scuffing his feet back and forth across the floor. "Ask me anything. I swear I'll answer."

"That's better," said the monk—then he made a small noise like a hiccup. He looked down at the serrated steel point protruding from his ribs. He looked up at Praxle for a moment, a questioning look in his eyes, then his eyes dilated and focused on the hereafter.

Jeffers, now visible standing behind the monk, let the tip of his sword drop, and the corpse sagged to the floor.

The half-orc wiped his blade on the monk's pants and sheathed it. Then he pulled a thin steel pick from his belt and started working on the locks of Praxle's manacles.

"It's about time you got here," said Praxle.

"I took the first opportunity," replied Jeffers.

"There was no chance yesterday?"

"It's only been two hours, master," said Jeffers. The lock of the first manacle clicked, and Jeffers freed Praxle's right wrist. "This was the first time since you've been captured that there was only one monk to overcome."

"I bought a bodyguard who's afraid of two unarmed monks?"

Jeffers shrugged. "They are very skilled in weaponless combat. I have little experience facing such techniques. While I would be certain to kill one, I could not be positive of my defeating the other in a fair fight."

Praxle threw Jeffers a weary and angry look. "I hire you to keep me safe. If you die, I can always buy another half-orc."

"You hire me to keep you alive, master," responded Jeffers. "Were I to die, I could not free you. And where, then, would you buy yourself another chance to escape?"

Praxle considered this, then collapsed to the floor when Jeffers opened the second manacle.

"Time to go, master," said Jeffers. "I've made some preparations." He slung Praxle over one shoulder, stepped to the doorway, looked out, then sprinted out the door and around to the back side of the outbuilding. He adjusted Praxle's position to one that Praxle found even more painful, then sprinted again.

The gnome bounced along on the half-orc's shoulder, too exhausted to resist or protest. The sun-washed red grass and ruins swooped by beneath the gnome's exhausted gaze, then Jeffers hauled him into a building. The stable, by the earthy smell of it.

Praxle heard Jeffers open a latch, then found himself unceremoniously dumped onto a wooden floor. He banged his head as he landed, but the pain was nothing compared to what he had recently experienced, and he took no particular notice.

For a blissful moment, he was motionless. Then he heard Jeffers whip some horses into motion, and the carriage lurched forward, rolling Praxle under the bench. He tried to rise but banged his head. He managed to stabilize his position as the carriage accelerated, but soon the horses were sprinting down a little-used cart track at full speed, and Praxle found himself unable to climb out from his spot.

In the wake of his torture, he wanted nothing else but to relax, yet he couldn't. The carriage rattled and jolted, and the door swung open and shut, banging loudly and bathing Praxle in either bright sunlight or near-total darkness. Praxle could not even rest his head on the bucking floorboards, nor raise it too high lest he knock it against the bench seat above his head, over and over.

His head lolled in resignation. "Jeffers," he said, his weak voice buried by the din, "I am docking your pay."

CHAPTER 7

Teron leaned against the windowsill of the infirmary, looking to west, at the golden hues of the sunset. The crescent horns of Eyre, Aryth, and Sypheros sailed above the horizon, reminding Teron of a stack of bowls or hands cupped in meditation.

He turned away from the view as he heard someone enter the room. Keiftal shuffled in, shutting the door behind him. He saw Teron, and a broad, happy smile broke across his aged face. "It is good to see you up and about, my boy," he said, not quite meeting Teron's eyes. "Are you feeling well?"

Teron grinned in spite of himself. Keiftal's wrinkles, his slurred and creaky voice, and his slightly stooped frame all stood in stark contrast to the pure, almost childlike joy that shone from his countenance. "I feel hale, master, thank you for asking," he said, leaning against the windowsill. He ran one hand down his abdomen, stopping so that his fingers could investigate a fresh pink scar that puckered his skin. "But I must ask: what happened? Was I struck down? Poisoned? Did I have the ague? I remember fragments, then . . ."

Keiftal shook his head, sadness darkening his features. "No, my boy. You were very badly wounded, and . . . well, Prelate

Quardov prayed over you for the intercession of the Sovereign Host. You were healed by divine providence."

Teron blinked several times in surprise. "Prelate Quardov? Prayed for me?"

Keiftal nodded.

"Perhaps I have misjudged him," murmured Teron with an abashed smile.

"No, my boy, I am afraid you have not," said Keiftal with a heavy sigh.

"No?"

Keiftal shook his head. "His motives were far from altruistic, I am afraid."

Teron shrugged. "Be that as it may, his prayers worked."

Keiftal sat down at the foot of Teron's bed. "Do you know what those people were doing down in the catacombs?"

Teron shook his head.

"They stole something," explained Keiftal, "an item of great power. It was . . . a . . . a *weapon* . . . used during the War. We had a visitor, you see, from the University of Korranberg. Perhaps you heard. His name was Praxle d'Sivis. Well, at least that's what he told us, but I think it is true, because he seemed a very cocksure gnome and the papers that we found in his room seemed legitimate. He had a half-orc companion named Jeffers with him, who acted as his servant. They came here, ostensibly for University research, but it has become apparent that they were actually here to search for this relic."

"What's it called?" asked Teron.

"We don't know if it has a proper name, but we've always called it the Thrane Sphere," said Keiftal. He paused and picked at his nose. "Anyway, while we were entertaining Praxle, Jeffers and some others broke into the catacombs to steal the Sphere. You chanced, somehow, to catch them in the act."

"I had a little help," said Teron.

"I wish you could have stopped them, but alas, they got away. We captured Praxle, but they freed him—and stole the prelate's carriage to make good their escape."

"It was right after that that Quardov agreed to intercede for me, wasn't it?" asked Teron.

Keiftal nodded.

Teron folded his arms and crossed his legs as he leaned against the sill. In contrast to his still pose, his eyes darted about studying Keiftal's face. "And the two of you want me to go after them and recover the Thrane Sphere." It was not a question.

"That is exactly it. You see, there is no other choice. You are the only one who has the training to deal with the thieves on their terms—eye to eye in the alleys and secret places. And you are the only one who has seen them."

Teron drew a sharp breath through his nose and sucked on his lips as he considered this. "I can't," he said at last.

"You are the only one who can," said Keiftal. "If they try to escape overland, it will take them enough time that we can notify the military and the Arcane Congress. If, however, they take the lightning rail, they stand an excellent chance of slipping our border before we can set up measures. Our only hope is to send someone to run them to ground."

Teron narrowed his eyes, casting his expression in a more defensive tone.

Keiftal waited for a moment, then added, "I recall a little while ago, you said that you were a tool of war that had no use in a newfound era of peace. You lamented your very existence."

"I do," said Teron. "I should have died with the others."

"I have only met one other person with the same foolish opinion of your life," said Keiftal, "and that is Prelate Quardov."

Teron closed his eyes and pinched the bridge of his nose with one hand.

Keiftal leaned forward, raising his blurry voice. "You are a uniquely talented individual, Teron, even for a member of the Quiet Touch. You are a national treasure"—he paused, drawing a breath—"even if we dare not let anyone know you exist.

"The Last War may be over, but the struggle is not, the fight against evil is not. The peace is a fragile one, and there is at least as much a need for killing as there ever was. You did amazing things during the war. I know. You killed key people, destroyed critical targets, but in truth you accomplished nothing that could not have been done with a large enough supply of soldiers. Today, however, there is peace. We cannot send any soldiers at all. We can only send you. You can accomplish things that can no longer be done any other way. The crown needs you. Our people need you. Everyone on Khorvaire needs you, lest the Thrane Sphere be unveiled again. We need the last member of the Quiet Touch!"

Teron slowly slumped, then fell to his knees on the bare floor. He leaned his head back against the wall, staring blankly at some random point on the ceiling. "You misunderstood me, master Keiftal," he said. "I didn't say I *would* not do this. I said I *can* not do it. I realized something down there in the catacombs . . . among the dead." He drew a shuddering breath. "The Last War made me who I am. I . . . I chose my course, and the war shaped me, honed me, preserved me. But the war's been over for two years now, and I find that who I am is fading away. Evaporating, rusting like a fine blade left out in the weather. There is no way those . . . thieves—there's no way they should have gotten the better of me. Despite everything, I've gone soft."

Keiftal remained motionless, sitting on the bed, watching Teron grapple with his emotions.

Teron's larynx bobbed several times as he swallowed hard. Finally he spoke, his voice thick with grief, his gaze still roving the ceiling. "I can't even do what I was trained for," he said. "The forms, the routines, they . . . they were supposed to train me to fight. But for the last two years I've just sat here, and the forms became the fight."

"But what of your time spent in the Crying Fields?" asked Keiftal. "You've come back with bruises and other marks. . . ."

Teron sighed. "The challenge is not the same. Most of the time, the specters are ethereal, insubstantial. I do my best to convince myself that they are not, and I force myself to battle them, but my fists hit nothing but cold, dead air."

"But what of the rest of the time?" asked Keiftal.

"When the moon of the month is full," Teron said, his voice a hollow monotone, "they become more substantial. I can feel my fists striking something, like an echo of a body. I can see my fists leaving marks upon them, like a stone rippling a pond. Some I daresay I've even killed with my . . . talents." He looked down as he clenched one hand into a fist. "They can tear my skin, bruise my flesh, but they still cannot truly harm me. It's still not the same. That's why I watch the moons, master." He looked Keiftal in the eye. "My time is coming to see whether or not I am fit to live."

For a long while they sat there, Keiftal's piercing, fiery gaze trying to penetrate Teron's blank, dead stare.

"I would say that Dol Arrah, Mistress of Honor, Sacrifice, and Light, has deemed you fit to live, Teron," said the old monk.

The unquestioned conviction within Keiftal's words cast a slim ray of hope into the darkness of Teron's soul. Despite himself, he found his interest piqued. "Why do you say?"

"It's rare to claim to know the mind of a goddess," answered Keiftal, "unless you're full of conceit and vainglory like Quardov. But of this I am confident."

"Please don't bandy words." Teron sighed, feeling his despair dim the scant light. "Just speak."

"Dol Arrah answered Quardov's prayers. If she did not deem you worthy of her service, she would not have made you whole again."

Teron laughed, a derisive, voiceless hissing expression of disagreement and disgust. "I am far from whole, master," he said.

Keiftal leaned forward, forearms resting on his knees, fingers laced. "What do you mean?"

"I was far from whole when the monastery first found me. My home was . . . my . . . my family . . ." Teron struggled to find the right words, wanting to speak, but fearing the effect when the hidden, hated words at last flew free.

"We all lost family in the Last War, Teron," said Keiftal.

Thus given a reprieve, Teron's words flowed more easily. "Once I got here, it was easy for me to learn to kill. Every time I killed someone, it was to make the pain go away. I justified what I did by how it helped Aundair. Yet, as I assassinated more people, the pain never went away. Instead, I had to make myself numb just to cope, because I was killing for hate—and the killing only made the hate worse." Teron squeezed his eyes shut, then opened them again to look at his mentor.

Keiftal gazed back at him. His eyes, beneath his long, scraggly brows showed sadness, pain, and most of all understanding. Benediction seemed to radiate from every wrinkle of his compassionate features. "Teron," he said, "every soldier on Khorvaire—at least every one with a conscience—has struggled with the same thing. It's only natural to hate your opponent in a war. In many ways, we trained you to it—not to help you lose emotional control, but to make it easier for you to kill them without remorse."

Teron laughed again, a single black chuckle. "You did well, honored one, you and the other instructors. The things I've done . . ." Then his face turned gravely serious, even accusatory. "But I never did any of it because I hated the Thranes."

Within the darkest parts of his soul, Teron walked to the precipice. "I did it all because I hate myself."

Keiftal cocked his head to one side.

Teron steepled his hands over his nose and leaned forward until his hands rested on the ground. He took several deep breaths, then at last took the final step, the last desperate attempt to prove to his mentor that he was unworthy. "Master Keiftal," he said, "I killed my own family."

He heard only the nasal sound of Keiftal breathing. The rhythm did not change, indicating that Keiftal was not the least bit surprised at Teron's revelation.

Teron's disquiet grew, and he sat back up. "That's the truth of the matter," he said. He dared to raise his eyes to meet those of his mentor, but instead of cold reproach, he saw only absolution in Keiftal's gaze.

"Let it go," said Keiftal. "Leave it behind. Dol Arrah has counted you worthy of her intervention, as I have counted you worthy of everything I have to offer. If I do not hate you, if *she* does not hate you, do not hate yourself."

Teron pondered this, such all-embracing forgiveness in the face of his total self-recrimination. If his deity and his master held him in such high esteem, how could he add to his self-loathing by disappointing them? He wiped the corners of his eyes with his fingertips, trying to squeeze out the tension that had filled them.

He rose. "As you wish, honored one. I shall take this assignment."

"No," said Keiftal, "you shall complete it. Keep that in mind." He, too, rose. "We've prepared everything for you. Our best condensed rations, several letters of credit that have been carefully endorsed by the prelate, some gold and small gems for when you wish to use other methods of payment, maps, and the prelate's seal to prove that you are about official church business. And here are the portraits of Praxle and Jeffers. Some of the brothers copied them from the papers we found in their luggage. They're far from perfect, but they should help. That should be everything you need."

Teron smiled half heartedly. "That seems to cover everything I might lack, since it seems I still carry Dol Arrah's favor, blessings be on her for her beneficence."

"That I am glad for," said Keiftal, "for you shall need it."

"Yes, honored one."

"Quit calling me 'honored one.' "

❋ ❋ ❋ ❋ ❋ ❋ ❋

"Lathleer!" Oargesha gasped as she looked at the settlement atop the next hill. "At last."

"No, I don't think so," said the Fox. She spotted a farmer working a nearby field and hailed him. "Heyo!" she called. "Which town is this?"

The farmer cupped his hand, propping his hoe in the crook of one arm. "Bluevine," he answered.

"Bluevine?" asked Oargesha. "Where in the night is that?"

The Shadow Fox shrugged.

Oargesha called back to the farmer, asking, "How far to Lathleer?"

The farmer scratched his head. "A hundred, maybe a hundred fifty."

"Sovereign bitch!" spat Oargesha.

"Watch your tongue, my friend," said the Fox, waving to the farmer and urging her horse forward. "It's hard enough to get the gods' attention. You might want to ensure that when you do get it, it's the kind of attention you want."

"Give me some leeway here, will you?" said Oargesha. "It's dinner time, the horses are run out, my butt feels like it's on fire, we lost three people for Host's sake, and here we are at some provincial little Aundairian hamlet a hundred or more miles from nowhere! We can't keep this pace up, Fox. It'll take us another three days to get to Fairhaven, minimum, and that's if none of the horses die on us. By that time, you know everyone will be looking for us."

"You're right. This route was probably a mistake."

"Probably? What do you mean probably?" said Oargesha. She growled in irritation. "Maybe we could press eastward from here. I know we don't have any camping equipment, but the Thrane border can't be that far, and—"

The Shadow Fox reined in her horse. "Hold up, Gesha. What's that over there?" She stood in the saddle and squinted her eyes. "Is that an airship on the other side of town?"

Oargesha raised a hand to shade her eyes from the sun, hovering just above the horizon. "I can't tell from this distance," she said.

The Fox leaned over her saddle horn for a moment, tempting herself to relax, perhaps even slide off the horse, then she straightened up again. "Just a two miles' hard gallop," she said.

"No," murmured Oargesha. "I can't."

The Shadow Fox summoned up what energy she had left and slapped the haunch of Oargesha's horse. *"Heiya!"* she yelled and kicked her horse to a reluctant gallop.

A hulking shaggy shape sank into the bushes, beady eyes squinting against the waning light. "Hey! Snouts up!" the creature hissed. "Here comes one!"

Two other gnolls, bestial canine-headed parodies of humans, crept up and joined the speaker, hiding behind a sprawling thornberry bush.

"I told you we should start early tonight," said the first.

"He's running very fast," said the second. "Do you think he's running from something?"

"I hope so," said the first. "That way he's already scared."

"He doesn't even have any weapons," said the third. "This will be easy."

"Let's get ready."

Two gnolls moved over by the road while the other stayed at the lookout's post. In this particular location, the cart track crested a hill between two thickets of thornberries, making an excellent choke point for highway robbery. It was far enough from Ghalt to avoid town militia, and the hilltop location made it easy to spot marks or law enforcement a good distance away.

The lookout watched as the lone figure drew closer. He was lightly clothed, holding a small pack under one arm, but the speed at which he ran indicated that he was in fear of losing his life or of losing whatever valuables were in the pack. The gnoll smiled. Both would be lost very soon—or from the gnoll's point of view, gained.

As the lone human passed him, the lookout broke from cover and ran around behind him, penning him in the ambush site. The other two gnolls broke cover ahead of the human and blocked his path.

The human slowed then stopped. He didn't stumble to a stop as one afraid, just controlled his deceleration. Breathing heavily, the human put his hands on his hips. He looked at the two gnolls ahead of him, then turned halfway around to lock eyes with the lookout and check that his escape was, indeed, blocked.

The lookout smiled cruelly.

The human leaned forward and set his pack down, then placed his hands on his knees, his chest heaving as his tired lungs burned through huge gulps of air. The lookout noticed that large patches of the human's tunic and pants were drenched with sweat. This is good, he thought. He'll be tired.

The three gnolls closed and displayed their weapons, carefully chosen for their barbaric appearance. One hefted a halberd, one swung a spiked chain, and the lookout spun a war pick in his great pawlike hands.

The gnoll's leader stepped forward and raised himself up to his full seven-plus feet. A patchwork of leather, stitched together from bloodstained articles recovered from previous victims, covered his shaggy hide. "Give us your pack, flatface," he said, grating his voice to sound more animalistic.

The human straightened up and stretched, still panting heavily. "I only . . . have time . . . to kill . . . one of you." He waved one finger back and forth, pointing side to side. "Who'll it be?"

The lookout felt an unnerving sensation in his gut. The human neither smiled in jest nor shouted in bravado. The gnoll felt as if his presence was almost an annoyance to this tired man. He felt the first trembling of fear. Sensing this, and not wanting to lose his privileged status in the tribe, he buried his fear beneath a feral snarl and advanced. The human nodded, a gesture of acceptance.

The lookout heaved his war pick high then slung it hard at the human. Propelled by his great strength and the angular momentum, the pick's head whistled through the air.

Even as the pick descended to split the human's torso wide open, the gnoll saw the little man move. He kicked out with one foot, displaying a startling limberness, and struck the gnoll's left elbow, locking it. The lookout felt his joint give between the impact and the downward force of his blow. The war pick kept moving, however, and the handle pried itself against the gnoll's thumbs, loosening his grip. Time slowed as the lookout realized that the human's bravado had nothing to do with bragging. He also realized that there would be no time for pain.

The human's hands darted out, one grabbing the butt of the handle, the other grabbing the haft. With a sharp pull, he levered the pick out of the gnoll's hand and spun it upward. The lookout felt his own weapon strike him right in the jugular. His taloned hand tried to rip at the human's throat, but the world spun away before it reached its target.

❊ ❊ ❊ ❊ ❊ ❊ ❊

The Shadow Fox and Oargesha rode up to the Lyrandar airship, which hung thirty feet in the air near the outskirts of town. She was an elegant ship, with smooth curving lines and a wide hull for stability. Even the struts that held the elemental ring in place amidships had been built to accentuate her grace.

The Cyrans reined in their horses. Oargesha slumped forward, wrapping her arms around her horse's neck and falling into a numb doze. The Shadow Fox dismounted stiffly, stumbling and falling to her knees. She rose and lurched over to the crewmen beneath the airship, wobbling on her sore and unstable legs.

She pushed her hair out of her face. "Is there an officer here?" she asked.

"I'm the second mate," said one. "Jendro of House Lyrandar at your service. The captain's in town, bargaining for water, and the first mate's up on the ship supervising. What can I do for you?"

"Well, I hadn't expected to find an airship here," said the Fox, smiling.

"Oh, yes, well, I suppose it's a bit of a novelty out in these provincial locations, isn't it? We hadn't expected to be here ourselves. Rather thought we'd be approaching Fairhaven by now."

"What happened?" asked the Fox, making an effort to keep her eyes bright and perky despite her exhaustion.

"Well, we're running from Sharn to Wroat to Fairhaven, but it seems we put in a load of tainted water back in Cragwar. Half the crew are down with dyse—um, that is, they're indisposed, if you please, young miss. We'd hoped to be able to resupply with water here, but the farmers aren't much for letting us have any."

The Shadow Fox reached out and brushed an imaginary fleck of lint from the petty officer's jacket. "Well, Jendro," she said, dropping her eyes, "I was hoping I might be able to purchase a passage to Fairhaven, for myself and my friend. Would that be possible?" She looked up at him from beneath her dark eyelashes.

"Well, um, miss," said Jendro, "we're not precisely a passenger vessel."

"But it would be an excellent chance to add five fine horses to your manifest. And I'm a very good cook." She raised her eyebrow suggestively. "I'd be happy to show you. If the horses aren't enough, I can pay extra for our passage." She turned her body not quite halfway around, reached into her blouse and pulled out a small stone, very pretty but ultimately worthless. She handed it to the second mate with a self-conscious smile.

"Um, it seems like a very . . . very logical proposition," said Jendro. "I'll, um, make arrangements for everything."

"Thank you," said the Fox. "And if you could arrange for a hot bath, too, I'd be very . . . grateful."

The second mate flushed slightly. He touched his brow with one finger, turned, and began to climb the rope ladder that dangled from the airship's gunwale.

The Shadow Fox turned and walked back over to Oargesha. "Up," she said. "We need to get moving."

"What?" grumbled Oargesha. "Why?"

"I've got us an easy ride to Fairhaven," replied the Fox. She heaved a bemused sigh. "Men. When they're young, they're just so easy to manipulate."

❂ ❂ ❂ ❂ ❂ ❂ ❂

With the sound of a click and a creak, a shaft of red light struck Praxle across his unconscious face.

"Master? You need to wake up, master."

"Mwha?" asked Praxle. He raised his head from the polished floor of the carriage. There was a small ripping sound as his cheek peeled way from the smooth varnish. He wiped the drool from his lips with his sleeve and tried to sit up, striking his shoulders on the bottom of the bench seat. "Damnation," he cursed. With a grunt, he pushed himself out from under the seat, sat up, draped one arm across the padded bench and let his head fall sideways upon his shoulder. He looked at Jeffers, bleary eyes topped by an unkempt mass of tousled hair. "Where in the dark dragon's dungeon are we?"

"Five miles east of Ghalt by the best of my estimation, master."

"Why are we stopped?"

"It was necessary to the furtherance of our current disposition, master," said the half-orc, scanning the horizon for any activity.

"Right," mumbled Praxle. He tried to stand, but failed. "I feel terrible."

"You had a most difficult afternoon, master," said Jeffers, and a hint of compassion crept into his voice. "If you don't mind my speaking out of place, master, I doubt I could have resisted any better, despite my stock."

Praxle managed to stand, and stepped over to lean against the doorframe. "That's because magicians have an advantage in that regard, Jeffers," he said, exhaustion sagging his voice. "We are trained to concentrate, and to endure many distractions, both expected and unexpected, while preparing our spells I was able to focus my mind on reciting cantrips in my head, and that blunted the worst of their efforts." He hung his head, blew out, and drew a deep breath, then he descended the carriage's stair very carefully. "It's one of the many inherent advantages of being a mage."

He lurched around, finding his legs, and looked about at the rolling, empty landscape. "With the Sovereigns as my witness, Jeffers, I do not know whether I hurt or just think that I hurt. Which will help? Should I try to stretch or relax?"

"I am afraid we have not much opportunity for either course, master," said Jeffers. "We must be about our business if we are to elude pursuit. They believe we have stolen something from them, which, in fact, we now have, as I purloined the prelate's carriage to effect our departure. I sincerely doubt that they will refrain from using every means at their disposition to prevent us from crossing the frontier. Among those methods would be the employment of the speaking stone at Ghalt to alert the guards at all border crossings, and using airships and shifter scouts to patrol the empty areas. I thought first of pressing eastward, but it is a wide and empty place, and one scout with a dragonhawk could locate us. I considered westward into the Eldeen Reaches, but we are ill prepared for such an expedition, having had most of our supplies seized at the monastery. I opted instead to purchase passage aboard the lightning rail here at Ghalt, hoping to reach the border before word of our escape. Therefore speed is of the utmost import."

"Right," said Praxle, a hint of daze still in his voice. He turned and grasped the handrail to pull himself back into the carriage.

"Master?"

"Yes?"

"I have considerable doubts that the prelate's personal carriage would be a particularly inconspicuous conveyance for our departure."

"Right."

"I thought to set it ablaze here. My hopes were that the sun would set before the smoke became dense enough to notice from Ghalt. Obviously it is to our best interest that none notice the conflagration until the coach is well ablaze, lest it be identified. In the meantime, we shall press into town using the horses we rode to the monastery."

"Where are they?" asked Praxle.

"I tethered them to the rear of the carriage just prior to our escape, master. I preferred not to leave the opposition with any advantageous equipment. Our tack, harness, and saddles are in the back of the coach. I shall have the horses ready to ride shortly."

Praxle sat heavily on the step that folded out from the carriage door. "That sounds fine," he said. Then, more to himself he mumbled, "Maybe I won't dock your pay after all."

"Pardon me, master?" asked Jeffers.

"Nothing, Jeffers," answered Praxle. "Nothing to concern yourself with."

CHAPTER 8

Darkness had fallen when Teron staggered into the outskirts of Ghalt, exhausted. He stumbled into the first guesthouse he saw, falling through the door more than walking through it. He placed his pack on the table then leaned back against the doorframe. Panting heavily, he threw a weary glance over at the proprietor.

"Great Sovereigns," said the innkeeper, "what is that all over you?"

Teron let his head flop forward so he could look down. He looked back at the innkeeper, and his head fell back against the doorjamb with a thump. "Gnoll blood," he said between gasps. "They . . . don't listen."

The proprietor thought about this for a moment, then an artificially cheery smile erupted across his face. "What can I bring you, stranger?"

"Broth. Whatever you have. Big bowl."

The innkeeper hustled for the back. Teron pushed himself off the jamb and opened his satchel. A very woozy-looking cat stumbled out, panting. "Hold on, Flotsam," said Teron, ruffling the cat's fur.

Teron staggered around the room to keep his blood flowing

as he tried to catch his breath. The place was largely devoid of customers, and those few present had little desire to interact with someone who looked like he had been hit by several buckets of blood. One young couple made a quick exit through the back.

A nervous serving boy arrived, carrying a large bowl of weak chicken broth. Teron sat, picked up the entire bowl, and drained most of it, downing several gulps between each panting breath. Once that was done, he set the rest down for Flotsam, who sniffed at it uncertainly. Teron called the boy back over and handed him a sovereign. "That's yours if you bring me the innkeeper, a bowl of hot water, a towel, and a new shirt—all right away. And there will be more, if you're very fast."

The boy's eyes grew wide, and he scampered into the kitchen, yelling for his father.

The owner ran out of the kitchen, wiping his hands on his apron as he came. "What else can I do for you, my good man?"

Teron locked gazes with the older man, impaling him upon the intensity of his stare. "A gnome—about this high, wealthy clothes, pale hair and a thin beard about his chin—and a half-orc servant—tall, large, well-dressed, oiled hair—traveled this way. Did they stop here?"

"No. Ain't seen anyone like that sort at all. No one wealthy here at all tonight, more's the pity."

"There's the ruin of some sort of carriage about four miles east of here. Know anything about it?"

"I heard someone saying something about it earlier, but I didn't pay no heed, being busy serving dinner as I was."

The boy arrived with a large basin of hot water and slid it onto the table, spilling only a small amount. Teron stripped off his crusty tunic and started washing his hands and arms as the boy ran across the common room and up the stairs.

"Lightning rail. What's the schedule?"

"Well, master, I do believe the next southbound run is—"

"No," interrupted Teron. "Tell me which runs left most recently."

"Well, let me see. The most recent northbound run would have left about an hour or two ago. The southbound run would have been about an hour past noon, I believe."

Teron ducked his head and washed his face in the water, then wet his short-cropped black hair. When he raised his head again, he saw that the boy, panting, had placed two lumps of cloth on the table. Teron had to shake them out to figure out which was the shirt and which was the pathetic imitation of a towel. He dried off his chiseled torso and quickly donned the ill-fitting peasant shirt.

"Your boy. Reliable?"

"Aye, he is," said the innkeeper nervously. The boy nodded, his eyes filled with awe.

"Good. Speaking stone in town?"

"Aye."

"Paper and quill. Now. I need a message run to the stone station."

The innkeeper snapped his fingers and turned around to smack the boy, but the lad was already off and sprinting to gather the supplies.

Teron flexed and stretched while the innkeeper fiddled with his apron and kept a fearful eye on the young monk's routine. Flotsam snuck off into the kitchen.

The boy came back with a few pieces of cheap parchment, a frayed quill, and an inkpot, much of which had spilled onto the boy's fingers in his haste. The innkeeper rounded on the boy. "Careless wretch! I should—"

"Smack that lad and you'll be cooking left-handed," said Teron as he smoothed out the parchment and dipped the quill. Then, as he started writing, he distractedly added, "Treasure your family while you have them."

He scribbled the ink across the page, occasionally pausing to rewrite words that might have ended up illegible in his haste.

Captain of the Night Watch
Passage
Most Vital

Turn out a special detachment to the lightning rail station prior to the arrival of the Passage run, which arrives before midnight. Watch for a gnome named Praxle d'Sivis and a half-orc called Jeffers, both male. And two humans named Fox and Oargesha. May be traveling together or separately. Check all papers.

Should this not reach you in time, cordon the town, looking for anyone seeking to escape into the Eldeen Reaches.

Specifically, look for a black globe of two spans' width. We urgently seek its recovery. Whosoever finds it and the thieves shall be generously rewarded.

By Order of Prelate Quardov

Then, when he finished, he rubbed an impression of the prelate's seal onto the paper.

"There." Teron passed the paper to the boy and took the boy's chin in his hand. "Take this to those who operate the speaking stone. This is for them," he said, pressing a gold galifar into the boy's hand, "and this is for you," giving the lad another sovereign. "I want this in their hands before I finish my last letter. If it is not, you'll wish it was only your father smacking you. Is that clear?"

The boy, too foolish or too amazed to be fearful, nodded. As soon as Teron released his grip, the lad turned and bolted out the door and up the road.

Teron took another sheet and wrote another letter at a more relaxed pace.

Captains of the Border Patrols
Starpeaks, Marketplace, Arcanix, Lathleer, Passage
Most Vital

At the behest of the Church of Aundair, you are to turn out additional forces to pay special attention to the borders. Look for Praxle d'Sivis, a gnome male; a half-orc called Jeffers, a male who acts as his servant; and two humans, named Fox and Oargesha. They may travel in a group or separately. Especially check the gnome and half-orc for papers; their papers were confiscated.

The aforementioned individuals have stolen a priceless artifact from the church. It appears as a black globe, two spans wide. We urgently seek its recovery, as well as the apprehension of the thieves. Under no circumstances attempt to use the relic. The church will handsomely reward anyone involved in the recovery of this item or the arrest of the thieves.

By Order of Prelate Quardov

Teron looked over his work then handed it to the inn-keeper. "When your boy returns, have him take that to the speaking stone."

He pulled a third sheet and wrote:

Master Keiftal,

I followed the carriage tracks to Ghalt. Found the carriage burned, the harnesses empty. Hoof prints indicated that they took the horses and continued west. Lost the trail but believe they continued into Ghalt, else why burn the carriage? I have alerted the military via speaking stone as of an hour past dark. I will check the station to see if they are waiting for the next southbound rail run, but I believe they have most likely taken the first available, which would take them north to Thrane. This worries me. Might they escape into the Eldeen Reaches? If so, we may already be too late. If not, could they be helping the Thranes to get the Sphere back? I do not know which I fear more.

Pray for me. Pray for us.

T

He flipped the paper up and reread it for good measure, then handed it to the proprietor along with a gold coin. "Post this to the Monastery of Pastoral Solitude. This should pay for the services. Keep the rest for your troubles."

"Yes, of course," said the innkeeper. "Thank you."

Teron stepped closer to the old man. "And tell no one I was here."

"Yes, absolutely. Have no fear of that at all."

"Good. I'd hate to have to come back."

The lightning rail station outside of Ghalt was, as usual, quite slow between runs. The local merchants, beggars, and thieves had by and large dispersed, as had most of the debarking passengers. A few travelers remained, one pacing back and forth, waiting for those he was to meet, the rest lingering in the café and savoring their Aundairian wine. Outside the depot building scattered clots of locals exchanged goods, monies, and stories.

Teron moved among the stragglers, scanning for a gnome paired with a half-orc and listening for the voices of the thieves he'd encountered in the catacombs. He doubted the latter two would be foolish enough to stand around together, although he also hoped they'd never believe someone was capable of running all the way from the Monastery of Pastoral Solitude, and therefore that they might be a little lax in their circumspection.

He satisfied himself that none of his suspects were present and headed to the building. It was a small structure, set well back from the trail of conductor stones to avoid the potential of a strike of elemental energy as the caravan moved past. It was a new building, the Ghalt stop being one that had seen much use during the Last War. The structure had been built with military efficiency and therefore military ugliness. Unlike most buildings in Aundair, it was strictly utilitarian and devoid of ornamentation.

One end housed the offices and the counter at which passage was purchased. The center was a large, open waiting area, ideally suited for marshalling small units of troops but too loud and open for a crowd of civilian passengers to pass the time peacefully. The far end held a small kitchen and restaurant, mercifully separated from the waiting area by a solid, noise-dampening wall.

Teron stepped up onto the building's porch. The cuffs on the innkeeper's peasant shirt hung annoyingly low on his wrists, and he pulled back one sleeve as he opened the door to the waiting area. He walked across the open room to the counter where a solitary clerk fiddled with a small skinning knife.

Teron laced his hands and leaned his wrists against the counter.

The clerk looked up. "May I help you, traveler?" he asked, his voice as limp as his half-lidded eyes.

"I seek information," said Teron. He tried to fix the clerk with his steely gaze, but the clerk was more interested in the way his blade was spinning on the countertop. "The most recent northbound run," said Teron, pressing forward, "did a gnome and his half-orc servant book passage?"

The clerk favored him with a brief, weary look. "We do not give out information on our other passengers. House Orien bylaws."

Teron proffered the prelate's seal. "This is very important. Church business. I need an answer."

"Look, friend," said the clerk, almost looking at Teron, "I work for House Orien, not the church. And House Orien says, 'Don't give out information on our passengers.'"

"You don't underst—"

"No, you don't understand I can't tell you anything."

"Actually, you can."

"Actually, not a kobold's chance," said the clerk. "If there is a problem with this, take it up with House Orien."

"All right," said Teron, "I will. Let me speak to your supervisor."

The clerk gave Teron a brief, long-suffering glare. "He's not here."

Teron raised one eyebrow. "You're the most senior employee here?"

The clerk nodded.

"I'll go check, shall I?" said Teron, and he placed his hands on the counter, preparing to vault over.

"No! No, wait right there," said the clerk. "I'll fetch him and send him around to speak with you. Maybe he can make you understand."

The clerk shuffled away from the counter to the door to the rear office. He knocked, cracked the door open, and stuck his head through. Teron heard him speak to someone else, and then, after a moment, a well-dressed elf appeared. He walked around the counter and approached Teron, looking the monk up and down as he closed. Teron smiled grimly—the only smile he was capable of generating on command—and extended a hand.

The elf took Teron's hand to shake it, but Teron shifted his grip at the last instant. He pressed the elf's middle knuckle in with his thumb and squeezed his hand, flexing the elf's slender hand backward. The elf drew a sharp breath in through his nose, but to his credit he held his composure.

"I'm here on official church business," repeated Teron. With his left hand he pulled his satchel around to the front and fished through it to find the portraits. "I need to know whether this gnome and this half-orc boarded the northbound run a few hours ago."

The elf pressed his lips together. "House Orien policy is not to provide any information on the itineraries of our passengers."

Teron squeezed the elf's hand more tightly, and he felt the elf's tendons creaking under the strain.

"However," added the elf through clenched teeth, "perhaps we can make an exception. For the church."

"Thank you," said Teron, bowing slightly. He released his grip and clapped a friendly hand on the elf's shoulder so that it rested at the base of his neck. One finger probed the weak point between the elf's neck and clavicle, and Teron felt the elf tense up again. "Why don't we look through your books?"

"I didn't see no passengers like he's looking for, master," said the clerk, the boredom utterly wiped from his face. "But I can check the other ledgers, if you like."

The elf supervisor nodded quickly.

"Praxle d'Sivis," said Teron. "Look for that name."

After a several minutes' search, the clerk returned with a ledger. "Here you are," he said. "D'Sivis, party of two, booked passage to Thaliost, Thrane."

"When will that run reach Fairhaven?" ask Teron.

The clerk fumbled about for a schedule, traced his finger across the grids, and said, "It reaches Passage a few hours before dawn, leaves again about an hour after sunrise, then reaches Fairhaven just after sundown."

"Wait—did you say it remains in Passage for . . . three or four hours?" asked Teron.

"Indeed it does," replied the elf stiffly. "We depart after dawn for the convenience of our passengers." He paused and looked at Teron with a pinched expression. "Speaking of convenience, master, would the church mind terribly if you removed your hand from my shoulder? I find it inconvenient."

Teron mumbled something incoherent and let go his grip. The elf immediately began massaging his neck with his left hand.

"Passage is about a hundred miles away, maybe a bit more," said Teron.

"Rather more like 140 miles, I believe," said the clerk helpfully.

"Understood. I have five or six hours to get there. I need something fast to take me there. Or to Fairhaven; I should be able to intercept them there. A Lyrandar airship, perhaps. Suggestions, either of you?"

The clerk and supervisor looked at each other. "Well, we don't ever get airships in here," said the clerk. "At least, not often. I mean, every month or two maybe one will drop by for provisions or trading, but there's no telling when that'll happen. Maybe you could buy yourself one of those magebred horses . . ."

"Ten miles an hour at best, buffoon," snapped the elf. "He'd never reach Passage in time. There's no animal that . . ." The elf's voice trailed off as a sudden realization dawned on him. "You want Hatch Vadalis. He'll get you there."

"Who?"

"Hatch Vadalis. He has a fast service that crosses all of southern Aundair," said the elf, nodding in approval at his own idea. "He flies everywhere from Arcanix to Tower Valiant to Marketplace, and every little farm on the way."

"He has an airship?"

"Of course not," said the elf. Then he backed away slightly, just to be safe. "Hatch rides a bird."

"That's right!" piped in the clerk. "It's a beauty too, it is. Some kind of giant dire magebred dragonhawk or something along those lines there. *Real* big. Moves like the wind. Shepherds don't much like it, though, and sometimes when he takes off . . . well, some people around here don't fancy it a whole lot, but they'll always take the gold he spends."

"Where is he?"

"Head toward the west end of Ghalt," said the elf. "Look for the three-story house. It's the only one around. You can't miss the coop smell, either."

"Thank you," said Teron, bowing his head.

The elf simply gave a pained smile as he massaged his right hand.

❀ ❀ ❀ ❀ ❀ ❀ ❀

Lying on the top bunk, Praxle stared out the window of his private room, trying to reconcile the idyllic countryside with the horrific torture he'd endured at the hands of the locals. Could the blight that lay upon the Crying Fields have twisted the minds of those who lived there?

Praxle snorted. How could it not?

Technically, the room was not private. It had three berths in it, but since Praxle no longer had enough money handy to pay for a first-class room, he'd opted to pay for an extra bed in one of the second-class coaches. He dreaded the coming of night, for he feared that Jeffers might snore. The very thought gave him chills.

"Done, master," said Jeffers.

Praxle peered over the edge of the bed. Below him, Jeffers had laid out the varied supplies that he'd managed to gather before their escape from the monastery. It was nowhere near everything they had arrived with; just a few items left in the room when the monks pilfered it, another few items quickly gathered in the outbuilding where Praxle had been interrogated. The blade that, for a brief moment, was the most beautiful thing that Praxle had ever seen.

"Olladra's outhouse," cursed Praxle. "Those monastic bastards still have our papers."

"Yes, master, they do."

"You couldn't have managed to, shall we say, pick them back up, you half-moron?" snapped Praxle.

"I had quickly to choose between following the papers and following you, master," said Jeffers unapologetically. "Had I known you'd be making so much noise, I—"

"Shut up, Jeffers," snarled Praxle, bitter at the memory of his screaming and begging, a weakness that had eclipsed his discipline until, at last, he had lost all hope and simultaneously recaptured the ability to resist. He tried to force the memories out of his mind but couldn't, and his stomach began to churn.

"How shall we cross the border, then?" asked Jeffers. "We could perhaps claim that our papers were stolen. It is not entirely untrue."

Praxle's mind seized on Jeffers' question like a drowning man grasping a rope. "We must make new ones," he said. "We must have papers, or else the Thranes will turn us back. If we get turned back, the Aundairians will take notice of us, and I cannot allow that. I need folders, nice ones. High-quality paper. Quill, and ink. I can forge a reasonable facsimile of our papers, then cast a durable glamer upon them as we approach the border." He chuckled. "Thank the gods I'm a son of House Sivis," he said. "Otherwise I seriously doubt I could create a good enough forgery, even enhanced with my best illusions."

"As you wish, master," said Jeffers. "I shall undertake to acquire these necessities when we arrive in Passage. The conductor led me to understand that we'll have a several-hour wayside stop at that location."

"Several hours?" Praxle groaned and rolled onto his back. "Several hours, wasted sitting in some gods-forsaken station."

"Problem, master?"

"The monks are looking for us. They now have several more hours to alert the soldiers at the border crossings." Praxle slammed his fists into the bedding at his sides. "I don't think we're going to make it."

CHAPTER 9

Bang-bang-bang!

Startled by the pounding at his door, Hatch Vadalis jumped from his chair, banging into the table and scattering some of the food on his plate. He growled at the interruption. Just before he left the room, he pointed one finger at his dog and said, "Don't even think about it, Stinker."

Bang-bang-bang-bang-bang!

"I'm coming, I'm coming, don't split your gizzard!" he yelled. He opened the front door to his home and saw a young man panting on his porch.

"Hatch d'Vadalis?" asked the newcomer. He shifted a small bag in his arms.

"Just Vadalis," said Hatch. "I married into the name."

"My name's Teron," said the man, bowing. "I have an important parcel I need delivered to Passage as soon as possible." He proffered a letter of credit from the church treasury in Fairhaven.

Hatch took the paper and scrutinized the arcane mark upon it. "Looks legitimate," he said. He glanced at the amount written and nodded approvingly. "Very well. I'll head out at first light."

"No," said the man. "Now."

"But I can't—"

Teron pulled a second letter of credit and handed it to Hatch.

"Well, um, let's see," the old man said, greed and concern warring in his mind. "Flying at night, it's—"

Teron snatched the two letters of credit from Hatch's hand. Hatch gasped, but then Teron provided a third letter, larger in sum than the previous two combined. "Final offer," he said. "Accept it."

"I think this will do nicely," said Hatch. "Come in, Tayrum."

"Teron."

"Teron. Right. I was, um, just eating my dinner, and— *Damn it, Stinker! Get off the damned table!*"

"Eat quickly," said Teron.

"Right you are," said Hatch. He crammed food into his mouth, chewed, then swallowed. "If you don't mind, put the kettle on the fire, will you? I'll be wanting some tea to see me through the night."

"You might want to brew some for your bird, as well," Teron said with a chuckle.

"What's the package, by the way?"

"Me."

Hatch stared at him for a moment, then nodded. "That'll keep me honest," he said.

The old man wolfed down the remainder of his food, leaving the scraps for the dog. Teron quietly appropriated a few pieces and let Flotsam out of the bag to eat on top of the table.

Hatch gathered several waterskins and poured a handful of tea leaves into each of them. Catching a clue from Teron's pacing, he filled the skins with water that was merely warm, proclaiming them, "Good enough."

Grabbing a lantern to light the way, he exited the house for the roost. Teron scooped up his cat and followed. Hatch walked over to the large barn next to his house, handed the lantern to the monk, and pulled open one of the large doors.

As the light spilled into the barn, Hatch turned to look at the monk's expression. Sure enough, the young man gaped in amazement at the creature within. The expression of bedazzle-ment never failed to warm the old man's heart.

The great bird was perched on a tree trunk hewed for just that purpose. Even without the stand, it stood almost twelve feet high, with large, intelligent golden eyes set on each side of a cruel gray beak. Its breast was a cloudy gray that blended well with autumn skies, while rich mottled brown feathers covered its wings and back.

It blinked at the unexpected onset of light and raised a single long feather set at the front of its black-feathered head. It balanced on one great claw to stretch out its other wing and leg, displaying its huge talons as well as the bony horn that pro-truded from the wing's wrist.

"That's impressive," said the monk.

Hatch brought a stepladder over to the great bird. It bent its head down as he fitted the bit and reins. Then he coaxed the dragonhawk to stand horizontally while he mounted the saddle. "Soarwood," he said as he tightened the hitches. "Makes it a bit easier on the old girl."

Teron held up one hand. "I'm just glad we'll be riding on its back."

Hatch stopped his preparations and stood up. "Back? You're riding in its claws, son."

Teron blinked. "You're . . . joking, right?"

❀ ❀ ❀ ❀ ❀ ❀ ❀

Wakened by one of the deck hands, Oargesha shucked off the canvas tarpaulin that had served as her blanket, gathered what gear she had, smoothed her hair, and climbed up onto the bow deck.

The sky in the east was just starting to lighten, silhouetting the Shadow Fox's slim figure leaning on the railing. Oargesha walked up to stand beside her.

The Fox pointed to the north, and Oargesha looked. The airship was just cresting a large hill, and the vast panorama of Fairhaven lay sprawled across the rolling terrain in front of them. The Aundair River parted the city down the center, and a massive complex of buildings dominated the left bank.

"Will you look at those," said Oargesha quietly, somehow hesitant to make any noise in the quiet predawn hour. "Those towers have to be at least a hundred-fifty feet high. And they're so slender!"

Fox nodded. "Impressive, aren't they? And they say the towers of Sharn are even taller." She sucked on her teeth for a moment. "Metrol used to be that large," she said.

"I know." Oargesha dropped her head. "It's hard to think of that many people all dying at once. And just lying there like they say they do. . . ."

"That's why we did this," said the Fox. "That's why we're doing this. I want it all back. Even if it takes a hundred years."

The ship drew closer to the Aundairian capital, just starting to come to life with the growing dawn. The Shadow Fox craned her neck and then dashed for the forecastle. Oargesha followed, wondering what the alarm was.

"Belay there!" ordered the second mate as the two women climbed the short ladder. "I told you not to come up here! I got into enough trouble already just bringing you aboard."

"Just for a moment, Jendro, I promise," said the Shadow Fox. "I just wanted to borrow your glass, and I didn't feel right bothering an officer like you to bring it to me."

Jendro lost his bluster. "I'm not really an officer, of course, but—"

"Just for a moment," said the Fox with a wink as she gently pulled the small scope from his hands. "I'll give it right back." She put the glass to her eye and scanned the cityscape. She gasped in delight. "I was right! Gesha, the lightning rail is at the station! We ought to be able to catch it!" She handed the glass to Oargesha and pointed. "See? It's that large building with all the light, just over there."

Jendro snatched the glass from Oargesha's hand. "You said you've give it right back!"

The Shadow Fox smiled. "I'm sorry. I just got too excited.

Can you—could you please, could you debark us at the lightning rail station?" she asked.

Jendro shook his head. "Sorry, I can't do that."

"Why not?" asked Oargesha.

"Aundairian law requires us to go to the airship dock at the west side of town. We'll be able to let you down after the dock opens for business, an hour or two after dawn. That's of course assuming that no one else is ahead of us."

"Wait a moment," said the Shadow Fox, grabbing Jendro's arm.

The second mate yanked his arm out of her grasp. "Unhand me," he said, "and clear the forecastle! You're not supposed to be up here in the first place! We'll get you down as soon as we can, assuming you give me no more troubles. You," he added, pointing to a burly half-orc deckhand, "make sure they stay off the forecastle, understand? And if they cause any more trouble, send them below decks."

The two Cyrans withdrew from the bow and repaired to a spot on the rail amidships. They watched in silence as the airship crossed above the outskirts of Fairhaven. The details of the city grew in size and detail as the sky grew lighter and the airship gradually descended.

Oargesha looked wistfully at the glowing lightning rail station, slowly drawing nearer as the airship cruised to the appointed dock. "So much for catching this run," she said. She leaned over the railing to look at the ground below. "Who would have thought that such a short distance could be so far away?"

"What do you mean?"

"I mean the ground. It's right there, and yet it's too far away. We can't jump. It'd be the death of us." She sighed in exasperation. "I just wish I had a spell that could help us, but that's not my kind of magic."

The Shadow Fox turned, a wry smile brightening her face. "It is mine," she said. "Gather your belongings and meet me right back here. Quickly."

Oargesha went back below and quickly stuffed her clothes,

personal articles, and spellbook into her bag, then sauntered back across the deck to the railing.

The Shadow Fox was at the aft end of the airship, her bag over her shoulder. She walked up the length of the beam, idly trailing one hand over the railing.

As she approached, Oargesha looked past her to the stern, and the parcel that had been left unattended at the rail. "Hey, Fox, isn't that the—"

"Yes. Walk with me."

Oargesha turned and walked alongside the Shadow Fox up the length of the airship. The half-orc deckhand glared at them as they approached the forecastle.

The Shadow Fox stopped and looked over the railing. "This looks good," she said. "Face me. Hands on hips."

"But—"

"Obey me!" hissed the Fox.

Oargesha turned to the Fox and placed her hands on her hips. As irritated as she was becoming, it was easy to do.

The Fox pulled her hand up over the side of the airship to reveal the end of a rope that arced sternward. She quickly slipped it around Oargesha's waist and secured it with a square knot. She shoved Gesha's bag against her belly and handed her what little slack there was left in the rope. "Grab tight," she said.

No sooner had the Cyran wizard grabbed the rope than the Fox wrapped her arms around her, grabbed the rope in both hands, and flopped the pair of them over the railing.

Oargesha shrieked as they tumbled through the air toward the city streets below. But almost immediately the rope went taut, and the two women glided in a smooth arc. They reached the bottom of their pendulous path a mere ten feet above the streets, but instead of rising again, it felt like their path started to flatten out.

The Shadow Fox looked up and said, "Here we go!" She let go and pushed off slightly.

Instead of the reverse swing that she expected, Oargesha felt herself start to fall freely. Her throat tightened; she was too terrified to scream again. She dropped to the ground, landing hard on the packed dirt.

She lay there in pain, wondering if anything had been broken in the fall, when she felt the Shadow Fox grab her under the arms. "Here it comes," she said as she dragged Oargesha along the ground.

The wizard opened her eyes and saw the bag with the black globe crash belatedly to earth a few feet in front of her, its aberrant inertia finally bringing it down to rest upon the rope it had supported a few seconds earlier.

Oargesha's hands were trembling; her heart raced. "Clever," she panted. "But couldn't you have given me some warning?"

"There was no time," said the Shadow Fox, gesturing with her thumb at the lightning rail station that stood less than a hundred yards away. "We have a run to catch."

❀ ❀ ❀ ❀ ❀ ❀ ❀

Hatch turned and elbowed the person sleeping behind him. "Time to wake up," he said.

Teron stirred from his slumber. He sat in the portion of Hatch's saddle ordinarily used for luggage, which, in a sense, he was. His arms and legs were lashed to the saddle and to Hatch. Although Teron hated to be constricted in any way, he saw the sense in so doing, for the extra security it afforded allowed Teron to catch some much-needed sleep.

Teron straightened up and blinked his eyes open. He tried to stretch, but the lines restrained him. He undid the knots that held his arms, leaned back and stretched out, popping his back and shoulders in several places. He grabbed his head and twisted his neck, eliciting more pops. Then he drew a deep breath and looked around.

They were flying some five hundred feet in the air. The air was cold, crisp, and very clean, and the only sound was the steady swoosh swoosh of the great raptor's wings. The sun was rising behind him, casting the countryside in a marbled pattern of golden glow and blue shadow. The whole rolling landscape was cut by a patchwork collection of hedges, roads, and wooded margins, dividing the land into farms for as far as he could see, broken by tiny villages and large wooded tracts. A low-lying mist lingered at the edges of the fields below, but it was a healthy, clean white, not the malign haze that so often lurked over the Crying Fields.

Teron leaned way over to look straight down, stabilizing himself with the end of one of the ropes that had bound his arms. Below, for an instant, Teron saw the dragonhawk's reflection as it crossed a calm stream. Then they crossed over a large, very green meadow, and he saw a flock of sheep stampede in panic as the great dragonhawk flew over them. Their bleating reached his ears, at once clear and tiny.

"I'm surprised I can hear them all they way up here," said Teron.

"You can hear all kinds of things up here," said Hatch. "There's nothing to block the sound."

Teron looked around some more, surveying the vast panorama that receded to a curving horizon. "This is utterly amazing," he said, and a genuine smile of pure delight crossed his face for the first time in many long years.

Hatch smiled and nodded. "Delivering mail," he said. "The job may be boring, but the work is very enjoyable."

Teron laughed, "I envy you," he said, and with those words, darkness rolled back over his disposition. "I envy you your job and the ability to enjoy it."

Hatch said nothing. They flew for a while in silence, then, as they passed a particularly large residence, Hatch reached into his satchel and pulled out a rock. Tied to the rock was a small scroll, and a long, bright red streamer. Hatch tugged at the bird's reins, and it slipped down and to the right. Hatch tossed the rock overboard, and it fell to the residence, trailing the bright red streamer all the way down. "It wasn't much out of the way," said Hatch. "Hope you don't mind."

Teron did mind, of course—any delay could prove crucial—but it was too late to do anything about it. Instead, he asked,

"So Hatch, is that a nickname, or your real name?" Despite his dark mood, the beautiful morning made him feel more sociable than normal.

"It's short for Hatchling, and that came from the first bird I owned. It wasn't as big as this one, but it was big enough. Of course, I was a bit lighter of girth at that time. Anyway, I called it my Hatchling once, as a joke, and, well, you know how people are when they think they're clever. The joke never got old, not to me, at least. And after the old thing died and I got a new bird, the name kind of stuck to me. You know, they start out saying, 'Look, it's Hatchling,' meaning the bird, and then it ends up being, 'Look, it's Hatch,' meaning me. Ah, I loved that old bird. That's how I met my wife, too. I needed some help with my bird, and she was there to give it. Can't say it was love at first sight, but after I'd seen her enough times I decided to ask her if I might court her."

"So what happened?"

"She slapped me."

Teron laughed.

"No, really, she did," said Hatch. "A couple months later, though, she finally agreed. I can be rather persistent. Damn it!"

"What?" asked Teron.

"Look over there," said Hatch. He pointed to the west. Teron looked and saw the conductor stones, a long strand of white pearls that marked the lightning rail's path. And farther west, near the town of Passage, he noticed something that looked like a white, actinic caterpillar inching its way along the path.

"I thought we'd made better time," said Hatch. "Either that, or they kicked the elemental a bit early this morning."

"Let me make this clear, Hatch," said Teron. "I must be on that run."

"It can't be done," said Hatch. "They aren't going to stop for us. Even if I dropped you right on one of the stones, it takes the rail a good long time to come to a stop. You'd be crushed and roasted long since, Tayrum."

Teron chuckled. "I've done many things that can't be done, Hatch. I will be on that run. Have your hawk dive for it, match speeds as best you can and as low as you can. I'll handle the rest."

"Not on your life," said Hatch. "I don't want my bird's wings to get caught in that lightning wreath. The last thing I want is to crash under a burning dragonhawk."

"Final offer, Hatch," said Teron. "If you won't, I'll break your neck and pilot this bird myself."

Hatch turned and cast an uncertain look at Teron. He checked forward again to ensure the sky was clear, then looked back again, his eyes wide and fearful. "You wouldn't." He gauged Teron's expression. "Oh, Fury's finger, you would. Damn it!"

He turned to look forward again, and Teron was pleased to notice that he now hunched his shoulders.

"All right," said Hatch. "You paid me well enough. I'll do it."

Teron rolled his eyes at the rationalization.

"We can dive to match its speed, but I can't get too low. It'll be a long jump for you."

"Extra height I can handle," said Teron. "It's the left-right leeway I can't manage."

Hatch giggled nervously. "I hear you," he said. "But you'll be just fine. I've been flying this bird for years. I'll get you on target." He urged the bird to the north, positioning themselves to intercept the lightning rail. "You'll only get one shot, I'm afraid. My bird isn't as fast as the rail, although I do believe we can outpace it while diving—at least for a short period."

Teron shrugged. "I'm used to only having one chance."

"Maybe so, but if you blow this chance, you die."

"I'm used to that, too."

Hatch looked back over his shoulder and raised one eyebrow. Seeing Teron's bland expression, he pursed his lips and returned to piloting.

They flew closer to the lightning rail line. Miles off to their left, the harness coach flew over the conductor stones, gaining speed. As the caravan accelerated, the number of energy bolts writhing over the coaches' surfaces increased, as did the intensity of the individual strands. Then Teron heard the sounds of the rail, crackling like a distant fire.

Hatch looked to the left, hissed, and urged his great raptor faster, guiding it into a slight dive to increase its speed without losing much altitude. "You'd better untie and hold on tight!" he yelled. "Probably best if you got straight off the end of the tail. Sit yourself behind the parcel backboard, right on the bird's arse, then when I pull her up, you let go and slip right off. Got that?"

"Got it," said Teron. He climbed over the back of the wooden parcel holder and stepped onto the dragonhawk's huge, feathered rump. He turned around to face forward, and kneeled down. "All right, Flotsam," he said as he hitched his satchel around to the front. He tightened the straps until it sat securely against his chest. "You're not going to like this."

He heard a small yowl of dread emanate from the canvas bag.

Long moments passed as the great bird moved to intercept the coaches. Teron took a firm grip on the wooden partition. Teron calmed his mind, purifying it of all distractions, then he felt the sickening lurch of weightlessness as the bird swooped. Adrenaline surged into his blood, making his mind ring like a newly drawn blade.

"Hang on . . . get ready . . . Damn it! The rail line turns up ahead! Jump!" Teron felt the dragonhawk spread its wings, and it changed its dive to a climb. Teron pushed off the rear of the luggage carrier and slid off the bird's tail. Its stiff, soft tail feathers brushed against his face as he fell, and suddenly he found himself in midair, abut thirty or forty feet over the lightning rail.

He had a scarce heartbeat or two to appraise his situation before he landed, and the moment seemed both preposterously long and dangerously short. He saw the top of the lightning rail coaches, and was relieved to note that they had a flat surface down the center suitable for walking . . . or tumbling from a height. Lightning flashed across the surface, and just as quickly disappeared. He had to rely on luck to get past the arcs without injury.

He realized that the lightning rail was moving faster than he was; Hatch had lost too much speed pulling the dragon-hawk out of its dive. This meant that Teron was positioned all wrong—he'd planned to tumble forward on a slower-moving coach, now with a faster target he had to tumble backward when he landed. With no time left to turn his head and look, he'd be operating blind. All he knew was that he was near the midsec-tion of the coach.

Fear and exhilaration fueled his reflexes. To control his backward acceleration, he kicked out with his feet as he landed. He rolled himself into a rear tumble, whacking the back of his head nastily as he rolled head over heels. Stunned for the briefest instant, he did nothing to decelerate. Instead, he pro-tected Flotsam, secured to his chest, and kept rolling. He felt his hair stand on end and wondered whether a blast of energy was about to rip through him. It didn't, but the distraction caused him to lose more control of his tumble. He rolled to one side, kicked himself away from the side of the car toward the center again, then flipped off the back of what turned out to be the last coach.

There was a short, sharp cry as Teron disappeared over the end of the string of coaches, and the lightning rail sped into the dawn.

THE LIGHTNING RAIL
CHAPTER 10

The Shadow Fox and Oargesha sat in their seats oblivious to the passing scenery as the lightning rail cruised through the bright morning. They rode in the third-class coach. It was not as crowded or dismal as the steerage cars, but beyond the fact that the two women had seats, there was little to recommend it. Their seats faced each other. The Fox sat with her arms tightly crossed and her head sunk to her chest. Oargesha sat with her head back and her mouth open. Occasionally small snores escaped her throat.

The black globe sat in its bag on the floor between them, pressed up against the coach wall. Each of the Cyran women had one foot on top of the bag, and another touching it on the side. No one could move the bag without shifting at least two of their feet.

From beneath the Shadow Fox's seat, a small, thin hand reached out. It gently lifted the Fox's heel a scant eighth inch from the top of the bag, and then a broad dagger slid out from the shadows and inserted itself between the Fox's boot and the bag she guarded. Then a second thin hand appeared and started quietly undoing the clasps on the bag, first one, then two, then three.

The hand paused in its endeavors as Oargesha smacked her mouth noisily a few times. "Pull back your hand while you still have it, halfling," she said without opening her eyes.

The hand remained frozen in place.

"I think I'll have to put my sword through this seat," said the Fox. "That'd be about where a halfling's kidneys would be, don't you think?"

"Absolutely," said Oargesha. She let her mouth sag open again.

The hand closed the hasps, and then gently pushed the Fox's foot off the dagger.

The Fox stepped down firmly, trapping the blade between her boot and the bag. "Leave it," she growled.

The hand withdrew from sight. The blade remained.

* * * * * * *

With the exception of one limb, Teron was curled into a fetal ball. Only his right arm extended out, the hand tightly gripping the railing of the last carriage in the caravan. His left arm tightly cradled his yowling cat to his chest—the cat had taken the first opportunity to force his way out of Teron's bag—and his legs pulled in as tight as they could to avoid getting clipped by the landscape that passed rapidly beneath the levitating coach.

"Easy, Flotsam," he murmured as calmly as his adrenaline allowed. He forced the cat away from his body, a direction the disheveled tom was loath to take. He clawed at Teron's peasant shirt, trying to remain in the secure sling of Teron's body. The monk gritted his teeth and forced the cat to the small platform that extended from the rear of the carriage. Once on the comparatively stable balcony, the cat oozed pitifully to the rear door and hunkered down.

Grimacing with effort and unable to use his tightly curled legs, Teron strong-armed himself up. His left arm grasped the rail and he pulled his body up. His skin trembled with the electric energies that coursed all about, but the railing was designed to keep harmful energies away from passengers who came out here to view the scenery.

Teron climbed over the railing, stood upright, and brushed himself off, despite the fact that his tumble hadn't made him any dirtier. He drew a tension-purging breath, then took just a moment to look for Hatch and his dragonhawk and wave in thanks.

Teron took another deep breath, then placed his hand on the latch of the door that led inside the carriage. He glanced down at his cat.

"I just hope they've already checked everyone's passage," he said.

❀ ❀ ❀ ❀ ❀ ❀ ❀ ❀

"What's on your mind, master?" asked Jeffers. "You've hardly touched your breakfast."

Praxle glanced up at the half-orc with a grim set to his smile. "I face several problems, Jeffers," he said. "They vex me. And I'm wondering which of them will ultimately stand between success and me, that I may be the best prepared.

"First, we have had the Orb of Xoriat stolen out from under our very noses. Second, we do not know who stole it—other than, I surmise, that they are the selfsame Cyrans who assassinated Caeheras back in Wroat. Third, the Aundairian authorities believe I collaborated with the Cyrans, and therefore they are searching for me. Fourth, I don't even know if my new papers will see me successfully across the border. Fifth, the Thranes still possess the investigative notes on the function of the Orb. The Cyrans may potentially know this as well and could well be closing upon the Thranes ahead of us. Sixth, the Thranes have no idea that people are coming. Granted, that last point could work for me or against me.

"I need to reach Flamekeep and acquire the Thrane mages' notes before the others do. If I don't . . . then the Cyrans will have both the Orb of Xoriat and the knowledge to use it, yet lack any reason to stay their hand." Praxle thumped his fist on the table. "This means I have to move fast and alone. It's not my preferred method, but it will have to suffice. I dare not wait for reinforcements."

"As ever, master, I am more than delighted to provide any assistance I can," said Jeffers as he refilled Praxle's water. "Especially if it means that we can obviate another singular cataclysm such as the disaster that befell the area around that monastery."

Praxle looked at the half-orc with hooded eyes. "Your job, Jeffers, is to keep me alive and comfortable. Thus far, you've proven to be quite effective at the first and reasonably good at the second, recent events notwithstanding. So long as that remains true, I can see no other duties more valuable than your current tasks."

"As you wish, master," said the half-orc with a slight smile.

❦ ❦ ❦ ❦ ❦ ❦ ❦

The coaches lurched as the lightning rail began its deceleration heading into the Starpeaks River Valley. Oargesha nudged a toe to wake the Shadow Fox, who'd been sound asleep with her head leaning against the window for the last fifty miles.

The Fox stirred and rubbed the sleep from her eyes. "I'll be glad when we get to Flamekeep," she said. "This whole trip is very discomfiting."

"Your heart and mine," said Oargesha. "I wish we still had the others with us." She swallowed hard. "I keep seeing their faces, hearing . . . do you think there's any chance Roon made it out?"

The Fox looked Oargesha square in the face but said nothing.

"I know," said Oargesha glumly. "I knew that. But I still have hope, right? I saw Grameste get . . . well, I saw Grameste. So I know she's dead. And Rander . . . well, he got it first. But I still can't help but wonder if maybe Roon beat that . . . that monk, or whatever he was and made it out after we'd left. Do you understand? I just can't help but wonder. I mean, maybe he beat him, but say his leg was badly hurt, and . . ."

The Fox shook her head ever so slightly.

Oargesha broke eye contact and looked out the window, her eyes welling with tears. "Well," she said, "at least they're not trapped behind the mist."

The Fox chose to say nothing. Instead, she opened the window, letting the chill northern air blow through her hair and bring a flush of red to her cheeks. She looked out at the countryside as the lightning rail continued to decelerate. Here the line followed the Aundair River on its winding course through the Starpeaks, and she looked out on fertile river-valley fields dotted with farms and paddocks. On the far side of the river, there was another narrow band of farmland, and then the Starpeaks thrust out of the ground, steep, rugged evergreen-encrusted mountains capped with remnants of snow. "We'll be crossing the border soon," she said. "Now's as good a time to pray as any, Oargesha."

Oargesha started to bow her head, then paused. "Aren't you going to pray, Fox?"

Without turning her head, she answered, "Given the life I've been leading lately, I'm more than a little concerned about which god would answer."

Oargesha murmured a series of supplications under her breath as the Fox watched the countryside roll by.

In this corner of Aundair, close to the Thrane border, the marks of the War became more and more prominent. They passed through the ashen wreckage of a small rural village, ruins so old that sizable trees had grown up within the empty frames of houses, only to be burned themselves when war swept through a second time. Now dead stalks of wood, bleached white like skeletal hands, clawed at the sky among overgrown squares where an entire community once had lived its collective life.

Closer to the border lay fieldworks, long barricades of earth and wood that once had protected the defenders of the realm from the incessant attacks by Thrane armies and Karrnathi undead. Fronted by trenches filled with long stakes and supported by towers equipped with ballistae, the fieldworks showed signs of breaches and reconstruction. They stretched across the river bottom and even up onto the lower parts of the mountains, a livid scar that demarked the hostility that yet remained between the nations.

The Fox saw other, less obvious marks, as well—veteran soldiers missing limbs, wrecked wagons and carts abandoned by the sides of overused country lanes, reckless holes torn or blasted through centuries-old hedges, rotting structures where a command post once stood in the middle of a fertile field.

The lightning rail slowed further, and for a moment the Shadow Fox considered jumping out the window with the black globe and trying to sneak across the border on foot. Then she noticed a blue-tabarded longbowman across the grassy field, scanning the passing caravan for any such questionable activity. A few score yards farther on and she saw a second guard and then a third.

The Fox placed a hand on Oargesha's head. "This doesn't look good," she said. "I'd say your prayers aren't being answered."

"Patience," was all Oargesha said in response.

The sun set behind the curve of the mountains. The land lay in shadow, while the sky still shone brightly above. The lightning rail pulled into the border station and came to a complete stop. The border station was a small encampment for Aundairian military personnel and tax collectors. A rough-hewn boardwalk ran along the side of the rail and led to a sizeable platform near a plain, wooden office. Several barracks sat behind it, removed from direct access to the passengers, as well as a stable and a couple of buildings.

The two Cyrans looked out the window and saw well over a hundred guards with spears and halberds standing alongside the rail. Farther back, cavalry armed with longbows lurked, waiting for the opportunity to run down and pierce anyone who managed to break through the cordon. As the last of the lightning rail's actinic flares died away, an officer of the guard blew a shrill whistle. "Everyone off," he said. "Queen Aurala and the

Church of the Sovereign Host are compelling a detailed search of papers and belongings!"

"They're onto us," whispered Oargesha, her voice filling with fear.

"Perhaps," said the Shadow Fox, "but perhaps not. This may be a random stop, some newly appointed officer whipping his blundering troops through their paces just to bloat his ego. Or maybe, my dear Oargesha, this is the way things are up here at this end of the world. I've not taken this route before, so I don't know, but this is the most direct path from Fairhaven to Flamekeep, and you know that relations between Aundair and Thrane are anxious at best."

Oargesha leaned over and whispered, "So?"

"So maybe they're looking for someone else."

"But they may still catch us in their net. What are we going to do?"

"For one, do *not* cast any spells," said the Fox. "If they have this kind of force turned out, you know there are mages, priests, familiars, and more all prowling these premises. They'll be looking for anyone who tries a magical means of bypassing the search, just as the guards are looking for anyone who tries to sneak something past them. We need to look haggard. Don't hold your baggage too efficiently, so it looks like more than it is. Try to give the impression of someone who wants to cooperate but is too exhausted to care much. Beyond that . . . Cyre's spirit, I wish I knew. Just follow my lead. Try to keep in the thickest part of the crowd, and we'll see what I can do."

The two gathered their luggage and followed the flow of passengers out of the coach. They proceeded down the boardwalk, staggering and occasionally stopping to readjust their bags. Every time they did so, the Fox struggled with starting or stopping, as the black globe continued to demonstrate a mind of its own with regard to motion.

They approached a cluster of guards, and one stepped over to them.

"Papers?"

The two Cyrans handed over their papers, stolen in separate incidents a year ago from some Brelish adventurers of similar appearance and who, having been assassinated, would never report their loss.

"Who is in your party?" the guard snapped.

"Me and her," said the Fox. She allowed one of her bags to slip, then wrestled it back into place. "What's this all about, soldier?"

"Routine tariff check," he snapped as he handed back their documentation. "Over there. Line to the left."

The two Cyrans followed the soldier's command and ended up in a long line of unhappy people. They looked at the others in their line, then checked out those in the much shorter line.

"Do you see that, Oargesha?" asked the Fox.

"Yes, I do. What do you suppose is happening? Do you think maybe Aundair is having some trouble with Droaam or Darguun?"

The Fox tilted her head and narrowed her eyes. "I rather doubt it," she said. "Look around. We have goblins over here in our line. Why separate them from the half-orcs?"

"You're right. Everyone over there is either of orc or gnome blood." Oargesha smiled. "They're looking for someone else. Hey, what's that? They're leading someone away."

The Fox nodded. "A gnome and a half-orc. That's interesting."

"And you said my prayers weren't being answered."

"I'd hold the celebration until we get ourselves through this," said the Fox. "We're not free yet."

As they approached the front of their line, the Fox watched the guards questioning the passengers at the head of their line. It looked like the passengers were running a gauntlet. The crowd moved between two sets of guards, two pair of guards on each side. Each pair questioned a party, then those who had been inspected made their egress through the far end of the gauntlet and returned to the boardwalk where they awaited permission to reboard the lightning rail.

"I have an idea, Oargesha," said the Fox. "The guards on this line are processing people fairly swiftly. Let's go separately, with you going first. I'll pass the globe over to you. I think we can do this without having this bag opened."

Oargesha nodded her approval.

The lines kept crawling forward, amid grumbling in the long line and high-tempered moments between the guards and the passengers in the gnome/half-orc line. Finally Oargesha reached the head of the line and stepped forward with her bag. The Fox waited, having faded back a spot in line. She gauged the progress of the various passengers, then let one more slip ahead of her. As Oargesha spoke with the guards about something in her papers, the Fox step forward. She had to strain, stiff-armed, to pull the globe along behind without it being obvious. She'd been holding it motionless at her side, and it resisted getting under way.

She walked slowly to one of the guards, and "accidentally" dropped her shoulder bag. As she moved to retrieve it, she let go of the bag holding the globe. The bag sagged around the globe within it, but the globe itself kept moving in the same direction, slowly gliding between the luggage of the various passengers. Oargesha caught its motion out of the corner of her eye and planted one of her feet in the bag's path.

The Fox's aim was true. The globe glided into Oargesha's foot and almost came to a stop before she let it continue sliding ever so slowly onward. Any noise the impact made was lost in the general brabble of the crowd. The guards waved Oargesha on, and she picked up her bag and the globe's bag and proceeded onward with none the wiser to their ploy.

GENTLE TOUCHES OF DISCOMFORT
CHAPTER 11

Praxle and Jeffers walked down the hallway toward their second-class room. The sleeping berths were on their right side, and on their left a long bank of windows allowed them to view the landscape of central Aundair. The cloud-dotted sky was stained in reds and blues in the wake of the sunset.

Wrapped in an ever-shifting cocoon of magical energy that constantly fought against gravity and inertia to keep the lightning rail on its plotted course, the coach trembled beneath their feet. They reached their door, and Jeffers cut around Praxle in the narrow hallway. Jeffers pulled the key from his pocket—for security's sake, he had two of the three copies and Praxle had the third—and undid the lock.

Jeffers opened the door and scented the air with his keen nose. Smelling nothing amiss, he entered and turned the ever-bright lantern mounted in the wall by the door from a bare glow to full brightness. Praxle followed close behind, shutting and locking the door behind them.

Jeffers raised one hand. "Hsst!"

Praxle raised his hands preparatory to a spell. "What is it?"

"Someone has intruded upon our cabin," said Jeffers, "via the window."

121

Praxle glanced at the window and saw nothing amiss. "How do you know?"

"I placed a piece of down near the window for just this purpose," said Jeffers as he turned to scan the cabin. "Someone pried open the window, and the breeze blew the down." He checked the ceiling and beneath the bottom bunk that served as their table. Satisfied, he retrieved his sword and swept the room again, seeking anything invisible.

"I am unable to locate any manner of intruders, master," said Jeffers.

"Can you tell what they were doing here?" asked Praxle.

"No, I cannot," said Jeffers. "It appears that whoever it is was able to spend no short time here, as they were able to return everything they touched to its original state. Nothing save the down appears to have been disturbed. They accomplished whatever they desired then left the cabin again, either by the window or by the door."

"Did they steal anything?" asked Praxle, his hands still raised.

"Allow me to check our inventory, master. I suggest that you search for any lingering magical effects."

Jeffers investigated their bags, while Praxle cast a spell and scanned the room with his arcane sight. "I find nothing amiss, master," said Jeffers at last. "How did you fare?"

"Nothing at all," said Praxle. He sighed in frustration.

"I take it, master, that you do not surmise this to be a common burglary."

"Naturally," said Praxle. "A common burglar would not have cared for leaving evidence of his passage. These people knew that we were going to the dining coach and how much time we were likely to spend there. They used that time to search our room." He paused, hands on hips, licking his lips and tapping one foot in irritation. "Now how will we figure out who dared to invade our room?"

A loud knock sounded at the door.

Jeffers raised one eyebrow. "Answering the door sounds like one option, master," he said.

Praxle's face scrunched up in confusion. "It can't be them.

It makes no sense. Why take all the time to sneak in only to come knocking at the front door?"

"Perhaps it is someone with information?"

"That could be," said Praxle. "Nonetheless, be ready for anything."

The knock sounded again, and a firm baritone voice said, "Open up."

Jeffers picked up his sword from the bed and moved to the door. Praxle stood against the back wall away from the window. Jeffers opened the door with his left hand, then pulled it open with a finger of his right hand so that it concealed the sword while giving the impression his right hand was empty.

Standing in the hallway was a smallish human with short, dark hair, simple pants, an oversized peasant shirt, and a gray cat on his shoulder. The cat leaped down as the human stepped into the room. "Praxle d'Sivis," the man said and closed the door.

At the mention of his master's name, Jeffers sprang into action. He grabbed the human's wrist and cocked his sword arm for a thrust through the kidneys. But as he pulled the human's arm toward him, the stranger twisted his wrist and yanked his hand through Jeffers's grip, leaving the half-orc with nothing but sleeve. The human stepped sideways, pulling the half-orc's arm to the right, spoiling the aim of his thrust, then he flipped his arm around and bound Jeffers's hand with the excess sleeve. He stepped in, lifting the surprised half-orc's arm and striking him hard in the ribs with an open palm.

The man stepped back, freeing his hands and sleeve. The half-orc opened his mouth then slumped to the floor and gasped for breath.

Praxle's eyes widened at the brutally efficient dispatch of his bodyguard. His hands flew into motion, and he intoned the words for the quickest combat spell he knew as the human stalked across the all-too-small cabin. Praxle formed his hands into a circle, and a magical light shimmered between his fingers, glowing like a still pond at sunrise. Then the pond rippled, and a winged serpent with rainbow-hued scales slithered its way through and took flight, aglide on broad, feathered wings and baring its long, poisonous fangs.

The human spun in place as the bright serpent circled the room, its scales glinting as the lamplight played across its surface. Then, to Praxle's extreme displeasure, the intruder stopped and faced Praxle. Praxle guided the serpent to intercede, but the human closed his eyes. Praxle drew a breath between his teeth in anger and fear. The couatl illusion was a fast-casting spell in part because it had no aural component.

Although the lightning rail had a constant background noise of crackling energy and creaking linkages, the human turned his head at the small noise Praxle made. One hand shot out and grabbed Praxle's lapel, and before the gnome could react, the second hand clamped around his windpipe, restricting but not entirely blocking his breath.

"Praxle," said the human, opening his eyes. "My name is Teron." He glanced over at Jeffers, slumped in the corner, a serrated sword unattended on the floor. "I see that you were expecting me."

Praxle shrugged as best he could with a huge hand clamped over his neck.

"Here's what we're going to do, Praxle," said Teron. "First you dispel your illusion, then we're going to sit and talk. I'm going to hold your right hand, and any time you lie to me, I'm going to break one joint of one finger. If you try to cast a spell or do anything else untoward, I'll break your finger joints one after another until you stop. Is that clear?"

Praxle's eyes narrowed. "You can't do anything to me that they didn't already do at the monastery," he spat.

"Actually, I can," said Teron. "The brothers used the Biting Thumb techniques to cause you pain in such a manner that it would leave no bruises, because Quardov didn't want to create an incident between Aundair and Zilargo. I have no such qualms. In fact, I am expected to use every means necessary to accomplish my task. Therefore, you should consider how many spells you could cast, and how many scrolls you could scribe if you had fifteen dislocated joints on your right hand."

Praxle opened his mouth to answer, but no clever remarks came. Rather than sound boorish, he closed his mouth again.

"And," added Teron, "after such a painful trial, do you think that you could convince your masters that you didn't spill every secret you know?"

Praxle shook his head.

"Very good. I'm glad we're in accord. Shall we begin?"

"Do I have a choice?" asked Praxle.

"Of course you have a choice. You may choose how many fingers I break before you cooperate."

Praxle grimaced. "That will end up being all of them if you only want to ask me where it is," he said.

"Oh, I am very clear that the Thrane Sphere is not here with you. But . . . I wish to better understand the situation. First let's talk about your visit to the monastery. Why did you come?"

Praxle looked into Teron's eyes to gauge the young monk's resolve. He saw nothing but a blank slate—no hatred, no firmness, nothing. He considered his options, then opened his mouth to answer. Teron immediately started flexing his little finger backward, and Praxle's face pinched in pain. He gritted his teeth, and his eyes found the resolve behind Teron's empty gaze.

"All right, monk!" he said. "You win. In part because you seem more reasonable than those black-hooded thugs of yours at the monastery."

"They were just ordinary acolytes, Praxle. It's customary to wear black when using the Biting Thumb."

"They wore black, and they were thugs. If you have difficulty accepting that, then let me hold your little finger."

Teron nodded. "Continue," he said.

"You have probably been told that I stole the, er, the item you call the Thrane Sphere. Unfortunately, that is a fallacious assumption based on spurious deductions."

Teron frowned in disappointment and started flexing the gnome's finger again.

"Wait!" grimaced Praxle. "Hear me out, then break as many

fingers as you want! If your 'brothers' had been that patient, I could have told you everything yesterday!"

Teron paused, looking askance at Praxle. At last he relented and released the pressure on the gnome's finger, although he maintained the grip. Jeffers began to stir in the corner, still clawing for breath. "If you want proof," said Praxle, desperate to be believed and to maintain the sanctity of his hand, "wait until Jeffers rises, then send him from the cabin. I will tell you everything I know, and you can question him separately. He will tell you the exact same story! I swear!"

Teron considered this for a moment then nodded. "Jeffers! First, breathe all the way out then take a deep breath in—as much as you can." The half-orc did so. "Now get up, leave your sword, and walk to the very rear coach. Then come back here."

The half-orc climbed to his feet, using the door latch and the walls to keep himself from falling over. He glowered at the monk with hatred and shame, then opened the door and let himself out.

"Leave it open," Teron said.

Jeffers lurched off, right hand tightly holding his left side. As he went, the cat glided out of the room, hopped up onto the sill of the long windows in the hallway, settled down, and napped.

Praxle drew a deep breath and blew it out noisily, puffing his cheeks. "You can let go of my finger, now," he said.

"I know," said Teron. "And I might. After you talk."

Praxle's nostrils flared. "As you wish," he said. "As I am sure you are aware, I have been accused of stealing the Orb of Xo— the, er, Thrane Sphere from the monastery. This I did not do, though I did consider it." Praxle glowered at his interrogator through narrowed eyes. "I hope you understand how hard this is for me. I deal in information, which means that I acquire it instead of dispense it. On those rare occasions that I give knowledge to others, I charge my clients dearly for the privilege."

Teron tilted his head slightly. "I deal in death. No charge." He reflected for a moment, then added, "Pain is just a hobby."

Praxle drew a deep breath and abandoned all hope of building a false history of events. "Well, then," he said. "The Orb—that's what we call it—is originally the property of the University of Korranberg, recovered during an expedition to Droaam over two millennia ago. It was . . . lost during the Last War, due in part to a gross blunder on the part of my forebears. We located it at last in your monastery. I came to recover it on behalf of the University. When I met with Prelate Quardov to broach the subject, he would have none of it."

"You asked him about it?" asked Teron.

Praxle shook his head. "I had no need to. He was most uncooperative. He had the very aura of an ice mephit."

"That sounds like Quardov," said Teron.

"That put me in a bit of a quandary, so I retired to my rooms to reconsider. I shall admit that I used some"—Praxle winced with shame as he confessed—"sleight of eye, if you will, to acquire some additional information for my own use. With the information I managed to glean, I had a fair idea where the Orb was secreted. Keiftal mentioned the catacombs, and Quardov was happy to give me details of where previous heroes of the faith were buried. At that point, I was sorely tempted to steal the Orb and bring it back home to its rightful owners. My intent was to send Jeffers into the catacombs that night to explore. I might well have joined him, depending on what demands the prelate or your master placed upon my time. However, I never had the chance to follow through on that."

Teron flexed Praxle's finger. He rolled his head toward the gnome in weary disbelief. "Stop spinning this yarn," he said, "and speak the truth. Do you seriously expect me to believe that someone else just happened to steal this Orb of yours the same day you arrived at its location?"

"No," said Praxle, breathing hard to resist the pain, "I don't expect you to believe that. Not without the rest of the story."

"Proceed," said Teron, an untrusting look in his eye. "But just so you know, you're running a ledger of five breaks thus far."

Praxle tugged at his collar and cleared his throat before continuing. "About a week ago I met with someone in Wroat."

"A friend?"

"No," said Praxle, "not in the slightest. I only befriend a very select sort of person, monk. He was merely a contractor." He coughed in a vain attempt to clear the nervous tremor from his voice. "A freelance investigator. Our meeting was disrupted. My associate was killed, and someone stole the information he had for me. To the best of my knowledge, this person is called the Shadow Fox and is a notorious Cyran thief."

"Really?" Teron leaned forward.

"There were others," continued Praxle, "and the story is rather convoluted, but it appears that my associate had leaked his information to a Cyran who tipped off this Shadow Fox person. The stolen information pointed to your monastery as the place where the Orb was hidden. This I learned from my associate's dying breath. I made to reach the monastery as soon as I could, hoping to beat the Cyrans there. I could afford the lightning rail. I hoped they couldn't." Praxle paused a moment and marshaled his thoughts. Now that he had warmed to his subject, he was quite oblivious to the fact that Teron still held his hand in a grip that could easily break several fingers. "I don't know how much detail was in my associate's report. Perhaps everything. Perhaps not much, and the Cyrans were spying on me at the same time that I was prying secrets out of your people. Perhaps both. There's no way to know. Now let me tell you what I don't know, monk." He looked Teron square in the eye. "I don't know who stole the Orb, nor how, nor even when, other than the loss was discovered while I was at the monastery. I don't know how they escaped. I do know that I was arrested, tortured, and then I escaped, and I do know that you followed me, which means that you monks don't know who actually stole the Orb, either."

Teron leaned back against the wooden wall. "I do," he said. "I was there."

● ● ● ◉ ● ● ●

Across the border in Thrane, the lightning rail accelerated into the waning day to Thaliost. Oargesha basked in the success of their ploy, her feet straddling the bag that held the Black

Globe. She wished to talk, to joke, to celebrate their minor victory (and the answer to her prayer), but after waiting so long on the platform, Fox excused herself to use the privy as soon as the lightning rail got underway again.

Oargesha looked down at the large, leather bag and relived the moment in her mind. The easy glide the bag made, thanks to the curious counterintuitive properties of the Globe within. Fox's perfect aim. Her flawless movement as she gathered the bag along with her other luggage.

She started to play with the bag between her feet. She pressed against it with one foot, hard, then as soon as it started to move, released the pressure. The bag glided across the floor to her other foot, and she had to apply counterpressure for a few seconds before it slowed its progress. She batted it back and forth several times, trying to apply just the right amount of pressure to negate its momentum, without reversing the direction of its travel. Eventually she tired of the little game—or, more accurately, the muscles on the inside of her legs tired of it, and she pressed the bag to the floor until it stopped moving.

Her mood darkened as she remembered those who had given their lives for this artifact. Rander, Roon, and Gram, all killed by that monk in the catacombs. The once-fine team had dwindled to Fox and herself, but if the Globe was as powerful an artifact as the Fox said it was, it would be worth the sacrifice for the rebirth of Cyre. Or so she told herself as the tears welled up once more.

Just a few more hours until they reached the rail stop at Daskaran Ferry. Then it was across the sound and off to Fox's safe house in Flamekeep.

Oargesha swayed to the right as the rail line turned. At her feet, the bag drifted to the wall, carried by its own peculiar inertia. Its unnatural motion piqued her interest. Slightly bored from the long day, and looking for anything to distract herself from replaying the deaths of her friends over and over in her mind, Oargesha studied the bag on the floor.

It looked so ordinary. Just a black leather bag, neither polished like new nor worn as if old. The straps were heavy and sturdily attached. It bulged slightly with the valuable relic inside. Oargesha leaned forward and undid the snaps that held the bag shut, one by one. As the last snap opened, the bag opened slightly, like the inviting lips of a lover . . . or the mouth of a hungry black toad.

Oargesha pushed the bag open wider, curious about the mail lining that Fox had mentioned. The sides of the bag were indeed lined with fine-mesh chainmail. The rest of the bag was filled with the heavily swaddled Globe as well as padding to fill the empty portions.

Oargesha ran her finger inside the bag, near the top edge, feeling the soft rippling sensation of the chain links passing her fingertip, one by one. As her hand passed close to the Globe, she felt the little hairs on the back of her wrist start to stand on end. She held her hand closer to the Globe, not daring to touch its pale shroud. Her palm felt alternately cold and rashy.

Her hand seemed to move unbidden, and her fingernail traced a fold on the drab fabric that swaddled the Globe. She felt a tugging, as of a whirlpool, drawing the tip of her finger closer. Her chin began to tremble as though she might cry.

She caressed her fingers across the fabric then spread her hand like a claw and clutched at the Globe's wrappings. She gasped, although she did not know if it was a gasp of surprise, revulsion, or ecstasy. Despite the fact that the material was clearly dry, it felt greasy to her touch and seemed to move beneath her fingers.

Fearful, she pulled her hand back, but despite her intent her curling fingers clutched at the fabric, undressing the Globe, pulling away its mask. All light seemed to fall into the ebon surface of the ancient artifact as it was exposed, devouring the coach, the countryside, even her own hand, leaving her with nothing else to see. Her eyes were drawn in fascination and anguish to the ancient creation, lacquered so deep a black that it seemed to swim with colors. Her hand reached out, and she gently stroked one of the many curved, sliding segments that covered the surface of the Globe. It started to move . . . .

CHAPTER 12

So you believe us," said Praxle with some relief. He looked to Jeffers, who had just come back into the room and was eyeing the monk warily. Praxle saw him glance to the blade, which still lay on the floor, and he gave his head a sharp shake.

Teron drew in a sharp breath and let it out. "Not necessarily," he said, letting go of Praxle's fingers, "but I cannot locate anything that you have said that does not mesh with what I know." He scooted back on the berth and leaned his shoulders into the corner.

Praxle pulled his hand back and cracked his knuckles one by one, relieved that he could still flex all his digits without pain. "Then let us play all of our cards on the table," he said. "You were wronged, for you had the Orb stolen from your monastery. I was wronged, because the University's rightful property was taken. And everyone stands to be wronged, because the Cyrans now hold the Orb of Xoriat. If they can figure out how to use it, the destruction they could cause would be . . . unthinkable."

"What does it do?"

"It does everything you saw at the monastery—and then some," said Praxle. "We at the University have some theoretical knowledge about why it works but not about how it works. The Thranes seem to have figured out how it works—or at least they did so at one point during the Last War. If the Cyrans can seize those notes, all of Khorvaire could become as blighted as your Crying Fields—or worse."

"I believe that you and I need to work together, monk," he continued. "The University will compensate your monastery handsomely for your time and trouble—and for the safe return of the Orb to its proper hands."

"Why do you want it?" asked Teron.

"I know that look," said Praxle. "It says, 'I don't trust you.' Well, then, let me tell you, monk, we gnomes first acquired the Orb two, maybe even closer to three thousand years ago. We believe it is a relic of the Daelkyr Wars. It's had who knows how many names over the years. The druids who first recovered it called it the Ball of Ineffable Madness, or so I am told. If we'd wanted to use it as a weapon, we'd have done so a hundred times over, and done so with far more circumspection than did the blundering Thranes."

"Meaning you wouldn't have lost it the first time you used it," clarified Teron.

"Precisely."

"Somehow that does not fill me with confidence."

Praxle shook his head and smiled. "You misunderstand me, monk. We could have used it. We could have used it to great and terrible effect. However, we didn't, partly because we're cautious about anything dealing with Xoriat and partly because it's irreplaceable. No, our desire for the Sphere is just this: it is an amazing relic of transplanar magic, and we wish to study it. It's that simple. Well, no, transplanar magic is very complex, but I think you understand my point. The University of Korranberg is an institution devoted to knowledge, not war."

Teron mulled this over, chewing thoughtfully on the inside of his cheek.

"Do we have a deal, monk?" asked Praxle.

"I will work with you to prevent the Cyrans from gaining the Thranes' knowledge of the Sphere," said Teron. "In exchange, you will help me recover the Thrane Sphere. Once that is completed, we will see to its disposition."

"Excellent. Jeffers, explain my plans to the monk."

The half-orc rummaged among their gear and pulled out a map, exquisitely rendered but heavily worn on its creases. He spread it out on the berth between Praxle and Teron. No sooner had he done that, than Teron's cat hopped up onto the berth, sauntered to the center of the map, and flopped on its side. Teron scooped up the tom and dropped him in his lap.

"We are approximately here," said Jeffers as he brushed some stray cat hair from the parchment. "We shall debark the lightning rail here, at Daskaran Ferry. From there, we shall book passage aboard a vessel that heads through Scions Sound to Flamekeep."

"There's no direct lightning rail route?" asked Teron.

"Curiously, no," said Jeffers. "I surmise plans for such an extension fell with the Kingdom of Galifar."

"And why Flamekeep?"

"The Thrane college is there, including their research library," said Praxle. "University agents confirmed the existence of a book containing their compiled notes on the Orb some years ago. We considered stealing it then but thought it best to leave the Thranes in the dark about our knowledge until such time as we discovered the fate of the Orb itself."

"Why?"

"They'd know we were the ones to steal it," shrugged Praxle. "No sense in offending them until we had both pieces handy."

Teron studied the map. "The collapse of the White Arch Bridge made Thaliost a dead end. It offers no access to Scions Sound. So whether the Cyrans are going home to Cyre or they're after the Thrane book as we are, they'll debark at Daskaran Ferry."

"It does seem the most expedient choice," said Jeffers.

Teron paused for a long moment, petting the cat that purred in his lap. "Done. We're in this together. We'll retrieve the

Sphere from the Cyrans and the notes from the Thranes. Then we'll head back to Aundair and you can haggle with Prelate Quardov over who gets what. Does that sound fair?"

"Fair enough, monk, since our other choice is to have you start breaking fingers and such."

Teron smiled humorlessly, pushed the cat off his lap, and rose. "Then I will see you when we arrive at Daskaran Ferry," he said, and departed the cabin without further ceremony.

Praxle and Jeffers stared at the closed door for a long time after Teron left. Finally Jeffers broke the silence. "Dare we trust him?" he asked.

"I don't have much choice," answered the gnome, "at least not at the moment. But I'll have to watch my step, especially when we finally get both pieces together. I believe that's when he'll make his play, to try to take it all for himself. And I have to make sure I stop him."

❂ ❂ ❂ ❂ ❂ ❂ ❂

The Shadow Fox walked slowly down the aisle of the lightning rail coach. Her eyes were unfocused, and she ran her hands through her hair, trying to stave off the exhaustion that pulled at her.

Just hold out until dawn, she thought, then we can be aboard ship making for Flamekeep. All we have to do is stay alert for a little while longer, and then we can hole up in our safe house. It would be so much easier if we still had five. Even three would be better than just Oargesha and me.

With a heavy sigh, she flopped onto the bench beside her traveling partner. "Just another hour and we—" Her words stopped abruptly, the rest of her statement vaporized from her mind as she saw her friend and cohort.

Oargesha sat, leaning over the open leather bag at her feet. One hand reached into the open bag, doing something that the Fox could not see. The other white-knuckled hand rested on her knee for balance; the strongly clawed fingers digging deep into her thigh. Her eyes were open very wide, staring into the bag, and her pale face was torn with emotion, displaying a mix of rapture, disgust, and horror.

Not a single muscle on her entire body moved, save a peculiar twitch in her left eyelid.

"Gesha?" whispered the Fox. "Oargesha." She leaned closer. "What did you do? What did it do to you?"

She reached out with the toe of one foot and tried to usher Oargesha's hand out of the bag. She met with limited success, however, for the mage's muscles were all as rigid as iron. The Fox did manage to move her arm enough to slide the bag away from her reaching hand.

The Fox pulled Oargesha's bag from beneath the bench, opened it, and pulled out a skirt. Then she pulled on a pair of gloves and, averting her eyes, stuffed the skirt across the top of the bag to conceal the unknown relic inside. As she did so, she could feel the device shifting beneath her fingers. It was surrounded by a tangible aura of malevolent thrumming.

Once she was certain that the skirt had been well placed, she closed the bag up. She still avoided looking directly at the opening, relying on her peripheral vision and her sense of touch to find all the clasps and seal them.

She looked at her compatriot. As she feared, there was no change. She slapped Oargesha, tickled her, even poked her naked eyeball with a fingernail. Nothing elicited a response. She pulled off her glove and touched Oargesha's lips then her teeth. They were dry. Only the rear portion of her tongue still had any moisture.

The Shadow Fox's heart started racing, fearing that Oargesha's unnatural death would attract the attention of the other passengers, bringing the Silver Flame down upon her. She looked around quickly to see if Oargesha had garnered any notice. Fortunately, it appeared not. It was well after dark, the coach was sparsely populated, and the other passengers seemed content to stay in their chairs and doze as the rail approached Scions Sound.

Fox leaned Oargesha against the wall and pulled her travel cloak over her like a blanket. Then she sat next to her friend, put her feet up, and draped another cloak over herself in an effort to conceal the fact that the mage's feet stuck out awkwardly, like those of an upturned crustacean.

The Fox sat and watched as the coaches rolled onward. All exhaustion had left her, replaced by a dread fear.

※ ※ ※ ⊛ ※ ※ ※

As the lightning rail pulled into Daskaran Ferry, the Fox turned her haunted eyes on her former traveling companion. Setting her jaw to guard against crying, she rummaged through Oargesha's belongings for valuables and removed the mage's coin purse.

She took a deep, trembling breath, leaned over, and kissed Oargesha on the temple.

She pulled Oargesha's cloak a little higher up in an effort to hide her face better, but it slid back down again, dropping to her shoulder and revealing her frightful rictus to all.

"Farewell," said the Fox.

She glanced both ways to ensure that no one was looking in her direction then departed the coach. By the time she stepped off the bottom step and onto the platform, her stride was graceful and sure, and she wore a bemused smile. She paused to look up at the night sky, but despite her demeanor, her eyes saw nothing but her friend's terrified face.

"Care for a hansom, lady?" asked a young lad. "Two crowns to ride over the ferry and anywhere in the city, if you like."

"That would be wonderful," she said with a brightness she didn't feel.

She followed the lad to a waiting hansom. She paid the driver two coppers, and he tossed one down to the boy.

Despite her veil of tourist pleasantry, she struggled to raise her foot to step into the hansom cab, for doing so was the final step in her abandonment of her team.

※ ※ ※ ⊛ ※ ※ ※

The lightning rail pulled into the Starpeaks border crossing under the watchful eyes of a hundred or more Aundairian guards. Before it stopped, even as the last flickers of the conductor stones played across the coaches' surface, one of the doors opened and Teron stepped out.

"You there—" said one of the guards, but Teron pushed past him and walked swiftly across the boardwalk to one of the officers at hand.

The officer was resplendent in a long blue robe embroidered with a beautiful dragonhawk's head. Tucked under one arm she held a high helm plumed with dragonhawk feathers and gold-inset engraving. She was surrounded by aides and junior officers.

As Teron made to walk through the circle of military personnel and approach the officer, one of the petty officers barred his way. "The lines form over there, citizen," he said, grabbing Teron's peasant shirt with one hand.

Without breaking stride, Teron snapped one hand up to pin the soldier's fist against Teron's shoulder. The other struck up under the soldier's elbow, locked the joint, and forced the hapless warrior forward and down. He fell flat on his face.

The other soldiers jumped in surprise, and their hands flew to the hilts of their swords, but before anyone's weapon cleared its scabbard, Teron had already stepped over the downed soldier. He bowed respectfully to the officer.

"Captain," he said, proffering with both hands the prelate's commission. "Prelate Quardov Donrain, High Archdeacon of the Cathedral of the Heavens in Fairhaven and Keeper of the Divine Wrath, sends his holy regards."

"Holy?" muttered the junior officer as he started to regain his feet. "Maybe if you mean 'holy havoc my arm hurts,' they're holy. What in the—"

"You are dismissed," said the captain.

The soldier saluted and departed, still rubbing his arm.

The captain studied Teron for a long moment, then took the commission from his hands and scanned it. "It says here that you act with the authority and support of the prelate," she said. Her words were a statement, not a question. Teron remained silent, his hands folded placidly at his waist. The captain studied him some more and licked her lips. "For someone acting on behalf of the church, you have less than ecclesiastical manners."

"I apologize for your aide," said Teron. "It was pure reflex. He startled me."

The captain's eyes narrowed. "No," she said, "I think you planned for it. You have had extensive monastic training, and I surmise that if your reaction were truly pure reflex, then at least one bone would have been broken. Am I not correct?"

Teron dropped his gaze for a second, giving the captain all the answer she needed.

"I have great respect for your kind," she said. "Personally, I would not dare to face a battlefield full of Thranes without a broadsword and a full suit of fine chain. You and your kind are either very brave or very mad."

Teron nodded. "Most likely both, Captain."

The captain laughed—a genuine if brief expression of mirth—before her face became the cold countenance of a military officer again. "What business brings you here, citizen?" she asked. "What help can I offer the prelate?"

Teron pulled out the folded drawings of Praxle and Jeffers from the waistband of his trousers. "Yesterday I, upon the orders of the prelate, personally put forth an alert to watch for a gnome named Praxle d'Sivis and a half-orc named Jeffers, who is a retainer. Here are portraits drawn from their papers, which we confiscated. I have been pursuing these people and have located them on this very run. I request that you therefore detain these two and clap them in irons. I also request that you gag them immediately. The gnome is certainly an illusionist, and the half-orc may have an arcane bent as well."

The captain looked at the two illustrations, one after the other, then folded the papers and slapped them across the chest of one of her junior officers. He immediately took the papers and ran to where the guards were sorting the passengers, gathering a squad of soldiers as he went.

The captain inclined her head slightly toward Teron. "It is

always a pleasure to be of service to the Sovereign Host and their ordained mortal servants," she said.

"I will report your efficiency and accommodation," said Teron. He bowed again and departed to await the capture of his quarry.

❧ ❧ ❧ ❧ ❧ ❧ ❧

"Well, then, what's all this to-do?" asked Praxle as they debarked the lightning rail. He stepped to the side, out of the flow of passengers, and surveyed the depot. "Look at them. There must be at least a hundred soldiers or more. I've never seen a border guarded like this."

"I am completely confounded, master," replied Jeffers. "I would surmise either that there are diplomatic tensions between the lands or else that the crown is throwing a dragnet for certain people. Might they be searching for us, master?"

"Yes, they might well be looking for me," said Praxle, gauging the odds and reaching a result that did not please him in the slightest. "One can only assume that the prelate, thinking I stole the Orb, sent out an alert."

"Would they then be searching the travelers for us personally, or searching our packages for the Orb? If the one, master, then we are safe, but if the other, we may have some difficulties."

Praxle waved a hand dismissively. "Not a worry," he said. "I have that monk working for me. I'm sure he can get me through this with no problem."

Jeffers looked all around. "Where is our monastic companion, then?"

The steady stream of passengers parted up ahead, and a squad of a dozen soldiers cut through the line. Several had long bows, several had drawn swords, and one held two sheets of paper, one in each hand. The squad leader looked around, then he pointed directly at the pair and the squad started walking toward them purposefully.

"Maybe we can ask these soldiers where he is, master," observed Jeffers dryly. He reached for his sword, strapped to his waist. "Shall I—"

"Don't bother," said Praxle resignedly. "I can't afford the time to look for another bodyguard right now." He rubbed his head slowly. "He betrayed me. That monk is more intelligent than I gave him credit for."

The guards surrounded them, and Praxle and Jeffers dispassionately held out their wrists.

Praxle noted that the manacles were, like Teron's betrayal, cold.

❁ ❁ ❁ ◉ ❁ ❁ ❁

"And what would you wish to be done with these two?" asked the captain. "Shall we send a detachment to take them back to Fairhaven for you?"

Teron looked over at Praxle and Jeffers, who stood amid a quartet of guards with their hands locked securely behind their backs. Jeffers looked stoic as ever, although Teron noticed him flex his arms to test the stiffness of his bonds. Praxle's eyes burned with deliberate hatred, standing out sharply above the large ragged gag that filled his mouth.

Teron rubbed his fingers along the corners of his mouth, trying to wipe out the smug smile that lurked there, ready to splash across his face. "No, captain, that will not be necessary," he said. "These two are smugglers, wanted by the Thrane authorities. We've been pursuing them in Aundair for some time, and thanks to you we have caught them.

"I will be bringing them to Daskaran and handing them over to the authorities there. The Thranes will doubtless take them to Firehaven for trial."

The captain tilted her head. "Why go to all that fuss just to make the Thranes happy?"

"Two reasons, captain. First, anything that can help ease tensions between Thrane and Aundair will be good for everyone. Second, and more importantly," he added, "we could try them here, but the Church of the Silver Flame has . . . more creative solutions in the realm of justice."

The captain raised her eyebrows and wagged her head,

although Teron could not tell if her gesture was one of assent or merely acceptance of a tale she did not believe.

"I thank you again, captain," Teron said, bowing. "Your assistance will not go unnoticed, I assure you."

He walked back toward the lightning rail, and as he passed Praxle and Jeffers, he gestured to the soldiers. "Bring them this way, if you please," he said.

The soldiers each took an arm of one of the prisoners and impelled them toward the waiting coaches. They hauled them back aboard, pushed them into the second-class sleeper cabin that Teron indicated, and turned to leave.

"You'll be all right, then?" asked one of the guards. "That orcblood looks pretty tough, and that gnome, well, he looks downright vicious. We'd be happy to lend the church one of our swords, if you like."

"I'll be fine, soldier," said Teron.

The soldiers nodded and departed, and Teron closed the door to the cabin. He pulled a key from his belt and waved it.

"Back in Ghalt I alerted the military to arrest you if you appeared at any border crossing," he said. He offered up two pieces of parchment. "They had excellent descriptions, based on these pictures of you, drawn from your papers by one of the brothers at the monastery. The search edict was given in the name of the Prelate Quardov, and would have been obeyed. You would have been detained and sent back, and I doubt he'd believe your version of events. The only way I could think of to get you two across the border without raising suspicion was to have the military actually arrest you."

"Why did you not inform us of your scheme?" asked Jeffers.

"It was a gamble," said Teron. "I thought it best to keep your reactions honest and to proof your minds against telepaths."

"I knew that," said Praxle. "You didn't have me fooled, monk."

Teron glanced at Jeffers. The half-orc rolled his eyes.

CHAPTER 13

The lightning rail glided slowly to a halt, wreathed in energy. Steam rose from the coaches, the watery remnants from a brief shower being vaporized by the powerful magical effects of the conductor stones. The mist glowed whenever the slanting mid-afternoon sun broke through the scudding clouds.

The last of the flickering bolts died out as the caravan came to a halt. Stewards stepped up to the carriages and opened the doors, setting wooden steps in place for the convenience of the passengers.

"Daskaran Ferry!" bellowed the conductor. "Debark for Daskaran Ferry, Daskaran, Scions Sound, Flamekeep, and points south! Boarding, eastbound run to Thaliost! One hour to board for Thaliost!"

Jeffers stepped off the coach, down the small wooden bench, and onto the platform. His head swiveled side to side, taking in the entire area. He nodded, and Praxle followed him off the coach, using the handrail to help him take the steps that were uncomfortably large for a gnome. Teron followed the other two off, his scraggly cat Flotsam perched on his shoulder.

He walked up to stand beside Praxle and Jeffers. "Where to now?" he asked.

"Not now, monk," said Praxle quietly. "We've got trouble by the conductor's hut."

Turning his head as little as possible, Teron glanced over toward the small outbuilding that served as the conductor's office. There he saw several Thrane soldiers listening intently to a ragged-looking goblin. The diminutive humanoid gestured to his wrists, shook his fists, and then pointed directly at the threesome. Eight veteran eyes followed the goblin's finger and studied the travelers like raptors.

"What is your wish, master?" asked Jeffers calmly.

"Let's disperse," Praxle said. "Some, but not overmuch," he added, walking casually away from the others and picking up an abandoned broadsheet of the *Flamekeep Mirror* that lay on a slatted bench.

Jeffers kneeled down to adjust a nonexistent problem with his boots, and Teron simply turned the other direction and sauntered away.

The guards moved briskly over. Two stopped at Praxle, who was the nearest, and one of them used a spear to usher Praxle's reading aside. "Your papers," said the guard with no hint of respect in his voice.

Praxle smiled and pulled out the small case holding his forged identity papers. The case was made of lacquered ebony edged with polished silver, a fortunate find when Jeffers went shopping in Passage. The Thrane guard inspected the beautifully calligraphed identity papers and matched the illustration with Praxle's beatific face.

"May I enquire as to what this is all about, good soldier?" asked Praxle.

The guard grimaced. "We received a report, citizen d'Sivis, that you'd been clapped in irons just the other side of the border. We, uh, we needed to pursue the matter."

"Folderol!" said Praxle, his eyes wide with surprise and indignity. "Me? In irons?"

"Did you have any difficulties with the Aundairian law, citizen d'Sivis?" pressed the guard.

"Why, no, of course not," replied the gnome. "I don't understand—" His eyes narrowed suspiciously. "Say," he said, leaning forward, "this . . . report, did it come from a goblin? About yea high, kind of a, a burgundy coat?" asked Praxle.

Flustered, the guard replied, "We can't make any—"

"Because if it did," interrupted Praxle, "that would be the gambler I took to the woodshed over several hands of sovereign setup. See, he'd get this little tic in his left eye when he was bluffing, and I drained his purse until it was as empty as a Karrn's heart. He said I'd regret it, but I paid him no mind, as I have my domestic with me," he added, gesturing to Jeffers.

"Right," said the guard, handing back the papers as he looked past Praxle to his fellows. One was holding Jeffers' papers, looking back for confirmation. The other had just garnered Teron's attention. "My apologies for the interruption."

He placed his hand on the shoulder of his compatriot. "You stay with the gnome," he said. He strode across the platform. "Stay with him," he said to the guard with Jeffers.

He broke into a trot after Teron.

❁ ❁ ❁ ❁ ❁ ❁ ❁

"Hold up there," said the guard as he closed.

The human in the peasant shirt did not slow down, although the cat jumped off his shoulder and scrambled away.

"You there, halt now!" barked the soldier.

The human stopped and slowly turned around.

The guard quickly peeked over his shoulder. His sergeant and one comrade were speaking to the gnome, the other had the half-orc bowing submissively and proffering his papers. Yet somehow he was nervous approaching this one, even if the traveler was unarmed, unarmored, and a good six inches shorter than he.

"Papers. Now," demanded the guard.

Without any acknowledgment, the young man pulled a very plain leather fold from his satchel and handed it to the guard.

The guard inspected the papers. "From Aundair, huh?" he asked. "Heard there was some trouble on the other side of the border. Heard some of you folks were in irons. Is Queen Aurala throwing out her garbage across our border? What crime did you commit,"—he glanced at the papers—"Tuh-rone?"

"It's Tehr-ron," said the man.

"Mind your mouth, Aundairian, if you like all your teeth." The guard looked Teron up and down. "Did you fight in the War, t'Rone? Huh?"

"Why? Afraid I killed someone you knew?"

"I'm not afraid of any Aundairian. Answer the question."

"I was not in the army, no," said Teron. He readdressed his body so that he faced the guard squarely. He steepled his fingertips together and raised his hands to his solar plexus.

"Look me in the eye, Aundairian!" barked the guard.

Teron looked up and the guard took an involuntary step back.

"All right, Aundairian dog," said the guard as he leveled his spear, "you're going with me to see the captain. Don't try anything you might regret."

"It's far too late for that," whispered Teron.

The guard nervously shifted his grip on the spear, then let out a tense breath as he heard his sergeant trot up beside him.

"Trouble, soldier?"

"Aye, sergeant. This Aundairian's got trouble written all over him," said the guard. "I think he fought in the Last War. He's got a killer's look about him."

"I was in the Last War myself, soldier," said the sergeant. "But last I heard, that war is over."

"That still doesn't mean I want Aundairian soldiers prowling our countryside, sergeant. Just look at him. He's all tensed up, like a lurker ready to spring."

The sergeant crossed his arms. "And look at you, soldier. You've got your spear leveled at someone for a routine check of papers. He's unarmed."

"That's right, sergeant," stammered the guard. "I think he's one of those monk warriors."

The sergeant stiffened and looked at Teron anew. He saw the balanced stance, the poised hands, the dead eyes. "I think you may be right," he said slowly. "The Monastery of . . . Provincial . . . oh, what was it?" He thought for a moment, trying to remember. "No matter," he said suddenly. "I remember the gold altar that my regiment plundered from it well enough." He smirked. "Do you want to know whether or not this is one of those monks, soldier?"

"Well, yes and no, sergeant. I heard they were pretty treacherous."

"True enough, but my regiment did all right." The sergeant drew his swords and smiled mockingly. "Let's find out, shall we? Repeat after me, Aundairian. 'Dol Arrah is a rancid whore. All praise the Silver Flame.'"

Teron's eyes flared, then he snarled, "Dol Arrah is a rancid whore." He paused, then added, "All praise the Silver Flame," with a rather confused expression on his face.

The sergeant pushed out his lower lip in frank amazement. "I guess you were wrong," he said. "Now quit being so skittish and give the man his papers."

"What do you mean?" asked the guard, still edgy.

The sergeant leaned close and said, "Over the course of the Last War, our inquisitors were able to bring the light to a number of Aundairian captives. But despite their best efforts, they never succeeded in coaxing a single monk from the Monastery of the Provincial Whatever into saying the least positive token about the Silver Flame." He shrugged. "Just part of their vows or something. Let him go," he added with a yawn. "He's no monk. He's nothing more than a street tough. This is all just an angry goblin gambler getting some petty revenge."

The soldier tossed Teron's leather fold back to him and walked away warily.

* * * * * * *

"Hold on there—what's this?" asked Praxle under his breath. He nodded his head to a woman who sat by herself on the platform, a look of entranced horror on her face.

Jeffers stepped over and kneeled in front of her. He noticed papers in her lap, and inspected them. "Three different identities. Neshryk of Darguun, Oargesha of Cyre, and—"

"Oargesha?" said Teron. "That was one of the people I fought in the catacombs."

"And you let her get away?" goaded Praxle.

"One of them stayed to slow me down while the other two fled," explained Teron. "They got away. He didn't."

"So whatever has happened to her?" asked Jeffers.

"Perhaps she toyed with the Sphere," offered Teron.

"She sure has the face of one who did," said Praxle, and chuckled. Intrigued, he placed his palm against her forehead, intending to set her to rocking, but as his hand touched her skin, he gasped and pulled his arm back as if bitten. He cocked his head, curious, and studied the woman more closely.

Praxle felt for Oargesha's pulse. Then he pulled out his timepiece and held the polished golden ring up to Oargesha's mouth, shaking his head. "She's definitely dealt with the Orb of Xoriat," he said hollowly.

"I guess this proves we're still on the right trail," observed Teron.

"Judging by her state," said Jeffers, "I'm uncertain whether or not 'right' ought be applied to this situation."

* * * * * * *

Daskaran Ferry was little more than a service hamlet built alongside the venerable chain of conductor stones that marked the lightning rail's route through northern Thrane. Aside from the platform and office, Daskaran Ferry boasted merely two stores that sold a variety of durable goods, three purveyors of fresh-cooked and/or preserved foods (those sold by the kobolds being of highly questionable quality), a cheap lodge, and the ferry for which the tiny hamlet was named.

A few miles upstream, the Aundair River flowed into a finger of Scions Sound, a writhing hydra of a saltwater inlet that, among other things, separated Thrane from her enemies to the east:

Karrnath and Cyre. The ferry had been the only means to cross the sound since Karrnathi sappers destroyed the arching span of the Trader's Bridge during the Last War. The ferry operated under the auspices of the Thrane government, providing free passage in hopes of improving trade and travel through the area.

Teron, Praxle, and Jeffers walked down the packed-dirt slope to the ferry's marginal dock. The sun, peering through the dissipating clouds, continued its descent to the horizon, a hazy and colorful display that cast a rich orange hue over everything.

"All right, Praxle," asked Teron, "what was that?"

The threesome made it to the dock and stepped out. The heavily weathered boards creaked and flexed under their feet. Their brief detention put them among the last of the passengers to board the ferry, but no one paid them any extra attention; the aggressiveness of the Thrane soldiery was well known across Khorvaire.

"Hm?" Praxle said distractedly, inspecting the ferry as they approached.

The ferry was a large barge equipped with weatherworn wooden benches. Tarps lay bundled at the gunwales in case of rain; the barge was definitely not equipped for luxury. But most curious was the gaping circular hole cut in the center of the deck. Next to the hole was a silver paddle, looking rather like a rudder raised up on a pivot and secured out of the water. Within the hole, the sound's salty waters roiled aggressively, even rising up to a foot in the air, yet none of it spilled out, and, despite the weight of the passengers, the barge did not sink.

"I said, what was that?"

"Oh, that's a binding seine for a water elemental," said Praxle. "Very curious design, I admit. There must be something below the hole to afford the elemental a better grip to get this scow across the sound. Perhaps a keel, laid sideways. Very clever."

"No," said Teron. "What was that up there? That had to be you."

"Hm? Oh, indeed it was," said Praxle with a pompous smile. "You seemed like you were getting ready to spring, monk."

Teron shrugged. "I could have taken them."

"I know," said Praxle. "I saw how you handled my so-called bodyguard. But I didn't want that kind of trouble. It would be inconvenient, especially since we are liable to remain here for several days at best." He sat on one of the benches, drawing one leg up and leaving the other dangling. "So, since they were done with me," he continued, waggling his fingers in the air, "I used my magic to throw my voice into your mouth. Judging by your reaction, monk, it even made you think twice about whether or not you said it."

A sailor dipped the silver rudder into the roiling water at the center of the boat. The turbulence settled down as the barge accelerated from the shore, gliding smoothly and quickly across the sound toward Daskaran on the far shore.

"I know," said Teron, a steely tone entering his voice. "I am very displeased to have been associated with such words."

"Drop it in the river, monk," said Praxle. "You should know by now that all Thranes are religious zealots beholden to the Silver Flame and itching for the next Great Missionary War. You'll hear a lot worse during the next few days, so count this as your first lesson in accepting an insult to stay out of trouble."

"I don't need a les—"

"Yes, you do, monk," snapped Praxle. "You're the most hotheaded, fight-focused, cold-hearted, socially inept mendicant I've ever laid eyes on. Everything you do, you do with fists and fierceness. You barge your own way through everything like it's a war and you're a warforged juggernaut. If you had the discipline of magical training, you might be great. As it is, you're a pair of fists looking for a face to punch." He exhaled explosively. "You've shown that you're smart, monk," he admitted, more softly now, "but you have to learn to relax, as well. The war ended, you know."

Teron raised one hand, fingers tensed somewhere between a gesture and a strike. He tried to say something, but his seething anger kept his lips pressed together, so instead he steepled his hands in front of his solar plexus and walked slowly to the side of the barge to look out at the setting sun reflecting off the rippling waters of the sound.

Jeffers looked over at the sullen monk and shrugged. "That could have progressed more congenially," he commented.

"He needed it," said Praxle. "He's far too suppressed. I hit the mark dead-on. If I hadn't he'd have been able to respond."

"I must confess, master, that I was thoroughly impressed with your ability to replicate his voice."

Praxle waved a hand dismissively. "All I had to do was speak in a flat tone through clenched teeth. It was easy."

❦ ❦ ❦ ❦ ❦ ❦ ❦

In the darkness of midnight, a cloaked figure debarked from a carriage, laden with two bags. The moon Vult shone its scarred face on the city, casting ghastly shadows in the streets.

The figure sauntered toward a doorway, then darted down a narrow alley. The high walls concealed the figure from the moons and Ring of Siberys, casting shadows that meshed with the dark cloak and wrapped all within the alley's narrow, inky embrace.

Somewhere in the night a rat scuttled for shelter, the scratchy sound of its claws upon the cobbles sounding like a small hail of bone shards.

The cloaked figure stumbled, looked around, and slid down another alley, a thin canyon between large stone edifices. The figure looked once more to ensure that no other soul was in sight. A hand reached out, touched a miscolored stone, the knot in a large timber, and then pushed on a rusty spike embedded in the wall. The spike slid in, clicked, then slid back out. The figure stepped to the side and pushed up on a windowsill. It gave way, moving up an inch before settling back into place. After a moment there was a soft grating sound as a section of the stone wall backed into the building, revealing a short, narrow hallway.

The figure entered, and the secret door slid shut again.

Utterly fatigued, the Shadow Fox pulled back her hood and slumped to the floor. She sat in the claustrophobic darkness, her head leaning back against the wall, and cried tears of relief and exhaustion. At last the awkward position made her lungs and stomach ache, so she roused herself once more. She abandoned her shoulder bag there in the hall, bringing only the large black leather bag.

Navigating by touch, she staggered down the hall, trying to keep the bag as far from her as possible in the tiny space the passage allowed. At last she entered a larger, open chamber illuminated by an everbright lantern.

Her team's secret den. Then she realized that that label no longer applied. It was just her secret den, now.

She moved over to the side wall, opened a well-concealed hatch in the paneling, and placed the bag containing the Sphere of Xoriat behind the wall. Closing the hatch, she moved over to the bunk farthest from the concealed compartment.

She sat heavily on the bed and kicked off her boots.

Safe at last, she thought.

She glanced at the secret panel. Or am I? she wondered.

Not even bothering to strip off her sticky travel clothes, she flopped onto the bed. The pillow still smelled of Rander, but she was too weary to move. The smell permeating her senses, she cried herself to sleep.

❋ ❋ ❋ ❋ ❋ ❋ ❋

Praxle, whistling happily, led the quiet Jeffers and sullen Teron through the quiet Daskaran streets. Teron cradled his cat in his arms, idly scratching Flotsam's head.

Teron, unable to seethe in silence any longer, spat out a question. "Where are we going?"

"To the Daskaran docks," said Praxle. "Hire ourselves a small ship or a berth to Flamekeep."

"Why by sea?"

Praxle snorted. "Because it's faster. Monk."

"We should go overland," said Teron.

Praxle stopped in his tracks, then turned around wearily. "That would be slower. Monk."

Teron put his cat down and rested his hands on his hips. "If the Cyrans went by ship, we won't beat them to Flamekeep," he said. "If they went overland, we might overtake them on the road, all alone and away from Thrane sentries. If we get good transportation and travel fast. Given the choice, I'd rather take a small chance than no chance."

Praxle drummed his fingers on his chin as he considered this. "Well, then, that's a very good point," he said. "In fact, that makes a lot of sense. You killed, what, two Cyrans in the catacombs? Then there's that frozen one we saw on the platform across the way, and I dropped one when we were bushwhacked back in Wroat. So that's four Cyrans dead. I'd wager there are naught but two or three left. They wouldn't have the strength or courage to try to prize the notes from the Thranes until they had more support from their fellow Cyrans. But if we caught them on the open road when their numbers were so depleted, that would make life ever so much easier."

He reached out and clapped Teron on the hip. "You're still pretty smart, monk. At least about things that involve killing. Let's see what we can find, shall we?"

Praxle looked about and spotted a cluster of Thrane soldiers a few blocks away, lazing underneath an everbright lantern, leaning against the wall and chatting. One of them puffed on a pipe, and the smoke rose up like an ethereal serpent in the cool nighttime air.

The trio walked over to the guards. "Excuse me, my good fellows," said Praxle sweeping his hat as they drew close, his tenor voice resonating in the street, "we were hoping you could direct us to where we might be able to hire some overland transport to Flamekeep."

One of the guards stood, scratching at his unshaven cheek. "Who's asking?"

Praxle, ahead of Jeffers and Teron, stepped into the circle of light cast by the everbright lantern. "Praxle Arrant d'Sivis, of the University of Korranberg," he said with a bow.

The guard straightened. "At your service, friend gnome," he said. "You'll want to go three more streets that way, then turn right. That's Procession Road; you can't miss it, it's very wide and well cobbled. Go maybe a half mile, and you'll see a sign pointing you toward Caravan Square. There's caravaneers, drovers and the like looking for hirelings and passengers, House Orien has an outpost there, and such like. You should be able to find something that'll leave in the morning."

Jeffers and Teron stepped up beside Praxle. "Would there perchance be a representative of House Vadalis there as well?" asked Jeffers.

The guard's answer was interrupted by one of his companions, who suddenly stood bolt upright and confronted Teron with wide, accusatory eyes. His mouth worked fiercely, but the only noise that came was an airy whisper punctuated by sharp sibilants and plosives.

"Is he ill?" asked Praxle, backing up. Jeffers stepped forward between the gnome and the apoplectic guard.

Hissing, Flotsam darted out of Teron's arms and scooted for the protection of the wall.

The guard, seeing the confusion in the eyes of his compatriots, whipped out his sword with startling speed and, in one continuous motion, slashed at Teron's neck. Teron leaned backward, taking a grazing slash across the cheek. He tried to back up, but his heel caught a jutting cobble and he flopped to his back.

The guard brought his sword around, up, and down, intent on splitting Teron's belly open, but Teron used the velocity of his fall to propel him into a backward roll. The sword sparked on the street, and Teron continued his somersault to land back on his feet at a safer distance.

The guard was big, and the way the everbright lantern illuminated the sneer of hatred that smeared across his face made him seem larger still. He stepped forward with his sword extended aggressively.

Praxle and Jeffers backed up as the other guards unlimbered their various weapons. "Hold it right there," barked one of the guards, pointing at the twosome. Jeffers paused, standing with poise and dignity as the scene unfolded. Praxle cowered somewhat less proudly close behind the large half-orc.

The guards fanned out, two warily watching Praxle and Jeffers, the other two moving to assist the guard facing Teron.

Seeing three guards facing him, Teron straightened up and tentatively raised his hands in surrender, shaking his head ever so slightly. The mute guard moved in, his face held somewhere between a grin and a snarl. He prodded Teron in the sternum with the tip of his broadsword, and the monk flashed into action. His hands, held to the side, jerked in, striking the mute guard's sword arm and hand, and suddenly Teron, his arms crossed in an X before him, held the broadsword in his left hand. The guard looked in shock at his empty hand, then up at Teron's calm eyes.

"Nobody move!" boomed a voice. Nine more Thrane guards stepped out of the night and into the shadowy periphery of the everbright lantern's glow.

Frozen in position, Teron looked at them, gauging the odds. Jeffers raised his chin defiantly, but left his serrated sword sheathed. Praxle hid himself beneath the tail of Jeffers' overcoat.

With the appearance of reinforcements, the guards' surprise and wariness were replaced by a cold, gloating superiority. One of the guards facing Jeffers stepped in closer. "I dare you to draw now, orc-thing," he mocked, his face so close that Jeffers turned his head.

The reinforcements spread out to surround the group, their steely arms and armor glimmering in the darkness, reflecting stray shards of light.

Teron slowly lowered his arms, still holding the sword and keeping his hands defensively crossed at the wrists.

"Well, now," said the newly arrived officer with a dark chuckle. "It seems we have some people here who think they're dangerous. Ludicrous, don't you think, that they dare take on the followers of the Silver Flame?" The soldiers laughed. "You three are under arrest," continued the officer in his bold tenor voice. "And don't even think of resisting. You'll find my guards to be rather more of a challenge than a group of spelunking Cyran thieves or handful of overzealous border guards, wouldn't you say . . . monk?"

Even as the officer finished speaking, Jeffers acted. He turned his cultured gaze on the guard facing him, and head-butted him in the face. The guard staggered back, hand rising to his broken nose. Jeffers snatched the guard's spear away and struck him on the side of the neck with the shaft, cracking it. The guard went down.

Teron reversed his grip on the broadsword and gave a backhand thrust, swinging his arm low and guiding the point of the sword upward, to pierce the mute guard's abdomen below his cuirass.

Startled by the sudden revolt, the patrol sergeant looked to the officer and the other eight reinforcements for assistance. To his amazement, they faded from sight. He glanced about, saw the human engaged with three guards, the half-orc fighting one as well, and the gnome pointing a small wand at him. There was a magical flare of red, and the sergeant saw no more.

Teron ripped the bloodied blade back out of his mute victim and tossed it handle first to another of the guards facing him. As the guard's eyes rose to follow the weapon through the air, Teron jumped forward. His leg snapped up and delivered a debilitating kick between the legs. As the guard doubled over, Teron lanced his fingers at the guard's throat. The guard's head dropped, and Teron reached out and grabbed the guard's head. Holding the guard's neck secure, Teron spun around him, interposing the hapless soldier's body between him and the rest of the melee.

The third guard that faced Teron stepped forward, hefting a large double-bitted axe. Teron shifted his position, keeping the incapacitated guard between them. With a rip, he twisted his captive's head sharply and broke his neck, looking to goad the axe-wielding guard into a reckless attack.

The attack never materialized, however, as a serrated blade decapitated the guard before he charged. Teron dodged aside as blood gushed from the wound.

"That could have proceeded more auspiciously," said Jeffers, slinging blood from his blade. "We'd best get our transport quickly."

"What was that all about, monk?" asked Praxle.

"Did you see his throat?" said Teron. "I think I must have crushed his voice box during the war."

"Strange that he'd remember your face," said Praxle.

"I must have been in a hurry," said Teron, scooping up Flotsam unceremoniously under one arm. "I usually don't leave survivors."

CHAPTER 14

Look here now, if it isn't the Shadow Fox."

The Fox shut the door quietly behind her, shutting herself in with the pungent odors that permeated the arcanium. "Good afternoon, Rezam," she said. She crossed the room and sat in a large chair at a stained table, turning it so she faced the wizard.

The aged elf pushed his tome aside and leaned back, lacing his fingers across his belly. "It's been a very long time since you've come to visit our little nest here," he said.

The Shadow Fox fidgeted with her fingers a moment, then looked up, all business. "I've been busy with one of the other nests. We ended up traveling across half of Khorvaire."

"Mm," said Rezam, batting his thumbs against each other.

"It was difficult, but we were successful. We acquired a very old relic. It's called the Black Globe, but I'm guessing that's an alias. It's reputed to come from the Gatekeepers, which means that it could have powerful protective magic. I'm hoping that we could somehow use this to restore Cyre to where it's supposed to be, maybe drive the curse off the land."

Rezam lolled his head from side to side as he considered. "It could also be planar magic," he said. "If so, we could theoretically use it to reach back to moments before the Day of Mourning and snatch the whole country forward to our time. Hm. Say, who knows? Maybe we already did, eh?"

"What?"

The elf leaned forward, craning his neck out, his eyes wide with the possibilities. "Maybe the dead gray mist and all of that is the lingering effect of us in the future having saved our country from its terrible fate. Maybe we've wasted all this grieving, because we're just moving through the patterns of things that had already happened when Cyre was taken, hey? Did you ever think about that?"

The Shadow Fox slowly blinked. At last she replied. "I'll bring you the Globe then, shall I?"

The elf spread his arms wide. "You will do as the patterns of prophecy require, for the dragons will not abide a paradox," he intoned.

The Fox curled her lip skeptically. "You're a little odd," she said.

Rezam's face fell. "You've said that before," he said, tracing his finger around a stain on the table. Then a small smile touched his lips. "But you know as well as I that investigative magicians must envision the whole realm of possibilities when trying to unravel arcane secrets."

The Shadow Fox rose. "I know. I didn't bring you on because you were an average person. I brought you on because you're so good it's scary."

Rezam grinned. "Then bring it over. I look forward to seeing it."

As she Shadow Fox left the laboratory, she glanced one last time at Rezam. Sometimes, she thought, you're a little too scary.

* * * ⊛ * * *

Inside the Phiarlander Phaire the atmosphere was raucous and jovial. The tavern was filled to capacity with drinkers and diners, sampling some of the best wares to be had in Flamekeep outside of House Phiarlan's magical feasts. A thick haze of tobacco and incense lurked about the rafters, and the clink of tin plates and flatware fought a hopeless struggle for dominance with the sounds of laughter and conversation.

Zabettia Besdal stepped through the front door and immediately felt as if she were drowning in an excess of civilization. Her body already starting to sweat, she loosened her cloak, then worked her way across the floor. She had to wriggle between chairs filled by overstuffed patrons and plot her course to avoid the many servers working the crowd.

She wound her way to the service counter and caught the attention of one of the staff, an old man with one eye. A long scar, a keepsake from a Karrnathi scimitar, draped across the other half of his face. He nodded at Zabettia in recognition.

"The Shadow Fox is back," said Zabettia, raising her voice to be heard above the brabble.

"It's about time," grumbled the old man. "Where's she been?"

"You know she never talks about that. But she did say that several other Cyrans lost their lives in the service."

The man spat on the floor. "I hope they weren't home when it happened," he groused. "That just wouldn't be right."

"I wouldn't know," said Zabettia. She looked around the room, taking in the wide variety of people present. "She said to be on the lookout for Aundairian monks, or a Korranberg gnome traveling with a half-orc servant. She's not sure whether or not they might have managed to follow her here."

"That's not much to go on," said the man.

Zabettia nodded. "I know," she said. Then she slapped her hand on the countertop. "Better than nothing, though," she said with a smile. "Have to go make the rounds. Keep your eye open."

The old man touched his brow in farewell. "By the fifth nation," he said, then spat on the floor again.

❋ ❋ ❋ ❋ ❋ ❋ ❋

"Well, that was a waste of time, monk," said Praxle as they climbed off one of the caravan's wagons.

Teron shrugged. "We took a chance. It didn't pan out."

"Instead we spent two and a half days getting sore kidneys bouncing on a cart in an Orien caravan."

Teron didn't bother to reply. He stretched out, as did his cat. Then he hopped out and placed one hand on the side of the wagon, and Flotsam walked up the length of his arm to perch on his shoulder.

"That has got to be the ugliest stray I've ever seen," said Praxle, warming to his sour mood.

"He's sort of my pet," said Teron. "He just kind of likes me. We get along."

"Look at him, monk. His head is way too flat and wide, his hair . . . well, he sure doesn't bathe himself often, and I swear he takes two steps with his front legs for every three he takes with his rear. He's built like a hyena."

"He's growing into a tom," said Teron. He kneeled down to put the cat within reach of Praxle. "Here, feel his muscles at his shoulders."

With a look of disgust, Praxle complied. The cat's muscles were dense and powerful. He ran his hand down the cat's back, and partway down the ribs, the muscles turned smaller and softer. He felt the terminus again, the sudden shift from thick to thin. "That's . . ."

"Strange, isn't it?" said Teron. "It's like he's maturing front to back." He chuckled softly. "You should have seen him when he first started. First his nose grew all out of proportion to his face, then his head got big like this but he still had the body of an older kitten."

"That sounds very ugly."

Teron stood. "I guess that's why we get along."

"If you'll pardon me for interrupting, Teron," said Jeffers, "I have something that I've wished to enquire of you. I believe we are safe enough to ask you now."

"What's that, Jeffers?"

Jeffers glanced about and lowered his voice. "Back in Daskaran, you took a sword away from that guard. I was most curious as to how you accomplished that."

Teron smiled, a brief but genuine expression. "Pick up that stick. I'll show you," he said.

Jeffers picked up a larger stick and held it like a dagger.

"Look. My hands are out to the side, right?" said Teron, placing himself squarely in front of Jeffers and raising his arms partway up. "It looks like I'm surrendering, but I'm not. My hands are ready."

Jeffers nodded.

Teron flashed his hands together, striking Jeffers and stripping the stick from him.

Jeffers blinked, and rubbed his now-empty hand. "My apologies, but I didn't quite follow that."

Teron handed the stick back. "It's an advanced technique," he said. "Let me show you the foundation move. Watch." He raised his hands again, and started moving them slowly towards Jeffers' wrist. "I bring my hands in. My right hand strikes you on the inside of the wrist. My left hand strikes you on the back of your hand." He paused, his hands just making contact with the half-orc's larger hands. He started applying pressure. "As I move them in, what happens?"

"You bend my hand forward."

"And how strong is your grip now?"

Jeffers tried to grip the stick firmly. "Very weak."

"Right. Now if you do this fast enough, you actually make the other person toss the weapon from their hand. Here, try it on me." He took the stick from Jeffers and held it.

Jeffers raised his hands to the sides of Teron's hand, and aligned them with their targets. He took a deep breath, then slapped Teron's wrist and hand, and the stick flew out of his grasp. "Why, that's child's play," said Jeffers, pleasantly surprised with his success.

"Essentially, it is," said Teron. "It's basic body mechanics. The strike you saw me do is tough. You have to know how hard to strike, you have to power your hand through the enemy's without overpowering the blow, and you have to have precise timing to grab the weapon's handle as it flies from your opponent's hand. There's a few other points, too, but I think you get my point."

"Fascinating, my good man," said Jeffers, slowly moving his hands to strike at a number of imaginary weapons. "I do appreciate the instruction."

"If you two are quite finished playing children's games," interrupted Praxle irritably, "I wish to find us some good lodgings that provide strong drink, good food, and a large, hot, soapy bath."

"Lead on," said Teron.

Praxle stomped off, followed by Teron with his cat, and Jeffers, who continued to practice martial arts in his mind.

⊛ ⊛ ⊛ ⊛ ⊛ ⊛ ⊛

With a relaxed sigh, Praxle climbed out of the brass bathtub. It had been designed for someone of larger size, so he had to climb awkwardly over the edge, but the inconvenience was a small price for being able to float in steamy hot clove-scented water until his skin was bright red all over.

He dried himself off and dressed in the new attire he'd purchased earlier that day. Bright red breeches, a gold tunic with puffy sleeves and black highlights: bright and cheery attire to buoy his mood. He was determined to have a good time tonight, to forget that some damned Cyrans stole his relic, that some damned Aundairians hid it from him for decades, and that some damned Thranes stole it from his people years before that; he was determined to enjoy his bath and his dinner and his drinking despite the fact that he'd be dining with an Aundairian monk in an establishment that served Cyran dishes located in the very heart of Thrane itself. And, as he slid the silken tunic over his bare chest, the caress of the cool fabric on his overheated skin succeeded, for a moment, in eclipsing all other considerations.

He walked into the common area of their room. Jeffers sat at the table writing a letter, attired in his usual dapper but nondescript clothing. Teron, dressed in new but plain trousers, soft boots, and a sleeveless leather vest, looked out the window, arms crossed.

"I . . ." pronounced Praxle loudly, "am ready!"

Jeffers nodded deferentially. Teron remained at the window.

"Well, then, monk, I rather liked that peasant shirt, though it was too large. But the women are going to fall out of their bodices after one look at you."

"What do you mean?" asked Teron.

"What do you mean, 'What do I mean?' Look at you. Thin, agile, muscles like a Valenar stallion . . ." he stopped short as Teron turned around. "Yipe, hold on there, monk!"

"What?"

"Clean up your face. You've a big smear of blood where that Thrane cut you."

Teron raised one hand to his injured cheek. "I must have reopened it when I washed."

"Jeffers," said Praxle, snapping his finger. "See to it. I'm starving."

Jeffers acquired a large ceramic bowl of hot water and a clean rag. He daubed at the blood, cleaning the skin as well as the wound itself, until all that was left was a red slice across Teron's cheek and its partner nick just above the tip of his nose.

"Would you like me to stitch those closed, Teron?" asked Jeffers.

"Don't bother," said Teron. "I've suffered worse."

"It will be less likely to scar if I do," persisted Jeffers.

"I won't notice one more scar."

"So I see," said the half-orc, casting an eye down the various pale lines that marred Teron's sun-darkened arms.

"All right, monk," said Praxle cheerily. "You're looking almost civilized. Let's go."

The gnome led them out of their rooms and down the hall to the large staircase. "You've probably never been to a popular guesthouse before, have you, monk?" Hearing no answer, he continued. "You're in for quite a treat. The people were fascinating. It's like watching a herd of sheep all milling about, each thinking that it's the bull ram. Or maybe wolves. Depending on the mood of the evening, and the quality of clientele, a pack of wolves might be more appropriate."

The trio descended the staircase. "But remember," added Praxle, lowering his voice to avoid attracting the attention of the others in the lobby, "we're in Thrane now. I'm guessing that you were only in Thrane as part of the Last War, right?"

Teron nodded.

"Well then, let me be the first to educate you, monk. Thrane is the bastion of the Church of the Silver Flame, the beacon that will change the world, or so they think. The church is stronger here than the entire Sovereign Host is in Aundair. Everyone in the country sees themselves as a warrior-proselyte with a divine duty to usher in a new age."

The threesome exited the inn. The nighttime streets in this area of town were well illuminated by everbright lanterns and light spilling from various restaurants and inns. The sounds of merriment washed into the streets from a dozen establishments.

"So you're saying that they're a bunch of violent heathens," said Teron.

"Well, in essence, yes. I'm also telling you to keep calm. We got lucky with those guards in Daskaran that there was no one else around, monk. You need to rein in that temper of yours or the whole town will turn on you. Understand?"

"I will be as a flower in the breeze."

"Fine," said Praxle. "I just hope you're a flower that didn't leave too many other Thranes remembering your face."

· As they continued down the street, Praxle gestured to one particular establishment. "There it is, the Phiarlander Phaire," said Praxle. "It was recommended for its good food and boisterous atmosphere."

Jeffers walked over and opened the door for the others. Inside, the common room was crowded and noisy. Every table was filled. Teron turned to leave again, but Jeffers gently restrained him.

After a brief scan of the room, Jeffers pointed out a table currently occupied by two half-elves obviously deep into their cups. Praxle nodded. The half-orc led the small gnome toward the table, plowing a clear path for the small illusionist through the careless throng. Teron walked just behind.

As they closed, Praxle cast a spell, conjuring an illusion of a very attractive pair of elf women. He sent the illusion walking around the table. The two drunkards looked up, and the illusory elf maidens winked bawdily and headed for the stairs in the rear. The men stumbled out of their chairs and staggered after them.

"Well, then, here we are," said Praxle as the threesome took their seats at the vacant table.

After several minutes, a young lass with thick auburn hair stopped by the table. She smiled and brushed a lock of sweaty hair from her face, pulling it behind her ear. "May I help you, gentlemen?" she asked, her voice brassy with the need to speak loudly.

Praxle nudged Teron beneath the table, then remembered that the monk probably had no idea what to say. "Bring whatever the kitchen has the most of," he said, "and bring it fast. We're famished. I'll have a tall mead. What about you, monk?"

Teron shook his head and waved off a drink. Jeffers ordered a tankard of ale.

As the young lass departed, Praxle rounded on Teron. "What's the matter with you, monk?" he asked incredulously.

Teron looked genuinely confused. "What?"

"That tawny young filly thinks you're the dragon's shard, and you didn't give her two blinks! You didn't see that?"

Teron crossed his arms and glowered.

"Her smile brightened like the sun coming from behind the clouds when she laid eyes on you. The intense eyes, unshaven face, fresh scar worn raw, she senses you're a dangerous and exciting man, I'd wager."

"No, she doesn't."

"Yes, she does," countered Praxle. "Her hair was in her face when she came to the table. She saw you, and pulled it back. Only on the side facing you, I might add. And she used her tray to hide a stain on her apron."

Teron turned his head away.

"She wants you to ask her to dance, monk," finished the gnome. He laughed. "Hardly have your hook in the water, and already the trout are swarming!"

When the young lady returned with their drinks, Teron averted his eyes. Praxle spoke with her a moment, then gave the lass a knowing smile and tossed a sovereign on her tray for good measure.

"Hey, monk! Her name's Kelcie!"

Teron ignored him.

By the time the serving girl returned with their food, three musicians had taken the small stage and the sounds of spirited music cut through the noise of the crowd, lightening the mood and, at the same time, making it harder to talk.

Praxle leaned over and said something to Teron. The monk shrugged in reply. Praxle repeated it. Teron shrugged. At last, Praxle cast a small spell, his swift and delicate fingers spinning the arcane sapphire energies into a specific shape. He mouthed some words, and he finished, magical motes flew to Teron and Jeffers alike. Praxle's voice sounded in their ears, quiet yet clearly audible: "The stage must be magically enhanced."

Praxle and Jeffers put away a prodigious amount of food between them. Teron ate lightly, tense to be surrounded by so many Thranes and uncomfortable in the unfamiliar environment.

As the last patrons finished their dinner, the pace of the evening slowed considerably. The servers supplied everyone amply with drinks, and the crowd submitted itself to the sway of the music. The musicians broke into a slow song, a melancholy instrumental piece that hushed the crowd almost entirely; only a few coughs and brief exchanges broke the melody and countermelody.

Kelcie stopped by the table again to check on the three. Teron nervously waved her off, but Praxle tugged on her sleeve and asked, "What is this song they're playing? I've not heard it before."

"It's the Song of the Argent Stream," she answered, and her melodious voice whispered like satin. "It's a song of destiny, sacrifice, and redemption. The horn represents Tira Miron, and her calling. The lute represents the couatl, who pleads for her aid amid the terrible battle it fought with the demon. Do you like it?" she asked the table in general.

Jeffers nodded.

"It's very beautiful," said Praxle. He tilted his head to the side. "What do you think, monk?" he asked, reaching out to tap Teron on the shoulder.

Teron simply leaned forward and rested his chin on his interlaced fingers.

Kelcie's shoulders slumped slightly as she rose.

"Another round," ordered Praxle. He watched Kelcie leave, glanced at Teron, then quickly cast a small spell. As before, a flickering trail of cerulean motes whooshed from his hands, but this time the spell arced over the room to strike Kelcie's ear.

She stopped in her tracks, pulled her hair back, and looked over her shoulder at the table. Praxle caught her eye and nodded wearily, an apologetic half-smile on his face. Kelcie smiled brightly and left to fetch their drinks.

The evening passed with Teron sitting tensely, Jeffers sipping herbal tea and scanning the crowd, and Praxle diving with reckless abandon into mug after mug of mead.

After several other religious pieces, the minstrels started playing a rollicking, boisterous tune that hailed from somewhere in the early years of the Kingdom of Galifar, a catchy melody that had been hijacked for any number of lyrics over the past few centuries.

"Come now, everyone!" bellowed the minstrel playing the tambor and drums. "Let's Fight!"

The crowd cheered, adding the clashing of tankards and the thumping of tables to the rolling rhythm. Their drunken voices boomed cacophonously, filling the walls of the tavern with the heady sound.

> Fight, right! I do love to fight
> Face evil and smite it with valor and might
> Find a thief or a liar
> And make them expire
> There's no glory higher
> Let's fight!

Praxle leaned over to Teron, his head wobbly from too much drink. "What in Khyber's corset is this?" he yelled, and the crowd charged into the second verse:

> War, more! I love a good war
> And whetting my mettle 'midst chaos and gore
> To some it seems chilling
> But nothing's as thrilling
> As wantonly killing
> To war!

"This is a far cry from that Song of the Silver Hooplah," Praxle said. "They—"

> Kill, kill, it still gives a thrill
> To pierce something fierce and watch blood start to spill
> Karrn, Cyran, Aundairian
> Or Brelish Lord Baron
> I really don't care and
> Let's kill!

"I told you they were bad," yelled Praxle over the din. "I swear this is all they ever think about!"

> Crush, crush, it gives me a flush
> Put a mace in their face and the blood starts to gush
> Why bother with pikes
> When I love to take strikes
> With the iron and spikes
> They crush!

Praxle stood up. "Right!" he yelled. "That's it!" He stomped off quickly for the minstrels, carrying his mead and casting a transmutation spell as he walked. Jeffers, scanning the room for potential trouble, didn't sense him leave until it was too late to prevent him without making a scene, and with it, a bar fight.

Teron pushed his seat back and sat at the edge, ready to leap to his feet.

> Chop, lop, no reason to stop
> Take whacks with an axe at the bottom and top
> To watch the limbs flying
> And hear your foe crying
> Just give it a try and
> Let's chop!

Praxle leapt up onto the stage and signaled the musicians to keep playing. Surprised, but sensing the attention of the crowd, they obeyed. Praxle turned to face the audience. "Are you ready for new verse?" he asked. His magically augmented voice, combined with the enchanted effects of the stage itself, carried unnaturally well. The crowd cheered. "I said, are you ready for new verse?" he boomed, nearly pitching himself off the front of the stage with his effort. The crowd cheered again, much louder.

Praxle drew himself up as far as his three-and-a-half-foot stature allowed, and broke into a hearty tenor rendition.

> Drink, drink, I do love to drink
> Swill ale by the pail 'til I'm too drunk to think
> This inebriation
> Is quite the sensation
> So fetch a libation
> And drink!

The crowd roared its approval as Praxle drained his mug. Then he spread his arms wide in thanks and fell face first off the stage, the smile never leaving his lips.

Teron stood, but Jeffers was already moving toward the intoxicated gnome, so he sat back down. The half-orc picked up Praxle gently and carried him out, stopping by to collect Teron on the way.

The monk stood and followed Jeffers out of the Phaire. Jeffers kicked the door open and stepped outside with his master, but just as Teron reached the door, he felt someone grab his right elbow. He jerked around, right arm moving to break the grip, left arm readying to strike.

He found himself face to face with a pretty oval face framed by a mane of rather disheveled auburn hair.

"You're leaving?" Kelcie asked, her eyes pleading. "Don't you want to dance with me?"

Trapped in an utterly unfamiliar situation, Teron fought his way out of it as he had been trained to do: aggressively and without reservation. "Yes," he said with a candor that startled him. "I'd love to. But I've never danced."

He opened his mouth to say something else, but then turned away and moved purposefully after his two companions.

Kelcie stared after him, speechless. Then she turned back into the Phaire, walked over to the service counter, and slammed down her tray. "Roadapples!" she spat.

The one-eyed man behind the counter nodded.

CHAPTER 15

Eyes bleary, head swaying side to side, Praxle strained to focus his intoxicated brain as he worked his way through a spell. At last the tendrils of mystic energy coalesced properly, and he raised his hands to his face. The energies swirled around his head, then wormed their way into his hair and disappeared into his scalp.

"I didn't pass out," he said slowly, concentrating on his diction. "I took a bad step."

Teron leaned against one wall, his arms crossed. "Your legs weren't moving," he countered.

Praxle sighed deeply. "Tea, Jeffers, very strong."

Jeffers nodded, and left the room to procure the tea. He shut the door quietly behind him.

Praxle turned around slowly, swiveling on the rotating stool on which he sat, then leaned back against the table. "I don't understand you, monk," he slurred.

"How so?"

"That wench wanted your touch," said the gnome. "The string of her blouse got looser and looser as the evening went on."

"It was hot in there. She was working."

"She was offering a lot more than drinks every time she came to our table and leaned over," snarled the gnome, venting all his physical discomfort into the utterance.

Teron looked down, trying to forget her touch on his arm, the look in her eyes.

"Are you truly that blind?" asked Praxle, rubbing his eyes with the heels of his hands. "If you spent half the energy on pleasure that you do on exercising and causing yourself pain—"

"Pain is the mortar of my life," said Teron. "I could not build myself without it."

"That," slurred Praxle, "may be the wisest thing you've said yet, monk."

Teron looked up. "My name is Teron."

"But why do I even bother? I'm trying to show you there's more to life than abusing yourself and meditating on your navel, and what kind of gratitude do I receive?"

"Use my name."

"Be quiet, monk. I don't feel well at all."

Teron strode over and planted his hands on each side of Praxle, penning him in against the table. "You call Jeffers by name. He's your servant. I'm your partner. Show me the same respect."

Praxle's momentary surprise gave way to an inebriated smirk. He guffawed, then broke into a near-hysterical drunk laugh. He slid off the stool to the floor. "Oh, monk," he said, rolling onto his back, "He's not *named* Jeffers. He's just . . . my Jeffers. That's what he is. He's . . . I think he's the third one I've had. All my Jefferses . . .ses."

Teron stood and took a step back. "What?"

Just then the door opened, and Jeffers stepped in with a teapot. "May I enquire as to what you gentlemen find so amusing?"

"Oh, look," said Praxle, giggling. "My dear Jeffers is back with the tea."

❀ ❀ ❀ ❀ ❀ ❀

"I seen them, yes'm," said Squints, a tremor in his voice. "There's no doubting it." The old man hated being away from his familiar kitchen and his cleavers, more so hated being here, way out of his element. He fidgeted with his hat, turning it in circles and trying to make out some semblance of shape in the darkened recess of the private booth. The *Coal Scuttle* was known as a place of discretion even at noontide; in the wee hours of the morning its darkness was all but impenetrable.

"What, exactly, did you see?" asked a voice from the darkest shadows.

The old man scratched at the scarred eyelid that hung over his empty socket. "I work at the Phiarlander. I saw a little gnome, all gussied up, take the stage and sing a bit. Then he passed out, on account of being very drunk, I do believe. A half-orc carried him out. And behind them walked a human, too. I'd wager gold to gonads that he were a monk type. He had muscles that moved like . . . like there was weasels under his skin."

"Muscles do not make a monk."

"Yes'm," replied the old man, "but Kelcie, she's one of the girls that works the tables, er, not like a whore or anything, you understand, the Phiarlander is classier than that, but she brings drinks and food and other needy things, she said the monk guy was all flustered and such that she talked to him, like he ain't never been with a woman or anything."

"I see." The Shadow Fox leaned forward, her face concealed by a large, drooping hood. The old man could only see the point of her jaw; the rest was concealed by shadows or black material. It was hard to tell which. "Anything else?" she asked.

"No, that's all I done saw." The old man stared at the shrouded figure. The Fox didn't move. At last the man couldn't withstand the silence any more and stammered, "I thought you were wanting to know, is all. I came right as soon as I'd finished up the cleaning."

He looked around for some support, but no one else in the *Coal Scuttle* was paying him any mind. He started crumpling his hat and twisting it.

The Fox reached forth with one gloved hand and placed a gold coin on the table with a clack. "You did well to bring this to me," she said. The glove retreated, and soon a second galifar clinked onto the first. "Very well," she said. And then, as she reached out and deposited a third coin on the table, she added, "Three enemies. Three rewards. Thank you."

The man hesitantly reached for the coins, then snatched them up as avarice overcame timidity. He clutched his fist to his chest, feeling the beautiful weight of a month's wages. "Welcome, kind lady," he said, his voice trembling with fear and relief. "It weren't nothing." He tittered. "Nothing at all." So saying, he backed halfway across the floor, turned, and made a brisk escape into the night street.

He didn't notice that one of the other patrons tapped thrice on one of the tavern's windows just as he exited.

● ● ● ◉ ● ● ●

Praxle rolled a string of vowels from his mouth in one last incoherent attempt to communicate as Jeffers shoveled him into bed. He continued to babble for a few moments, his slack jaw pushed to the side due to the angle at which his face rested on the pillow, but in a short few moments the droning voice was replaced by snoring.

Teron lay on the floor, his head propped up against the wall. Flotsam sat on his chest, paws tucked in contentedly beneath him, and purred loudly.

"That was . . . educational," said Teron.

Jeffers, seating himself at the table with a quill and papers, raised his hands helplessly. "The pot did not contain tea, I'm afraid. I find that on evenings such as this, a mild narcotic makes for a simpler existence."

Teron snorted with amusement. Flotsam opened one eye in annoyance at the disturbance.

"So why do you stay with him?" asked Teron.

"I am a bondservant. I sold myself to his service as butler and bodyguard for a period of ten years. He paid my family quite well for my time."

"Is that who you write letters to?"

"Indeed. I keep them abreast of our adventures. They mean the world to me." Jeffers tapped his lips with the quill for a few moments then set it down and walked over to sit at the edge of the bed nearest Teron. Teron glanced up out of the corner of his eye and noticed the half-orc's posture was perfect.

"If I may be so bold as to enquire, good Teron," asked Jeffers, "there seemed to be some tension between you and my master with regard to the young woman at the guesthouse this evening. What, precisely, was the source of the problem?"

Teron considered for a moment, then decided to answer. "I think you, as a bondservant, would understand." He gently ushered his gray cat off his chest, and sat up, legs folded, hands on his knees. "I swore a vow when I joined the monastery. I dedicated my life to Dol Arrah. In a sense, I married her that day."

"Dol Arrah?" echoed Jeffers. "She seems a trifle unusual a choice for a deity of warrior monks. Please take no offense, but the goddess of honor and light does not mesh well with the impressive acts of puissance that I have witnessed you undertake."

Teron nodded his head to the side in concession. "True, but Dol Arrah is also the goddess of sacrifice. That aspect is the centerpiece for my . . . my school. It's an ancient path, one that hadn't been seen for a long time. I shouldn't say any more on the subject."

"I understand, master. Rest assured I shall exercise the utmost discretion in this regard. None shall hear of your path from me."

Teron tipped his head respectfully. "Thank you, Jeffers."

For a while there was only the sound of Praxle snoring and the cat noisily cleaning his fur. Then Jeffers got up and began gathering the teapot, cup and spoon to return them to the proprietor.

"Jeffers?" asked Teron.

"Yes, Teron?"

"What's your real name?"

"Whatever makes you ask, my good man?" asked Jeffers, eyebrows raised in curiosity.

Teron looked at him and realized that the half-orc didn't know. "I just figured that it wasn't the name you were born with."

Jeffers smiled. "You are correct, master, though Master d'Sivis has insisted on using 'Jeffers' from the day he hired me. He did not treat my cousin well when she used my real name, and I have not mentioned it to anyone else since."

"You don't have to worry on my account," said Teron.

"You don't know master d'Sivis," said Jeffers as he let himself out the door.

❦ ❦ ❦ ❦ ❦ ❦ ❦

"Where are you going, old man?" asked a sniggering voice that slithered from the shadows of the alley behind the *Coal Scuttle*.

"What?"

The mugger stepped out of the shadows of the alley. He slid one arm out from beneath his cloak, turning his short sword so it caught the light. "I said, where are you going, one-eye?"

"Home," he stammered, desperately wishing he'd brought his mace from beneath the service counter. "I'm no trouble to you."

"No, I don't suppose you would be. Too old and timid. You sound like a foreigner, too. Where are you from?"

"C—Cyre. At least, that's where I was born." Without the comfort of the familiar establishment and several Cyran compatriots nearby, Squints found his courage utterly void.

"Ohh," mocked the mugger, in an exaggerated show of grief. "Poor Cyre. Where the weak of soul let their whole country just die in one short day. No wonder you're such a coward." He waved his blade slightly, and held out his left hand. "Come now, grampa, unload your saddlebags. I know you've got coin, and I'll take it from your hand now. It's up to you whether your hand is still attached to your arm."

A tear rolled down from the old man's good eye as he slowly extended his hand and, by an act of will, forced it to open and release the gold. Clink clink. It fell into the mugger's hand. Clink. As the last coin fell, the old man bowed his head in defeat.

The mugger spun his short sword once, sheathed it, and jingled the gold in his hand. "Thank you so much," he said with another snigger. "You have a nice evening."

He turned to go but found his path blocked by a woman in a hooded cloak. She stood, her weight all on her right foot and her hip thrown to that side. Her cloak was thrown back on the left, showing that her left hand was balanced lightly on her thigh.

"You have my money," she said simply.

"What are you blathering about, woman?"

"You have my money. I gave it to him, and you took it from him. Give it back."

"Oh, I don't think so," said the mugger, chuckling.

The woman started stepping forward, slowly, her hips swaying gently like a great cat on the prowl. "I don't care what you think," she said. "Give. My money. Back."

"You listen here, lady—"

The Shadow Fox stepped right up to the mugger, her face still concealed by her hood. "Draw steel," she demanded.

"You're asking for big—"

Smack! Her left hand darted out and struck him full across the face. "Air that sword and start fighting, boy. I'm only a weak-souled Cyran. You said it yourself."

His eyes widened and rolled like a panicked horse. He wavered for a moment, then he drew his blade and swung a mighty chop at the Fox.

She stepped forward and ducked, sliding neatly under his initial flailing blow. She turned to face him again, flipping her cloak off her right arm. She concealed both her hands behind her back. "Try it again, boy."

Angered and nervous, he slashed at the Shadow Fox again. She stepped to the side and extended one arm to deflect the blow. The mugger's blade landed a glancing blow, shuddering and sparking as it traveled the length of her arm.

Stupefied, he paused for a moment. The Shadow Fox chose to give him his answer. She revealed the weapon in her hands: in her right a kama, a small weapon shaped like a miniature scythe. A chain led from the butt of the kama's haft up to her neck. With a casual shrug, she let the links drop. She held the other end of the chain in her left hand; she'd had it pulled taut over her shoulder and down the arm to protect against an overhead slash.

"What's the matter? You look like you've never seen a woman with a weapon before." She slung the kama toward him, then yanked on the chain. The horn-shaped blade snapped like the tip of a whip, drawing a gash across the back of the mugger's calf. With another snap, the Fox slung the kama back to her hand.

Trembling with rage and fear, the mugger attacked again, swinging for her neck. The Fox deflected the first strike, stepped back from the second, and at the third she stepped in and locked his hilt with the haft of her kama. There was a brief pause, and she flicked their weapons apart.

He yelped and stared at a second gash across his wrist, just starting to well blood.

"You fight like you learned how to swing a cleaver from your mother," said the Fox. "Didn't your father teach you anything?"

He charged and thrust. She gave ground quickly, raising her kama just in time to steer his point away from her abdomen. He pressed the attack, and she parried, her chain jingling with every move. Then, as he drew back his blade for a third thrust, she yanked her arms up and out, pulling on the chain. It had looped around his ankle as he'd pressed forward, and her sudden move made him lose his balance on his injured leg. He dropped to one knee. Quick as a cat she lunged forward, pressing her blade into the flesh under his chin, ready to slash his jugular from the rear. The kama's razor tip drew a bead of blood from the soft skin.

He froze in place, mortal fear in his eyes.

"Drop your blade." The short sword first dangled, then dropped and embedded its point in the packed-dirt alley. "Give him back my money." The mugger's left hand extended, and the old man came out from hiding to recover his wealth.

With a quick sneer, the Shadow Fox drew her blade across the mugger's throat. He clapped his hands to his jugular, his eyes wide with panic. He rose and turned to run, but the Fox slung the weighted tip of her chain around his ankle and tripped him up. He rolled on the ground and she stepped on his chest to hold him in place.

"Your throat will heal," she said. "But I want you to remember this, and tell all your little friends: I work for the Shadow Fox, and he's very protective of his fellow Cyran. If anyone harms a Cyran, the Shadow Fox will find them. Do you understand?"

The mugger nodded with as small a motion as possible.

The Fox cleaned her blades on his cloak, concealed the chain beneath her cloak, and walked away.

"And crawl home on your hands and knees," she called over her shoulder. "You never know: I might be watching."

* * * * * * *

Praxle groaned and pulled the blanket over his head. "Wake me after you've broken your fast," he mumbled.

"I already have," said Teron.

"I also partook," added Jeffers. "And, if history is to be a guide, master, we should be just in time for midday meal."

Praxle moaned again and rolled over, trying to curl into as small a ball as possible.

Teron stepped over to Praxle's bed, grabbed it firmly, and heaved it onto its side just as Jeffers blurted out, "Wait!"

With a yelp, the sleeping gnome tumbled to the floor, pulling the blanket off with him. He ended up on his stomach, the blanket beneath him, wearing naught but his underclothes. "Who—this—" he sputtered, as he pushed himself up. He rolled onto his back, reclining on his elbows. "You vicious little bastard!" he spat.

Teron loomed over him, staring back, unafraid. "Get dressed," he commanded. "Let's get moving."

Praxle glared up at him. "I should—"

"Try me," said Teron, gesturing Praxle up with one hand. "Your illusions won't help you."

Praxle smiled cruelly. "Bravely spoken by someone who only knows how to hit people," he said. "But illusions are the first step in creation." Magical energy coursed around his hands, arcing out to encompass his body and the area around. Teron took a step back as sudden winds blew in the room, buffeting Teron's clothing and sending Praxle's blanket flopping across the floor. The window rattled as the winds gathered beneath the gnome, whipping his underclothes and hair, and pushed him to an upright posture floating a hand's span above the floorboards. Then all at once the wind cut off, and he landed gently on his bare feet.

Praxle gestured again, creating a sea-green flash. The sound of a dozen clashing sabers resounded in the room. An aura of pale energy surrounded him.

Teron stepped back again and adopted a ready stance. "Be careful, Praxle."

"Careful?" said Praxle. "My power grows every year, monk. Your power will fade as you age. I can create. You can only destroy." He gestured again, his hand flaring crimson, and Teron felt a forceful blow strike him in the midsection. The impact shoved Teron backward into the wall of the room with a loud slam. He managed to keep his balance, however, and stepped forward, ready to launch an attack to immobilize the gnome. He drew himself up short, however, when he saw that Praxle was once more his casual self, and wasn't even looking at him.

"Well, then," the gnome said, "now that I'm up, I suppose we may as well get to work." He got dressed, idly bantering about the day. "All right, first, food. And then I'll show you the place the Thranes keep their research notes. And, uh, let's leave the mangy cat behind, right?"

As the threesome left the room, Praxle paused. "We do understand each other, right . . . monk?" he asked, but before Teron could answer, he turned and headed down the hall.

❂ ❂ ❂ ❂ ❂ ❂ ❂

A cold wind blew in from Scions Sound as Praxle, Teron, and Jeffers walked toward the heart of Flamekeep. Unseen behind them, a nondescript person paced their progress, almost a block to the rear.

"All right, here it comes," said Praxle. He cleared his throat with mock dignity and swept one arm out in a grand gesture. "The Great Library of the Congress of Alchemical and Magecraft Academics of Thrane," he intoned. "That's what the Thranes call it, at least. Down in Zilargo, we refer to it as the Camat Library."

"Why?" asked Teron.

"It's an acronym. Made up of the initials. It's a lot faster than using their long-winded and pompous name."

"We're taught to respect names," said Teron.

"I might respect the name if I respected the people or the institution," said Praxle. "But the Thranes are a bunch of warmongering zealots, and the Camat is an ideologically dominated school that focuses on application over theory."

"I see," said Teron. "Better to have something you can daydream about than something you can do."

Praxle looked up at Teron with scorn. "Shut up, monk. You don't understand."

"Ah. Right. Debate is application, not theory."

"Shut up, I said."

"Your superior intellect shames me."

Praxle growled as he led them to the front doors of the soaring structure. As they approached, Praxle began to gesture widely and spoke in a louder voice with obvious fascination. "The architecture is of the dynamic Flamic school. Observe the saw toothed minarets that soar above the corners of the building; notice that each moves sedately, rotating about the base of the bridge that rises to it. Obviously, magical enhancements maintain their elegant courses, and the bridges use some of the finest engineering techniques to swivel with the towers. Thus at once this grand edifice showcases the skill of Thrane magewrights and architectural engineers, the glory of the Church of the Silver Flame, and the prestige of such a vaunted institution."

They climbed the large stairs that ascended to the library, and Praxle pointed to a variety of adjacent buildings. "Well, then.

Over there you see the Dormitorion, the building that houses students of the school. Behind us lies the Assembly, which contains the magical laboratories, the circle of regents, and proving grounds for students seeking advancement within their craft."

They reached the top of the stairs, and the massive granite doors of the library, each twenty feet high, swung open noiselessly to admit the visitors. "In case you hadn't noticed, the doors open automatically to admit those with magical ability," Praxle said, doffing his cap with a sweeping bow.

They entered the building and walked across the wide marble floor of the foyer. The foyer was tall and wide, and very dark compared to the afternoon sunshine. Other than the narrow shaft of sunlight spilling in, the only light came from a small fire burning atop an eight-foot-tall silver oil stand, polished to a mirror shine. Any features in the walls around were lost in the shadows.

As they drew closer to the oil stand, some of the flame spilled over the side and onto the floor. It trickled across the floor toward the visitors, then pooled ten feet in front of them. The flame grew, and gathered itself into an oval shape that hovered a foot and a half above the floor. Only a single thin strand of flame reached down to touch the oil.

A voice issued forth from the flaming ovoid, a strange mix of whispering and growling. "What help may I provide, esteemed visitors?" it asked. The hard consonants sounded like the popping of a fire.

"I was escorting these gentlemen around, showing them the wonders of this library," said Praxle.

The fire elemental flared. "The library is open to all spellcasters, although pursuant to our concern for safety and our position as guardians of the nation, we have certain strictures in place. Followers of the Silver Flame may bring tomes from the shelves to the reading tables. Students of the Congress of Alchemical and Magecraft Academics of Thrane may bring materials into private reading rooms. Only members of the faculty can remove items from the building. However, this library generously provides any spellcaster in Khorvaire with new incantations for personal use for a nominal fee.

"The library's resources are divided by the schools of magic. The schools are arranged about the perimeter of the building, with more advanced resources available on higher floors. For the safety of all, librarians are on hand to ensure that novice spellcasters do not endeavor to research techniques that are beyond their capacity." The fire elemental dimmed as it finished its recitation.

"What about the physical sciences? Alchemy, artifice, topics like that?"

The fire elemental flared briefly and said, "The physical and paramagical sciences are located in the center of the library. In this way we ensure that there is as little interaction as possible between members of opposing schools of magic."

Praxle smiled. "I would like to tour the library, if you please."

"Of course. I shall be happy to make an appointment for you," said the fire elemental, pulsing. "I can arrange for you to apply as early as next week."

"Apply?" said Praxle. "What does that involve?"

"In the interests of the safety of all, we check every applicant carefully. We do not wish to provide enemies of the peace with additional potentially damaging resources."

"Enemies of the peace," muttered Teron. He snorted.

"No, thank you," said Praxle. "We have no need. I doubt we shall tarry that long. I believe we have seen enough to impress our friends back home. Thank you."

The fire elemental flickered away, leaving nothing in its stead. No trace of oil remained on the floor.

The threesome turned and departed the building. The great doors opened, then closed behind them. As they descended the great staircase, Jeffers asked, "You didn't wish an appointment, master?"

"No," said Praxle quietly. "There's no sense in leaving them with my identity when I plan to burgle them in a day or two."

CHAPTER 16

As Teron, Praxle, and Jeffers turned the final corner on their way back to their lodgings, a squad of a half dozen soldiers stepped out from beneath the eaves of a storefront. The soldiers spread out as they approached, weapons drawn and chain mail chinking.

"You three. Hold," one of them said.

Teron looked around. Broad daylight, major city street. The odds were fine, and chain mail provided negligible protection against joint locks and blunt impact, but the result of any resistance would be their exposure as "enemies of the peace." They'd have to abandon Flamekeep immediately, which would make recovering the Thrane notes and the Sphere itself much more difficult.

Teron looked at Praxle and gently shook his head. Praxle nodded.

"What can we do for you on this chilly day?" asked Praxle, sweeping his hat in greeting.

"You'll come with us." It was not an answer, but a demand. "Lady Stalsun wishes to speak with you."

The six guards escorted the wary travelers to a waiting carriage, a large and elegant vehicle that sported the family crest of Stalsun on the door. The three climbed in, followed by a few guards. The other guards climbed on the back as footmen, and the carriage lurched forward as the driver cracked the whip over the horses' heads.

Praxle stared out the window as they progressed through the city. "These are the widest streets I've ever seen in a city," he said, to no one in particular. He turned to one of the guards. "Why are they built this way?"

The guard looked at her comrades, then decided to answer. "The Voice of the Silver Flame commanded that the city be built this way, with wide avenues so that all feel welcome," she said. "The city is only five or six hundred years old, and the Voice had seen the choking streets of the other so-called great cities."

"That's interesting," said Praxle. "One would think it would make the city more difficult to defend."

"Not at all," said the guard. "Flamekeep was briefly besieged after Shadukar was razed. We found that the wide avenues allowed us to move our forces quickly and easily through the city, to counter attacks or to launch forays of our own. Meanwhile, the Karrns had to march their troops all the way around the city, out of bowshot of our archers. It took them four or five times as long to react. We broke the siege from within with a series of raids, always striking where the Karrns were weakest. Of course, we had to burn the bodies so they wouldn't raise them again. Nothing's more annoying than having to kill your enemy twice."

Praxle pursed his lips as he considered this. "It also makes the city appear cleaner than other large cities I've visited," he said.

"The city is cleaner," responded the guard.

"Of course."

The carriage traveled to a smallish estate on the wealthy side of town. Ivy-covered masonry walls surrounded the house, and a guarded gate admitted the carriage. The carriage rolled up a nicely paved path to the front of the house.

A doorman dressed in elegant formal attire gestured Praxle, Teron, and Jeffers from the carriage and led them into the house. He required them to remove their boots and don slippers "to preserve the polish of the floors."

He then led them into a drawing room and seated them on some comfortable chairs, though not until after he carefully covered the chairs with extra fabric to prevent them from becoming soiled by the companions' clothing. There was a long silence in which the doorman stared at them dully, and they were forced to remain in their chairs silently.

At long last, the heavy latch to one of the other doors clicked, and as it swung open, the doorman announced, "Lady of the House Hathia Stalsun, Duchess of Shadukar."

Praxle and Jeffers rose and bowed elegantly. Teron hesitated, then grudgingly rose to match his companions.

In walked a Thrane noblewoman, dressed in an exquisite royal blue gown brocaded in black and gold, finery that had been fashionable five years earlier at best. The hem of the dress hissed across the floor, and the sleeves of the gown covered the backs of her hands. A high stiff neck held her head in a perpetual pose of arrogance, and her half-lidded eyes only added to the appearance. Pale makeup covered her face, obliterating her wrinkles and turning her lipstick a harsh color in comparison; her mouth almost looked like a puckered spear wound. All this was topped by a towering upswept wig adorned with small, dangling jewels.

In spite of the heavy-handedness of her attire and posture, she still exuded the image of a womanly core. Her arms were graceful and long, her features fine, and even the exaggeration of her corseted middle and the hoopskirt could not totally overshadow the fact that a feminine figure moved beneath the fabric.

She carried a walking stick in one hand, and it tapped the floor regularly as she moved to the largest chair in the room and seated herself quite primly. Once she was seated, twenty guards entered the room. Ten took up positions against the wall behind the lady, while the other ten took up positions uncomfortably close behind the threesome.

The lady delicately raised one hand to cover her mouth as she cleared her throat, then laid it atop the other, which rested upon the head of her walking stick. "My introduction has been made, gentlemen," she said in a voice that was smooth and full, as if she has been trained for singing. "You will now introduce yourselves to me."

Praxle gestured the other two to their seats. "Am I to understand that this is an official inquiry, Lady Stalsun?" he asked.

"I take it you have not crossed the path of the Crown Knights," she said. "If you had, you would know the answer to your question. The Council of Cardinals demands swift justice for wrongdoing in Thrane, and their methods of interrogation are effective, if zealous. While I have no concern over this in cases of the guilty, I do believe that their enthusiasm is often misapplied to those who may actually be innocent. Therefore I give you this one opportunity to speak with me civilly, unofficially, but also candidly. Another such offer shall not be forthcoming, either from this house or from any other citizen in Flamekeep."

"But, if I may ask, Lady," countered Praxle, "if this is not an official inquiry . . . who are you? What is your interest in us?"

"My interest, gentlemen, is the safety of Thrane. I am a lady with a meaningless title. Shadukar was burned to the ground during the Last War. The battle destroyed my family's entire estate, all their holdings, and all who had sworn them fealty. Of my family, I alone survived, by virtue of having been elsewhere. Fortunately, my family had a number of investments that have provided a helpful stipend. Thus I was able to relocate to this place and survive. Since then, I keep my fingers in a lot of events. It gives me something to do, and I can serve my nation by watching the comings and goings of interesting people." She shifted her hands on top of her stick. "You will now introduce yourselves to me," she said, "or I shall be forced to see you to an official representative."

"That will not be necessary," said Praxle. "I am Praxle Arrant d'Sivis, of the University of Korranberg. My domestic Jeffers accompanies me everywhere. My traveling companion is Teron, who hails from Aundair. These you may verify with our papers, if you wish."

Keeping her hands atop her cane, Lady Stalsun pointed with one finger. A guard stepped forward. He glanced at each of their documents, nodded in confirmation, and handed them back.

"May I ask why you have an interest in us?" asked Praxle.

"Word of several incidents has reached my ears, the most recent of which concerns the death of a young woman riding the lightning rail at Daskaran Ferry. Let us start there, for while I have no prejudice against Cyrans dying, I don't like it happening in my country with no explanation."

"We had nothing to do with that," said Praxle.

Hathia raised her chin imperiously. "You would have me believe that you—"

Praxle interrupted. "And . . . she wasn't dead."

Hathia paused. Her eyes narrowed. "What do you mean?"

"You're referring to the young Cyran that was paralyzed as she sat, is that correct? Frozen rigid with that unseemly expression on her face?" Praxle waited for confirmation, then continued. "I tell you the truth. She wasn't dead."

"But—but my sources told me that she was stiff with the rigor, and her skin blued. What other explanation is there?"

"Her state is the effect of the darkest magic," said Praxle. He sat down and locked eyes with the lady to press the import of what he was about to say. "Let me tell you what she suffered. What she suffers still. Her heart was still beating, but too slowly to hear. She still breathed, too, though it took her a minute or two just to draw a breath.

"But most important, I could sense what had happened to her soul." Praxle paused, looked at the ceiling, then looked back and continued. "I am blessed with the dragon's blood, Lady. I am a practitioner of magic, and of no small skill, if I may be so bold. As such, I can discern certain aspects of magical auras; the more powerful the effect, the easier it is to analyze. And the effect on her was . . . notable.

"Her soul was elsewhere, lost, and yet still tied to her body. She'll die soon. In fact she's probably already dead, perhaps from suffocation for breathing too slowly, or maybe chilled to death if the guards left her outside. Once she dies, her soul will remain trapped wherever it is."

Lady Hathia leaned forward. "What do you know of where her soul might be?" she asked. The appalling truth of the situation crept through her façade of composure and tainted her expression with horror.

"It's on another plane of existence. I don't know exactly where, but it's somewhere terrible. I could hear the echo of her screams. And not of pain, either. More like . . . I don't know if I can find the right word. Fear, maybe. Anguish, revulsion . . . madness . . .

"Allow me to confide in you, Lady," continued Praxle, running his fingers through his hair. "You've been very patient and accommodating to speak with us personally instead of turning us over to the Inquisitors. The reason we are here is that I believe that this woman is part of a team of Cyrans that stole an artifact that rightly belongs to the University of Korranberg. This is a very powerful artifact and could be utterly devastating in the wrong hands, as this woman's fate shows.

"I believe that the Cyrans may have fled to this very town. We are hoping to recover this relic before the Cyrans unleash a calamity of legendary proportions upon Thrane. If you could see fit to help us, Lady Stalsun, we would be most grateful, and the whole of Khorvaire would be the safer for it."

The Thrane woman sat unmoving for several long minutes before finally shifting her position. She glanced down at the armrest of her chair and brushed an imaginary fleck of dust away, then looked back at Praxle. "That does not explain why you visited the Great Library of the Congress of Alchemical and Magecraft Academics."

Praxle responded without hesitation. "Well, it should," he said, then chuckled. "I went there hoping that I could find some assistance in locating the thieves. A scroll, a diviner for hire, a magewrought seeker I could rent."

"Why not hire a finder from House Tharashk?" asked Hathia. "Surely those with the Mark of Finding could be of some service."

"If they realized the true potential of the relic, they'd be tempted to steal it for their own use," said Praxle. "The University of Korranberg held this artifact safely for a few hundred years, and then within twenty years of us losing control if it, someone started using it as a weapon of war. I hired someone, and he died, yielding his discovery to the Cyrans. I trust no one else in this matter, not any more."

"I see," said Lady Stalsun. "Then you're telling me that I should trust you and abet you, when you freely admit that you lost control of an ancient artifact to a rabble of displaced Cyrans?"

"They were no rabble," said Teron. "They were skilled and disciplined. Not excellent fighters, but they were quick thinkers and stealthy spies."

"Their leader was amazing," added Praxle. "Fast, clever, and deadly, and probably the best planner I've seen, outside of myself. But for some good luck on my part, the Cyrans might have effected the theft perfectly."

"I would not expect to hear anyone speak of the Cyrans so highly," said Hathia. "For myself, I find them wearying and contemptible, like those who pine away over a lover whose memory death has turned into a fairy tale."

"Then you understand why we must find them and this relic before they try to unravel its secrets," said Praxle.

Hathia raised one hand to silence him. "What I understand, my persistent guest, is that this interview is now at a close. Rest assured that our eyes will be upon you whilst we reflect upon your tale."

* * * * * * *

Dark had fallen over Flamekeep. Teron pulled back the window curtain and peered out. The Siberys ring hung in the heavens, its elegant light contending with the unsubtle glow of the everbright lanterns in the streets of Thrane. Dravago, one of the larger and hence brighter moons, shone like an amethyst, but was not yet near zenith. Eyre, also large, was moving toward the horizon, and its slanting light no longer penetrated the city streets. Only distant Vult hung overhead, and its wan light was of little concern.

Teron let the curtain fall shut again. "It's time," he said.

"Right," said Praxle. "Let's go."

"No."

"No?" asked the gnome, puzzled. "Then what's it time for? I thought you wanted to scout out the Camat Library."

"I'm going alone," said Teron. "Not you."

"Look, monk," said Praxle, "that place is probably crawling with magical wards and alarms, to say nothing of traps."

"Of course it is," said Teron, pulling on his soft-soled boots. "And many of them are likely keyed to guard against the use of magic. You, gnome, can't sneak around there without using magical enhancements. I can."

"You can?" scoffed Praxle.

Teron turned and headed for the corner of the room. With a leap, he jumped up the wall, planted a foot and a hand on it, and pushed himself to the other wall. He braked his momentum with his other foot and hand, stopping himself three feet above the ground, held in place by his hands and feet. He bowed his head to avoid knocking it against the ceiling. "Yes, I can," he said. "You've honed your spirit to work magic. I've honed my body to do the same thing."

Jeffers looked at Teron with an appraising scowl. "That outdoes any theatrics of mine," he said.

Soft as a cat, Teron dropped back to the floor. "As for the rest of the wards, I can take care of those. I have training."

"You'll need help," persisted Praxle. "We're in the middle of the capital of Thrane, for the Host's sake!"

"No. I need solitude," said Teron. "I'm trained to work alone, even in the middle of the enemy camp. Allies can only fail you."

Praxle narrowed his eyes. "What was it you trained to do, monk?"

"I trained in the Way of the Quiet Touch," he replied. "I break things noiselessly."

"Things? You mean like magic staves and the like?"

"Or bridge supports, necks of enemy generals, whatever I was told. Whatever Aundair needed broken I broke."

"So you're an assassin," said Praxle.

"I'm someone who took a vow," answered Teron. "And I always keep my word." The two stared at each other for a long time, testing each other's will. At last Teron broke the silence. "I'm going to scout the library," he said. "And I'll do it alone."

He turned to leave the room, then patted his shoulder and tsked with his tongue. Flotsam stirred from where he slept in the corner, rose, stretched, then leapt up Teron's vest and clawed its way the last little bit to perch on his shoulder.

"I'll be back in an hour or two," he said.

Praxle twisted his mouth into a crooked, angry sneer. He pulled a chair over to the window, climbed up, and peeked out between the curtains. He watched Teron leave the building, walk down the street, then turn a corner.

He hopped off the chair and grabbed his coat. "I don't care, monk," he growled. "I don't trust you. Jeffers? Come."

❧ ❧ ❧ ❧ ❧ ❧ ❧

Teron glided silently in the shadows of an alley across from the Camat Library. The building loomed over his head, illuminated a ghastly shade of yellow at the base by the ubiquitous everbright lanterns that shone in the street, and fading to a dark shadow against the starlit night sky. Vult did its best to bring a healthy shine to Flamekeep, but its light was no match for mortal invention.

He turned his head slightly and nuzzled Flotsam, perched on his shoulder. "Time for me to go," he whispered, and gave the cat a little push with his head. The cat hopped down, landing rather more heavily than a cat perhaps ought. It rubbed up against Teron's leg for a moment, purring, then sauntered off into the night.

Teron looked at the library again. Various shrubs ringed its base, lovely vegetation grown with magical assistance to be large, dense, and beautiful. It also served as a first line of defense against someone trying to approach the building, but at the same time it provided cover to those who managed to get past. Teron got his bearings, then walked down the side of the library, angling his path to draw close to the spot he had chosen for his infiltration. He stretched as he walked, using the motion to camouflage a quick check to the rear to ensure no one else was near enough to see him. At his chosen spot, equidistant between the nearest glowing street lanterns, he dropped into a shoulder roll and ended up on his belly almost under the shrubbery.

He lay beneath a robust evergreen shrub with prickly branches and a pervasive odor of compost. He oriented himself toward the wall, and then scooted under the shrub using the "snake walk," a technique that involved propelling oneself forward using hands, feet, elbows, knees, hips, chest, and head. It was awkward and slow, but required minimal overhead clearance (when the head was turned to the side) and left no telltale drag mark trail.

There was a good two-foot clearance between the shrubbery and the masonry of the library wall, but Teron did not enter that gap. He shifted his position, then gently extended one hand. Slowly it moved forward, almost too slow for the eye to see. He began to feel a bit of static pressure on his palm, a tingling sensation of warning: a ward of some sort, a magical barrier to deter intruders, either by raising an alarm or direct application of power. Teron pulled his hand back.

As part of his training in the Quiet Touch, Teron had had to learn to bypass security measures both magical and technical. "All traps have triggers," Keiftal had taught him. "The body triggers tangible traps. Magical traps are more dangerous; many wards are triggered by the soul. You can bypass a physical trap by avoiding the trigger: do not do the action that the trap awaits. Bypassing the magical triggers is much the same; you must ensure that you use nothing that might set off the spell. You must have an empty soul."

Achieving that had been always the hardest part of training for Teron. Most of his peers in the Quiet Touch emptied their soul by becoming as placid as a morning lake. Teron had always emptied his soul through sheer force of discipline: he willed himself void. Of course, once empty, he no longer had the will to force his soul to quiescence, so his window of opportunity was always small.

The evergreen shrub afforded him enough room to rise to his knees without entering the zone of the magical alarm. He did so, forcing his head into the resistant, prickly branches of the magegrown shrub. He placed his hands in front of him until he felt the pulse of the magical ward again, then he crushed his thoughts beneath ritual discipline. They fought, as always, stray concepts and ideas that demanded he remain focused and alert, but he forced them out, hooking them aggressively with every available tool, in much the way that he might force a pack of hungry dogs back out the door of a building.

For a brief moment, all was at peace. He relaxed utterly.

The shrub pushed him forward, seeking to extend its branches once more. Teron felt himself fall. He tried to will the doors of his mind to remain closed, but the dogs charged back in, baying their alarm. His hands flew up to the wall, deflecting his fall so that he landed beside the building instead of cracking his forehead on the stone. He yanked his feet to him, out of the zone of the magical ward, hoping that the instinctive reflex of the motion did not hold enough intent to activate the spell. He lay on the ground and waited, unmoving, one bare arm pressed up against the cool stone of the library. Vult slowly crawled across the sky directly over his head, and he remained motionless until its glow had been utterly hidden by the Camat Library's roof.

Satisfied that no alarm had been raised, Teron stood. Even standing, he was well concealed by the high bushes that landscaped the perimeter, so for the moment, he felt secure.

The exterior of the building was ornate, as one might expect for the centerpiece of all magical scholarship in Thrane.

Aside from Flamic ornamentation, periodic narrow ridges adorned the walls, each long vertical strip engraved with symbols of fire. Teron approached one of these ornamental crests. The ridge did not even extend so much as a full span from the wall, but for Teron, that was enough. He grasped the ridge with his hands, gave a slight jump, and gripped the ridge with the flats of his feet.

He scaled the narrow ridge, hand over hand, scooting his feet up as a pair. He reached the top, pulled himself over, and took a moment to flex his tired muscles and look around. A selection of statues graced the perimeter of the rooftop, neither as grotesque as the gargoyles of Karrnath nor as beautiful as the half-attired deities of Aundair. They were idealized martial sentinels that watched over the streets below, tirelessly bearing their greatswords aloft.

The roof had an orchard of jagged iron spears pointed skyward to protect the library from being assaulted by sky brigands. At the very center of the roof, a small fortified tower stood guard.

At the four corners of the roof, stairwells, rotating about their bases with a slow grinding, extended up and out to small towers. Judging by their small size, the towers were likely not used for research or storage. Teron thought it most likely that they were just for show, an exhibit of expertise.

Teron crept up to the tower, keeping low to avoid silhouetting himself against the night sky. The tower was clearly built for defense, short and squat, with arrow slits for windows. Looking up as he circled the base, Teron saw the tips of three ballistae jutting forth, illuminated by a weak light from inside the tower. He presumed some other defensive weapon fired directly up, an alchemical bomb thrower or a battery of magical wands.

There was one door into the guard tower, small, solidly built, and shielded by an enclosure of heavy stone. The door lacked any external mechanism to open it. Teron gently placed his hands on the door and opened his awareness. He felt no tingling sensation to mark a magical aura, so he surmised that the lack of an external latch was a simple mechanical security measure, not an indication that the door was opened by a special password or arcane trinket.

He placed his ear to the door to listen, hoping to be able to discover the number of guards inside. He heard a few murmurs, then he heard a bell start to jangle insistently. Teron pulled back from the door and hid on the far side of its protective enclosure. Within a few breaths, bells rang throughout the building and the guards within the tower began moving with speed and purpose.

Teron gritted his teeth and ran for the edge of the roof. Behind him, he heard a shout and the distinctive snap of a crossbow. He veered to the side, and the quarrel whistled by. Next he heard the gears of a ballista rattling as someone cranked it to full cock. Not relishing the idea of an inch-thick piece of hardwood impaling his torso, he mixed his zigzag run with occasional tumble. The ballista didn't fire, perhaps due to his skillful evasion or possibly for fear of sending a pike flying through a student's window in the Dormitorion.

Teron reached the edge of the roof and had to pause to find one of the building's decorative spines. Crouching low to spot one, he heard the loud crack of the ballista. In the dark, he had no hope of seeing the projectile in time, so he used his crouch to jump up into a back flip, twisting to the side to present the minimal silhouette. He heard the low whoosh of the pilum zipping past, felt its breeze as it narrowly missed him. He landed on his feet, and a second later he heard the wooden shaft splinter itself on the Dormitorion wall.

Teron scuttled a few feet across the roof's edge to one of the ridges that climbed the building's side. He heard the tread of numerous feet on the rooftop; without hesitation he dropped off the edge of the roof and grabbed the ornamental spine with his hands and feet.

He let his feet slide along the carved sides as he lowered himself hand-under-hand as quickly as he could. This was where he was the most vulnerable; there was no room to maneuver when one hung from one thin projection. He heard voices above him, but thankfully none seemed to have any missile weapons.

About twenty feet from the ground, he halted his descent and pushed himself forcibly from the wall, diving to leap all the way over the wide greenery below. He twisted in the air, then pinwheeled his arms to get his feet beneath him. He hit the street and tumbled into a roll. His arms slapped against the cobbles to devour his momentum. He finished by handspringing to his feet, then took off running to the alley. Crossbow quarrels spattered in the street about his heels.

He glanced back toward the library from the concealing shadows. Lights were springing on all through the building, and he heard the chorus of many alarmed voices. One voice from the rooftop boomed out insistently: "The alley by the Dormitorion!" As if to provide punctuation to the cry, a small, bright bead appeared at the roof's edge, arcing right for the darkened alley. Teron waited, tensed to spring, and as the speeding mote got close, he leapt into the street and dodged to the side.

A massive flash of fire erupted from the alley as the glowing ember struck the ground, but as soon as the flames spat past his shoulder, Teron ducked back into the alley and sprinted past the burning debris.

CHAPTER 17

In the pre-dawn hours, Praxle opened the door to their rented room, only to find Teron standing there, fists clenched, a grim set to his jaw, and a dark fire burning in his eyes.

"Dolgaunt!" he spat.

"What?"

"I told you I'd scout the library myself!"

"Well, I—" started Praxle.

"Reckless idiot! Do you have any idea what you've done?" shouted Teron.

"I've done nothing!" yelled Praxle.

The guests in the next room pounded on the wall.

Teron leaned down, almost to Praxle's height, and gestured with an extended finger. "I was almost in," he hissed. "I had almost figured out the best way to enter. Instead, you raised the alarm and almost got me killed!"

"I did no such thing!" persisted Praxle.

"Then where were you when I got back? Were you at the library?"

"Well, yes," admitted Praxle, "but—"

"But nothing!" yelled Teron. "This is why I operate alone!"

"Yes, fine, I left for the library, but I had every reason to!" said Praxle. "This is my artifact! It belongs to my family! The Thranes took it from us, you lot hid it from us, and the Cyrans stole it from us, and I absolutely will not let you cheat it away from me again! Grouse all you want about it, that's fine, but let me say this: Nowhere between here and Khyber did I raise the alarm!"

The neighboring guests pounded on the wall again. Praxle's eyes flicked to the wall for just a second, and in that eyeblink Teron shot out a hand and grabbed the gnome by the neck, lifting him off the ground. Praxle kicked and clawed at Teron's wrist, his tongue starting to extend out of his mouth from the pressure.

"Gentlemen!" said Jeffers. He stepped forward and gave both parties' ears a brutal tweak, then stepped back out of range. They both glared at him. "I may be speaking above my station, but you will, the both of you, desist this ruckus and listen! Teron, put my master down. Master, shut up."

Teron set Praxle down and took a wary step back. For his part, Praxle seemed utterly content to massage his neck, swallow repeatedly, and stay out of arm's reach of the monk.

"I accompanied my master upon his sortie, Teron," said Jeffers. "I assure you that we had only just approached the street opposite the library when the klaxon rang out. Thus, while my master did indeed intend to pursue some exploration of his own, he was unable to consummate the deed. I tell you this upon my word of honor. Now that you know the truth, you may opt to judge or forgive such trespass as you wish.

"As for you, master," continued the half-orc, "in my appraisal it would be better not to round upon your fellow, but rather to work together. We were not close, and Teron was almost in. Therefore someone else must have caused the hue to be raised. We should endeavor to deduce the identity of said interloper."

Teron's eyes darted back and forth between Praxle and Jeffers, fading from loathing to righteous indignation to suspicious calculation. "The Shadow Fox," he said at last.

"I'm inclined to disagree," said Praxle. "I was rather thinking it to be Lady Hathia Stalsun."

❧ ❧ ❧ ◉ ❧ ❧ ❧

The Shadow Fox quietly admitted herself through the arcanium's secret entryway and closed the door behind her. The everbright lanterns had not been shuttered in the room ahead, and she heard low discussions. She knocked on the wall as she entered the arcanium proper. The magicians present—Rezam and an assistant were left at this hour—looked up.

"Did you get the papers?" asked Rezam.

"Not this night," she answered, shaking her head. "I had just gotten past the hedges and was pulling out my nullifier ring when this damned cat leapt out of nowhere, hissing and clawing. It startled me, as you might imagine, and I touched the library's warding. Roused the guards and gave me a vicious shock—I wasn't sure my legs would even let me run after that; they were trembling and weak—but the guards started chasing after some beggar or small-time burglar instead. Never even looked for me."

"Lucky."

"Yes, I had a lot of luck," she agreed, "both good and bad."

She walked over to the laboratory table that stood in the center of the room. The Sphere sat on a silver pedestal, shrouded with a gossamer cloth. A nimbus of olive energy swirled around it, the shifting energy fraying into paisley patterns like stirred smoke in a shaft of light.

"What's the field?" asked the Fox, leaning her hands on the back of a chair.

"Abjuration," said Rezam. "You were right about it; it has certain disquieting qualities when viewed with the naked eye. It . . . enticed our eyes and hands. We needed to make it less distracting to get on with our work."

"So it . . . called to you?" asked the Shadow Fox.

"Oh, yes. Very much so. We resisted, of course, but those without training in the mental disciplines of high magic could easily fall prey to its allure."

"But Oargesha had training."

"True, but she had no warning. We did, and we had no wish to suffer her fate."

"Mmm. So . . . I know it's only been three days, but . . . have you discovered anything about it?"

"It is definitely a planar device," said Rezam. "As, you may recall, I originally conjectured. Cautious divination indicates that it is either 10,000 years old, or else it was created two weeks from yesterday."

"We're putting our wager on 10,000 years," said the other wizard.

Shadow Fox nodded. "Which plane?"

"Xoriat," said the two wizards simultaneously. Rezam's assistant continued, adding, "Once we knew roughly what we were looking for, knitting the stray facts together was not that difficult. It all fits together. That would be about the time of the Daelkyr War. I'm guessing that this is a means of opening a rift of some sort, either to let those from Xoriat here, or else maybe to harvest folks like us and send them into Xoriat."

"For what purpose?"

Rezam snorted. "You're assuming that anything having to do with Xoriat will be logical. Even if I knew their plans and could explain them to you, the concepts would probably drive you to claw your own eyes out."

"And swallow your tongue," added the other.

"Is there any way to get Oargesha back?" asked the Fox. "Any hope?"

"Listen," said Rezam, "even if we knew how to operate this device, and even if we could somehow use it to get to Xoriat and back, and even if we were able to find Oargesha in that mess, when we brought her back here, there'd be nothing we could do for her but tie her up tightly and put a gag in her mouth."

"Because otherwise she'd mutilate herself," added the second. "In fact, killing her would probably be a mercy. Unless somehow that would drive her soul back to Xoriat. Which it probably would."

The Shadow Fox sat heavily and buried her face in her palms. "Great gods," she said to herself, "what have we done?"

"What have we done?" echoed the first wizard. "We've managed to procure perhaps the greatest weapon imaginable! If we can just get those notes you were talking about, why, we could bring Khorvaire to its knees!"

"I know. Just the threat could—"

"Threat? How could you have something like this and not use it?" exclaimed Rezam. "Think of it. Everyone who's slighted us, Thrane and Karrnath and Breland especially, you know they were involved in the Day of Mourning, and House Phiarlan, they had to know that Cyre was going to die, how else do you explain the fact that all of their most senior members managed to be out of our country when it died? Just imagine how they'll pay with an eternity of torment for what they did to our homeland! And then anyone else, if they don't bow to our demands, boom! We pull their souls to Xoriat and listen to them scream."

"But it does such unspeakable—"

"For that matter, we'd have to use it just to test it, make sure we understood its function properly."

"Right," said his assistant. "Test all the settings, all the permutations of the controls. Of course, first we have to figure out how to operate it."

"That's certain," Rezam said. "It's a very interesting puzzle. Very interesting. I could probably start a whole magewright school based on this alone. I wonder if we could duplicate it."

The Shadow Fox looked at the two mages in disbelief. "You're mad," she whispered.

"Mad?" quipped the second. "No, the people trapped in there, they are mad. If you could hear them, you'd know what I mean. We're trying to make sense of it."

"But you just said that Xoriat makes no sense to the sane."

Rezam leaned forward, thrusting his face far too close to the Fox's. She recoiled from his bulging eyes as far as she could in the chair. "I did say that. But this . . ." he said, gesturing one hand dramatically to the Sphere, "this is a device. Devices work by mechanical and metaphysical laws. Laws that can be understood. And I think I am starting to understand some of how this device works." He waggled his eyebrows, and the Shadow Fox felt a knot tighten in her stomach.

She slid out of the side of the chair and stood, backing away from the wizards. "All right," she said. "I'll leave you to it. But I think you all ought to cover that thing completely and call it a night. Get some rest before you continue. Understand?"

The wizards looked at each other quizzically, then nodded in agreement. "Absolutely," they said unconvincingly. "Smart idea."

The Shadow Fox let herself out of the arcanium, sliding back into the city streets. She prayed that she knew what she was doing.

* * * * * * *

Dawn was just breaking over the western horizon when Teron sat bolt upright in bed, awakening with a gasp, his hands raised for combat.

Praxle rolled over and looked with bleary eyes. "Nightmare, monk?"

Teron ran his hands over his eyes and across his ears. "Yes."

"Well, put a cork in it. I'm trying to sleep." Praxle rolled back over and pulled the blanket up high.

Teron sat in bed for a while, calming himself as the overpowering images of his dream faded in the pre-dawn light. His breathing slowed back to normal, and he lay back down, his hands clasped prayerfully over his nose as he meditated.

A few minutes later, a long, low moan carried through the room.

"I told you to cork it," grumbled Praxle.

Another moan, and Praxle threw his pillow at Teron, who sensed it at the last minute and partially blocked it, then sat up in annoyance. "What was that for?"

"Quit your yowling nightmares, monk, I want to get back to sleep," grumped Praxle from beneath a shapeless pile of covers.

Teron started to say something, then arrested his tongue. He stood quietly, went to the window, and pried it open. He leaned out.

"Flotsam!" he said gently, with a ghost of a smile on his face. "And I see you caught yourself breakfast!"

* * * * * * *

A misshapen homunculus prowled the perimeter of the Camat Library, grunting, hissing, and squealing with every painful move of its malformed limbs. It lurched about the brush on its two legs, using one of its arms for balance and the other arm to shield its uneven, piggy eyes from the sun.

It scratched in the dirt, muttering to itself and wiping its nose. Then it moved on, snuffling the leaves and gurgling in its throat. Every so often a horse and carriage clopped along the cobbled street close to the undergrowth, and the pitiful creation hunkered down and covered its head mournfully, shivering in fear.

It hobbled along, doubly-forked tongue dabbing the dirt, frail hands picking up twigs and other detritus for inspection, wet nose sniffing insistently at every thorn and leaf.

Then at last it found what it was looking for: a long, sharp thorn darkly stained. A wail of gleeful spite squeezed out of its angled throat, nasal and reedy. It grabbed the thorn by its base and tried to pry it off, to no avail. The homunculus barked and growled, then cursed a string of incomprehensible syllables in some unknown language. It renewed the attack on the thorn, clawing and biting at the stalk of the plant, prying, tugging, twisting, ripping, cursing. At last, the thorn started to pull free, resisting like a youngster's tooth, but the eager homunculus exerted its asymmetric body ever the harder, and soon the thorn came loose. The creature yowled its deviant delight, a noise loud and guttural enough that it caused even the daylight traffic to pause in unease.

It loped along the ground to the front door of the library, holding the darkened thorn aloft like a torch. Every galloping movement of its body forced out some small utterance from the beast, small wheezes and grunts of discomfort.

It climbed the long set of stairs leading to the doors, each step half as high as it was. Its barrel ribcage expanded and contracted laboriously, panting with the heroic effort of the ascent. Its jaw, filled with needle-like teeth, hung open with its tongue lolling out.

The massive granite doors swung open as it reached the top of the stairs, recognizing the power of the magician's blood that had been used to create the beast. It stumbled through the door, croaking its triumph. It scrambled toward the brazier, and hopped about clumsily until the fire elemental manifested and gushed forth.

Faced with the tall fiery guardian, the homunculus hooted wordlessly, displaying the thorn, and within a minute, three Thrane mages teleported to the library lobby, looking at the homunculus with curious eyes.

One of the mages squatted down, holding out both hands just off the floor. The homunculus scuttled over and climbed onto his hands, still proudly displaying the thorn. The mage stood, lifting the homunculus. He placed it on his shoulder and took the thorn from the creature.

The other two wizards drew closer as he studied the thorn. "Blood," he said at last. "Fairly fresh. Probably drawn from the intruder of last night during the flight from the premises."

He held the thorn forth for the others to inspect. "I do believe this will give us enough to pay our respects, will it not?"

The other two wizards nodded.

"Excellent. Then we are off to the summoning circle."

The homunculus hooted and clapped its paws in sadistic delight.

❋ ❋ ❋ ❋ ❋ ❋ ❋

"I can't believe you, monk," groused Praxle. "You've been lying there in bed almost all day long—"

"So were you until past noon," commented Teron, stroking Flotsam's outsized head. The cat stared at Teron's face through half lidded eyes, and the only noise it made was the heavy breathing that whistled through its nose.

"Sure, but I was asleep," said Praxle with exasperation. "And so were you. But since then, all you've done is lie in bed and pet your ugly cat and do nothing!"

"Don't judge things you don't understand," said Teron quietly.

"Are you planning on doing that all day long?" asked Praxle, pacing and gesticulating wildly. "Why am I even asking? It's already been all day long! The sun set an hour ago! What about preparations? Are we going to get those papers together, or are you going to sit here and pet your damned cat while I go get the papers myself?"

Flotsam growled deep in his throat.

"We'll go together," said Teron. "I'll get up soon, limber up. We'll get it done by midnight."

"You're a pathetic, stone-faced, lazy-backed thug, you know that?" yelled Praxle.

Flotsam put his ears back and growled again, louder. His slitted eyes dilated as his claws slid out and started clutching Teron's vest.

"You'd best watch your tongue, Praxle," Teron said, a stern tone creeping into his soft voice.

"Or what? You'll set your fearsome attack kitty on me? That mangy mongrel stray is the most detestable part of you!"

Flotsam dropped his ears flat against his skull, and he hissed loudly.

"Hold up there, Praxle," said Teron, concern edging his voice.

"Oh, right, I'm dreadfully sorry if I wounded your cat's feelings," said Praxle. "Why do you lug that stinky beast around, anyway? It's nothing more than a walking spectacle of spontaneous hairball generation!"

Flotsam leapt off Teron's chest and ran to the corner of the room, arching its back, puffing out its fur, and spitting. Its tail lashed back and forth violently.

"Praxle! Shut it!" said Teron.

The gnome stopped in mid-rant. "What's with your cat?" he asked.

"Can't you feel that?" asked Teron.

"Feel what?" asked Jeffers, rising from his chair at the far side of the room. "Everything appears to be perfectly regular to me, gentlemen. Present dialog excepted, of course."

Praxle turned a slow circle in the center of the room, hands tentatively extended and eyebrows furrowed. His eyes darted right and left. "He's right," he said distractedly. "Something's happening. A focus is coalescing in this room."

"Whatever does that mean, master?" asked Jeffers.

Praxle held up one finger to silence his bondservant. "The library?" he asked.

Teron turned out his hands. "But how? How did they know we were staying here?"

"Maybe one of Lady Stalsun's agents?" offered Praxle. "She seemed to know a fair amount about us."

The air grew tangibly tense, and a rainbow halo emerged around the two glowlamps in the room. "We can't stay to figure it out," said Teron, scooping Flotsam up. "No telling what they're sending after us. Come!"

Jeffers opened the door for the others as they hurriedly left the room, then he grabbed his sword and followed. The three of them ran down the hall, swept down the stairwell, and quickly crossed the foyer into the street. Once in the comparative darkness of the Flamekeep urban night, they slowed down to a jog, then to a brisk walk once a couple blocks separated them and their lodgings.

"What do you think they'd send?" Teron asked, his voice calm and even despite the sudden exertion.

Praxle panted for several breaths before he answered. "I don't know," he gasped. "I hope it was something normal, though. I'd hate to face an archon of the Silver Flame or some equally deific creature."

Jeffers looked up at the clear night sky, then back down to the everbright lanterns that illumined the street. "Pardon me, gentlemen, but it is a clear night, is it not?"

Praxle looked up at Sypheros and Vult, chasing each other serenely across the starry sky. With the ambient light, the Ring of Siberys was all but invisible. "Yes it is," he said irritably. "So what?"

"So can anyone explain to me why the street lanterns appear to have halos about them as if it were a foggy eve?"

"So they do," said Teron. "I can feel it coalescing again. How are they doing this, Praxle?"

"They need something to use. Hair, clothing, blood, something like that. Did you hurt yourself at the library last night? We didn't; we didn't even get close."

"I dodged a ballista," Teron said. He turned around, looking over his shoulder. "Did it get a scrap of my vest?"

"No, master, your clothing looks to be in perfect order," said Jeffers.

"But—" started Praxle, confused.

Teron stepped toward one of the everbright lanterns and rearranged his grip on Flotsam. He started ruffling the cat's fur against the grain, inspecting it beneath the lantern's glow. Two quick passes and Teron looked at his fellows. "Scab," he said. "They're after Flotsam."

"Great!" said Praxle, looking skyward. "Pitch the cat!"

The air started tangibly trembling, a spell waiting to burst.

"They'll get one of our hairs sooner or later. I'd rather face whatever it is now and get it over with."

The air continued to tremble, but nothing manifested. "What is this?" whispered Teron, turning in a wary circle.

"The spell needs some sort of trigger," said Praxle. "It's waiting for us to do something."

"Like what?"

"There's no way to know," said the gnome. "And I have to tell you, that vibrating is making my stomach feel funny."

Teron put Flotsam down. "There's not much we can do," he said. "We can stay, or we can move. If we move, we either trigger the spell, or perhaps move out of its range."

"I say we move, and move away from the library," said Praxle. "Jeffers, stow the sword."

The three proceeded down the city streets, tensely watching the other pedestrians and wondering if the spell would explode into being. Those who passed near them recoiled from their presence as they sensed the mysterious effects of the spell. "This is doing wonders for our anonymity," muttered Praxle.

They took familiar streets, thus their path led them by the Phiarlander Phaire, where, as usual, the business was hopping. A group of older men hung outside the tavern, smoking pipes and flirting with a group of bawdy younger women who fetched them drinks and lavished affection on them in exchange for tips. Inebriated and in good spirits, the group hailed the passers-by, and one of them even lurched toward them, a saucy wench on his arm, and bade them join the company.

As the gregarious man neared the threesome, the supernatural dam broke. The dottle in his pipe glowed brightly, then flared, then flames shot several feet high out of the bowl of his pipe, igniting his beard in the process. The man cried out in terror and dropped his pipe. The other bystanders screamed and fled in a panic.

Flames spilled out of the abandoned pipe, pooling in the street. The fire of the hapless man's burning beard also grew in size and intensity as it spread across his head and ignited his clothes.

Praxle, Toron, and Jeffers closed ranks in the face of this unexpected development. Flotsam cowered behind their ankles and hissed.

The flames from the pipe coalesced into a whirling column. The vortex pulled the ashes of tobacco up into the air, and the spinning motes provided the embers from which a fire elemental spawned. A thread of fire rose from each of the bits of burning tobacco, and as the summoned beast moved the whirling created a look of several insectile legs writhing in the air.

The flames from the burning man formed themselves into a second creature, spiraling around the screaming man until he collapsed and the fats rendered from his body spilled forth and ran in the street. The second flame elemental rode the rivulets of fat toward the trio, gliding along the ground like a curtain of fire.

"With all due respect, master," said Jeffers, "I do not believe my expertise will avail us much in this situation."

"Distract them, Jeffers," Praxle yelled, panic seasoning his voice. "Keep them away from me!"

Teron looked at the two magical creations. For a moment he wondered whether the mages behind this assault expected to get two fire elementals, or whether the dead man had provided a convenient bonus. He checked the two creatures again and chose his first target. "Watch that one!" he ordered Jeffers, shoving him toward the oily fire.

He closed on the soaring elemental, then quickly hopped forward and slung his leg around in a roundhouse kick, aiming for the motes that fed the flames. He felt his foot pass through the fire; there was a moment of resistance, like the flame itself was thick as Brelish pudding. He felt the searing heat, but his foot swept right through the collection of tiny coals that kept the thing alive. The kick snapped half of them away from the flames, tearing them from feeding the fire. For a moment, the elemental had but three fiery legs twirling beneath it, but as Teron recovered his balance, he saw the vortex draw the other motes back into itself, and the flame leapt to them once more.

"Right," murmured Teron, and braced himself for what must be done.

He stepped back, ignoring the cries and curses from his companions; they were far enough away that Teron felt no threat from the fire they faced. He focused his spirit, turning his will inward and forcing his viscera to comply. He pulled energy from deep within himself, an agonizing draw that sent bile into his throat, but he steeled his face to a calm mask.

The fire elemental drew closer, dancing in the air on its six fluttering embers. It closed, then veered away, pursuing Flotsam. Somewhere behind him, Teron heard a sound akin to slowly shattering glass as Praxle unleashed a spell.

Teron forced his energy out to his fists, feeling the energy burning as it descended down his ligaments and veins. A scarlet glow emanated from his palms. It started to break free, but Teron clenched his fingers like a dragonhawk's talons, forming them into cages. The energy struggled to explode outward, but his will kept it in check, straining at once to force it out of his palms but keep it within his grip. It felt like trying to hold onto a fistful of acidic baby eels.

As the fire elemental passed in front of him, Teron unleashed himself, lunging forward and striking the fire elemental with a double thrust. He opened his fists at the last second to attack with open palms, and the energy erupted.

The fire elemental reeled. Teron pulled back and saw that three of its embers had been disintegrated by his attack, and the other three fluttered in the wake of the concussion; the flaming creation struggled to maintain its shape, dancing on a tenuous trio of flickering legs.

The elemental's attention shifted away from Flotsam to Teron, clearly it considered him a greater threat than the skittish feline. It whirled toward him, the embers that anchored its magical existence braiding a complicated trail that defied prediction.

Teron staggered back, his stomach twisting and preparing to heave from the torment of evoking such energy in a controlled manner. He leaned forward as he backpedaled, an acrid belch forcing its way out of his stomach. Behind him, he heard exclamations from Praxle and Jeffers, but he had no time to sort the sounds into something sensible as the fire elemental closed.

With an agonizing effort, he summoned more energy from deep within him. A luminescent streak of magical energy erupted from his hand, but he grabbed the tail end and spun his hand to wrap it around his fist. It strained to be free, to fly and destroy, and he had to concentrate to pull its tail back within himself and contain its head. He gave an involuntary moan of feverish discomfort and his head swayed slightly as a wave of dizziness swept over him.

At that moment, the fire leapt toward him. He brought his hands together in a violent clap, spattering the magical force at the flying coals at the creature's base, and then it was on him. His instincts screamed at him to run, but his training pushed him forward through the flames, and he tumbled across the ground, rolling to put out any parts that might have ignited.

He looked back at the elemental. It moved away, as if it had expected him to flee its fiery wrath. It reversed it course, and he noted that two embers remained to fuel it. He summoned some more of his rapidly depleting energy to his hands as it closed. He tried to contain the fury of the power, but it slipped his fingers and flew at the fire elemental, passing through the main body of the flames. The energy punched a brief hole in the fire, but the fire burned as brightly after it passed through. The elemental closed on Teron, and he crawled backward, the torsion in his bowels slowing him considerably.

I never thought I'd burn to death, he thought, and steeled his will to avoid screaming as he died.

Of a sudden he saw something leap through the air at the flaming conjuration, twinkling against the night sky, and with a splash and a hiss, the fire elemental vanished. Teron blinked in surprise. There, just behind where the flaming beast had danced, stood Kelcie, the barmaid, holding an empty bucket in her trembling hands. The two locked eyes for a long second, each equally startled.

Teron heard Jeffers cry out, and it stirred him from his brief reverie. With an agonized roar he stood, knees rather wobbly. He saw Jeffers rolling along the ground, his clothes aflame. The other fire elemental slithered near him like a flaming viper.

Teron spared just an instant to look Kelcie in the eye once more, and he gripped her shoulder with a brief, strong gesture of thanks. Then he sprinted down the street for Jeffers.

Praxle was nowhere to be seen.

CHAPTER 18

Having extinguished the flames that were consuming his clothes, Jeffers stumbled to his feet. The half-orc ripped the still-smoking jacket from his back, panting out a series of grunts in what appeared to be impending panic. Unseen behind him, the fire elemental turned, writhing its way in for the kill. Teron dived for Jeffers, tackling him shoulder to midriff, and the two of them crashed to the hard, cobbled street as the flaming snake shot past, singeing their ankles.

Teron rolled off Jeffers and saw the thing coming around again. With a cry he pushed his energy, willing it down from his center. He knew he could not restrain the power any longer once it started to seek escape, so he timed his effort to coincide with an arcing swing of his foot. His stamping blow hit the leading edge of the fire elemental as it drew near, releasing his spiritual power and spattering shards of ice across the cobbles. The burning beast recoiled momentarily, then gathered itself for another attack.

Teron knew he was spent; he had drawn so much from within himself that most of his remaining energy now went to keeping his dinner from making an appearance. Jeffers—burned, stunned, and not at all equipped to deal with a supernatural foe like this—was all but useless. Kelcie, well, her bucket was empty.

He had to draw the fire elemental away from him somehow. And then an idea struck him. He crawled away from the fire elemental and called, "Flotsam! C'mere!"

The cat bounded over, then flailed to a halt and hissed as the fire elemental noticed its proximity. Teron looked commandingly at the cat and pointed down the road. "Go. Run! Now!"

The cat bounded down the street, and the fire elemental turned and pursued it, a flaming rectilinear string of fire rapidly cutting its way between the cobbles.

The last thing Teron saw was the cat zigzagging as it ran. Then he felt himself lose the contents of his stomach, and with them, his consciousness.

❦ ❦ ❦ ❦ ❦ ❦ ❦

The bright, full morning sun spilled in through the colored windows of the Phiarlander. The smell of cloved ham slowly roasting in the oven pervaded the dining room, competing with the lingering smells of spilled beer and stale sweat. Kelcie moved about the room, shifting tables to their proper position and righting chairs that had been toppled during the panic in the wake of last night's incident in the street.

She hadn't thrown any of the windows open, for the odor of burnt hair and charred flesh still lingered outside the door. Although the old man's body had been removed just before dawn, the stench lingered near the black scorch marks that marred the paving stones.

Kelcie picked up a chair and set it upright. As she released it, she noticed that it wobbled, so she tested it again with both hands. She curled her lip in displeasure. Turning the chair over, she saw that two of the struts that held the legs secure were broken, and the chair leg they supported had cracked near the top, threatening to split entirely. She adjusted her grip on the chair and started taking it to the back when the main door opened and a severe but well-dressed woman walked in.

"I'm sorry, lady," said Kelcie. "We don't start serving for another hour yet."

The woman strode briskly across the floor, leaving the door open. Kelcie noticed that someone outside pulled it shut again. She also saw the shapes of two others silhouetted against the windows.

"I am not here to dine, girl," she said perfunctorily. "I am Lady Hathia Stalsun of Shadukar. I've come to enquire after a monastic gentleman from Aundair. I must see him at once. Where is he?"

"I'm sure I don't know who—"

"I'm sure you do," retorted the lady. She stepped threateningly close. "I have already visited with his traveling companion, a University gnome from Zilargo. He told me that the Aundairian and he dined here the second evening prior. I'm certain you can recall them. He said that you and the Aundairian fair hit it off. Then yesternight, it appears that there was some manner of grave affair outside this very establishment. Although the gnome espouses otherwise with his tale of events, I surmise that he fled the scene. He also claims, and this I do believe, that he has not seen his Aundairian companion or his half-orc butler since that time.

"I assume that the Aundairian remained here afterward. Thus I come here, young woman, to speak with him. The matter is pressing." She nodded slightly, as if giving Kelcie permission to respond.

"I didn't work last night," said Kelcie, "so I didn't see anything of the fire and such."

"I never said fire was involved," said Hathia.

"I, uh, heard it from the cook," explained Kelcie.

"Mm hmm," said Hathia dubiously. "And what did you do with him afterward?"

"Teron? Nothing," blustered Kelcie. "I said I didn't work last night."

"I never mentioned Teron's name, either," said Lady Hathia. "Enough of your dissimulation, girl. Bring me to Teron right now."

Kelcie quailed for a moment beneath Lady Stalsun's icy

glare, fearful of her wrath, horrified to betray the reserved young Aundairian. She started to nod and lead the way . . .

But then she remembered the fearless calm in his eyes when he touched her, how his resolve gave her courage and how his grip stilled the trembling in her heart and made her actions seem perfectly normal. And she remembered that on the first night they met, however he tried, he failed to avert his eyes from her every time she passed . . .

"No," she said firmly, raising her chin and narrowing her eyes in defiance.

"Listen, girl," said Hathia sternly, "I do not brook disobedience from my lessers. You will take me to see Teron, and you will take me now."

"Squints!" called Kelcie. "We got a high-and-mighty lady here who thinks she has the run of our boardinghouse. Do you want to escort her on her tour of the building?"

From the kitchen came the cook bearing a cleaver and wearing a blood-spattered apron. He looked at Lady Hathia with his single untrusting eye. "I'd be happy to, Kelcie. You," he said, gesturing with the dirty cutlery, "The first part I'll show you is the exit."

"You do not intimidate me," said Lady Stalsun.

The cook walked right up to her, showing no deference for her station at all. "Woman, I'm a Cyran. Nothing you say can frighten me. But everything I say should scare you to death. Because I'll poison a whole tavernful of Thranes just to kill the one that bothers little Kelcie."

Hathia studied the look in his eye, then the horrid scar that marred the other side of his face. At last she made up her mind. She turned to Kelcie and said, "Tell Teron that Lady Hathia Stalsun was here to see him on an urgent matter, and requests he pay a call immediately." With that, she snapped her fingers in Kelcie's face and small keepsake locket appeared in her hand as if by magic.

Kelcie held her ground and took the jewelry. "May I tell him what this regards?" she asked.

Lady Hathia dropped her eyelids halfway. "It's personal," she said. "He'll know." And with a knowing smile, she turned and left the building.

After the door closed, the cook spat on the floor. "Damned highbrow Thranes," he growled. "I hate 'em all."

Kelcie looked at him with concern. "Um, Squints," she said, hesitantly, "I'm a Thrane, you know."

He tossed her a gruff smile and slapped her roughly on the shoulder. "Aw, Kelcie," he said. "You're one of the good ones."

Her look of concern didn't fade. "But Squints . . ." she started.

He dropped his gaze. "Don't you pay me no mind, Kelcie. I was just trying to run her out. It was just talk."

He hefted his cleaver and returned to the kitchen.

* * * * * * *

Teron woke up to find the afternoon sun slanting through the window onto his bed. He rolled onto his back and stretched, vague memories of Kelcie's presence replaying themselves in his mind. He remembered her earthy beer-hall scent as she and another carried him upstairs, and he remembered drifting back into a light doze as she gently cleaned the sword wound on his cheek and applied salve to his hands and ankles to counter the minor burns he'd incurred during the fight.

He remembered waking up at some point in the morning to find her pulling the covers back over his shoulders, tucking him in nicely, and just for a moment he thought it was his mother, and he reached out and held her hand. Then unwanted thoughts of reality rolled back into his mind, and he withdrew back into himself, but somehow she seemed to understand, and as she rose to leave, she gently traced her finger down his nose and lightly touched his lips.

But with that last thought reality returned, along with its requisite tension. He sat up and looked around. Flotsam lay stretched out at the foot of Teron's bed, splayed out decadently in the sunlight. Teron stroked him gently, impressed with the warmth of his sun-drenched fur. The exhausted cat didn't even stir at Teron's touch.

The other bed in the room was empty, the blankets neatly folded at the foot. Teron remembered hearing Jeffers' voice several times through the night and morning; seeing his bed so neat, he realized that the dedicated half-orc must be in good health. The thought brought a small smile to his lips.

Teron saw his pants and vest, cleaned and arranged nicely on a chair beside the bed. A momentary flash of shame washed over him. He checked; he was still wearing his undergarments, though that fact did little to ease his self-consciousness. He wondered who, exactly, has taken off his pants.

He inspected his injuries, little more than shallow abrasions and some light reddening from minor burns, then dressed himself. He stretched out his stiff muscles extensively until he felt fully alive again. And as he stretched the last of the stiffness and nausea out of existence, he realized that he was ravenously hungry.

The door to his room opened. "I thought I heard the up-stairs floor creaking," said Jeffers. "It is delightful to see you up and about, young man. I must also offer my most heartfelt thanks that you were able to intervene between me and the fiery creature," he added, bowing. "I do believe that you saved my life."

Teron snorted. "Well, that's a switch," he muttered.

"May I enquire as to why you remained, master?" asked Jeffers. "You could have withdrawn easily at the same time as my master."

Teron paused. "I should ask you why you stayed," he replied.

"I stayed because I am paid to preserve my master's life," said Jeffers. "Once he had made his escape from the threat, I could not extricate myself from the combat."

"I could," said Teron. "Extricate you, that is. I don't know whether I saved you so much as helped me. If it had killed you, I would likely have been next."

Jeffers smiled. "Whether you doubt your motives or not," he said, "I appreciate the end results." He bowed again and let himself out. "I'll see you in the common room once you're dressed," he said as he closed the door.

Teron pulled on his pants and vest, then lurched downstairs, his muscles still achy from the previous night's events. He found Praxle and Jeffers waiting in the large common room. Praxle sipped a glass of wine, while Jeffers drank a mug of tea.

"Teron!" bellowed Praxle in his tenor gnomish voice. The volume of his greeting filled the room despite his small size. He hopped from his chair and strode briskly over. "Good to see you've returned to the land of the living!" he said, pumping Teron's hand.

"I'll feel a lot more alive once I've had something to eat," murmured Teron quietly.

"Of course, of course," said Praxle. He led Teron over to the table, where Jeffers politely pulled out a chair for him. "Your young filly has kept a whole plateful of various foods ready for whenever you should make an appearance."

"She's not my filly," said Teron.

"Well, you're sure her stallion, I tell you that," said Praxle. He climbed into his human-sized chair as Teron sat down at the table. "See?" added Praxle. "Here comes the wench now."

Sure enough, Kelcie made an appearance, coming out the kitchen doors with two plates laden with food. Teron waited just long enough for her to get within earshot, then turned to Praxle and said, "She's not a wench, Praxle." The gnome let out a gasp of exasperation.

Kelcie set the plates down, two large platters filled with rolls, ham, potatoes, oatmeal, hard-boiled eggs, fruit, smoked fish, and salad, as well as a tall mug filled with weak beer. "I didn't know what you might like to eat, so I saved you a little bit of everything," she said.

Teron thanked her, looking up just in time to see her give Praxle a withering look of vindication. Praxle turned his head and rolled his eyes.

Praxle waited until Kelcie had gone back into the kitchen. "You need to watch your timing when you open your mouth, Teron," he said. "Impolitic comments can cause all sorts of trouble when given at the wrong time."

"I know," said Teron. He found it easy to suppress a smile with a mouth full of food.

"She is a wench, and you know it," said Praxle disparagingly. "She's just an average human, low class at that, and certainly no mage. But I'm sure she'd be a good ride." He leaned forward on his elbows eagerly. "So why didn't you tell me you were a magic user?" he asked. "That's great! How could you hold out on me like that?"

Teron shrugged, holding up one finger. He chewed the large pack of food that filled his mouth, then swallowed and said, "I don't talk about it. I don't much like to use it."

Praxle rested his cheek on his fist, his eyes narrowed with rapt attention. "Fascinating. I didn't think they taught arcane techniques in the monastery. I thought it was all chanting and such."

"They don't," said Teron as he crammed another forkful of ham in his face.

"You might consider eating with greater moderation and forethought if you wish to be ready for another such fracas," observed Jeffers gently. Teron nodded in acknowledgment.

"So if they don't teach that in the monastery, where did you learn it?" asked Praxle.

Teron looked at Praxle blackly. "It's just a skill, understand? I don't want to say any more about it."

"Just a skill? You mean you've always been able to do this?"

"I said I don't want to talk about that!" snapped Teron.

Praxle held up his hands. "I understand," he said. "I'm not trying to probe. I'm just trying to understand what it is you have here. Is that all right? I'm just trying to clarify what you mean." He paused, and for a long moment the only noise that broke the uncomfortable silence was that of Teron chewing some nuts. "So . . . it's not something you learned from a scholar or anything," said Praxle.

Teron wagged his head side to side noncommittally. "It's . . . internal. I focus my spirit's essence. Master Keiftal worked with me on it. He helped me to concentrate enough to alter the energy when it came out. Made me practice timing and control. He said he'd never seen anything like it."

"I'll bet he hadn't!" said Praxle's. "That's sorcery! You're a sorcerer!"

"No, I'm not," said Teron. He shook his head. "It's not even really magic, Praxle. Master Keiftal said I was discharging spiritual energy."

Praxle snorted in disbelief. "What in Khyber do you think sorcery is, then? Riddle me that!"

Teron thought about it for a moment during a more sedate mouthful of food. "I don't know," he said. "I only studied magic because some of my targets might be mages. I studied what it did, not how it got there."

"What kind of stupid approach is that?"

Teron slapped the table hard, right in front of Praxle's nose. The gnome jumped back, startled.

"It is not stupid," said Teron. "You're being the fool, here. Do you have to know about prospecting, mining, smelting, or even blacksmithing to understand how to fight someone armed with a sword? No. I have been extensively trained in sensing magic, resisting magic, and counter-fighting mages of all types. Wizardry, sorcery, divine magic, even dragonmarks, they're all the same as far as I'm concerned."

Praxle chuckled. "Now you're being stupid, Teron. They are all very different. You need to know the differences, because I don't believe it—you don't understand the gift you have here! You! Are! A! Sorcerer!"

Teron tossed up his hands in a gesture of pointlessness. "Fine," he said. "I'm a sorcerer. I'm also hungry. Hunger I can solve. So let me eat."

"All right," said Praxle. "Let me put everything into a context you might understand."

"Might?"

"Will," said Praxle. "You're pretty smart." He cleared his throat and organized his thoughts. "The world was created by three great dragons: Siberys, Eberron, and Khyber. Siberys is the dragon above, who is the stars and the great ring that encircles us. Khyber is the Underdark, and the dragon below. Eberron is the dragon between, whose body is the land we live on, whose blood is the rivers, and whose breath is the wind that we breathe."

"You're not telling me anything I don't know," said Teron.

"Be quiet and listen," chided Praxle. "Being made of the stuff of dragons, the world is infused with magic, but the various systems of magic use very different methodologies. Wizards are the most common form of mage, but not the most well known. They learn to manipulate magic through extensive schooling, rote memorization, and strict practicum. It takes them years to master their craft. Let me say that again. It takes them years of practice to manipulate that which pervades the world all around us. Clearly, then, they make up for a lack of talent with an excess of application. Do you understand?"

Teron nodded slowly.

"Artificers are the best-known of the magic-using disciplines, at least in the Five Kingdoms. Everyone knows artificers. They make the lightning rail, the everbright lanterns, all that rot. Basically, though, they need material items as a kind of magical crutch. They can make magic items do interesting things, and they're very good a creating them, but you won't see them slinging fireballs."

Teron looked askance at Praxle. "What about divine casters?" he asked.

"Bah! A bunch of mewling pawns," Praxle said, "hardly even worthy of the title of magic user. They are nothing more than a conduit. They don't cast spells. Their god casts spells for them. They just channel a higher power through their body by bowing and scraping and fawning all over a being that, frankly, wouldn't give a Karrnathi carcass whether they live or die. And I include druids in that. Especially druids. All that circle of life and death tripe they spew out, and they think that their deity cares a mite for them? They're just as useful sprouting mushrooms out their back."

Praxle drained the rest of the wine in his glass and handed it to Jeffers, who rose from the table to procure a refill.

"So let me get this straight," said Teron, shoving the food to one side of his mouth. "Wizards have no talent. Artificers need crutches. And clerics are lapdogs."

Praxle nodded, a half-sneer of exasperation on his face. "Can you believe it? Pathetic, the lot of them."

"Psions?"

"Their major flaw is they don't see the big picture. They focus on evolving themselves, whatever that means. Perfecting their craft. They remain fundamentally mortal. They don't see that ascension is the issue. Sorcerers, however, at least some of them, understand." Praxle paused in mid-thought, finger to thumb as he prepared to make a point. Instead, he asked, "Do you know where a sorcerer's power comes from?"

Teron shook his head, and then pulled a draught of weak beer to wash down his bread.

"A sorcerer," said Praxle, leaning forward and whispering, "has dragon's blood. Now the catch is that most people think that this means blood from *a* dragon. But they're wrong. It means blood from *the* dragon."

"The dragon," echoed Teron.

Praxle shrugged. "One of them, yes—although there's no telling which one. Or perhaps all three."

Teron narrowed his eyes. "You're talking about . . . Siberys. Or Eberron."

"Or Khyber. Yes, I am. I am talking about the fact that sorcerers don't need crutches. They don't need books. They don't need to wheedle the gods out of a favor. They can work magic because the blood of the dragons flows in them, and the dragons are the very essence of magic itself. It's the challenge the dragons give to the best of us, to see if we have the mettle to pull ourselves up by the scruff of the neck to stand above the mere mortals of the world!"

Jeffers returned and set a full glass of wine by Praxle, and then sat back down.

"What about dragonmarks?" asked Teron. "That seems a more definite gift of the dragons than this magical blood."

Praxle laughed, a disparaging, long-suffering laugh. "Dragonmarks are a decoy. In fact, they're a curse. They're no challenge! They're something that the dragons hand out just to make people shut up. They're even worse of a crutch than an artificer's . . . crutch. A person gets a dragonmark, and that's a sure sign they'll never go anywhere. Sure, they may be important in this world, but all their ability, all their potential, all their attention remains focused on scratching out a better hovel in the dirt.

"Look at it this way: If you have a dragonmark, you get to do one magical thing. One. That's it. It's like . . . having a crossbow that can only shoot at targets twenty-three yards away, no more and no less. For my part, I'll take the challenge. I'll take the hard path, and I'll take the dragon's blood! It just irks me that all those other schools of magic get the same respect, if not more, as sorcerers. They're pathetic!"

Teron leaned back and pushed his plates away. "I think I'd better not eat any more of this," he said.

"I'll get the girl," offered Jeffers, but as soon as he started to rise, Kelcie exited the kitchen and came to the table. With a dazzling smile she gathered the plates and retreated back into the kitchen.

Praxle chuckled.

"What?" asked Teron.

"That's why you have that stupid mangy cat, you know," said Praxle with a laugh. "That's your familiar!"

Teron looked confused. "What do you mean? He's a pet. He just showed up one day and started following me everywhere. He . . . he understands me. . . ." His words trailed off as he considered the implications.

Praxle laughed again. "Well, then, aren't you the worldly one?" he said with a huge grin.

Kelcie reappeared, bearing another mug of weak beer for Teron. She sat down beside him and gazed at him warmly. "Is there anything else you need?" she asked. "You liked the food, right?"

"It was wonderful, Kelcie," said Teron, nervously trying to keep her rapt gaze, but the intensity and beauty of her gaze was too difficult and open for him to bear. "Um, thank you."

"Oh, I almost forgot," said Kelcie, reaching into a pocket in her apron. "Someone came by to see you, but I didn't let her. She seemed like kind of a shrew, and I wanted you to get your sleep." She reached into the pocket of her apron, pulled out the locket, and handed it to Teron.

"What's this, Teron?" asked Praxle. "Does the Silver Flame want your godlike body now?"

Teron turned to show the gnome the crest on the locket. "Hathia Stalsun. Kelcie, *why* didn't you tell me?" He rounded on the serving girl. "What were you thinking?"

"Well, I—"

"I have to go see her. She's important."

"But—"

"Let's go," said Teron, standing up and heading for the door. "We can't keep her waiting."

"But Teron, I—"

"Don't try to interfere, Kelcie," said Teron. He turned and paused at the door. "You don't know what you're doing."

Praxle and Jeffers followed him out. Jeffers paused at the door and said, "Allow me to apologize for the ill manners of my companions, young lady."

But Kelcie's head was turned, and Jeffers could not see the pain in her eyes.

●　●　●　◉　●　●　◉

A hired carriage rolled up to the front of the Stalsun manor. The door opened, and Jeffers, Praxle, and Teron stepped out. They entered the manor and found themselves escorted once more to the drawing room to await Lady Stalsun, although this time the furniture was left without protection.

Lady Stalsun entered, her long dress hissing across the polished wooden floor, with a squad of guards as escort. She sat, and gazed upon her guests imperiously. "Do you know why I have summoned you here today?" she asked.

The three shook their heads.

"I have a suspicion that you returned to the Great Library of the Congress of Alchemical and Magical Academics," she said.

"Only a suspicion?" asked Praxle. "That's a weak statement. I don't think your informants are earning their pay." He paused and scratched his cheek. "We went there the once," he added, shrugging, "you know that. We decided it would be too much trouble for not enough help."

Hathia traded long stares with Teron and Praxle alike.

Teron broke the stalemate. "Why do you believe we'd waste our time returning?" he asked.

She smacked her lips once. "Last night, there was a fire at the Great Library of the Congress of Alchemical and Magical Academics," she said. "It appears that somehow the entirety of the landscaping surrounding the building was set afire. Our mages were compelled to intervene, casting spells to extinguish the flames and dismiss the outsider that had been summoned to ignite them." She paused and traced the contours of the carving in her armrest before continuing. "I find it curious that one day after you visit the Great Library, there is a magical fire there. Ill fortune seems to hound your heels." Her look dared a response.

"Lady Stalsun, I understand your implication," said Praxle, "but I am an illusionist, not an evoker or a conjurer. I have no talent in creating energy from nothing."

"I had supposed that you would avow neither knowledge of nor complicity in the arson," she said.

"How did you know that an outsider was involved?" asked Teron.

"I have sources within the Congress," said Hathia. "The fires only subsided after a powerful dispelling."

"If you were to do some more research," said Teron, "you will find that it was not an outsider, but an elemental. Two originally manifested in the Guild Quarter. Apparently one ran amok and made it as far as the library before being destroyed."

"And the other?"

"We took care of it," said Teron.

"So you were nearby?"

"You might say that."

Hathia tilted her head. "You think you were the targets."

"I think you were the instigator," said Teron. "You or your subordinates in the Congress."

Hathia smiled and dropped her head slightly. "My dear monk," she said, "my associates are prone neither to carelessness nor failure. I must wonder whether the Cyrans themselves might have unleashed this upon you. Certainly it displays the sort of recklessness I have come to expect from Cyran mages of late."

Praxle and Teron looked at each other. "But how would they know where to find us?"

Hathia clenched her lips, as strong an expression as the visitors had ever seen her display. "The Cyrans have eyes, as well, feeding their information to a man known as the Shadow Fox."

Praxle leaned forward. "What do you know of him?" he asked.

"Very little. Rumor has it that he gave up his name after the Day of Mourning, saying that if he had no country, then he had no name. Reports also indicate that he has made inroads among the Cyran expatriates as well as elements of the criminal underworld, and has established independent nests of Cyran agents throughout Thrane.

"Some of those agents are known to mine. We are piecing together the information we have in an effort to discern where this Shadow Fox might have sequestered the artifact in question." She looked at them. "When we do, and I assure you we shall, I will send for you."

"You'd hand that information to us rather than to your own government?"

"This artifact has lain in the hands of Zilargo for unknown centuries, as well as within Aundair for decades. In neither of those spans have those who controlled the relic endeavored to use it. The same could not be said of the limited time in which my government held it. Based on what you told me about the Cyran woman at Daskaran, this is something that I would rather never see used again."

"So you trust us?" asked Praxle.

Hathia stood and moved to the door. She turned and appraised the trio one last time. "Trust is not the issue," she said. "I simply have no other choice."

CHAPTER 19

Praxle, Teron, and Jeffers stood by a water fountain in uptown Flamekeep. Praxle stood on the rim that surrounded the fountain, placing him at roughly the same height as Teron. Jeffers loomed over the other two, but his deferential posture made him seem smaller. The splashing noise of the fountain helped keep them from being overheard, they covered their mouths to protect against spies who could read lips, and the presence of a large quantity of water lent a feeling of security against fire elementals.

"What did you think of Lady Stalsun?" asked Teron.

"I don't trust her," said Praxle. "I think she knew more than she was letting on."

"But masters," asked Jeffers, "if she did know for a fact that both of you tried to approach the library a second time last night, why did she not endeavor to catch you in a lie?"

"I don't pay you to think, Jeffers," said Praxle.

"But he's got a point," retorted Teron.

"She was probably just gauging our honesty and openness," said Praxle. "Seeing how much she's drawn us into her web of lies."

"I don't agree," said Teron.

"Regardless," persisted Praxle, "I don't like her. I don't like her, I don't like this city, I don't like this country, and I don't like the way things are going. Anyone we meet might be a spy for the Cyrans. And it's a sure bet that almost everyone is a spy for the Silver Flame. I say we strike against the Camat Library tonight, while things are still unsettled, and before someone makes another try against us."

"That, I can't argue," said Teron. "But can you find the Thrane notes?"

"If you can get me in, Teron, I can get the notes."

"I can get you in," said Teron. "And I can get you out."

❧ ❧ ❧ ❧ ❧ ❧ ❧

In the dark of night, three shadows moved through the streets of Flamekeep, avoiding the larger avenues and their attendant lanterns. A small, dark cat flitted about them, occasionally meowing in the darkness. Bright Eyre descended toward the horizon, but unfortunately that meant that both Sypheros and Vult ascended the sky, bloated and bright like a pair of eyes. It wasn't a good night for darkness.

The three slid through an alleyway toward the library, passing the charred wreckage of barrels and other detritus. The stink of ash still lingered in the air.

"Right," whispered Praxle. "Jeffers? Remain here, watch our escape. You'll be the most use if you draw away any patrols that threaten to cut us off."

Jeffers nodded.

"Ready, Praxle?" asked Teron.

"Naturally."

The monk and the sorcerer scooted across the street and into the ashen remnants of flora that now surrounded the library. Teron moved slowly forward until he felt the air grow taut with the magical effects of the warding spell. Since the brush had largely burned away, he stood up, looked around, and aligned the posture of his body to a narrow angle to the wall. He hyperventilated. As he felt his lips start to tingle, he sealed his lungs, leaned slightly to the right, and clenched his abdomen as hard as he could. The extra pressure and oxygen combined to push his brain over the edge, and he allowed himself to slide into unconsciousness.

His body fell forward, buckling to the right, and he flopped past the warding without incident. He came to a moment later, and sat up, scanning the area for any alarm.

A gnomish whisper slithered out of the darkness. "That can't be good for your brain, Teron. You need to take care of it, if you intend to practice more magic."

"I'll be fine," said the monk.

"All right. Start your climb. Hopefully the warding ends about twenty or thirty feet up. Otherwise, this could be a real problem."

"Not at all," said Teron, "I'll just chop your neck and roll you through."

"I'm not particularly fond of the idea of you hitting my neck," said Praxle.

"I've knocked out plenty of people," said Teron.

"I thought you just killed folks," hissed Praxle.

"It's easier when they're unconscious."

"Somehow that answer does not make me more inclined to let you knock me unconscious."

Teron chuckled, a slight hissing noise in the shadows. He gripped one of the ornamental spines of the library and ascended, pausing every five feet or so to extend one hand and check the height of the ward. At the third floor, he found nothing. He tsked twice, getting Praxle's attention.

Praxle unlimbered a coiled rope. He glided his hand over the thin cord, murmuring under his breath. The rope started to pulse a deep blue as Praxle's spell worked its way through the fibers. He set the coil down and one end of the rope began to rise like a cobra, slithering upward into the sky. It rose as high as Teron, then looped itself and moved toward the wall of the library. When it reached the wall, it coiled against it, creating a circle of enchanted rope for extra stability.

Praxle began to climb the rope. As he ascended, the rope wriggled from side to side, always presenting extra coils for Praxle's hands and feet, creating an ever-shifting ladder to ease his climb. He reached a height that was even with Teron, then shimmied across the five-foot span to reach the wall.

As he reached the wall, he grabbed hold of Teron's vest. The monk grunted with the extra weight, having only the ornamental spine for support. Praxle whispered to the long strand of rope, and it writhed its way like a serpent for the roof, weaving around the Flamic carvings that adorned the spine. The two intruders waited until at last the tail end of the rope appeared and wove itself into a small step beneath them.

Praxle climbed off Teron's back, then worked himself to the side so that the monk could ascend first.

With coils of animated rope dangling about the spine, Teron reached the rooftop quickly. He scanned to either side. The sword-bearing statues stood their silent watch to either side, while the rotating towers spun slowly around. Nothing moved in the forest of spears that threatened the stars above.

Teron peered back down at Praxle and waved him up. Once he'd climbed to just below the roof, Praxle coiled the rope beneath him and cast a spell that wrapped around him like a blanket. The spell contracted enough to become a second skin. As it did so, Praxle's color changed to a shifting dark gray, difficult to see in the night.

"How long will that last?" asked Teron.

"Over an hour." Praxle climbed up to hunker next to Teron, and took a few moments to help the writhing rope coil itself neatly at the edge of the roof.

Keeping low, the two of them scuttled across to the central tower, then slid into the nook that protected the single door. They could hear the muttering of voices inside, dull, bored. Teron stood, clenched and cocked his fist . . .

Then Praxle quickly stood in front of him, blocking the way. Teron looked at the gnome quizzically, but Praxle waved him to the latch side of the door. The gnome moved to the hinge side and slowly worked his hands, tying a knot of arcane opalescent energy. His motions completed, he opened his hands and the energies floated for a moment, then they contracted.

"Mew!" a plaintive kitten's voice sounded in the air.

Teron looked at the gnome, but all he could see in the shadows was the light of the spell reflecting off the gnome's teeth. The spell pulsed twice more, looking rather like a beating heart. "Mew! Mew!" The small voice whined louder, more insistently.

Praxle leaned forward and scratched at the door with his fingernails, a mischievous grin shining in the darkness. "Meww!"

Inside, Teron heard the voices grumbling among themselves, some confused, some complaining, but one or two sounding reasonable and concerned. He heard a chair scooting back, and approaching footsteps. He braced himself, and shaped one hand into a spear.

Behind the door, someone slid a heavy bar to the side. Praxle's spell redoubled its crying, and the gnome scratched some more at the door. A key turned in the tumbler, and the latch clicked. The door opened, spilling light in the entryway, and a guard stepped partway out, looking toward the ground.

Teron thrust with his spear hand, striking the guard with the point of his finger right in the voice box. The guards gagged, raising one hand to his throat in surprise, and Teron stepped forward, grabbed the man's head, and gave it a sharp jerk. A single loud pop resounded in the night.

Holding the dead man up by the head, Teron pulled him away from the door and lowered him quietly to the ground.

Teron moved into the tower, Praxle following. The interior of the tower was a single common room, and five other armored guards stood in surprise as they saw the strangers enter. The nearest lunged for his sword, leaning against his chair, still sheathed. Teron snapped a kick upward, smacking the guard in the face and driving him upright again. The monk spun with the kick, turning a full circle and arcing around with a high spinning heel kick that took the stunned man on the temple, sending him to the floor.

Magic words spilled from Praxle's mouth, and they were punctuated by a small pop as a thick, billowing cloud of gray erupted from the center of the room and filled the entire interior of the tower with an impenetrable mist. Then Teron heard the door shut as Praxle secured the area. He smiled and stood perfectly still.

Somewhere in the mist Teron heard a guard babbling confused and panicked questions. Relying on his four basilisks training, the monk swept a path to the speaker with kicks and punches; none of them met with any resistance until his foot connected with a knee, breaking it. The speaker cried out, but Teron finished him off without hesitation. As the guard's last breath escaped, Teron heard the soft jingle of chain mail close at hand. He dropped low and swept his leg at ankle height, dropping another guard. He quickly pinned the guard's weapon and killed him, as well.

Teron rose silently and stalked the cottony fog like a panther. Betrayed by the noises of their armor and their hissing attempts at communication, the other three Thrane guards fell just as quickly as the others.

As the last of them fell, Teron turned a full circle, listening for any noise from his companion, but the gnome was utterly silent. "Praxle!" he hissed. "Praxle!"

There was no answer for a short while, but then Teron heard hinges creak as the door swung open again. A small tenor voice murmured in the mist. "Are they all dead?"

"Indeed," whispered Teron. "Now get rid of this mist!"

"Let it run its course," suggested Praxle. "I'd rather not waste energy dispelling it. We may have greater need later."

Teron heard Praxle step across the floor, then a clatter and a curse as the gnome tripped over a Thrane corpse.

A few moments later, the mist cleared away, vaporizing into nonexistence in a complicated series of intertwining tendrils, stirred into that chaos by the passage of Teron and the guards.

Praxle whistled. "Your body is impressive, Teron," he said. "Now we just have to whet your soul to be as fine, and you can be as powerful as I."

Teron ignored the comment. "Where now?" he asked.

Praxle pointed to the trap door of the tower. "There, first of all," he said. "I've spent many long, bitter years memorizing the architecture of this library and the location of the notes, all in preparation for this day."

Teron gripped the ring of the trap door and pulled. "It's locked from the other side," he said.

"I know," said Praxle. "But they designed the door with the hinges on this side."

Teron looked at the other end of the trapdoor. "Well, that was foolhardy," he said.

Praxle just smiled as he drew a dagger and worked the pins from the hinges. His gray skin shifted as he worked.

The mismatched pair worked their way down the central stairwell of the library. Praxle pointed to a certain door marked with a sign reading, ARTIFICE. Teron opened it, finding an open reading area with tables and chairs. No one was present. Three separate aisles led away from the area. Praxle pointed down the left-hand passage.

The two moved quietly through the magically lit aisle. Rows and rows of shelves lined each side, each covered with tomes, scrolls, and boxes, carefully catalogued and arranged. Signs describing the contents of the shelves adorned the ends of the cases.

"The library's quiet," said Praxle. "Aside from the guards up top, and they were too spooked by the mist to do anything." A brief pause. "Think our luck will hold?"

"Not a chance," said Teron.

"Over there," pointed Praxle. "That's where they keep the records."

Praxle ushered Teron over to a large, dark densewood door set into a thick wall of stone. "There it is. That's where they keep the research records for artifacts and relics that predate Galifar."

Teron appraised the area. "Looks like the walls seal a large room," he said.

"Indeed they do," said Praxle.

"Are there that many ancient relics they study?"

"Host, no," said Praxle. "They just wanted to ensure they had enough space. Many of the shelves within are empty, and much of what they have has been copied from records in other libraries."

"Is this the only door?" asked Teron.

"Yes, it is. And it's magically sealed. Give me a moment, let me handle it." Praxle cast a spell on himself, closed his eyes, and began to murmur under his breath. His voice gradually increased in volume until Teron could make out the words. It was a chant to build courage, used by the Church of the Silver Flame. Praxle flexed his fingers, and his skin sparkled, trailing tiny motes. At last, he reached down and grasped the door's handle. Behind the densewood, several bolts were thrown with metallic clicks, then the door vibrated as a heavy wooden beam glided out of the way. When the noise stopped, Praxle pushed the heavy wooden door open. It glided noiselessly on beautifully wrought and well-oiled hinges and revealed a large room, well lit from an indefinable source. Half-full shelves rimmed the majority of the perimeter; overstuffed chairs and large tables adorned with large magnifying glasses and bookstands filled the roomy center.

"How'd you do that?" asked Teron as the two of them stepped into the room.

"The seal is designed to open only to members of the Church," answered Praxle as he shut the door. "I had to replicate the aura."

"But how could you do that?"

"Teron," said Praxle with a smile, "I am an illusionist. It's child's play to deceive myself into thinking what I want me to think."

"But your soul is what it is."

Praxle stopped, turned, and gave Teron a pointed look. "No, that is never the case, Teron. Free yourself from such a thought, lest it be your death." He closed the door and looked around the room. "Over in that corner," he said. "I suppose now we'll find out how good our agent was."

The two of them moved to the designated shelf and began opening books and scrolls, flipping through the contents in search of telltale illustrations or notes.

"Is this it?" asked Teron. He pulled a leather-bound tome from the shelf. A chain rattled along behind the book as he lowered it to the gnome.

Praxle grunted as he took the book from Teron. "Dark six, this is a heavy thing! Did they wrap leather over byeshk for the covers?"

"And it's chained to the wall," said Teron. "Those are heavy links, too. They don't even want this book to go to the tables."

"This is it," said Praxle. He cradled the book in one arm, leaning it against a shelf for additional support, and flipped through the thick parchment pages rapidly. "Oohh yes, this is it," he crooned. "After all this time, I have it at last."

"You should not be here," croaked a small voice. Teron and Praxle spun and saw a small creature that sat atop the shelving next to the door. Its body was about the size of a human head, and similarly arranged. Four long, lanky limbs extended from near the back of the head, each sporting three joints and ending with a delicate, long-fingered hand. One hand rested on the latch of the door.

"But of course we should," said Praxle. "Otherwise the door would not have opened for us."

"I heard you talk," accused the creation. It smiled hideously. "You should have been quiet in the library."

Teron charged the creature, leaping up onto one of the tables that barred his path and flying through the air toward it, but it scuttled quick as a spider, opening the door a mere hand's span and spilling through, then pulling it shut just as Teron reached it. Latches threw and the heavy wooden bar began to slide back into place.

Teron thrust the bar to the side, grabbed the door handle, and yanked, but the door did not budge.

The monk rounded on the gnome. "What was that?"

"An arcane aide," said Praxle. "A magewrought creature to help fetch books and the like. They're built smart, agile and quiet, so as not to disturb mages during an experiment." Praxle glanced at the book, then looked back at Teron. "Listen, we have a few minutes at best before that thing raises a ruckus. You break this chain, I'll open the door."

Teron stalked back over to the book, and inspected the chain, as well as where it was set into the wall and attached to the spine of the tome. He gripped the chain and gave a few experimental tugs. He shook his head and chewed on his lip.

Across the room, Praxle cast his spell and focused, rapidly reciting the Silver Flame's chant. He reached for the door and boldly grasped the handle.

Nothing happened.

"Damnation!" he cursed. "I can't do it! I'm too upset about the notes! Get them loose, so I know we can go!"

Teron looked at the book again. He flipped it open, gripped a handful of pages, and gave a strong steady pull, tearing the pages from the binding with a loud rip.

"What in Khyber are you doing?" gasped Praxle. "That's priceless research!"

"And I'm taking it," responded Teron. He folded the parchments in half and stuffed them into his tunic. "Do you want the notes, or the cover?" He grabbed some more of the pages and tore them from the binding. He looked at them, then handed the majority of them to Praxle. "Here," he said. "This way, if one of us dies, they won't recover all the notes." Praxle took the proffered pages, rolled them up, and thrust them through his belt. Teron took the remainder and slid them into the back of his waistband, pulling his vest down over them. "The rest of the book looks blank," he said. "Open the door."

Praxle, bewildered and still horrified at Teron's cavalier attitude, shook his head to clear it. He turned back to the door, recast his spell, and started to chant. He interrupted his chanting to take a deep breath, then laid one hand on the notes that stuck out from his belt. He resumed his chant, calmer and more confident than before. He reached for the door's handle gracefully and gripped it.

The heavy wooden bar slid to one side, and the metal clack of dwarf-made bolts resounded. The door swung open easily, and as it did, the sound of a magical klaxon spilled into the room.

Teron vaulted over Praxle into the library. "Move!" he hissed.

The two ran for the main stairwell. As they approached, the door to the stairwell opened and a pair of Thrane mages stepped through. One pointed. "There!"

The first mage stepped forward, brandishing a staff, while the second stepped to the side and began casting a spell. However, Teron was moving faster than either had anticipated. The mage with the staff aimed it at the charging monk. Teron somersaulted, diving beneath a blast of intense cold.

Icy shards flew past Praxle. The gnome grabbed a handful of scrolls from the shelf next to him and flung them at the second mage. Three of them unfurled in flight, creating a fluttering flock of parchment distraction. The mage's spell fired a spray of energy pellets that flew at the scrolls instead of the small gray illusionist, hitting several of them and setting them ablaze.

Teron's roll brought him to the feet of the lead mage. He kicked up with his feet, catching the front end of the staff and knocking it toward the ceiling. The surprised mage staggered with the force of the unexpected blow, so he didn't see Teron's hand snake out and snag the bottom end of the staff. Teron yanked the staff toward him. The mage fought him, trying to pull it back. Teron obliged, thrusting the staff toward the mage, and their combined strength drove the tip of the magic staff squarely into the mage's teeth. He raised one hand to his face, leaving one hand holding the staff.

The second mage stepped forward, hands held in front of him, glowing with an icy blue the color of dead flesh. He scooted over the burning scrolls, looking for the gnome that had been there but a moment before.

Still on his back, Teron swung one leg up and hooked his heel over the top end of the staff. He drove his leg down, stripping the wooden staff from the Thrane. At the same time he snapped up a kick with his other leg and struck the mage in the side, knocking him down.

Startled by the cry of his companion, the second mage turned to check what kind of threat Teron posed. Teron rolled to his feet and spun the staff in a circle. He looked at the approaching mage, and the unnatural hue to his hands. Then he saw a shadow move from the shadows of the bookshelves, and Praxle lunged forward and planted a dagger into the Thrane mage's kidney.

The man stiffened, arcing his back against the assault, leaving himself open. Teron thrust with the staff, landing a brutal strike at the soft spot right below the breastbone, and following up with a spinning overhand blow that hit the mage on the back of the head as he doubled over. There was a loud crack as the man's skull broke.

Teron turned back to the owner of the staff. He was holding his face and crab-walking backward. Teron leaped forward, wielding the staff like a spear. He struck the mage in the gut, and then swung around and planted a heel kick squarely on the temple. The mage flopped dead.

Praxle wiped his dagger on the dead mage's robe. "We need to get going," he said. "Any chance of fighting our way through the lobby?"

"Never," said Teron. "Not with wizards and the guardian elemental. We're going up."

Behind them, near the door to the restricted research, a small explosion billowed forth as a Thrane wizard teleported in. "Hold!" she yelled.

Praxle aimed the hilt of his dagger at the new arrival and a blast of lightning split the air.

Teron turned, shocked. "Where did that come from?" he yelled.

"I went shopping," yelled Praxle. "Let's go!" The pair burst into the stairwell and ran for the rooftop. Below them, they heard the sound of multiple footsteps racing up behind. Teron moved quickly and easily, but Praxle, having to leap up stairs that were far larger than his body could easily handle, started to flag.

Teron burst into the guard tower, populated only by the cooling corpses of Thrane guards. He ran out the covered door and ran across the roof, weaving between the wicked weapons that defied the heavens. He made for the edge of the roof and grabbed the end of the coiled rope, looking for a good location to secure the line. He'd hoped Praxle's enchantment would still hold, but the rope lay limp and lifeless in his hands.

Then he saw the shadows move.

A dozen or more figures stalked across the roof, starlight reflecting off their huge naked blades. Teron grabbed the rope and ran back toward the central tower. He saw a shifting patch of gray in the darkness, faintly visible. "Take the rope!" he hissed. "The tower by the Dormitorion!"

"What?" Praxle whispered back. "What's the matter?"

"The statues," explained Teron, "they're animate! I'll distract them, you run to the corner tower, and pray your disguise holds!"

Praxle scuttled off, low and quiet, his shifting gray coloration making him all but invisible atop the unlit roof.

Teron turned and appraised the approaching constructs. Their anatomy had no nerves, thus incapacitating them with debilitating pain was not possible. Instead, Teron had to rely on striking weak locations to cause structural damage; no small feat for creations that were, in all likelihood, perambulating stone.

He hopped to the side, striking one of the upraised pole arms with the full weight of his body. The long weapon creaked, then snapped under the pressure, and Teron hefted it. It had a wide blade, covered with barbs and jutting spikes, a perfect weapon for use against unarmored targets, but against armored foes, it was less than ideal: the wide cutting edge dispersed the energy too much.

Two statues drew close, raising their greatswords for lethal strikes. He turned the pole in his hands, spinning the head of his weapon. He stepped in to one approaching statue, striking lightly to the face with the construct, and leaving his left side open to the second. The first statue balked as the razor-sharp spikes threatened its eyes. The second statue took advantage of the easy strike, swinging its heavy two-handed sword down to cut the monk in half. Teron sensed the approaching attack, and hopped into the air, bringing the head of his pole arm down and ushering the blade beneath him.

In the darkness, the construct warrior did not see the move in time to react. Teron guided the full force of the attack into the second, and the huge blade amputated the animate statue's leg at the knee. The injured carving collapsed silently, then made a weak swing at Teron's legs with its weapon. The monk hopped back and looked toward the tower where Praxle had run. He could see nothing, and decided to buy the gnome a few more moments before making his break.

The downed statue hurled its giant sword at Teron. The monk easily dodged, but the attack distracted him for a split second. In that time, the other warrior swiped its blade hard in a low, lateral stroke, cutting through the shafts of several of the upraised pole arms. They began to fall like timber, their sharpened edges arcing toward Teron. As they fell, the statue charged in.

Faced with so many attacks, and well knowing that the Thrane Congress was capable of using his blood to send magical attacks, Teron backpedaled rapidly, using his bulky weapon to deflect several of the falling shafts.

More statues closed in. He gave ground, but it became clear that the assembled creatures would wait until they had overwhelming force before attacking. Teron moved toward the central tower, but a statue blocked the way, whirling its sword in a defensive circle.

Knowing his time was almost up, Teron forced himself to press his energy lower into his body, pushing it uncomfortably into one leg. His stomach churned at the effort, complaining against the unnatural activity.

As he felt the energy start to course out of his body, Teron made his move. He used the pole arm to vault himself forward, snapping a kick out toward the face of the blocking statue. His kick was well short of the mark, but as his leg snapped to a full extension, the energy flew from the sole of his foot and struck the statue in the face. The creature staggered back with the arcane impact, and Teron took the opportunity to move. He tossed the pole arm right at the manufactured guardian while he himself dived to a roll, tumbling just past the creature's knee while its attention was drawn upward to the spiraling spear.

Several other statues were too close now; he had to flee. Teron tumbled back to his feet and leapt for the roof of the guard tower. He grabbed the edge and pulled himself up with one strong motion. He grabbed the shafts of two of the spears that jutted from the tower's roof and pulled himself forward, his feet clearing the edge of the roof just as three greatswords rang against the stone, spitting sparks and chips of rock with the ferocity of their strikes.

Teron ran across the turret's rooftop and jumped down the other side, sprinting for the corner tower that was closest to the Dormitorion. He heard the tread of two score feet in hot pursuit, nearly two dozen statue guardians chasing wordlessly after him.

He approached the corner tower, and Praxle was nowhere to be seen. The tower was swinging around toward the library building; in but a few moments the staircase would start to swing over the rooftop, and the means of escape would turn into a trap.

As he closed, he saw the rope knotted over one of the ornamental Flamic spikes that adorned the side of the soaring staircase. He vaulted over the side of the staircase and grabbed the rope as he fell. Several floors below him, he saw Praxle descending the rope as rapidly as he could.

Teron followed suit, glancing both up, for threats, and down, to follow Praxle's progress.

Above, the rotating tower started to pass over the rooftop, and as Praxle had tied the rope to the leading edge of the staircase, the rope started getting drawn up. Teron looked up and saw the silhouettes of two statues looking down at him. Just as he realized what they intended to do, he heard a metal clang and the rope went slack. He fell.

A mere five feet later, the rope stopped again, and Teron realized that the knot had, against all probability, hung up on one of the ornamental carvings that decorated the eaves. He glanced down. Below him, Praxle had reached the approximate location of the warding spell. As he watched, the gnome leapt out from the wall, hands gesticulating wildly. The gnome's clothes flapped as he fell, but Teron realized that he was falling slowly, buoyed by strong, magically manipulated winds.

Teron glanced back up just in time to see that one of the statues had thrown its greatsword at him, hoping to slash him as he hung all but helpless on the rope. Teron kicked off from the wall, swinging himself out of the way like a great pendulum, but as he swung as far as his momentum would carry him, he heard another clang from above, and he saw the end of the rope fling itself out from the rooftop. The knot had been cut away.

CHAPTER 20

Hunkered against the wall of the Dormitorion, camouflaged against the cobbles and stone wall by his spell, Praxle watched in fear as Teron tumbled from the side of the building. Up above, the guardian statues on the rooftop were lit from below as they leaned over and watched.

Teron hit, hard, grunting with the impact. He struggled to rise, stumbled, and looked up at the statues on the rooftop. Praxle followed his gaze.

One of the statues leapt. And another. And a third, even before the first one hit the street.

The first one landed badly, shattering both legs. Praxle saw its foot and ankle skitter across the cobbles, flung by the force of the impact. The second did not leap far enough, and landed heavily in the ruins of a large shrub. Praxle heard multiple cracks, but couldn't tell what sort of limbs might have broken. The third, however, took a more daring approach. It fell spread-eagled to the pavement, landing face-first on the cobblestones and dispersing the force of the impact over its entire body. Its greatsword clanged to the ground beside it. It lay motionless for a moment, then stirred and rose, smoothly regaining its feet. In the light of the everbright lanterns, Praxle could see that its stone surface sported multiple chips and cracks, but it acted none the worse for wear. It picked up the sword and moved toward Teron, who half-crawled half-hopped away like a wounded dog. The monk held one arm close to his chest, and one foot lolled to the side, badly broken at the ankle.

Even as Praxle considered what a small gnome like him might be able to do against the towering construct, Jeffers leapt out of the alleyway, swinging his serrated sword. He placed himself between the creature and the wounded Aundairian.

The half-orc engaged the construct, wielding his sword defensively, buying Teron time to make an escape. Praxle started to glide out from concealment to help, but from the alley Teron's cat hissed, and the sound gave him pause. As he hesitated, a second shadow slid from the alleyway, dressed head to toe in dark gray. Praxle's eyes went wide as he recognized the unmistakable attire of the Shadow Fox.

Chain kama in hand, the Fox moved with speed and stealthy grace to where Teron struggled to his feet. Seeing the threat, Praxle charged after, drawing his dagger.

The Fox reached Teron, grabbed his vest, and pulled him close, all the while brandishing the weapon. But before the Fox could strike, Praxle yelled, hoping to draw attention away from the wounded monk.

The Fox turned as Praxle lunged with his dagger. The Fox parried, partially turning Praxle's blade, but taking a long, painful cut along the buttock. The Fox dropped Teron and disarmed Praxle with a quick flourish, then turned and fled down the street.

Praxle checked on Jeffers. The half-orc was holding his own against the statue, but he wouldn't be able to for much longer. Two more statues had managed to survive the jump from the rooftop in operable condition. Glancing the other way, Praxle saw the Shadow Fox skid to a stop as armed guards turned the corner from the front of the Camat Library. The Cyran thief fled into a nearby alley.

"Run, Jeffers!" yelled Praxle, as he recovered his dagger from the pavement. Jeffers feinted, then disengaged from the

statue and sprinted aside. Praxle sidestepped quickly, aligning
the statue with the other two that were joining the fracas. He
reversed his grip on his dagger, aimed the hilt at the constructs,
and raised one hand to shield his squinting eyes.

A heavy bolt of electrical energy spat forth from the back
end of the dagger, destroying two of the statues outright and
catching a sizeable portion of the third before blasting a crater
in the side of the library. A quick turn and Praxle unleashed a
second blast at the guards coming from the front of the building. Satisfied that all opposition was dead, cowered, or seeing
a blinding afterimage, Praxle ran. "Grab him!" he yelled at
Jeffers. "He broke his leg!"

The half-orc heaved one of Teron's arms around his shoulder, and the threesome made a quick escape into the night,
followed closely by the cat.

❂ ❂ ❂ ❂ ❂ ❂ ❂

Praxle opened the door to their room, while Jeffers
helped the hobbled monk into the room. As Praxle closed the
door, Teron asked, "Who was that, that came up to me right
at the end?"

"You don't know?" asked Praxle. "That was the Shadow Fox!"

"Is that so?" mused Teron as he sat on his bed. Jeffers helped
him maneuver his broken ankle and arm onto soft pillows.
"Strange. He asked me to go with him."

"Did he?" said Praxle. He chuckled. "I think he knew we had
the notes. Trying to get them for himself."

"That makes sense," said Teron. He adjusted himself and
reclined on his bed. The papers crinkled as he lay down, so he
reached into his vest, pulled out the sheaf of notes, and handed
them to Praxle. "Here you go."

"Most excellent!" chortled Praxle. He danced around the
room with the papers, giggling manically. "After all this time,
at last, my moment is at hand!" With a sigh that bordered on the
erotic, he sat on his bed and combined Teron's pages with his
own, then started poring over them.

247

"I can endeavor to fetch a Jorasco healer for you, ma—Teron," offered Jeffers, "though I doubt that any shall make themselves available before morning."

"That's all right, Jeffers," said Teron. "If we contact one right now, it might cause questions. They might connect my broken bones and the break-in. I think we left no witnesses, but I'd rather be as safe as possible. I'll just take a tumble down the stairs in the morning to make it look good, and we'll get a healer then."

Jeffers drew a blanket over Teron. "You're sure about this?"

Teron nodded. "I've had worse." He sighed, half in relief and half in pain. "With all the ruckus we've caused, we'd better hope that Lady Hathia followed through on her promise soon, wouldn't you say, Praxle?"

But the gnome, engrossed in the notes, made no reply.

❧ ❧ ❧ ❧ ❧ ❧ ❧

The Shadow Fox limped into the Cyran hideout, finding her mages still hard at work trying to unravel the secrets of the Sphere of Xoriat.

"Fetch me the chirurgeon," she said.

"No time," said Rezam. "This is a fascinating problem, and we can't leave just yet."

She scowled and looked them over, haggard hair, dark circles under the eyes, yet a feverish look of excitement on their faces. "Haven't you taken a break? Gotten some rest?"

"No time! We're close! I can feel it!"

"Listen, you two, I need someone to stitch me up. Now."

Rezam rounded on her. "No! Get one yourself! You—"

The Fox whipped out her kama and slashed the wizard just above the eye, opening a long cut. Blood started welling from the wound, then dribbled into his eye. He cried out in pain and pressed his hand to the injury.

"Why you vicious little—"

The Fox dropped the tip of her kama to the soft spot between his collarbones, ready to pierce his larynx. "Now we both need a chirurgeon," she said. "Send your assistant to get one. Now."

The wizard's uncovered eye glared at Fox, filled with spite and fear. He gestured with his free hand, and a gecko suddenly skittered along the wall and out a door. "My familiar will bring one to us," he said coldly.

"Thank you."

"That was unnecessarily cruel," said Rezam.

"Cruel? Granted," said the Fox. "But unnecessary? I believe you have forgotten who is in charge of this operation."

Rezam did not answer, but his one open eye glanced briefly at the Sphere.

* * * * * * *

It was approaching noon by the time Teron was able to leave the Jorasco compound and return to the boardinghouse. He savored the feeling of having his arm and ankle hale once more. He walked briskly, enjoying the warm sun that shone through the cool air.

As he passed by the Phiarlander Phaire on the way back to his rooms, he saw a familiar sight: a carriage parked in front of the tavern, blazoned with the crest of the Stalsun family. Intrigued, he entered the Phaire.

The crowd was light, but it was still a bit early for a luncheon. As he stood by the entrance and surveyed the interior—dark by comparison to the noonday sun outside—he overheard snippets from a number of conversations about the incident at the library the night before. A fire the first night and lightning the second had sparked the curiosity of the populace.

At last he espied Lady Hathia at a tall table with Praxle and Jeffers, and began to approach.

Kelcie reached out for him from behind the service counter. "Teron—"

"Leave me be," he said absently. "This is important."

He smiled slightly as he approached the table; the elegant and haughty lady had obviously refused to debase her stature by sitting on one of the tall bar stools, and instead stood at the table. As he drew closer, Teron also realized that her posture kept the conversation more formal, which was probably exactly what she wanted.

"Good day, Lady," said Teron as he pulled out one of the stools and sat himself on it.

"You look well," she replied.

Teron shrugged. "I am."

"You're late, Teron," said Praxle. "I expected you back an hour ago. I could have been reading more of the notes!"

"Notes?" said Lady Hathia.

"We've gathered no small amount of information on the Cyran bandits and their methods, as well as a rota of Cyran expatriates in the city, their location, and employment," said Jeffers easily. "My master has been endeavoring to discern a pattern in an attempt to deduce who might be involved with the Cyrans, and where their safe house might be."

Lady Stalsun smiled thinly. "I see," she said. "My dear gentlemen, you should have saved yourselves the bother. I thought I had made my resources clear to you; I have been tracking all manner of questionable personages for some time."

"That's fine," snapped Praxle, "but—"

"With some selective application of pressure among those my people have been watching, we have pieced together the location of the Cyran hideout. We believe it to be where they are holding this relic you seek." She looked at each of the three foreigners in turn. "I surmise by your silence that you did not believe me capable of deducing its location, nor to be willing to share same with you."

"Wonderful!" bellowed Praxle. He hopped down from his stool and unceremoniously pumped Lady Hathia's hand. "My lady, you have earned my eternal gratitude, and I shall have an eternity in which to bless you for your assistance." He paused for a moment to regroup, and kissed the lady's hand. "And the gratitude of the Sivis family, and the University as well, of course. You will be handsomely rewarded for your efforts."

With a subtle look of disgust, the Thrane lady withdrew her hand from Praxle's grasp. "Be at my estate at sundown," she said. "Come prepared. You shall be taken to the location of the Cyrans' refuge. There, under cover of nightfall, you shall enter and recover your relic. My people cannot assist you; the political standing of my house is tenuous at best. However, I shall deploy them about the vicinity of the Cyrans' lair to ensure that any city watch patrols that threaten to interrupt your work are instead directed elsewhere. Is that clear?"

The other three nodded.

"Thank you for your assistance. The sooner this dangerous item is out of the hands of the Cyrans and safely away from Thrane, the better." She turned and started to leave, but stopped and looked askance at them. "I expect that I shall be able to prevail upon the church and the university alike for an equitable consideration in the future," she said. It was not a question.

Teron nodded. Praxle bowed, and said, "Most assuredly. You will have the favor of the most powerful of . . . of organizations to be found anywhere in Khorvaire."

She nodded slightly, eyes half lidded. Then she turned away and walked sedately out the door to her waiting carriage.

Teron sighed contentedly. "Time for me to break my fast," he said. He turned to the kitchen and called, "Kelcie?"

After a moment, the one-eyed cook appeared. "She done left, masters," he said. "What can I get for ya?"

❀ ❀ ❀ ❀ ❀ ❀ ❀

"How are you doing, Fox?" Two Cyrans entered the room and closed the door behind them.

"Who's there?" asked Fox, turning her head on the pillow.

"It's Dyen."

The Shadow Fox lay on her stomach on the bed, the bandage over her haunch pink with blood. "I'm not doing very well," she said.

"This is a nice room," said Dyen, taking in the comfortable bed, the sunlight streaming in the windows, and the overstuffed chair. "That should help."

Fox grunted.

"We brought you something to sup on. Thought you might like a tad for your stomach."

"Thanks," she said, and took a half a large roll. Her hands trembled as she drew it to her mouth.

"What's the matter, Fox?" asked Dyen.

She chewed her bread for a moment, then tucked it into one cheek. "I think that bastard little gnome had a poisoned blade," she muttered.

"Who is he? I'll kill him for you."

"Don't," said the Fox. "He's from the University. Pretty high up, I understand. We don't want gnomes chasing after his killers, prying into our business, right?" She looked at them and saw assent, if not agreement. "There is, however, something you can do to hurt them," she said. "I know they've been chasing the Sphere ever since we found it. And it appears that they, too, know about the Thrane notes."

"What notes are those?"

"Ah," said Fox. "Apologies; I forgot you didn't know. During the Last War, one of our agents discovered that the Thranes had an ancient relic borrowed from Zilargo. We believed it had been used against Aundair and subsequently lost. We also had strong indications that the Congress had extensive notes on the relic locked up in its library." She propped herself up on her elbows to get a better angle at which to look at her compatriots. "When we chanced upon the fact that the Black Globe might have been found, we pounced on it, and managed to grab it. Since I've been back, I've been trying to figure a way into the library to find those notes."

"But the library is battened down as tight as a Mrorian iron vault!"

"I know. It's been very frustrating. But I think finding a way in is no longer necessary. I think they—the gnome and his friends—I think they stole the notes from the library last night."

"Do you mean the instructions on how to use that relic you took?"

"Precisely," said the Fox. Her face paled, and she laid herself back down gingerly. She drew and exhaled a trembling breath.

"Now we don't need to break into the Congress Library," she continued. "Thank the Host, too, because there's no chance on Eberron that I'd be able to do it, not with these stitches in my hindquarters and that poison in my blood."

Dyen reached out one hand and pulled a stray strand of hair away from Fox's face. "Are you sure you're okay?"

"I'm as well as can be. The time for antidotes is long past, friends, and the treasury was utterly depleted by our trips to Breland and Aundair. I'll weather this storm, but it will be a while."

"So what can we do?"

"There are three of them," answered Fox, "staying at the boardinghouse on Fletcher Square, two blocks and a half from the Phiarlander Phaire. A human named Teron, a gnome named Praxle, and a half-orc named Jeffers."

"How'd you get all that?"

"I followed them to the lodge. The names came from Squints at the Phaire. Now shut up and let me talk." She paused to marshal her thoughts. "Second floor. I don't know their room. Find out exactly where they're staying. Squints said they've been eating at the Phaire, so break into their rooms when they're dining. Do it after dark, just in case you get caught. Bring one or two of the mages, and look for anything that seems arcane and take it. Are we clear on this?"

"Yes, Fox," the Cyrans said in unison.

"Good. Because now I want you both to leave," she mumbled as she turned her head away. "I'll kill anyone who disturbs me for any reason. I'm going to sleep to morning."

By the time the two visitors left the room, the Fox's breathing was deep and even.

* * * * * * *

Squints looked up as seven people entered the Phaire. Each carried a weapon—sheathed, thankfully—and several wore light armor. They entered with purpose, striding boldly in, not sauntering like regulars or hesitantly entering like those unfamiliar with the establishment.

They moved immediately for the serving counter, where Squints stood. He subtly grabbed the haft of the brutal spiked mace he kept behind the counter as insurance against bandits and the like.

"You must be Squints," said their leader, holding out one hand. "My name is Dyen. I hear you have some visitors frequenting this establishment."

"This is an inn," he said. "I get visitors."

"I'm sorry," said Dyen. He leaned closer, accidentally revealing the chainmail he wore beneath his tunic. "The Fox sent me."

At the mention of her name, the look in Squints' one eye eased considerably, and he gently set the mace back to its resting place.

"We're after a group of three: a human, a gnome, and a half-orc."

"I know them," said Squints.

"Great! We hear they're renting a room just down the street; do you happen to know which room is theirs?"

"No, I don't," said Squints. "But Kelcie over there, she helped them get back to their room the other day. She knows."

One of the Cyrans clawed his hand, and arcane power arced from fingertip to fingertip. "Let's go find out, shall we?"

Squints snapped his hand out and grabbed the mage's wrist. He leaned forward, his one eye flaring menacingly. "Don't none of you lay a hand on her," he demanded. "Do you hear?"

"Easy, Squints," said Dyen. "Just talk. Nothing else."

The magician rounded on Dyen. "Just talk? Is that all we do? Talk and wait? No! We find out where they are and we do this now!"

Dyen held up his hands placatingly. "Easy, Rezam. First things first. We can't do anything until we know which room is theirs." He glanced over to Squints, who gave him a meaningful glare. He nodded. "So you all just let me go and ask her, right?"

Dyen walked across the mostly empty dining room to the young woman. "Excuse me," he said, "your name is Kelcie, right?"

She nodded, pulling her hair behind one ear. "Please, have a seat," she said. "What can I bring for you?"

"I just need some answers," he said, placing a sovereign next to the dirty flatware on her tray. "Are you acquainted with a threesome visiting the city, I believe them named Teron, Jeffers, and Praxle?"

She narrowed her eyes suspiciously. "Why?"

He dropped his head for a moment, then looked back up. "It's embarrassing to say, but they have something of mine, and I intend to recover it before they exit the city."

"You?" Kelcie chuckled. "I sure hope you have a lot of friends." She turned away and headed for another dirty table. Without looking back, she added, "You're going to need them."

◦ ◦ ◦ ◉ ◦ ◦ ◦

Teron finished stretching with a satisfied sigh. He stood, walked over to the nightstand, and splashed his face with some water from the tarnished copper bowl, then ran his wet hands through his short-cropped hair.

He went back over to his bed and carefully picked up his vest. "It's closing on sundown," he said, "do either of you want to get yourselves something to eat before we go?"

"I'm too excited," said Praxle. "I can't eat. And neither can you, Jeffers." He paused to giggle. "Oh, to be this close, after all this time. I can feel the power!"

"What do you mean?" asked Teron pointedly, as he adjusted the waistband of his trousers and then pulled on his vest.

"Excuse me?"

"Power?"

Praxle walked over to Teron. "Do you have any idea what sort of power this will give me among my people, to recover this artifact? Right now I report to the doyen of the College of History and Archaeology. Next week, she'll be reporting to me! And that's just the beginning!"

"We may be working together," said Teron cautiously, "but we haven't yet settled the ultimate fate of the Sphere."

"Ah, but I am sure we will," said Praxle. "You're reasonable. Especially when you understand the Orb of Xoriat better, you'll be perfectly agreeable, I'm sure. For that matter, we can share."

Teron raised his eyebrows. He started to say something, but Praxle cut him off. "Pack it all, Jeffers," he said. "Don't leave anything. I want to be out of this town as soon as we have it back in our possession.

"That's wise," said Teron. "I was thinking much the same. Shall we leave by land or sea?"

"I arranged for a private carriage on the midnight run of the lightning rail," said Praxle with a touch of a gloat. "Jeffers, see to it that the staff here knows to deliver our bags to the rail tonight."

Teron was taken aback. "And here I thought you didn't have much coin," he said.

Praxle shrugged. "I didn't, especially after evading your friend the prelate," he explained. "But I was able to draw from the University and House Sivis accounts. It gave me some needed funds to shop for essentials. Like this." He picked up a long dagger from the dresser, flipped it in his hand, and slipped it into its sheath. "I rather like it. Creation and destruction, and a nice balanced blade, to boot. Noisy, though."

Teron shrugged noncommittally.

"Well, it sure beats your fists," said Praxle.

"Perhaps," said Teron, "but I can never be disarmed."

"Sure you can," laughed Praxle, "if your arms get chopped off!" He laughed uproariously at his joke, while Jeffers gave Teron a long-suffering look.

The gnome's hilarity was interrupted by a knock at the door.

"Teron?" called a familiar voice. "Teron, it's Kelcie! Are you there?"

"Kelcie?" Teron started walking over to the door. "What's the matter?

"There's some strangers at the Phaire; I think they're after you!"

"Who?" asked Teron, opening the door.

Kelcie smirked. "I brought them over to meet you, you bastard."

A NEST OF CYRANS

CHAPTER 21

A mallet flew around the corner of the doorjamb. Teron had a split second to react, and ducked just enough that the blow took him on the brow rather than square on the nose.

The next thing he knew, he was lying on the floor. He looked to the door, but Kelcie had already vanished. In her stead he saw two burly humans stepping through the door. One had a mallet, the other a small axe.

Instinct took hold, focused by years of intensive training. The man with the axe closed in, stepping between Teron's legs and raising his weapon for a killing blow. Teron hooked his right foot behind the man's ankle and drove his left foot into the man's knee as hard as he could. The angle was a little bit off, the man too close for Teron's kick to get the momentum needed to snap the axeman's knee, but the leverage of Teron's kick shoved the man to the ground. He fell into the mallet-wielding man and landed hard on his posterior.

Teron did a reverse somersault and rolled to his feet, his arms raised defensively.

Praxle grabbed the satchel that contained the Thrane notes. "Jeffers!" he yelled. "Get me out of here!"

Jeffers glanced at the door, now filled with three or four intruders. Two tried to push their way over their fallen comrade, while the third tried to help him to his feet. Trusting Teron to delay them for a few moments at least, Jeffers grabbed a chair and swung it into one of the latticed windows. It smashed through the wood and glass, sending shards toppling to the pavement a story below. Jeffers placed the chair right by the window.

"What the Six are you doing?" yelled Praxle, as his hands started flying through the motions for an illusion.

Jeffers declined to answer. Instead, he grabbed Teron's mattress and, with a growl of effort, heaved it around and thrust it through the window. It hung up on the shards and splinters, but Jeffers leaned into it with a roar. Glass creaked, wood cracked, and fabric tore in multiple places, but the half-orc forced it through. It fell to the cobbled street below, landing with a dull thump.

"Jump, master!" yelled Jeffers, "Before they notice!"

Praxle unleashed his illusory couatl, a feathery rainbow of serpentine danger, then turned and ran. Clutching tightly to his satchel, he leapt onto the chair and jumped headlong through the shattered window, passing cleanly between the shreds of fabric that hung on the jagged glass.

"Teron!" yelled Jeffers. "Follow!" He turned to the window as well, climbing out more slowly to ensure that in his haste he didn't land on his employer. He jumped, flopped onto the mattress and rolled immediately to the side.

A moment later, Teron burst through the window, lead leg extended as he hurdled the broken pane. He overshot the mattress, but landed into an easy tumble and rolled to his feet. "Flotsam!" he gasped, casting a glance at the broken window. "Did you—"

"Forget the cat!" said Praxle. "If it's your familiar, it'll find its way home." He grabbed Teron by the arm and pulled him away from the lodging. Jeffers added his weight, impelling the monk before any fireballs started dropping on them.

"If not," muttered Praxle as they ran, "then you won't have to worry about its smell any more."

❄ ❄ ❄ ❄ ❄ ❄ ❄

"They're getting away!"

"Dyen, take two and follow them," bellowed Rezam. "The rest of you, leave nothing unturned! I want those notes!"

Dyen grabbed two other Cyrans and ran downstairs, while the mage and the remaining Cyrans tore the room apart. Two broke open the packed luggage and tore the contents apart, while another overturned all the furniture, slitting cushions in her desperation.

Rezam stood in the center of the room, chanting quietly and turning a slow circle. As he did so, his anger and impatience grew rapidly.

"Nothing here," reported one of the Cyrans.

"WHAT?" bellowed Rezam.

"They must have taken the papers with them. But we'd better make ourselves scarce before the Crown Knights show up."

The Cyran mage growled. "Come!" He stormed downstairs with the others close at his heels. In the streets, he saw Dyen and the others scattered about. "Dyen!" he bellowed, arms wide in disbelief. "Where are they? Did you let them escape?"

"There's a number of people who saw what happened," answered Dyen. "They say the three of them ran to the end of the block and hailed a hansom. But no one here saw where they went after that."

Rezam roared in frustration. "How dare you hold out on us!" he bellowed to the crowd in general. "Where are they?"

"Easy, now," said Dyen. "Even if they had seen, there's no way we'd have any prayer of finding them. They have too much of a lead. They could have turned any number of ways a block from here. And now that we've tipped our hand, we need to go about this carefully."

The elf wizard turned about with a snarl, then suddenly his

voice turned sweet. "Of course we will," he said. "Anything for the Glo—anything for the cause, that is."

"Good," said Dyen nervously. "Because I did leave one of us down here, and the people say that he hired a trap and may have followed them. He'll tip us off later on, once he figures where they went."

Rezam sighed. "Then we shall wait a while longer." He looked at the gathered commoners that milled about the scene, staring, watching, muttering among themselves. He moved his hands, uttering foul words, and abruptly clouds of poisonous gases erupted at each end of the street. The noxious green clouds quickly billowed through the onlookers, obscuring them even as their voices choked and cried out in agony.

"What are you doing?" asked Dyen.

"No witnesses for the Crown Knights," whispered the mage conspiratorially. Then his expression buoyed up again, becoming positively jovial. "Come, everyone, let's depart through the rear of the building. Oargesha is waiting to show our enemies the secrets of the Black Globe. Soon we let everyone in, and the whole of Galifar shall pay the debt for its perfidy to Cyre."

❦ ❦ ❦ ❦ ❦ ❦ ❦

Darkness was starting to devour the sky to the east when Teron, Praxle, and Jeffers reached the Stalsun estate. They found a squad of three Thranes in House Stalsun livery, one of whom jumped aboard. He led them to a lower-class part of town and ordered the carriage driver to stop at a nondescript intersection. "Down the boulevard," said the guard, "then turn into that side street there. She's waiting for you."

They followed the guard's instructions, and found themselves on a little-used street with small service shops, all closed for the night. Lady Hathia Stalsun awaited them at the corner of the street and another small avenue, beneath the sole operative everbright in the area.

"Good evening, my lady," said Praxle eagerly.

"What happened to your eye, Teron?" she asked. "That's a nasty bruise."

"We had some trouble back at the lodge," said Teron.

"Which is to say," added Jeffers, "that a passel of ruffians chose to assail us in our room."

Lady Hathia narrowed her eyes and canted her head. "The Cyran thieves, perhaps?"

"Either that or friends of the serving wench," said Praxle, cutting in. "It seems our dear Teron doesn't have a way with women. I'm telling you, Teron, you should have ridden that filly when you had the chance. Made her feel like she mattered. Illusions are the first step in creation, you know."

Teron flushed and turned his head, but Hathia cut in. "You may have charm, d'Sivis," she said, "but you are a fool with regard to the female heart. Teron did the right thing by declining to take advantage."

"Can we quit this talk?" asked Teron, annoyance tinting his voice. "We're here on business."

"Indeed," said Lady Hathia. She gestured to an alley down the way. "Turn down that alley there," she said. "Take the first right branch. Then, after the alley turns left, you'll find their lair. There has been some activity tonight," she added, "and they've been a little careless. I do believe you'll find their door slightly ajar."

Praxle cackled, wriggling his fingers and bouncing on the balls of his feet as he led the way.

❋ ❋ ❋ ❋ ❋ ❋ ❋

Creeping quietly as a cat, Dyen slipped into the Cyran arcanium. The front room was empty, but light spilled from two doorways flanking the back hallway. "Psst! Anyone here?" he called out in a loud whisper.

"Sure, we're here," answered a voice, and a half-elf female sauntered out of one of the rooms. "Oh, hullo, Dyen. Back already? How'd it go?"

"Sh sh," said Dyen. "No time. I think they may be outside."
The half-elf hunkered down. "What?"

"I think they may be outside," repeated Dyen, hefting his mallet. "They may have seen me!"

"Careless dreg!" hissed the half-elf. She ran back into her room and returned a few seconds later bearing a Valenar scimitar, a long, vicious weapon with opposing curved blades at each end and a double leather-wrapped handle set in the center.

Dyen raised one eyebrow. "This will be interesting," he said.

"I hear someone," whispered the half-elf. She glided to one side of the corridor that led into the room and assumed a striking stance, her Valenar scimitar raised for a decapitation.

Dyen moved to an ambush position on the other side. He crouched low for a shot to the groin or knee. Or a face shot if the gnome happened to be the first one in.

After a few tense moments, a dark-haired human glided silently into the room, his bare arms raised, hands open, ready to strike or block. The half-elf stepped out and swept the double scimitar around in a dizzying flurry of sweeps, drawing the lead blade through the monk's neck and following with the trailing blade for good measure. A huge spray erupted as the monk's neck disintegrated, the thin strand of meat offering no resistance to the razor-sharp blades. For good measure, the half-elf reversed the spin and took the lead blade back through a third time to strike the head from the rear. The scimitar connected with the human's head before it had fallen more than a few inches, and as the blade sliced through, the head ceased to exist, spattering into a thousand multicolored motes that flickered away and died.

Shocked, the half-elf looked down at the little gnome who stood where the human had been a second ago. The gnome looked up and smiled. "Oops."

Then the half-elf saw Dyen spinning to deliver a reverse heel kick to the back of her head.

❂ ❂ ❂ ❂ ❂ ❂ ❂

Teron slid down the hall at the far side of the Cyran hideout. Light shone from two rooms; the one on the left he presumed was some sort of bunkhouse, presumably empty, because the half-elf had brought no additional assistance when she retrieved her weapon. He stood at the side of the door to the second lit room. The closer he got to the open door, the more he could sense the tension that resonated in the air.

He held the Valenar double scimitar in his hand to accentuate the adjusted illusory disguise that Praxle had given him. He did not trust the weapon; its opposing blades and asymmetric design clearly required years of training to master.

He listened at the door for several minutes, then signaled back to Praxle and Jeffers, holding up two fingers. They nodded, and Teron ambled into the room.

He saw two Thrane mages working on the far side of a large, heavy oaken table. Resting on a gold stand placed in the center of the table sat the Thrane Sphere. It looked like a mass of glossy black scarab beetles all huddled into a perfect sphere, occasionally shifting, and humming with vile intent. A pulsating shield of translucent green energy surrounded the sphere and prevented it from actually touching the stand; Teron recognized it as a protective spell, presumably one that did not protect the Sphere from danger but protected those nearby from the danger of the relic itself.

Teron walked up to the table, idly letting the double scimitar swing by his side, but as he approached, he sensed the aura of the Sphere press away the veneer of his illusory disguise, sending shreds of arcane energy wafting across the room. As one, the two Cyran mages turned malevolent eyes on him, burning with a hint of madness.

"Go!" yelled Teron, flinging the dangerous Valenar scimitar at one of the mages.

Teron tumbled over the table to attack the other mage, though, mindful of the Thrane Sphere's effects on the Cyran thief, he had to tumble quite wide of the mark. The mage was fast, however, and by the time Teron had landed on his feet, he saw a large flaming ball rolling toward him. He stepped to the side and retreated, and the ball swerved toward him. He thought of jumping it but was afraid it might reverse its course and remain beneath him, so instead he readied himself to punch it hard back at its caster.

Praxle entered the room with his dagger reversed in his hand and let loose a thunderbolt at the more distant Cyran mage. The blast flew out of the dagger, but its proximity to the Orb of Xoriat bent its path, and it smote the stone wall harmlessly. The Cyran mage made a series of gestures, each time sending blue tendrils of power all over his body. Angry, Praxle summoned his couatl illusion again as Jeffers lunged past and dived under the table.

The blazing ball rolled right at Teron, and he punched the fiery ball as hard he could with an open palm, but instead of a solid impact like he'd expected, his fist punched into a spongy mass that smelled of an alchemist's lab. Instead of deflecting the ball's approach, he'd buried his hand in the flames, and he could feel his flesh burning.

Teron pulled his arm back, and flopped backward as the flaming sphere rolled over him. He quickly batted at it with his hands and feet, keeping it distant as it overran him. The ball stopped trying to spin, content to be above him, and in that instant he moved. He let it drop to his side, guiding it with his hands, and then, kicking heartily with both feet, he managed to push the flaming ball just enough to wedge it under the table.

Praxle's couatl charged the second mage, who had retreated into the furthest corner of the room. It, too, shredded into nonexistence as it passed close by the dreaded Orb.

Jeffers surged up from beneath the table, waving his serrated blade and charged the second mage, now faintly shimmering with arcane effects. The mage gestured, and a staff flew across the room into his hands just as Jeffers reached him. He raised the staff to block Jeffers' initial chop, then spun the staff neatly to stop the second and third attacks of Jeffers' favorite combination move. Then with a speed and grace that made his mage's robes swirl like a dancer, the wizard spun around and cracked Jeffers on the back of the head with the inside of his staff, staggering the half-orc.

Praxle moved to an adjacent corner of the room to watch the duel. He prepared a spell.

Teron hopped back to his feet, ignoring the itching pain that was starting to throb in his burnt extremities. He lunged for the mage in front of him, but again the wizard was the faster. He finished another incantation just as Teron reached him. The monk landed a solid blow dead center to the wizard's breastbone, knocking him off his feet, but before he could follow through on his success, a miniature funnel cloud formed at the ceiling, reached down and surrounded the monk. Blinded by the winds and the dust they kicked up, Teron tried to wriggle free of the air elemental's grasp.

Gasping for breath from Teron's powerful hit, the first Cyran mage regained his feet. Satisfied that the monk was trapped in the elemental's embrace, he turned to assist his compatriot. A half-orc struggled with the other mage, each firmly grasping the mage's staff, a contest of orcish strength versus magical enhancement. The half-orc seemed to be getting the better of the fight, twisting the staff back and forth and brutally kicking the mage, while the wizard did nothing but tenaciously hold on to the staff.

Focused on their wrestling match, neither party considered outside threats, and thus the half-orc made a perfect target. The mage pulled a wand from his sleeve and aimed it at the intruder's head. With a mental command, a shaft of primal cold lanced out of the wand, striking true. In an instant, the cold had enveloped the half-orc's head, splitting the skin, freezing the eyes, and shattering a few teeth.

The spell also ruined the illusion that covered the pair; revealing a startled half-orc holding a staff, and a dead wizard lying on the floor.

"Sometimes I just love me," said Praxle to himself. He aimed the handle of his dagger carefully and let fly another bolt of lightning. As before, the Orb of Xoriat bent its path. Unlike before, Praxle had planned on exactly that, and the electric energy blasted the other Cyran mage before he could recover from his surprise.

Holding one hand over the huge knot on the back of his skull, Jeffers staggered over to the downed mage and stomped heavily on his neck. In that instant, the air elemental ceased to exist, and Teron dropped to the floor.

Praxle clapped his hands and rubbed them together. "Well, then," he said. "That was easy."

ESCAPE

CHAPTER 22

WHAT?" bellowed Rezam. His brow furrowed.

"I said the driver took them Uptown, and then back down to Old Central. That's where he dropped them. Then I saw them turn at Vintner's Avenue, and I came right back here to tell you."

Rezam's mouth twisted with anger, as if trying to chew the words that fought for freedom. "They're heading for the Sphere!" he said.

"That's impossible!" said one of the other Cyrans.

"No!" yelled Rezam. "They know! They followed the Fox here, and somehow they know! Damn it!" He swept his robe about himself dramatically. "Follow me," he said quietly, his eyes wide with intensity. "First we go to kill those who evaded us. Then we kill the one who led them here!"

✦ ✦ ✦ ✦ ✦ ✦ ✦

A rapid knock sounded at the door, followed impatiently by another. "Wake up!" called Dyen as he knocked. "Wake up!"

There was no response from inside the darkened room. There was a scratching sound of metal on metal, and then the door's tumbler slid to the side. The door swung open, and Dyen burst into the room. "Fox!" he whispered insistently. "We have troubles! Are you awake?"

He went over to the lantern that sat on the nightstand, the wick trimmed so low that it barely stayed ignited. "Fox," he whispered again, turning up the wick, "are you all—"

The lantern shed its slanting light on a vacant bed.

"Fox?"

❊ ❊ ❊ ❊ ❊ ❊ ❊

"We need to get out of here," said Praxle. "Someone will come looking soon."

"Agreed," said Jeffers, panting. "But we have to be careful."

With a groan, Teron pushed himself up to his hands and feet. He staggered, dizzy from the whirlwind. "Under the table," he said weakly, "there are some things that might help."

Praxle reached under the table and pulled the gear out. "This leather bag looks large enough to hold it," he said. "And look, it's lined with chain. That's smart; helps ground out arcane effects. And what's this?" he asked, holding the stained wrapping aloft. "It's a smothering cloth!" He swept his arms, flipping the cloth out. "That's sizeable, too," he added. He glanced sidelong at the Orb of Xoriat, sitting on the tabletop. "Wrap that in this, and place them in the chain-lined bag? That would certainly stifle its aura. No wonder we couldn't find it. Here, Teron, give a hand. Jeffers, you avert your eyes until we have it all wrapped up, understand?"

Teron took one end of the cloth, holding the corners out to keep it spread wide. Praxle wrangled the other two corners as best as he could with his smaller span. He clambered up onto the table and gently enveloped the Sphere with the end of the cloth. He held it in place as Teron walked around the table. He stepped over the cloth as Teron passed behind him, then the two of them ensured that the disturbing relic was wrapped thoroughly.

Finally the last of the cloth was set in place. Praxle took the two corners and tied them off against each other. "Good job,

Ter," he said. "You don't mind if I call you Ter, do you? Hand me that bag. There's a good man."

Teron picked up the bag and opened it, then swept it across and scooped the Sphere and its gold stand into it. But when he pulled the bag toward him, it didn't budge. "Hey," he said. He tugged again. And again, and the Sphere finally started moving slowly across the table. "This is . . . that's strange, very strange."

"You expect something with ties to Xoriat to act normally?" asked Praxle. He shook his head. "I have a lot to teach you, Teron." He paused to take a wand that lay on the floor. "Well, then, Jeffers," he snapped, "one would think that averting one's eyes would not preclude plundering the place. But no time now; let's go."

They left, Teron wrestling with the package all the way down the twisting passage to the outside.

❀ ❀ ❀ ◉ ❀ ❀ ❀

Blood draining down her leg, the Shadow Fox leaned against the wall. Ahead, she saw a group of her people, led by the elf Rezam, speaking vehemently with a trio of Thrane guards.

"Go!" she called. "Get out of there! They've got guards all over the place!"

But even as some of her people heard her and turned their heads, she saw Rezam pull a wand and unleash a flaming inferno. The wave engulfed the Thrane guards, as well as several Cyrans who happened to be in the way.

"Run!" she bellowed, but she turned and staggered off, forced to abandon her people before she fainted.

❀ ❀ ❀ ◉ ❀ ❀ ❀

Three simultaneous sighs of relief resounded through the opulent carriage when the lightning rail shuddered and started lumbering forward. The bag carrying the Orb sat in the center of the large, heavy dining table, and as the caravan started to accelerate, it stayed in place, slowly sliding toward one edge of the table and leaving long scratch marks in the polished wood. Jeffers moved to the end of the table to hold the bag in place while the caravan reached speed.

Slowly at first, then with increasing velocity, the rising spires of Flamekeep passed by the elegant windows, the flickering luminescence of the conductor stones reflecting off the building facades. Overhead, Dravago cast its cool lavender light upon their departure.

"We did it, Ter," said Praxle. "We recovered it. After all this time, I have the Orb of Xoriat back in my hands. It's finally back where it belongs."

"We haven't determined precisely where it's going, Praxle," Teron reminded him.

"I know," said Praxle. "But it's what, almost two days to Starilaskur? Until then, there's only one route for the lightning rail, unless you have a whim to head east from Vathirond."

"No," said Teron, "I have no desire to go to the Mournland."

"Well, then, then we have two relaxing days to talk things over and work out a solution. And once I understand this thing a little better, and I can explain it to you, I think we'll find a very good solution indeed."

Teron looked carefully at Praxle. He gauged his expression, then looked at the countryside passing by, then inspected the colorful map that was mounted in a frame on the wall. He decided he was fairly safe; the next major stop wasn't until noon. "I'm going to get some sleep," said Teron.

"You do that," answered Praxle, climbing into a comfortable chair beneath an everbright chandelier. "I'm going to read."

"Good night, master," said Jeffers.

Teron turned to leave. This particular luxury coach had private bedrooms at each end, and Teron chose the one at the front. He reached over to the lamp on the side table and adjusted it brighter, then closed the door behind him.

He stripped off his vest, then reached into the waistband at the rear of his trousers. He pulled out a few pages of folded paper. The last few pages of Thrane notes; the culmination of their research. He read them over, then again. Once he had them committed to memory, he spindled them and slid the roll into the oil lamp.

Within a minute, there was nothing left but ashes.

❦ ❦ ❦ ❦ ❦ ❦ ❦

Sometime during the night, Teron felt a massive weight settle upon him, crushing his brain, plugging his breath.

He saw the dragon. It turned to look at him, eyes afire with the flames of a thousand pyres.

It loomed closer, eclipsing the sun. "Teron," it said, its voice rolling like distant thunder.

Teron woke up screaming.

❦ ❦ ❦ ❦ ❦ ❦ ❦

Teron awakened slowly on the second morning of their trip. It felt odd to wake up in a large, comfortable bed with finely twilled sheets and a thick, downy comforter; they were a far cry from the cot and blanket that he'd had at the monastery. He was torn between a desire bordering on lust to enjoy this privilege while he could, and fear that such gross indulgence would undo his training and focus.

He rose, stretched, and ran through his morning exercise routine. In the midst of his chin-ups he heard a servant enter the car with their breakfast, but he finished all of his sets, each with an extra tenth tacked on to ensure that he wasn't going soft.

He exited his bedroom into the common area and saw Praxle reading through the Thrane notes. Black circles hung under his eyes, and a plate of food set on the table next to his chair lay unattended. Jeffers looked up from his letters, gazing at Teron with worried eyes.

Teron sat and broke his fast with the half-orc. As they ate, Praxle occasionally picked at the food next to him. "Has he slept at all?" asked Teron quietly.

"Not at all the first night, Teron," murmured Jeffers, keeping his head bowed to his plate. "Only a few times last night, and never for very long. Although I suspect he may have fallen asleep a few times with his eyes open. Sometimes it's hard to tell." He put down his fork and dabbed his face with his napkin to conceal his lips. "He's hardly eaten, and only gets up to use the privy. And even then he brings his reading with him."

"I know," said Teron.

"If you have any suggestions . . ." began Jeffers.

"I was about to say the same thing," replied Teron.

* * * * * * * *

After crossing the border into Breland and passing through Vathirond, the lightning rail shunned the line that ran through the dead lands of Cyre, and instead turned southwest toward Starilaskur. There the line branched: one went across the north side of the Dragon's Crown toward Breland and Aundair, the other led south along the Seawall Mountains to Zilargo.

Whether this particular caravan was branching south to Korranberg or continuing into Breland, Teron knew that the eventual confrontation with the gnome would come at Starilaskur. He knew Praxle would not let the Sphere pass so close to his home only to head back to Aundair. He debated the wisdom of postponing the confrontation, but at the moment things were peaceful, and he was concerned that an early debate could anger the increasingly unstable gnome. That, and he was curious why the sorcerer thought that learning about the Sphere would make a compromise easier for Teron.

The vast Brelish countryside rolled past throughout the morning and afternoon, occasional farms, rolling plains. Their course took them into a rainstorm that lashed the windows of the speeding caravan, but the trainer in the harness coach obstinately refused to slow down.

Shortly after lunch, Praxle finally stirred. "Right!" he said, negligently slapping the Thrane papers onto the end table beside him. The loose pages sprayed across the floor with the force, but Praxle paid them no heed. He stood and walked over to the bag that contained the Sphere. He gazed at the bag, his haunted eyes bulging above the dark circles that marred his cheeks.

"Now, Teron, allow me to show you what it is we have here," he said. He used a chair to climb up onto the large table where the leather bag sat, then walked around it, kicking off the candlesticks and other things. Then he undid the latches that closed the bag and pulled out the golden stand. He set it on the table. Then he reached in to pull out the swaddled bundle. He grunted and strained, but made no progress.

"Slow and steady pressure," said Teron. "That works best."

"What?" Praxle paused in his efforts and looked at Teron. Unnoticed beneath him, the Sphere slowly rose, responding at last to Praxle's efforts.

"Think of it as an angry mule," said Teron. "It goes where it wants to go. Guide it firmly, but with patience. Push too hard, and you'll just cause yourself more trouble."

"Oh," said Praxle. "It's a wife."

Jeffers snickered as Praxle ushered the Orb of Xoriat out of the bag and guided it to a more or less gentle landing in its golden cradle. He loosened the knot that held the smothering cloth tight, and began slowly unwrapping the artifact, a joyous smile gracing his face.

"I would have thought you'd be more impatient," said Teron.

"Some moments need to be savored," crooned Praxle. "Though the gods only know what awesome feats this creation was capable of before the druids drove Xoriat away from our plane, this is still a great moment." Then he whipped his head over to face his bondservant. "Avert your eyes, Jeffers," he snapped, then he returned to slowly undressing the relic. He had to raise the Orb a bit to get the cloth out from between it and the golden stand, but once it was raised, the unusual behavior of the Orb kept it hovering slightly off the stand with no further effort. Soon the last of the smothering cloth fell away, revealing the Orb in its unholy glory.

This was the first time that Teron had seen the Thrane Sphere not encased within a protective spell, and the image was disturbing. It seemed to be moving, either shifting its parts or crawling with thousands of microscopic ants.

Praxle ran his hands down his face, then clapped them together and rubbed them vigorously. He squinched up his eyes, shook his head vigorously, and heaved a deep sigh. "All right," he said, "this is going to be more difficult than I thought."

He looked up at Teron, then turned his eyes back to the Orb. "One thing you must decide, Ter, is where your loyalties lie," he said, as his fingers slowly manipulated the surface of the Black Globe. "See, I can use the Orb by manipulating the pieces on its surface, by organizing them into a pattern. The same concept is true for families, nations, worlds. Someone manipulates, arranges the pieces into a pattern that produces pleasing results. That's how a simple burglar works, arranging the tumblers of a lock to open a door. A general works by arranging the soldiers of the army, a king by adjusting the hearts of his people. Most of the inhabitants of the world exist to be manipulated for the benefit of others, even if it is to the detriment of those within the pattern. Me, I don't want to be manipulated. I want to determine my own fate. I want to be the hand that creates the pattern. Like this."

Teron stood, and saw that Praxle had arranged the shifting scarab-like plates of the Orb in such a manner that it looked like a black rose bloomed on one side.

"This Orb is an ancient relic, a door of sorts between here and the plane of Xoriat. Once, long ago, it allowed those in Xoriat to reach through to our plane and begin to rearrange the fabric of our world to suit their needs. That was the Daelkyr War. The Gatekeepers, they sealed the passages between here and Xoriat, but this doorway remains. While we can no longer reach into Xoriat, within this brilliant piece of work lies an antechamber to an alien place. And although the pittance left of Xoriat within this relic pales compared to its former power, it still has enough with in it to rearrange the pattern of life around your monastery. It has also allowed those here to reach through into the Realm of Madness, where, if they are careless like that Cyran mage we saw in Daskaran Ferry, they find themselves being worked into the inscrutable patterns of insanity."

Praxle leaned forward to the Orb, and Teron noticed that the rose that bloomed on its surface was now shifting of its own accord. "But doors open both ways, if you know how to work them. There are few indeed who could do what we're about to do," said Praxle. He leaned forward, drawing his face close to the growing bloom. It almost looked like the Orb was puckering to give Praxle a tainted kiss.

"What are we about to do, Praxle?" asked Teron suspiciously.

An orange vapor curled away from the Orb's lips, like the smoke from a smoldering log. Praxle leaned close and inhaled deeply, using his hands to waft even more up to his face. The writhing orange mist seemed to struggle against him but got drawn into his nose and mouth. He inhaled, swallowed, and smacked his lips. "Make patterns for ourselves," he said, "and not at the behest of the weavers."

The rose closed, and Praxle sat back on his heels. The dark circles beneath his eyes had faded, and his eyes were bright and alert. "You see, those who used the Orb at your monastery, they did so at the behest of others. They allowed themselves to become part of the pattern. That is why they suffered as they did and ended up devoured by madness. Their masters back at the Congress, they pulled the strings, manipulated events. Fortunately for us, they did not reap the benefits."

Teron shook his head. "I don't understand, Praxle," he said.

Praxle's hands flew over the surface of the Orb, and the rose started to bloom again. "It's all about patterns, Ter," he said. "That's how you learn martial arts, isn't it? You perform moves in patterns. Your patterns start out simple, and as you get more experienced, those patterns grow. Your body learns those patterns, and adapts itself to them." He inhaled deeply again, drawing another lungful of orange mist. Again he swallowed, smacked his lips. "Ah, the taste of success," he said to himself. He looked at Teron again, and the black bags beneath his eyes were utterly gone. "But what happens when the pattern becomes too complex?"

"I don't know."

"It drives you mad."

"You're not making sense," said Teron.

Praxle cackled. "Of course not! That is the point! Those who understand greater patterns seem mad to those beneath them, because they can unravel concepts that appear nonsensical to the uneducated mind!"

Even as he spoke, his hands flew about the surface of the Black Globe and opened the rose a third time. He breathed deeply, and this time the orange mist was sucked away without resistance. He moaned pleasurably as the rose closed itself.

"Teron," he said solemnly, "I have much to teach you now." He extended one hand. "You have shown yourself to be disciplined, focused, and clever. You have the blood of the dragon in your veins. You are worthy to be my protégé, and I can help you. You will walk with me as we ascend to power you haven't dreamed of!"

Teron stepped forward, completely unsure of where this was going but positive that either a confrontation or a very strange consensus was approaching.

"It all makes perfect sense now," said Praxle. "The Last War was not chaos. It was a pattern. Losing the Orb of Xoriat was not a tragedy. It was a necessary step in a convoluted sequence of events. Everything has unfolded according to a pattern that I am only now beginning to grasp. It has been a puzzle laid before us, Teron, a conundrum that we managed to unravel, a maze that we were able to solve from within. This, this beautiful blossom, it's like a puzzle box, and now that we have deduced our way out of the puzzle box that holds us prisoner, only now can we unlock this small puzzle box in front of us and escape."

His hands worked quickly on the side of the Sphere facing Teron. He didn't even look as he worked, but stared straight at the monk. Teron watched as the gnome's darting fingers pushed and slid, herding the beetled pieces and corralling them to bring forth the blooming rose again.

"Breathe, Teron," said Praxle. "Breathe and eat."

Teron looked down at the orange mist that crawled across the surface of the Sphere like an unearthed worm. "What will it do?" he asked.

Praxle held his palms up. Without warning, fire sprang forth from his right palm, while a fragile castle of frost formed in his left. "It will magnify you," he said. "It will feed the dragon's blood. Breathe, and we shall explore the Orb of Xoriat together."

"But . . ."

"But what? Will you crawl back to the monastery and let Prelate Quardov order your days while he lets your monastery rot? Will you adhere to the strictures given you by those long dead, remain what they made you while the world around you changes?"

The Quiet Touch, thought Teron. *None are left, save me, and they don't know what to do with me any more.* Curiosity nibbled at his brain, and he looked with renewed admiration at the display of Praxle's increased magical abilities. *It's my job to recover the Sphere,* he thought. *Shouldn't I know what it can do?*

He leaned forward, pursing his lips to suck in the orange mist that hugged the surface of the Sphere. It resisted being drawn in, but with a few deep breaths, he managed to inhale it. He felt it move within him, and he swallowed reflexively. He felt something slide down his throat, and a gritty sensation filled his mouth. He had a distinct sensation that a great vaporous snake was searching his innards for a way to freedom. He held his breath and salivated, trying to rinse his mouth clean with spit. Gingerly he started letting his breath out, but then again strange sensations moved within him. He coughed, then sniffed sharply to fight against a painful feeling that was growing at the rear of his sinuses.

Then everything changed. The awkward, unnatural feelings faded, as did the movements within. There was a feeling within his bones, a warm feeling that grew. For some reason he thought of watching tea infuse a bowl of hot water. He heard an indistinct screech, a wail ringing in his ears, but at the same time he felt his blood quicken within him, permeating his soul and enhancing his life force. His fists clenched instinctively as a wave of euphoria washed over him. His injured eyebrow tingled. He raised a hand to it, and found that the swelling had all but vanished. Then he looked at his hand, and saw that the red burn marks had faded considerably.

He looked at Praxle, his joints trembling slightly. Praxle swallowed and smacked his lips, a look of enjoyment and camaraderie on his face. "Doesn't that feel . . . good?" he asked, his hands opening the Orb again. He drew in another lungful of the orange mist, eyes closed. "I can feel my power growing. I can feel my blood pumping within me. I can feel the flow of the world, feel it moving into its pattern." He laughed quietly. "This must be what the dragons mean when they speak of the Prophecy." His eyes still closed, he proffered the Sphere, bloom opening, to Teron.

Teron drew in the orange mist, and he felt the supernatural effects once more, the shrieking noise, the crawling within, the infusion of power. He drew upon his training in meditation to look within himself, and found that he could better sense the energy that he used to fuel his magical strikes. He looked down at his hands and shaped them into claws. Flexing his muscles, he saw his palms turn bright white for just a moment as the energy within pressed to the surface and then retreated back within him. Only a slight nausea accompanied the evocation.

He looked up at Praxle. "What's happening?" he asked.

"I've opened the door in the other direction," said Praxle. He opened his eyes again, and Teron saw that his pupils had become somewhat elliptical, his eyes glassier. "I'm using the Orb of Xoriat to awaken the latent power of our dragon's blood. A while back, Ter, you said that pain is the mortar of our lives. That's true; I assume you learned that at the monastery. But your teachers fell just short of the mark. Pain is indeed the mortar of your life, but—here's the trick—it *doesn't have to be your pain!*

"That's the beauty of this device; it understands. The door is very small now; the Thranes apparently did not figure out how to completely open the Sphere. If only they had, I could already have drained every last one from within the Sphere."

"Every last one . . . of what?" asked Teron, fearing the answer.

Praxle gave him an incredulous look. "Why, souls, of course."

CHAPTER 23

Souls?" blurted Teron.

Praxle laughed. "Of course. What the Six else did you think was trapped in here, anyway? The druids sealed any ability to cross back and forth, so the souls in there are trapped on the threshold of madness, fragments of a greater pattern."

Teron pressed his palms together and raised them to his nose, stilling himself. There, in the black voids between his thoughts, he could hear faint screams of hysteria and gibbering words of madness.

"Don't look so surprised, Ter," said Praxle. "What else do you think would feed the dragon's blood within you? Why do you think everything has been ordered so that we could escape this prison puzzle box that holds us? This is our chance, our chance to seize the world by the throat, to force our pattern upon these souls within this ball and by ordering them within us, to ascend to greater power. The door has opened for us to become gods, ascending on the stairs of those who died for our benefit." He giggled and plugged one ear. "I think I can hear that Cyran mage."

For a brief moment, Teron wanted it. He wanted the power, he wanted the control, he wanted to stand up to the dragon, he wanted the chance to order the world to suit him instead of being a decaying relic of a dead war. And he knew how; the last few pages of the Thrane notes had spoken of opening the Sphere fully. Now that Praxle's words had given those cryptic notes a context, he understood that the Thranes wrote both of how to gather, as well as how to consume. He could harvest . . .

But then he thought of Master Keiftal, and of all those the old master had once called friends, now trapped within the extradimensional torment of the Sphere of Xoriat. Those who'd shared his trials, his training, those who'd called the monastery their home. And he knew that no matter how horrid their current state, he could not abide their essence feeding the megalomania of this egocentric gnome, or anyone else who would be a god.

Praxle sniffed deeply, devouring another tormented consciousness. His fingers tried to stop the petals of the black rose from closing, but the scarab plates squirmed in his grasp. "This is just so slow," he grumbled.

"That's because I burned about eight pages of notes," said Teron.

"You what?" shrieked Praxle. "How could you—"

"I blocked your path, Praxle," he said, "and I will not walk it."

"The dragon calls us, dares us to challenge it, and you're turning your back?" Praxle snorted derisively. "You're no warrior, monk. You're a coward. You don't deserve the dragon's blood."

"I cannot join you, Praxle, nor can I allow you to continue this," said Teron.

"Fine," said Praxle. He rotated the Sphere and began manipulating its pieces in a different manner. "I'll consume your soul, too. That should save me a little time."

Teron jumped up into the air and kicked at the table with all his force. The heavy table slid across the carpet. Though it did not move as far as Teron hoped, it was enough to throw Praxle off balance and slide him away from the Sphere, which remained in place.

Teron moved in the opposite direction and landed on his side by the wall of the carriage. He jumped back to his feet and saw Praxle crawling rapidly back to the Sphere, a fierce hatred in his newly reptilian eyes. Behind him, Jeffers reached out, grabbed the gnome's ankles, and pulled him away. Surprise and accusation filled Praxle's eyes as he stared malevolently at Teron, then the gnome grinned. Electrical bolts flared all about his body, wreathing him as they did the lightning rail's harness coach. Jeffers yelled in pain and released Praxle's ankles, and the sorcerer crawled up to the Sphere.

Teron snapped his arm like a whip, forcing energy to his fist. It spat out of his palm, but he closed his iron fist around it before it could escape. He leapt forward, windmilling his arm down to slam on the tabletop. He struck the table squarely on the centerline, and the arcane concussion split the massive table in half. It fell, taking Praxle with it. The Sphere remained in place, hovering just three feet off the floor.

With a primal roar, Praxle fired a bolt of raw arcane power at Teron. The monk dived to the side, and the blast took him across the back, charring his vest and blistering his skin. Teron rolled through the dive and ended up at one end of the sundered table. Praxle stood as well, feet awkwardly straddling the uneven table halves. With an immense surge, Teron grabbed the underside of the end of the table, where the cross bracing kept the legs from splaying, and heaved. He managed to lever the sundered end of the table a few inches off the ground, putting Praxle off balance again. The gnome fell, and Teron released his grip. The heavy table fell back to the floor, trapping Praxle's left hand beneath it and thrusting shards of shattered wood through the sorcerer's wrist. Praxle cried out in anger and pain.

With a growl of determination, Praxle placed his hand on the tabletop just above his mangled wrist. An explosion shattered the table, sending wooden shrapnel through the interior of the carriage. Teron felt several pieces cut into his skin as they flew past. Praxle rolled away from the table and around to the far side from Teron.

The monk forced his energy to his hands, but instead of catching the power in his fist as before, he clapped his hands together. He spun his palms until his fingers pointed in opposite directions, and then he ran his hands up to his elbows, simultaneously encasing each of his forearms in a sheath of raw energy.

Praxle stood, his injured left hand held tightly to his breast. He brought his right hand across his chest and back, then flung it backhand at the monk. A wad of fire snapped free from his fingers and flew at Teron. Praxle snapped his hand twice more, following the missile closely with a wad of pure acid and one of supercooled water. Teron blocked the fire bolt with his arm, extinguishing it. A rising block at the acid missile deflected it to the roof of the carriage, and it spattered about, eating away at the wooden paneling.

The bolts had come too fast, and Teron was barely able to duck out of the way of the third, which flew past his shoulder and into one of the large picture windows in the carriage, shattering it. Immediately noise and wind filled the carriage, loose Thrane notes flying about in the cacophony.

Praxle ducked around the corner of the table and out of sight. Teron knew his only advantage was to press the attack, using his physical training to prevent the gnome from employing his magical training, so he charged around the end of the table, arms raised defensively.

There was no one there.

Invisible! Teron jumped straight up, twisting in midair to remove his body from the target zone. As he rotated in the air, he saw a blast of flame gush forth from beneath the table, roasting the area where he'd stood a breath before. He slid down the sloped tabletop and landed on Jeffers, who was crawling toward the Sphere, one hand reaching out for the relic.

"No!" yelled Teron. He kicked Jeffers in the side of the head to stun him then rolled off the table and grabbed the smothering cloth. He flipped the cloth once to spread it out, just as Praxle stuck his hand out from beneath the table's end and shot a blast of lightning at him. The attack caught the cloth squarely. The cloth absorbed much of the bolt's magic, but enough electrical power remained to leave a large smoking char mark on it.

Teron flipped the smoldering sheet over the Sphere, concealing it from casual sight. Then he saw Praxle peek out from behind his cover to check on the effects of the lightning. The gnome ducked back. Quick as a cat, Teron charged the empty space beneath the end of the table, intent on killing the gnome at close quarters.

As he dived through the gap between the broken tabletop and the floor, Teron saw Praxle readying a wand. He struck with his elbow at Praxle's throat, but his arm passed through the illusion and glanced off the underside of the table.

He looked up and saw the gnome across the room, cocking his fist for a punch. Praxle punched at the air, and Teron had just enough time to raise his arms defensively before he got struck by a massive shockwave. He tumbled backward and slammed painfully into the table leg at the far end.

Teron rose to his feet and charged Praxle. The gnome still held his left arm protectively but wove a spell rapidly with his right. Teron jumped high into the air and tucked into a forward flip as Praxle extended his arm and launched a flight of baleful red spheres.

As he came down, Teron's excellent training allowed him to grab Praxle's extended arm with one hand. He turned his wrist around to lock Praxle's joints, then met the gnome's evil gaze. With his other hand he broke the gnome's index finger, then . . .

"Look out!" called Jeffers.

A flight of violent red spheres slammed into Teron's back, sending blasts of malevolent energy shuddering through his body and throwing him to the floor. He managed to break Praxle's middle finger before the gnome yanked his hand free.

Teron fought off the pain and got back up to his knees. He raised one hand to guard while the other steadied him against the wall. Praxle had run back toward where the Sphere of Xoriat hung in the air, its charred shroud fluttering in the winds from the shattered window. He studied his injured hands, one crushed and bloody, the other with broken fingers hanging awkwardly. "Think I'm finished, do you?" he said, glowering at Teron.

Grimacing in pain, Teron stood.

The gnome turned and drew his dagger with the remaining good fingers on his right hand. He aimed the butt end at Teron, and lightning shot out, turning Teron's whole world white.

Pain wracked the Aundairian's body, overwhelming his training and discipline. He screamed as the energy coursed up and down his body, dragging jagged razors along his nerves.

The wave of anguish passed. Teron forced his brain to stay awake, straining against the massive weight that threatened to press him into unconsciousness. He slowly rolled back to his hands and knees, mouth hanging open, head aching like it was fit to burst. His chest trembled so hard that he could barely draw breath.

He saw Praxle step closer, dagger held ready to fire another blast of energy and send Teron to the afterlife. Teron slowly pulled one foot underneath him, intent on dying on his feet.

Jeffers intervened. "A moment, master," he said, approaching Praxle with his hands out. "Think of what you're contemplating. If you slay him with that, you'll forfeit his soul, will you not? Would you not prefer to draw him into the Orb of Xoriat, to take full advantage of the situation, master?"

A flash of sanity crossed Praxle's eyes. "Of course, thank you, Jeffers," he said, and turned to look at the Sphere hanging in the air. "Well, then. Fetch that for me."

In the blink of an eye, Jeffers snapped his hands together, striking Praxle's outstretched right hand. The magical dagger flew from his grasp and imbedded itself in the wall. Then the half-orc grabbed the gnome's small body in his burly arms and, with a yell, charged across the carriage.

Praxle shrieked in terror. He clamped his injured hands on each side of the half-orc's head, gouging his eyes and pumping raw arcane energy into Jeffers' skull. Jeffers roared, grappling the gnome tightly and squeezing his torso in a bear hug. Jeffers slammed into the wall of the carriage, bouncing blindly.

Teron realized that Jeffers was searching for the shattered window, but blinded and wounded, he might not last long enough to find it. Drawing on the very last of his energy, Teron stumbled across the ruined carriage. He grabbed Jeffers by the tunic and used his weight to swing the two of them around. Jeffers did not resist, and Teron pulled them to the open window. Jeffers' knees slammed into the wall, and momentum carried master and servant out the window into the stormy night. A bolt of lightning and a blast of wind punctuated the evening.

Teron sagged against the wall.

Across the way, the Sphere's shroud billowed in the wind, making it look like it was dancing.

❂ ❂ ❂ ❂ ❂ ❂ ❂

Teron awakened to the sensation of the lightning rail slowing as it neared Starilaskur. The Sphere had moved to the opposite side of the carriage and lay on the floor. It took him a minute to figure out that the weight of the smothering cloth had dragged the Sphere slowly down, while the lightning rail's curving course had probably moved it from side to side several times.

Teron rose slowly, his entire body aching. He gathered up the Sphere and its cloth, and wrapped the relic up securely before placing it back in the leather bag. He gathered up what few pages of the Thrane notes remained in the cabin and burned them. Then he searched the carriage for anything of value, but since they'd abandoned what luggage they'd had when the Cyrans stormed their room in Flamekeep, he found nothing of note.

Other than the dagger.

Pulling it from the wall, he thought of Jeffers and his sudden, if sensible, change of loyalty. He wondered what chance the half-orc had of surviving the fall and the crazed gnome. He looked at the map on the wall and decided that the chance was nil. Falling from the lightning rail, an untrained person like Jeffers would certainly suffer injury, and in this portion of Breland hospitalers were few and far between. He might bleed to death, he might get savaged by wolves, but the chances of him making it to a town were slim at best.

Teron mused that the same applied to Praxle, as well, or at least so he hoped. It was possible that the gnome had been shielded from the impact by Jeffers' larger body, or that Praxle cast a spell at the last second to save himself. And if that were the case, the gnome would stop at nothing to recover the Orb of Xoriat. How long would it take him to find his way back to the monastery?

Teron scrutinized the map. He found the scale printed in one corner and, using a joint of his finger to mark off distances, did his best to estimate. He knuckled his way from Starilaskur to Vathirond: roughly 300 miles. He then did a rough estimate of how much time had passed before their fight, coming up with a guess that about two-thirds of that leg of the trip had passed. That left roughly one hundred miles. If Praxle survived the fall in good shape and went west instead of east, he'd reach Starilaskur in five to ten days, depending on how hard he could march.

Teron cleared the halves of the heavy table from the center of the carriage and began to stretch on the floor.

Five to ten days, he thought. Assuming he still lives, that's all the lead I have. But what shall I do with that time? Teron considered his options, trying to cover all possibilities.

I could run. But if I run, it's only a matter of time before Praxle or one of his associates finds me; the gnomes have eyes and ears everywhere. And they will corner me in a place of their choosing, with forces of their choosing, and they shall have the Sphere.

I could fight. I might win and kill Praxle, but even if I do, it's entirely probable that another gnome would pick up the trail, and then I'm back to the original choices. And if I lose the fight . . .

But at least, if I fight, I can choose the battlefield, position myself to my best advantage. Which would be at the monastery; that's where my knowledge is best and where I have the greatest number of trustworthy allies. The ground is broken and the monastery shattered so it affords a great number of places for ambuscades and traps.

What other choices are there? I suppose I could abrogate my responsibility, return the Sphere to Prelate Quardov, and leave it to him to determine its disposition. Teron paused in his stretching to snicker.

If only there were a way to destroy it, he thought. Remove it forever from the reach of Praxle, and others like him.

Once more he paused in his stretching. *Dol Arrah,* he prayed, *let the gnome be dead. Let what I do here be wasted time and effort. Let the Sphere never again fall into his hands, or into the hands of anyone like him.*

Any prayer I've raised that wished for my own death, he added, *let this prayer supercede it.*

❂ ❂ ❂ ❂ ❂ ❂ ❂

Shortly before sundown, the lightning rail pulled into Starilaskur. As it slowed, Teron took his satchel, Praxle's dagger, some leftover food, and the bag containing the Sphere and jumped out of the sundered window. The abnormal inertia of the Sphere yielded him a soft landing.

He glided into the drizzle, leaving the ruined carriage behind, empty of people, empty of answers.

Hoping to avoid detection, he passed the night resting in the shadows, for the most part quietly. A footpad tried to take advantage of a lone, unarmed man sitting in an alley, and instead received a lesson in how short life could be.

Well after sunrise, Teron located someone to buy the enchanted dagger and bought himself a hot bath, two days' worth of food, and passage on the lightning rail to Ghalt. He opted for a private cabin; he intended to stay awake for the entire trip back to the monastery. He had no intention of leaving the Sphere of Xoriat unguarded even for a moment; at best he would allow himself to fall into a light meditative trance from which he could easily awaken.

The days passed slowly for Teron, trapped within a cell consisting of a bunk and a writing table. He tried to spend time in meditation, but every time he did, he heard the faint echoes of screams in the back of his mind, lingering remnants of those whose souls he had unwittingly devoured. Instead, he spent long hours staring out the window of his cabin, watching the world pass by and wondering what had become of Flotsam. Every so often Kelcie's eyes would haunt his thoughts, but he drove her memory away by reliving her betrayal.

The rail cut through the more fertile portion of Breland, then turned north toward Aundair, skirting Lake Brey. Then at last it crossed into Aundair, and Teron dared breathe a sigh of relief.

The sky was dark as Teron debarked the lightning rail. He hitched the leather bag and its recalcitrant occupant under his arm, and began the long walk back to the Monastery of Pastoral Solitude. Part of his mind was aware that the weather was fine, with cool air and a clear sky, but the weight under his arm did not allow him to enjoy it.

He walked through the night and into the next day. He arrived at the monastery well after dark, thankful that the darkness had saved his eyes from having to see the vile red tinge of the Crying Fields. With a weary, satisfied sigh, he crossed the threshold of the Gallery and started to meander down to his small room.

Just as Teron passed the door to Keiftal's room, the aging master burst out, wild-eyed and frantic.

"What is it, my boy?" he yelled, the loudness distorting his nasal tone. "What's happening?"

Exhausted and startled, Teron whipped around, expecting to see a wave of gnomes pursuing him. "What? Where?" he asked.

Keiftal grabbed Teron's shoulders and spun him around face to face. "What's happening? Where's that coming from?"

"Where's what coming from?" asked Teron, edgy and confused.

"The screaming!" said Keiftal urgently. "I hear screaming, hundreds of voices, thousands . . ."

Teron's brow furrowed, and one hand flew to the black leather bag. He pulled himself out of Keiftal's grip and took a step back from the aging master. "I don't hear anything," he said warily.

Keiftal's eye dropped to the bag held protectively beneath Teron's arm, and his eyes went wide. "You have it?" he gasped, his eyes bugging out. He began to tremble. "The screaming, they're all begging . . ."

"What's going on, master?" asked Teron.

Keiftal stopped his rambling. "You can't hear them?"

"Hear who? Hear what?"

Keiftal put his hands to his ears. "The cries of the monks, the Thranes, the cries of people being devoured by madness . . ."

Teron pushed the bag down to the floor, and took his master's hand and led him away, down the hall. "I don't hear any screaming, master," he said, keeping one eye on the unattended bag. He ushered Keiftal around a corner, out of sight of the leather satchel. "Well, not much screaming, anyway."

The elder monk wagged his head. "I never thought that my prayer would be such a curse," he said.

"What do you mean, master?" asked Teron. "I don't understand you."

"My son," said Keiftal with a loud, trembling, brassy voice, "I can hear the screams of those devoured by that foul device all those years ago. I can hear them clear as a bell. For years I have prayed to Dol Arrah to let me hear something, anything, and now this . . ."

"What?"

"I've been completely deaf since the day the Thranes first opened the Sphere. The last thing I ever heard was the cries of the armies as the Great Maw drew them in. I haven't heard a single sound since. Not the crows as they ate the dead, not the prayers of my brothers and sisters, nothing. Not until just now. I can still hear their final screams.

"My boy, that thing is evil. We have hidden it for years, but now it has been found." He poked Teron in the chest and said, "We trained you to destroy. I tell you now, you must destroy that thing."

"But how?"

"Find a way. For the sake of the world, find a way."

◉ ◉ ◉ ◉ ◉ ◉ ◉

Under Keiftal's direction, a rotating guard was set up to watch over the Orb of Xoriat. When he was not standing guard, Teron thought on Praxle's words. Patterns. Patterns too complex for the human mind.

Why was it that the Crying Fields existed the way they did? Why did the ghosts of those dead manifest in the Crying Fields when the moon for which the month was named waxed full? The monks of the monastery had debated those questions for many years.

Some just dismissed the phenomenon as the result of magic, but Teron had always felt that that argument had been flippant at best. It was not understandable, therefore it was magic, because magic was incomprehensible. Yet Praxle's words had implied that even magic operated by patterns, and the fact that people across Khorvaire could cast spells indicated that patterns of magic could be understood and applied.

Other believed the occurrences were part of a rhythmic cycle that was very complex. A pattern of days and hours between manifestations that defied formulae; something predictable if not comprehensible. Yet the chance of such an equation randomly matching the cycle of moons and the calendar was infinitesimal.

Then it struck Teron: such answers looked on the alignment of the moons as a coincidence, or a marker. But what if the moons were themselves the cause? What if the manifestation in the Crying Fields occurred because of the moons, when the moons and the sun and Eberron itself all aligned into a pattern too large to be seen from the surface of the world? Was this a part of the prophecy that the dragons spoke of?

Then he started seeing other patterns, how his road had taken him on a large circle across Khorvaire. How he began pursing Praxle, then joined with him, then split from him, only to have Praxle—and he must assume the gnome was alive—pursuing him. How he easily outfought Jeffers at their first meeting to get to Praxle, then saved his life from the fire elemental, then Jeffers saved Teron's life from a lightning bolt, then Jeffers outfought Teron at the end to take Praxle away.

"I don't believe it," Teron muttered. "I'm starting to think like the damnable gnome." He snorted. "Maybe that Sphere is affecting me more than I thought."

But still, every night he stepped outside to watch the moons, Nymm, Therendor, Eyre and Aryth raced closer and closer to the full.

And he wondered where the pattern would end.

CHAPTER 24

Praxle seethed with anger. Not at his double-crossing bodyguard—that feckless animal lay rotting in a Brelish field—but at the one who'd turned his back on the dragon and wrenched Praxle's apotheosis from his hands.

He thought back on Jeffers' betrayal, how he'd slapped the dagger from his hands, how he'd used his overlarge body to pick up Praxle, and how, somehow, he had found the window and hurled them both out. In that moment of crisis, Praxle had proved his worth to ascend by drawing upon the power of the elements, lightning to obliterate the skull of his disloyal servant, and wind to save himself from striking the ground too hard. Conversely, Jeffers had proved with his action that he was indeed an insect, a worthless drone sacrificing itself for the benefit of the pathetic hive of so-called sentients, by striking at a pending god. Praxle hated being surrounded by those who couldn't work magic. There were so many of them, crawling everywhere . . .

But that monk. He had the potential. The dragons had blessed him with their blood. The dragons had called to him in his dreams. His mind had accepted the discipline, and his soul could sense the truth, but in the end he'd proved his heart to be merely mortal, recoiling in fear from the greatest test ever given to mortals. He'd refused to rise to the challenge of overcoming his own death.

Either that monk was apprehensive of the effort that it would require, or he was squeamish at the need to devour the souls of the underlings. It didn't matter. He had scorned the dragons. He had thwarted the new ascendant gnome. And he and his foul partner had done so by taking advantage of their larger size. Such a grotesque, fleshly advantage; Praxle was humiliated to have been undone in that manner. Such blundering size should be inefficient.

"It matters not," spat Praxle out loud. "I am more powerful!"

He stood on a hill, looking over the rolling red fields. In the distance, he saw the shards of the monastery defiantly reaching for the sky.

Soon, he thought, they will reach to me.

* * * ⊙ * * *

Teron stood outside and watched the fires of the setting sun stain the sky red. The color blended the horizon almost to nonexistence. The ring was faintly visible overhead. To the east, orange Aryth was at the full, its last sliver just being devoured by Eyre's silver disk. The faintest arc of Therendor rose beneath them in turn, eclipsing a portion of Eyre's face.

Teron watched as the sun fully set. Then he turned to the other direction, and for a long while he watched the moons in their gentle race across the sky. Aryth was devoured by Eyre's larger size, while Therendor's clean, white shape slowly overtook Eyre. At last Nymm also rose, hiding itself behind its larger kin.

He had planned for this night a long time, ever since the end of the Last War. If things worked out as he expected, he would give himself the ultimate test of his ability, proving to himself whether he was still worthy to exist. If he failed, he would die, and quite possibly never be seen on Eberron again. If he lived . . . well, he didn't expect to, but he'd deal with that when it came.

Odd, he thought, that Therendor, the moon of the month, should be called the Healer's Moon. And Eyre is the Anvil. There must be a message there.

Then he hesitated. If he should die, who would stand between the gnomes and the Orb of Xoriat? He looked back at the monastery, now starting to be lit from within. Would he trust anyone there with such a duty? Should he? Master Keiftal, of course, but how much longer would the old monk stay alive? And none of the other brothers had undergone the same intense training as the Quiet Touch had.

Then it struck him: He didn't have to abandon his position as the keeper of the Sphere.

He turned back to the monastery.

❃ ❃ ❃ ❃ ❃ ❃ ❃

"Praxle d'Sivis!" Master Keiftal, surprised in the middle of lighting candles in his room, all but dropped his taper. Wax dribbled unattended on the floor.

"Yes, I am back," said the gnome, menacing in presence despite his small size, "and I've come to get what I originally came for: the Thrane Sphere, the Orb of Xoriat." He walked right up to the speechless Keiftal and glared up at the old man. "Where is it?" he bellowed.

"I—I don't—don't know," stammered Keiftal, his gaze darting about.

Praxle reached up, grabbed the elder monk's scraggly beard, and yanked hard. "Don't lie to me!"

Thus affronted, Keiftal's courage rose to surpass Praxle's presence. His eyes hardened from surprised and fearful to solemn and determined. Praxle saw it and started to react, but Keiftal was quicker. He jerked his head up to pull the sorcerer's arm higher, stretching his body. Then he kneed Praxle as hard as he could, striking the gnome in the midriff.

Praxle stumbled back, snarling as he fell to the floor. Angrily he slammed his glowing fist into the floor of the monastery, and the paving stones exploded beneath Keiftal's feet, heaving him upwards in a geyser of masonry. Battered and thrown off balance, Keiftal fell to the floor. Sharp stone shards and heavy slabs up to a foot wide fell all about, some striking his frail body.

Keiftal started to rise, causing stones to clatter to the ground, but Praxle was faster. He grabbed the old monk's ankle with one hand, uttering words of power. Electrical charges raced through Keiftal's body, and the old man screamed.

"You're—you're too loud," he panted. "Help—will come."

"Really?" responded Praxle. "I think not." He turned to the doorway, left open to the hallway. Keiftal followed his gaze, and saw three young monks run right past the open door and begin pounding on the wall beside it. "Illusions are the first step in creation," he explained. "They see a closed door where the wall is, and a bare wall where the door is. Such a simple thing to deceive those without the dragon's eye."

Bruised, bloody, and trembling from the electrical shock, Keiftal turned his gaze back to the gnome, and fear returned to his countenance.

Praxle grabbed the old man's forehead and chanted his words again, sending another jolt of electrical power through the old man's body. "Now tell me, old man," he growled, "where is the Orb?"

"You're too late," Keiftal gasped. "Teron—he—he took it." He chuckled weakly.

Praxle grabbed Keiftal's throat, his hand tingling with unspent power. He pressed his face nose to nose with the old monk. "Where did he take it?" he hissed.

Keiftal reflexively glanced in the direction of the Crying Fields.

Praxle smiled beatifically. "Thank you," he said, standing. "I allow you to live." He whirled his hand above his head, making two full circles. He put his hands in his pockets and walked to the unattended open doorway, whistling softly to himself. And as he passed through the doorway, he vanished.

The monks continued to pound on the illusory door, calling Keiftal's name.

The spirits of the past writhed into being all around Teron as he walked the unnatural grass of the Crying Fields. Overhead, Therendor and Eyre shone brightly. The Healer's Moon, full and potent, slowly devoured the Anvil as they moved slowly toward conjunction. According to the astronomers, they would move into alignment at midnight, just as the day changed.

Just as the month changed. For an instant, the month's moon would be full in two months at the same time. It was the first time that had happened since the end of the Last War. He'd planned for this evening for two years, to test himself. And suddenly his planning had a second purpose. Teron wondered if this was that pattern that he and Praxle had been drawn to.

Of course, he thought, it's vain to think that *I* am being drawn to anything. More likely the Sovereign Host, or the Dragon Eberron itself was drawing the Sphere to this time and place, looking to remove it from this world by trapping it in its own corrupted pattern. I'm no more than a piece of the puzzle to make it happen.

Then he remembered Keiftal's words from seemingly so long ago: "You can accomplish things that can no longer be done any other way."

Midnight drew nigh, and the phantoms became more real. He knew from experience that the ghosts of those who fought and died here all lingered about the area, but tonight they took on the most substantial form he had ever seen, manifesting with a clarity he didn't expect. Heretofore, the apparitions had been ghostly, wispy, hideous caricatures of soldiers of all races. But tonight, they seemed like true ghosts.

Above, lit by a phosphorescent campfire, he saw the banner of Aundair, a resplendent dragonhawk on a blue field. A military camp resolved into being all around him, jumbled by the translucence of the spirits.

Repetitive experience over the last two years made it difficult for Teron not to attack the apparitions as they formed, but he restrained himself.

An Aundairian guard leveled a spear at him. "Halt! Who are you?" he demanded.

"I'm from the monastery," he answered.

"The monastery was destroyed last year," retorted the guard. "I heard there were no survivors."

"Destroyed?" echoed Teron, feigning surprise. "How?" The guard looked suspicious, so Teron held up his hands consolingly. "I was on a mission deep in the Reaches," he lied. He patted his hand on the black leather bag. "I was supposed to recover this, and I just got back. Here, here's my papers," he added. He showed his papers to the guard but put them away quickly before the guard saw the date written by the issuing official.

The soldier relaxed somewhat. "All right, move along."

"What happened to the monastery?" Teron asked.

The soldier leaned on his spear and shuddered. "We'd been camped just over there, about ten miles or so, waiting for the Thranes to move. Then . . . I don't know what it was, but one morning we heard this terrible row come over the plains, and this vast chill shadowed the air. Our scouts came in and told us not to go to the monastery. Now here we are anyways, and I wish we'd never come. This place just felt wrong, understand? There's this—"

A horn sounded in the night, and soldiers raised the rallying cry. "Thranes!" yelled the guard. "Sneak attack!" He turned and charged off into the night.

Teron continued moving toward what he believed to be the center of the Crying Fields. The battle spilled out near him, Aundairian soldiers engaging Thranes in a ragged, chaotic melee. One Thrane eviscerated his foe and charged Teron, waving a scimitar. Teron tried to dodge, but the Sphere he carried resisted the sudden movement, and the bag's straps held him in place. The Thrane swung his scimitar down to where he expected Teron to move, and the ghostly blade traced only a long, thin slice in Teron's arm.

Teron kicked out quickly, but his foot passed harmlessly through the ghostly form. The Thrane turned for another attack, and Teron quickly extricated himself from the bag's straps. The soldier swung overhand, intending to split Teron like a fish. The monk ducked and rolled beneath the hanging leather bag. As he rolled, he heard a loud clang as the Thrane's scimitar struck the Sphere and shattered. Teron rolled cleanly through the Thrane's legs and to his feet. He turned to strike the Thrane, but the soldier, seeing his weapon gone and a monk ready to strike, turned and fled.

Teron looked at the bleeding cut on his arm. He had never been wounded so . . . so physically before. Above, the last wisp of Eyre slipped behind Therendor's shield. They were not quite yet in conjunction, so he knew the dangers would only grow. And while he could strike back by focusing his magic, he knew he did not have the ability to fight all the way to his destination.

He grabbed the Sphere and moved on to where he believed the center of the Crying Fields to be, trying to stay low and unseen. He cowered like a camp follower, hoping that by acting non-threatening, he'd be ignored. He moved along through the fields, surrounded by knots of soldiers fighting, killing. In his years in the Quiet Touch, he never saw armies this large clashing, and he realized that indeed this area held the dead from many long years of war, all returned to fight once more.

He passed into a Thrane camp, curiously quiet but surrounded by the sounds of battle as its occupants fought against threats at all quarters. He looked around, but the ghostly remnants of tents, wagons, soldiers, and corpses littered the area, obscuring the terrain. He realized that he could no longer orienteer himself toward the center; he was as close as he could reasonably get.

"Psst! Brother!" He heard a female voice, speaking common with an Aundairian accent. In the darkness a shadow moved, hunkered low, silent as it walked. Teron moved over toward it.

In the moonlight he saw a young monk, probably just past the examination. Her head was shaven and her tunic ill-fitting.

The young woman darted her head back and forth. "Where are the reinforcements?" she asked. "Prelate Quardov said he'd bring reinforcements, but I haven't seen them anywhere! Have you seen them?"

Teron shook his head.

"I have to get out of this camp and back to the monastery," she said. "I think they're going to attack in the morning. But we can't prevail against these numbers. I fear the monastery will be burned . . ." She looked about, feverish in her determination, and snuck away without another word.

Her words gave him pause to think. Keiftal had often told of how the Thrane army had camped for days near the monastery before they used the Sphere. He was in a large Thrane camp. He just had to find the general's treasure tent.

He smiled. This was exactly what those in the Quiet Touch were trained for.

Thranes were nothing if not efficient. When on the march, the army always organized its camp exactly the same way. That way, soldiers could move easily about in any camp, no matter how the units or soldiers might get shifted around. It also meant that those infiltrating the camp had an easier time of it. Teron got some bearings by checking the arrangement of the wagons and scouting the pathways between banks of tents. Once he had deduced where in the camp he was, he moved toward the command center.

He moved along the open walkways, keeping to one side so as to seem inconsequential, shuffling his feet as though tired, hanging his head subserviently. He had done it often before, and he moved not simply as one who belonged there, but as one who was weary of being there and wanted to go home. In a sense, his posture was no disguise at all.

Ahead, he could see guards around the command center, illuminated by the flames of a ghostly fire. As he drew close, the fire grew stronger, starker, changing from an echo of a fire to what appeared to be the real thing. Teron looked up. Somewhere behind Therendor, invisible to mortals, Eyre moved closer to its appointed conjunction. Teron wished he could see it to better gauge what time he had left.

Regardless, he knew his time was running out.

Then a strong tenor voice broke through the darkness. "Drop it, monk."

Teron whipped around, shielding the Orb behind him. There was nothing to be seen in the darkness.

He heard Praxle chuckle in the moonlit night. "Now how will you use your big ugly fists, monk?" he asked mockingly. "How will you strike that which you cannot see?"

Teron spun in place as the Orb continued its sedate progress forward.

"You know, perhaps that's a good metaphor for your life," Praxle continued. "You couldn't see your potential, so you didn't reach for it. And now you can't see your death, so you won't stop it."

Crack! A blast of energy flew out from one of the tents and struck Teron squarely in the ribs, sending him tumbling to the ground. He looked up and saw Praxle through the adjacent tent flap, his smiling teeth reflecting the moonlight. Teron hopped to his feet, but as he did, Praxle vanished.

The Sphere continued on, but as the bag weighed it down, it also began to sink to the ground.

Teron stood, turning his head back and forth, searching the darkness. He heard the quiet scritch-scratch of Praxle's feet moving on the grass to his right. He feigned ignorance for a moment, and then stepped and delivered a low whirling heel kick at a level to catch Praxle right in the gut. His foot swung through the air without hitting anything, and the lack of impact threw him slightly off balance.

Then Praxle appeared on the other side and launched another bolt at the monk, wracking his body with pain. "Maybe you're not as smart as I thought you were, monk," he said, his voice dripping with sarcastic pity. "You've already forgotten that I threw my voice into your mouth. Moving my footsteps is nothing to me."

He vanished again.

Teron staggered to his feet and saw that several of the guards were running at him, weapons drawn. "Hold!" they yell. "Identify yourself!"

"There's a gnome assassin," yelled Teron, doing his best approximation of a Thrane accent. "He's after the general!"

The guards drew up around the bag, weapons ready, scanning the night. One of the guards grabbed Teron's arm. "Where? Speak!" he demanded.

Teron looked into the darkness. He could sense Praxle nearby, but the gnome had as much time as he wanted, and Teron had nearly none.

"Be ready," he said. He looked inward, pressing all of the energy he could into his fists. He focused all of his discord, the screams of the souls in his head, his self-loathing, and his painful past into the essence, then all at once he slung his hands around, pushing the energy out as he brought his palms together for a mighty clap. A bright white flash emanated from the monk, radiating out in a beautiful pattern of ripples. It billowed the tents and shook the grass, and it also shredded the invisibility that cloaked Praxle, reordering it into a series of disconnected arcs that flickered away.

"There he is!" yelled the guards, and they leapt to the attack as Praxle shrieked in anger.

Teron turned and ran. He struck the bag containing the Sphere as hard as he could several times to get it moving, and, after a few seconds, it responded, moving faster and faster. He ran over to the guards at the entrance to the general's tent and pointed back toward Praxle. Several flashes lit the night, and a couatl flew about, hissing its danger. "Gnome assassins!" he yelled. "Help them!" The guards ran to help their comrades as Teron got ahead of the Sphere and plied every ounce of strength he had to slow it down.

Inside the tent, he saw a large magewrought apparatus, a pair of iron-and-brass fangs that arced upward and held between them a bubble of vivid emerald energy some two feet in diameter.

The bubble was empty, as Teron had hoped. He pulled the leather bag off the Sphere and unwrapped the smothering cloth. The Sphere of Xoriat hovered there, drifting slightly to one side.

Teron aligned himself, the Sphere and the bubble of energy on the Thrane apparatus. Wrapping his hands in the smothering cloth, he grabbed onto the Sphere and pushed it toward the device. The Sphere crawled beneath his hands like he was pressing on a huge pile of large beetles. It seemed to struggle, flexing amorphous muscles to break his grip upon it, but he held firm, guiding it closer.

The Sphere of Xoriat began vibrating harder and harder until at last it touched the edge of the green field. Then suddenly the powers of the Thrane device took hold, and the magical bubble drew the Sphere of Xoriat into its protective embrace. In the last seconds the sliding pieces on the surface of the Sphere nearly boiled with activity.

Then it was in. Encased within the bubble, it sat motionless, the magewrought device somehow overcoming its odd inertial behavior. It almost looked like a beautifully carved gemstone of obsidian.

Teron exhaled with relief and draped the smothering cloth around his neck. He turned to go, but happened to notice the campaign map on the Thrane general's table. He looked at the map, and at the disposition of troops. Then, casting quickly about, he saw several intelligence reports. He scanned them quickly, and seeing the contents, he snatched them up and shoved them into his vest, offering a quick prayer to Dol Arrah that they might be spared from fading with the rest of the apparitions.

Just as he finished his prayer, he heard a familiar voice.

"Did you think it would be so easy, monk?" Praxle's voice rang out of the empty air.

"It's too late, Praxle," said Teron, "the pattern is complete."

Praxle popped himself visible with a snap of his fingers. Standing near the center of the tent, he surveyed the area and smiled. "Yes," he said, "yes it is." He walked over to the Thrane device. "An effective if cumbersome way to transport the Sphere," he said. He reached for the lever that controlled the inclination of the device.

His hand passed through it.

"What?" He tried again, with the same results. He jumped to grab the Sphere itself, and his hands passed through, leaving slight eddies of green and black mist behind as the device decayed into phantasm.

"Nooo!" howled Praxle. He quickly cast a spell upon himself and tried to grab it again. When that failed, he turned on Teron and shrieked. "You! You will pay for your treachery!"

Teron held up one finger. "Be careful, Praxle, or I'll tell your people what you've done. I don't think they'll be happy."

"You'll tell no one if you're dead, monk!" said Praxle, as he waved his hands and let fly a blast of arcane energy.

The brief moment it took for Praxle to gesture gave Teron all the warning he needed. He leapt high into the air, twisting and flipping as he arced. The blast of magical energy ripped beneath him, but as he spun upside-down, the edge of the searing blast smote his head and disoriented him.

Teron landed hard on his side, wrenching his neck. He instinctively kicked at the most substantial thing he could see, and heard Praxle emit a strained grunt at the impact. Teron's bleary eyes saw Praxle stumble backward through the side of the command tent, momentarily shredding the ethereal structure of the pavilion.

Teron rose to his feet. Outside a number of ghostly voices called out: "The assassin! He's after the general! 'Ware the gnome!" Through the hole in the tent fabric, Teron saw numerous Thrane guards closing in. Praxle started to stalk back through the main tent flap, but a Thrane apparition struck at his back with an axe, and Praxle cried out in pain and surprise. He turned and swept his arms back and forth in grand gestures, unleashing an entire thunderstorm of power in a matter of a dozen seconds, all the while cursing like a grave robber.

Teron shook his head to clear it fully, then grabbed the smothering cloth and wrapped it around his left arm, just in case. Moving as silent as a cat, he stalked up behind Praxle, fist cocked for a telling blow. Outside, he saw the shattered remains of scores of ghostly Thrane guards, blown by unseen winds.

As Teron closed in Praxle, the gnome spun about and hissed, his reptilian eyes flashing eerily in the spectral light of the Thrane torches. Praxle cast another potent spell at Teron, who reflexively raised his left arm for a block. The magical blast caromed off the smothering cloth and whistled past Teron's ear, giving him a painful if unthreatening glancing blow.

Teron spun and struck Praxle across the jaw with a spinning backfist, sending the gnome tumbling to the ground. Teron stepped out to finish the job, but as he approached, Praxle turned himself invisible once more.

Teron looked for footprints, but it was too dark to see any. Then, in a flash of inspiration, he snatched one end of the smothering cloth and snapped it around. He saw it graze something, and gave it a quick loop to drape it around his target.

He saw the unmistakable profile of Praxle's nose protruding from the wrap.

◦ ◦ ◦ ◉ ◦ ◦ ◦

Startled by the sudden appearance of a cloth over his face, Praxle started to duck. Then something struck him dead on the end of his nose with the force of the lightning rail. He saw a flash of white, heard the crunch of the cartilage of his nose shattering beneath the impact, felt himself weightless for a moment as the blow sent him momentarily airborne.

Praxle raised his hand to his bloodied nose. From his unimpressive position flat on his back, Praxle saw the hated Aundairian monk standing amid the fading Thrane tents, poised for another flurry of blows, and the smothering cloth dangling in his left hand. He realized that Teron's easy punch had knocked him clean out of the smothering cloth, and, better yet, the monk was scanning the area, eyes darting back and forth for some clue to the sorcerer's position.

With a vicious smile, Praxle rose silently to his feet. He drew a long poisoned dagger from his boot. Teron foolishly remained in place, merely shifting his feet as he looked around. Praxle crept around the monk's side, intent on stabbing the monk right in the kidney, then running out of the way until the poison took hold.

Then suddenly Teron took a jumping sidestep and kicked him in the side; he heard a pop that signaled his floating rib had broken. He writhed on the ground, trying to regain his breath.

Teron stepped over. "The cloth stripped your invisibility, you arrogant gnome," he said. "Surrender."

"I thought you were an assassin," grunted Praxle as he tried to get back on his hands and knees.

"That's part of it," said Teron. "But I've never gone out of my way to kill when I didn't have to. As I said before, I break things. Tonight I broke your ladder to godhood. Frankly, it felt good."

Wounded and exhausted, Praxle refused to concede the victory to one who had betrayed both his fellow sorcerer and his higher destiny. He summoned every last ounce of power he had left in him, gathering it near his heart. He rose to his knees.

"Don't make me kill you on top of everything else, Praxle," said Teron. "My job here is done."

Praxle sneered at the display of weakness. "And so are you." He raised his hands and let loose everything he had left in one massive surge of power. It struck Teron dead on and blasted him back, screaming. He flopped to the ground, motionless. All around, the ruins of the Thrane camp rippled and vanished in the wake of the magical eruption.

"Ha ha!" Praxle gloated, staggering to his feet. He walked over to where Teron's body lay. "Well, then, let that be a lesson to you, monk," he said. "Magic is superior to muscle, and wit is superior to size!"

Teron drew in a deep shuddering breath and pushed himself to his feet. His mouth hung open, and he swayed from side to side. Sweat plastered his hair to his scalp. Eyes burning with fury, he lurched forward.

Praxle gesticulated again, trying to draw forth another blast to finish the damnably resilient monk, but he could find nothing left within him. A few stray sparks of color wavered near his fingertips before frittering away.

Teron snorted. "Lesson to you, gnome. I never run out of punches."

◑ ◑ ◑ ◉ ◑ ◑ ◑

The bleary pre-dawn glow lighted a strange sight in the Crying Fields: an Aundairian monk walking side by side with a Zil gnome. Though from a distance one might think them to be comrades, the truth was very different.

"So are we going to walk all the way back in silence? Say something, damn you, monk!"

"I've been thinking," said Teron. "And all your grousing has made it harder for me to concentrate. But I think I'm happy with my solution now.

"So here's the deal, Praxle. We'll give you back your identification papers. We'll feed you. We'll put you back on the lightning rail. We'll even pay for you to have a private coach, as a measure of respect for the University. In return, you promise to remain aboard the lightning rail until it has left Aundair. You promise never to return to our country, and you promise never to harm any of the brothers you may meet elsewhere. Is that clear?"

"Yes, very clear."

"Do you agree?"

"Yes. Yes! I agree. Will you let go of my ear now?"

"No. Not until we're back at the monastery, and the brothers have been filled in."

Praxle growled. "Let go of my ear or you'll pay for your insolen— *Oooow!*"

"We haven't discussed penalties, Praxle," said Teron. "If you break any of these rules, the entirety of the Quiet Touch will hunt you down and kill you. We've been trained, Praxle. Trained to infiltrate, trained to blend in, trained to look just like people. The conductor on the lightning rail. The person who takes your garbage. A student at the University. Break your promise, and we will kill you, slowly and painfully. It may take a few years to infiltrate, but we will do it. You've shown me how better to blend in with the peacetime world, and I'll make sure to pass this knowledge on to everyone else in the order."

Praxle considered this. "So, uh . . . how many of you are there?"

"I'll never tell."

EPILOGUE

Keiftal looked up, his eyes alight with joy. "Teron, my boy, I'm so very glad to see you!" he said, rising slowly and painfully from his cot. "When that d'Sivis left after you, I feared for the worst."

Teron smiled shyly. "I can take care of myself, master," he said.

"I know that, but I feared you'd not be able to protect both yourself and the Thrane Sphere. But I am glad that you did. Tell me, my boy, where is it now?"

"I don't know," said Teron, but as the alarm rose on Keiftal's face, he added, "It's gone, Keiftal, and we need not worry about it for a long, long time. The Fields took it, and they will be loathe to yield it up again."

Keiftal began to sway slightly, and Teron gently led him back to his cot.

"Master Keiftal," said Teron, "I have something to tell you. I, well, I probably shouldn't tell you until you're healed, but I will not restrain the truth."

"What is it, my boy?"

"When I was in the Crying Fields, I chanced upon some Thrane military scouting reports. I took them from the command tent, but they faded just as I feared they would. But I knew you'd want to know what was in them."

"What did they say, my boy?"

"I didn't have time to read the whole of them, but the gist is this: When the Thranes used their Sphere, the prelate and his troops were just ten miles away. Waiting."

Keiftal gaped. "Our reinforcements, the promised help, just ten miles away?" He moaned, then raised his eyes to the sky. "Oh, Dol Arrah, why could they not have arrived earlier?"

"They did," said Teron. "There were several reports. The prelate and his reinforcements were encamped ten miles away for almost two weeks. But he never moved his troops in a position to assist in our battle. In fact, it looked like he avoided contact with the Thrane army when they tried to engage him."

"He swore!" spat Keiftal, disbelieving. "He swore to help us! If they had come as promised—"

Then the aging monk reconsidered this news for a while. "That was probably for the best, in the long run," he said softly. "That is, if his troops had been here, there would have been that many more lives claimed by the Thrane Sphere." He looked up at Teron but couldn't keep his gaze.

"That does not change the fact that he broke his vow," said Teron. "Nor the fact that he wanted the Thranes to destroy us utterly."

"But why would he want that?" asked Keiftal.

Teron walked over to the window and opened the curtain. He looked out on the Crying Fields with his arms crossed, then he turned back to Keiftal. "Because he didn't have the courage to do it himself."

Teron snorted once, smiling wryly. He turned and walked to the door, gripping Keiftal's shoulder affectionately as he passed. He turned at the door and looked back at his master.

"But I refuse to die."

ENTER THE NEW WORLD OF

THE
DREAMING DARK
TRILOGY

Written by Keith Baker

The winning voice of the DUNGEONS & DRAGONS® setting search

CITY OF TOWERS
Volume One

Hardened by the Last War, four soldiers have come to Sharn, fabled City of Towers, capital of adventure. In a time of uneasy peace, these hardened warriors must struggle to survive. And then people start turning up dead. The heroes find themselves in an adventure that will take them from the highest reaches of power to the most sordid depths of the city of wonder, shadow, and adventure.

THE SHATTERED LAND
Volume Two

The epic adventure continues as Daine and the remnants of his company travel to the dark continent of Xen'drik on an adventure that may kill them all.

AVAILABLE IN 2005!

TWO NEW SERIES EMERGE FROM THE RAVAGED WASTES OF... THE WORLD OF

THE
LOST MARK
TRILOGY

MARKED FOR DEATH
Book One

Matt Forbeck

Twelve dragonmarks. Sigils of immense magical power. Born by scions of mighty Houses, used through the centuries to wield authority and shape wonders throughout the Eberron world. But there are only twelve marks. Until now. Matt Forbeck begins the terrifying saga of the thirteenth dragonmark . . . The Mark of Death.

THE
DRAGON BELOW
TRILOGY

THE BINDING STONE
Book One

Don Bassingthwaite

A chance rescue brings old rivals together with a strange ally in a mission of vengeance against powers of ancient madness and corruption. But in the haunted forests of the Eldeen Reaches, even the most stalwart hero can soon find himself prey to the hidden horrors within the untamed wilderness.

AVAILABLE IN 2005!